I0710366

THE GARAGE HOUSE KIDS

STEPHEN HECKLER

Horner Douglas Publishing

HORNER DOUGLAS PUBLISHING
An Imprint of Horner Douglas, LLC
Post Office Box 341428
Beavercreek, Ohio 45434

Artwork by Aubri Heckler

First Edition: May 2024

For information about special discounts for bulk purchases, please contact Horner Douglas Sales at inquiries@hornerdouglas.com.

Manufactured in the United States of America

Library of Congress Control Number (LCCN): 2024938137
Cataloging-in-Publication Data has been requested.

ISBN 978-1-962861-01-4 (Hardback)
ISBN 978-1-962861-44-1 (Paperback)
ISBN 978-1-962861-00-7 (eBook-Kindle)

For my wife and daughters.
Without whom the Shadow would have claimed me long ago.

Between the idea
And the reality
Between the motion
And the act
Falls the Shadow.

- T.S. ELIOT, THE HOLLOW MEN

This story contains depictions of kidnapping, blood and gore, allusions to mental illness and ableism, torture, and murder of both adults and children.

You may skip Chapter 2, sections i and ii; Chapter 5, sections ii and iii; and Chapter 8, sections iv and v.

While some plot may be sacrificed, the resolution will maintain integrity.

This story also contains strong depictions of friendship, love, loyalty, devotion, courage, and resolve.

Please read with care.

CONTENTS

THE GARAGE HOUSE KIDS

PROLOGUE

In a quiet corner of Ohio, there stood a house. For thirty years it squatted in the small town of Brewster Falls, a place nestled in the map creases, lost between other places. According to the welcome sign, Brewster Falls was "A Nice Place to Bring Your Kids". Not raise. Not have. *Bring.* As for the house, it passed time in the kind of obscurity small Midwest towns are masters of preserving. Indeed, it and the town were adept at keeping secrets, nursing them along until the inevitable moment when quiet fractures and truth screams into the light.

Well, during the Fall of 1998 the inevitable moment came. Someone noticed the place and named it the Garage House. When that happened, a machine set in motion hundreds of years earlier bucked, snorted, and accelerated toward an unravelling that threatened the very fabric of reality. But for three decades it sat on the corner of Colonel Perez Road and Donovan Drive and did its job. So well, in fact, no one noticed Colonel Perez wasn't even real. The name was a nod to the ramblings of a delirious Marine many years earlier. Too many years earlier if you paid attention, which many were not. Who chose the name? Why, Leonard Philips, of course.

And it came to pass, as he drew back his hand, that, behold, his brother came out: and she said, 'How hast thou broken forth?' This breach be upon thee: therefore, his name was called Perez.

Biblical words uttered by Master Gunnery Sergeant Chaz Shammy after being blown into Midwatch by the first nuclear test. Leonard was nothing if not sentimental. Words carried meaning, so this gate was named Perez, and the structure that would become known as the Garage House was built on it in the fashion directed by the mysterious Ulrich. This was before Ulrich discovered Leonard's alliance with Midwatch, but we'll get to that. How was Leonard to know Midwatch would go back and destroy Ulrich's Congregate? Well, he couldn't have known, could he? Not that he would have cared.

Why call it the Garage House? Because while it looked normal from Perez, once you turned onto Donovan it was only garages. One set matched the house, and one set almost did.

In Hebrew, Perez means breach. When Perez shoves his brother Zerah out of the way to be born first. We've breached into this place. We're born again.

Chaz Shammy's brains may have been scattered that day, but there was genius in what he uttered. Interactions with Aesteria were oft recalled as religious experiences. What's Aesteria? The space between, but we'll get there, too.

Anyway, Leonard Philips built up this small corner of Ohio with his 'friend' Jack Nassem. Jack used his connections and influence, and Leonard used his guile and charisma. Leonard wormed his way into development and politics, and around 1960 or so, planned the joining of Alpha Falls and Brewster Township into one city known as Brewster Falls. The development commission recognized they needed a larger school to accommodate the growing population, so Brewster Falls High School was planned.

Leonard convinced the commission to change the name of the existing Alpha-Richmond Road to Colonel Perez, stating young people should be surrounded by things that inspire, like reminders of rich history. Only he knew the real history behind the name, though.

Another road was paved brand new to serve as entrance to the new student parking lot. This road passed right in front of the Garage House and was named Donovan Drive for no other reason than Leonard was fond of "Season of the Witch" by Donovan, which was released in 1966, around the same time all the final planning occurred. So, the house sat on the corner of Breach and Witch, right next to a buffet of young people and their friends.

For over twenty years, Jack and Leonard brought in the patriarchs of the most powerful families in the world. Founders of banks, newspapers, railroads. Their long lives and family continuance of power observed by the masses. Masses who believed it was merely due to their access to money and better doctors that they hadn't died off. Little did the proletariat know, as time went on, more and more influential 'world leaders' joined Midwatch through Leonard Philips. And the demand for children increased.

During the merging of Alpha Falls and Brewster Township, Jack Nassem's own son found his way into Midwatch, was harvested, and was made into an illimni for some oil baron out of Texas. What's an illimni? A terrible thing, you'll see.

It happened before he even knew it was happening. Jack had already been having more and more doubts about what they were doing, especially after having his own children. He and his wife couldn't reconcile the loss and separated. Leonard said it was for the best since she would age and die long before Jack.

Alas, poor Jack didn't make it a year after that. In the end, he had to kill himself a few times. He shot himself in the head, and his illimni took it. He couldn't bring himself to pull the trigger a second time, so he hung himself, and his illimni took it. He piped the exhaust from his Lincoln Town Car in through the driver's window. He passed out, but his illimni took that death, too. Finally, he stepped in front of a train passing through Brewster Station. His illimni hadn't had enough left for that mess, and to Jack's delight, the shadows finally took him.

Leonard kept his promise. When it was time to build Research Park Boulevard and the office complex at its terminus, he suggested they name it after his late partner, who had given so much to the programs they studied and whose life had ended much too soon. And so, Jack Nassem Research Park was born, JNR for short. And in Aesteria, near the boulder that an Aeraph known as Hesperus once sat, Nassem City was created. Poster-sized murals of Jack hung in both.

When Brewster Falls officially became a city in 1980, the party had been grand. So grand, Leonard ended up marrying a young lady he had taken to bed that night when he later discovered she was pregnant with his child. Her name was Stacey, and the child—the only thing he ever loved—they named Tiffany. He begged Midwatch to leave this child alone, to make her unwelcome in Aesteria and Nassem City. To his surprise, Midwatch agreed.

Most disconcerting to Leonard was how easy it all was. They had pipelines of kids coming in from all over the country. The network made the cowboys of the cocaine highways of the eighties look like amateurs. Milk cartons, post offices, and Unsolved Mysteries abounded. But as with most folks during the twentieth century's close, nothing could hold their attention long enough to make them care.

"Did you hear about that girl that disappeared?"

"Oh yes, how terrible."

"What it must be like for the parents."

"Mmmhm. Terrible."

A shake of the head.

And then, "Did you hear about the sale at Beerman's? They already have their Christmas stuff out. Can you believe it?"

"Earlier and earlier every year."

And just like that, the girl that disappeared was forgotten.

Everybody knew the dice were loaded, they just didn't care.

The good guys had lost.

July 1945

WHITE SANDS

HAMPTON

ALPHA FALLS

BREWSTER TOWNSHIP

AESTERIA

CHAPTER 1

Per Fretum Febris

"No weapon of destruction can usher in peace."

I – LEONARD PHILIPS

Leonard Marcus Philips was born on the 4th of July in 1903. It had been under two weeks since his forty-second birthday. A day on which General MacArthur declared Luzon secure from the Japanese even though it would cost several-thousand more lives from both sides before it was actually over in August. In Europe, both the U.S. and the reds were liberating camps full of Jewish people and other folk deemed undesirable by the Nazis. It had been over a month since V-E Day, but the Japanese were still causing trouble, and even when victories were declared large swaths of them didn't get the message and kept on fighting and killing and fighting and killing. In short, no one gave a shit about Leonard's forty-second birthday. And truth be told, neither did he.

Other than a slight temper, Leonard, or Lenny as his acquaintances called him, was not an emotional person. He had no real friends. He had only those which he owed something to, or those who owed something to him. If you called him Lenny, it meant one of you was in the other's debt. Ruthless as he was, he believed he acted for the good of mankind and the great United States of America. Until what transpired on this day and what it showed him. Even then, he kept acting in what he considered the peoples' best interest. For a while.

On this day, he had two Marines on his side: Master Gunnery Sergeant Charles 'Chaz' Shammy, and Chaz's First Sergeant, Gerald Montgomery, Sr. They lead a group of eight Marines placed here in secret at Leonard's request. A request made by someone higher up who of course owed him a favor and probably called him Lenny.

Leonard asked them to muster outside the barracks at 0445. They were standing at the ready at 0430. When Leonard arrived, he was not surprised.

"At ease, gentlemen," said Leonard Philips.

They didn't move. Leonard witnessed this before, and while impressive, it bothered him. He was the one in charge. Alas, only when Chaz relaxed did the rest of his team follow.

"Good morning, Master Gunny. Are there any concerns about today's mission?" asked Leonard.

"No, Sir."

Neither Gerald nor Chaz particularly enjoyed receiving their orders from a civilian, but Leonard had a certain gravitas that could not be ignored. He also had some power, enough for him to hold influence over the brass.

Also, he was damn likeable. Even Chaz, who was never much for emotion, seemed to like him, as though he wanted to impress him.

"Gentlemen, if this all goes according to plan, it will change your lives. Not only will our country be protected and this war over,"

Lenny told them, "you'll be heroes to your military, and while your deeds cannot be celebrated, there are other ways in which we can show appreciation."

I'll need to spend a few favors to get these guys houses, or land, or cars, thought Leonard.

"Do you understand your orders?" he asked.

"Sir, yes, Sir," the men answered.

That's more like it, thought Leonard.

"Any issues—" he began.

"Are to be brought here for interrogation and then addressed at your command, Sir," the men answered.

"Good, good," said Leonard. "And don't forget, no one is ever to discuss what is seen or heard here once the experiment begins. No one is to be seen by any of the other observers, or you yourself will become an issue to be addressed."

"Sir, yes, Sir," said the men.

II – GERALD MONTGOMERY SR.

On the morning of July 16, 1945, First Sergeant Gerald Montgomery Sr. awoke at 0347 Mountain Time, surrounded by his fellow sleeping Marines. He had been having a nightmare. His young son, Gerald Junior, apparated out of a shadowy setting screaming that he couldn't see. His face and shirt were covered in blood, his eyes were wide, and his head was gashed sufficiently for Gerald Senior to see his son's brains pulsating with thought.

When, in his dream, Gerald Senior turned away, his son's hands shot out and grasped him by the shoulders.

He has no eyes...

"Father, look at me! LOOK AT ME! DO you UNDERSTAND what you HAVE DONE? DO you UNDERSTAND what you SEE?" shouted Gerald Junior.

On the morning of July 16, 1945, at 0348 Mountain Time, First Sergeant Gerald Montgomery Sr. held his head and wept.

III – LENNY

Leonard didn't know what kind of test was being performed today. He had the brief, but he didn't read it. He never did. Why? It didn't matter to him. His job was simpler than that. Just don't let any secrets out. It was easy for him to not share secrets if he didn't even know what they were, right? Same with the men. They took orders.

(10)

They told him today was important and they were going to change the world. He liked the sound of that. They told him they may need to hold some people here if it didn't go quite right. No problem for Lenny Philips. And they let him choose his own team. He was in control, as he was used to being. As he wanted.

(9)

With the countdown sounding and the war horns wailing, and the look Chaz was giving him, he thought perhaps this was one mission brief he should have read. Unbeknownst to him, it wouldn't have mattered. The orders for him and these men were made up. Lenny and his team were a part of this important world-changing experiment.

(8)

They stood in a newly constructed house. He had seen enough that he didn't question the things the military and government sometimes did, but this one was Flash Gordon strange. Everything in this house was fake. No real water, no real electricity, no real fixtures. It looked real, sure. In fact, the only things that were real were the garage door and the windows. Even the front door was painted on. Their (incorrect) assumption had been this was a training ground for running operations in a civilian home.

(7)

A couple hundred yards away stood an odd-looking water tower with an oblong canister positioned at the top. Otherwise, they were surrounded by desert. Something new was being tested today which he had been told would end the war, maybe all wars, and change the world towards peace. Lenny didn't care about that so much but was happy to be a part of something important. Being part of important things always carried with it more leverage and influence.

(6)

"Sir, I think the water tower fell," said Chaz.

(5)

"What?" asked Leonard.

(4)

"Look," said Gerald Montgomery Sr. He pointed outside through one of the real windows in the fake house.

(3)

Leonard looked out and saw the tower, but the water tank was gone.

(2)

The ground shook, the light intensified, and Leonard Philips acknowledged many, many people did not like him.

(1)

"Shit," he said, but no one heard.

IV – HESPERUS

Hesperus sits.

He ponders the existence he occupies. The Temporans consider his kind all knowing, some even refer to them as gods. Like ants worshiping a boot as it squishes them to bits. The Temporan vassalage to time humors him. What small lives they must have. What did they call them? Seconds? Temporans saw Hesperus and the other Aeraph as dogs see their masters.

Yet, Hesperus does not feel like a god.

He feels like an outsider.

So, he sits.

The task given him by Michael is simple; guard this gate. In truth, the work requires much sitting and very little guarding. In the distance, other Aeraph train in the sky. They fly back and forth, honing their skills. Honing them for what? No attacks come against them.

Occasionally, a stray Temporan sneaks through the gate. The Aeraph herd them back whence they came, with a story or experience to take back with them. Upon their return home, their words are received as insane or as writ; either way working to ward off most potential intruders. But it never completely ends.

Aeraph have strict rules against harming Temporans, but no rules against scaring them. Hesperus wishes for one to sneak through for the chance to instill them with a story. Perhaps a frightening one with him as a fallen god, sent to suck their soul-energy from their body and use it to his will! What fun that would be!

Hesperus sighs, stretches his wings, and recalls his argument with Michael.

* * *

"Look at what is lost when they die!" Hesperus had shouted. "If they do not communicate their knowledge before death, it is lost. Lost! How do you not understand this! They must constantly start over, sometimes losing so much to a dark age! Michael, we know how to help them. Why let them suffer so?"

"Ah, Hesperus. It is not our place to interfere beyond the balance. You dance the edge of blaspheme. Except for the few born with a natural attenuation to Aesteria, none are to see this place. And we certainly cannot kill them, Hesperus! You know this!" responded Michael.

"Not our place! Not our place? Michael, we are gods to them. We need only harvest a few soul-minds to bring their next evolution. Is it not our place to provide this aid? Those left would be grateful!"

"Hesperus, we do not know the effects of leaving remnants of consciousness inside soul-energy. Conflicting consciousness in one mind could be catastrophic. It is too dangerous. You speak of urgency as if you are Temporan. Have you become a vassal of time as well?" Michael smiled.

"Do not smile at me and speak of blasphemy and time. We should try it. And if it fails, we eliminate the multi-conscious Temporans, if even created. Is it not worth the benefit of all to at least try? A few short Temporan lives is a small price to pay."

"Such ambition in you, Hesperus. I am wary for you to guard the gate, knowing your mind."

"I am fine to guard the gate. I simply wanted to voice my thoughts. I will not act on them, Michael. The shadows take you."

"Hesperus! Do not say this to me! Please, go in peace and be well. We shall speak on this again if you wish."

"I do wish, and we will."

* * *

How can I convince him to try?

He gazes across Aesteria. It is a beautiful place, a paradise. Every color is here.

As Hesperus surveys his home, the colors brighten.

What is this?

The greens become greener, the reds deeper, and the sky more vividly blue.

Hesperus soon finds himself unable to see.

The boulder beneath him vibrates and cracks.

"No," he says aloud. He screeches for Michael. They are being attacked. But by the *Temporans?*

It is not possible.

Hesperus stands and turns toward the gate. The light streaming from it burns his eyes. The ground shakes. He crouches to fly, but the last thing he sees before the gate flashes and blinds him is his own beautiful wings burning, his bones visible and disintegrating.

Hesperus screeches for Michael once more. Then, a shockwave shoots out of the gate and strikes the blind, wingless, smoldering Hesperus.

The boulder explodes.

The Aeraph in the distance fall from the sky.

When the dust settles, what remains in the place where Hesperus once stood, is a black, pulsating cloud.

V – THE ECHO SPACE

"Michael." *Michael. Michael Michael.*

What happened to me?

"We are being attacked!" *attacked! attacked! attacked!*

It is dark. What is this echo? Where is my body?

"It's me, Hesperus!" *Hesperus! Hesperus! Hesperus!*

The dark cloud of what used to be Hesperus hovers above the boulder fragments only moments ago it had been brooding upon. It pulsates darkly and violet. The gate is blown open. The Aeraph nearest it have fallen from the sky. The beautiful colors of Aesteria are scorched and twisted and grey. It can't see. It senses the color is gone and the Aeraph that were training nearby are dead on the ground.

The cloud senses something else, something... more.

It is... energy.

Yes. Yes!

It senses energy moving all around.

The cloud moves toward the energy it senses. It is a group of small creatures.

Yes. Yes! YES! thinks the cloud.

The cloud understands the small creatures are a group of hares. The cloud descends upon them and absorbs their energy. It becomes more powerful for it.

This power could be... limitless.

I must find Michael.

It senses a new energy. Many magnitudes larger than the hares. It craves it. It flies with haste back to the gate. Three Temporans lie next to the shattered boulder. They are unconscious, but alive.

So, it was an attack. But not much of one. And so... much... energy. Yes. Yes! YES!

The pulsating cloud of what used to be Hesperus feels itself going mad. Perhaps it is Hesperus' soul-mind fading away. Becoming a remnant. Yes. Except for his core thoughts, of course. Core thoughts of creating true neutrality. Balance. Forbidden thoughts.

A jolt of energy runs through the cloud. The order of magnitude compared to the hare is incalculable. Violet lightning shoots from the black veins within it, the sky darkens, and the smell of sulfur bursts forth. The cloud absorbs one of the Temporans, not yet knowing how to hold itself in one place.

Purple light showers Aesteria as far as can be seen. The cloud courses with unlimited power. For a moment. The charge begins fading as soon as it peaks. It craves more.

Aesteria. We are the space between. The middle ground. Measuring the cosmos and distributing balance. We are protectors, as owners to a pet. Watching for anomalies and dispersing energy where needed.

The middle ground.

The protectors.

The watchers.

"The Midwatch, perhaps?"

WHAT?! Who is here? here? here? here?

"Ah. I was recently known as Leonard Philips. I am not sure who, or what, I am now. I seem to have no body."

You are Temporan! I felt your power. I know your thoughts. I know your memories. Soon, you will be but a remnant. remnant. remnant. remnant.

"Remnant, you say? I would think you would be more grateful after I just named you."

Named me? Hah! Fool. I am Hesper... Hesp... Hmm. mm. mm. mm.

"Loss for words? I understand. You were caught in the same blast I was. My people tricked me into being near a bomb of some kind. Which begs the question, am I dead? Are we dead? Is this purgatory? Hell, perhaps?" Leonard is not too proud to understand where he is heading, assuming heaven and hell exist. He sacrificed his own eternity for the good of man. He could reconcile it.

Hm. Yes, I too was ordered to sit near your 'blast'. No, we are not dead. Simply changed. You have the most glorious dark energy. I need to take it now. I need to test a theory. theory. theory. theory.

"Midwatcher, being a man of science, could you please share your theory? I cannot escape, I have no body, yet I still think, so I still am. And I still yearn for knowledge. Would you please share this with me so that I may know what knowledge I will become for you?" Leonard Philips is still Leonard Philips, after all. His desire and need to influence and gain power are still intact.

Interesting. Even at your end you seek knowledge. Temporans are destined for more than they are given, I knew it. it. it.

"First, am I a Temporan? What is that?"

Temporan is what you are, yes. It is our name for beings that have not yet learned to transcend time. Beings with lives bound to it, like you. you. you.

"Ah, so all humans are Temporans. Are all Temporans human?"

Any life measured against time is Temporan. The Aeraph are not. We... they exist beyond time. time.

"Immortals, then, these Aeraph?"

No, not immortal. By your observation, yes, but in all the universe, no. Aeraph do expire. expire.

"So, Midwatcher, I find myself in a place *between* called Aesteria, where near immortal beings exist. Based on your thoughts earlier, a race called the Aeraph collect the souls of dead Temporans and re-distribute them to other places. And you, Midwatcher, were one of these Aeraph until the blast, as I was a Temporan. Is this correct?"

Yes, Temporan.

"Amazing. So, what is your theory?"

When a Temporan is brought alive into Aesteria and dies here, its soul-energy retains its consciousness, as you have. This creates a soul-mind. If we, the Aeraph, can influence and combine soul-minds with other soul-minds, and reason them into darkness, lightness, negative, or positive energy, then we could distribute the energy more evenly to new life in the cosmos and eliminate the constant misalignment against the balance we are charged to create.

"And once the soul-mind has been convinced one way or the other? Then what?"

Once the right alignment is achieved, consciousness is banished and what was the Temporan dies.

"Oh my. Midwatcher, how will you conduct this experiment with merely the three of us? You will need many more Temporans to realize your test."

I will go to Tempora and get all I need.

"Show me, please Midwatcher. Show me Tempora one last time before I go."

Are there others through the gate?

"Oh yes. Many."

What were you called?

"Well, my name was Leonard Philips. But my friends called me Lenny."

Very well, Leonard Philips. I will show you.

Midwatch passes the unconscious bodies of Chaz Shammy and Gerald Montgomery Sr. and goes through the gate.

VI – UNCLE ULRICH

On July 16, 1945, Ulrich was in New Hampshire tracking twin girls who seemed to have the connection he was looking for. The natural connection Jutte would have said made them witches. But they were hard to find. The powers of seeking would grow as the congregate grew, but for now, he was alone. And seeking children. Again. And they would be in danger. Also, again.

Midwatch grew stronger. If only he knew against time when Midwatch was created. In Aesteria, time was so slow it almost didn't exist. Midwatch didn't yet exist by human clocks but was moving in and out of time via the gates. It maddened him.

When? When does it come?

Today, Aesteria was still Aesteria and not yet Midwatch.

He sat in the lobby of a halfway house and waited for the Parkers to leave their room. Being a family, and one with a handicapped veteran father, the halfway house gave them the luxury of their own space. Ulrich had money and was going to offer Mr. Parker a job. He would then take them to his house, where he could train and protect the girls.

And then, all four Parkers screamed.

Pain flashed throughout Ulrich's body and mind. He fell over and convulsed.

Something terrible had happened.

As he seized on the floor, hearing screams but not seeing the nurses surrounding him, Ulrich understood it was this day. He was too late.

This was the day Midwatch was made.

VII - MIDWATCH

The house was gone, except for a few walls and the misshapen garage door frame.

The air was acrid.

Ash floated everywhere.

Midwatch and Lenny moved over to some crumpled piles nearby. Lenny recognized these were burnt uniforms fused to the remains of cooked human flesh and bone.

"They wanted to erase us," said Leonard.

Midwatch understood.

It was no longer a cloud. It was physical, but it was not Aeraph. Its view was low to the ground, and its movements unsteady, wiggling back and forth to move. To slither.

What am I?

"Not a cloud, to be sure. Is it me, or can we feel the air?"

Yes. What happened here?

"My team and I were to offer protection during a test, but we were deceived into being test subjects. They had us wait in this house. And, well, you see how it looks."

Such deception. There is much negative energy here. Dark energy. What was the purpose of this test?

"This weapon is supposed to be strong enough to end all wars. But it must be kept secret. I don't have all the details, but I know they called it Trinity."

Trinity? Interesting. Trinities are powerful. Aeraph use them often, but carefully. No weapon of destruction can usher in peace. Much soul energy traverses Aesteria this day.

Midwatch felt discomfort, a burning from underneath. It twisted and saw smooth black scale drawn out in a writhing line, shimmering not unlike satin.

"We are a snake?"

There is nothing more to see here but death. These souls have already departed.

The sky flashed followed by the scent of sulfur.

* * *

The form of Hesperus is no more.

"You were not surprised to be a snake?"

It is my chosen familiar form. We used to venture out as Aeraph, but it caused confusion, and sometimes worship, which would move certain species from their evolutionary paths. It happened to your kind as well. So, we chose forms that would be accepted and unnoticed for our travels. I chose a snake. snake. snake. snake.

"I have one more question, Midwatcher."

One more before you are banished. What is it, Lenny? Lenny? Lenny?

"How will you harvest what you need as a snake? How will you know you are getting the right mix of soul-minds? Would it not be better to have an ally selecting what you need?"

A snake can kill.

"Yes, quite. But you'll not be a snake for the killing, the snake will need to do the bringing. As you said, they need to die here. How will you, as a snake, get them here?"

The cloud pulses rapidly.

Do you consider yourself to be such an ally? ally?

"I do. But there are things I'll need."

Name them.

"First, I'll need me and my two men returned to Tempora. I'll need a body, my own if you can manifest such things, as you did your snake. And I'll need the power to punish those that sought to eliminate me and regain power within the leadership of my world. As payment for this, I will seek and deliver all the Temporans you need, for as long as you need."

I can manifest such things, but there is one problem with your plan.

"Which is?"

You only have one man.

Much to Lenny's surprise, Midwatch is correct. First Sergeant Gerald Montgomery Sr. is gone.

"Is this a problem? Can you find him?"

I do not sense his energy, and he could not have gotten that far from this gate to escape my senses. He is not in Midwatch.

"*In* Midwatch? Naming this place after yourself? As for the missing man, that's a minor issue. Do we have a deal?"

We do. I will need a Temporan to grant you the power and time you will need to complete these tasks. For you, it will be long. Aeraph once devised a way, although outlawed, of dampening the effect of time on Temporans. You will need this. Bring me one that is young, and dark.

"You can extend my life? For how long?"

As long as needed.

Lightning flashes and thunder cracks. Sudden intense pain flows throughout Leonard Philips as his body manifests and is thrown out of the cloud. He smacks his head on a boulder fragment.

"Ow, goddamit. Did you need to throw me?" Although he acts annoyed, he is overjoyed. This is the best deal he has ever struck.

He stands and goes to Chaz. He kicks him gently.

"Gunny, get up. We have work to do."

Chaz moans.

"C'mon Chaz. We need to go. Now."

"Sir? What happened? The men... Sergeant Montgomery..."

"I'll explain later. We need to go."

"Yes, sir."

Chaz very slowly comes around.

"How will I get back and forth between here and there?" Leonard asks Midwatch.

"When you go through now you will not return to the place we were. I will send you to a different location. The air and ground where we were is poisoned. Once through, the doorway you pass through will be the one you use to return. Guard it, and do not let anyone near it, for it will always bring those going through it to this spot. To me."

"Understood."

"You will have greater influence than you ever had," says Midwatch.

Leonard Philips receives a jolt of energy. He thinks he may be having a heart attack, but then he feels better than he ever has. Ever.

"What was that?" he asks.

"That was power. Lenny, if you fail me, I will find you, and I will harvest you," promises Midwatch.

"I understand. I'll return soon, with a child, as you said."

"I did not say child, but that is your choice. The younger the physical form, the stronger the soul-mind's effect."

Leonard nods and helps Chaz to his feet.

"Let's get you some help," says Leonard.

"Right on," says Shammy.

CHAPTER 2

Colonel Perez

The desire for power darkens even the lightest of souls.

I – LENNY

The air cleared of sulfur, and Lenny rubbed his irritated eyes. Master Gunny Chaz Shammy leaned hard on his right side, in and out of consciousness.

Where the hell am I? thought Lenny.

He did not think to ask, 'When the hell am I?', but it would have been appropriate.

"And it came to pass in the time of her travail, that, behold, twins were in her womb," said Shammy.

"What?" said Lenny.

"And it came to pass, when she travailed, that the one put out his hand: and the midwife took and bound upon his hand a scarlet thread, saying, 'This came out first'."

"Chaz, what the hell are you on about, son?"

"And it came to pass, as he drew back his hand, that, behold, his brother came out: and she said, 'How hast thou broken forth?' This breach be upon thee: therefore, his name was called Perez."

"Goddammit Chaz, what are you saying?" demanded Lenny.

Lenny was not a religious man, having always believed in himself more than any other power in the universe. That characteristic itself a sin. However, he understood Shammy quoted some sort of religious verse.

"Here, sit down buddy," said Lenny.

He set Shammy down against a tree and surveyed the area around him.

They were in a field. A road ran next to them, but no town. A faint glow shimmered in the air. This must be the gate Midwatch sent them through. He'd have to figure out a way to protect it.

He needed to find a telephone.

"We need to find a telephone," said Lenny.

"And it came to pass…"

"Jesus Christ."

"Yes, they were related."

"Chaz, I'm going to go look for a phone. Will you be alright here for a bit?"

"In Hebrew, Perez means breach. When Perez shoves his brother Zerah out of the way to be born first. We've breached into this place. We're born again," rambled Chaz.

"What are you talking about?"

"Perez and Zerah, sons of Tamar and Judah. Perez is the breach. This is a breach. We've been to Heaven, Lenny," said Chaz, and then recanted, "And it came to pass, when she travailed…"

"He's lost his mind," said Lenny, shaking his head.

"That wasn't Heaven, Chaz. You take it easy; I'll be back soon."

"Yes, sir."

Lenny Philips, for no reason at all, walked west.

* * *

He had walked about a mile when he came upon a schoolhouse. He approached the front doors and pulled. They were locked.

"Dammit," he said. It was July and school was out. Kids and families were working on their homes, gardens, and farms before the free labor was lost to classes.

Lenny walked on.

When he walked twice as far as he already had, he came to an intersection with a small grocery store and a filling station. Where was he? This was nowhere near the desert of New Mexico, he was sure.

He approached the filling station. An attendant checked the oil in a beautiful blue Oldsmobile 60 Series Convertible.

"Wowee," Lenny whistled. "That is one fine automobile."

The attendant looked up.

"Oh, sure is, mister."

"I bet you don't mind servicing these. Is that a '42?"

"Oh, no sir mister. Not at all. And yes, yes it is. Last year they were built before the war and all."

"Ah, the war," said Lenny. "Hey, you look like a man who can help me with something. Do you have a telephone in your station?"

In truth, the attendant looked about nineteen going on twelve.

"We sure do, mister. Let me finish here and I'll be right in to show you. Feel free to help yourself to a soda from the machine. Opener is on a string by the air hose."

"Thank you, sir. Will do."

Small town hospitality is something, thought Lenny. *That kid has no discernable accent.* Lenny shook his head.

As he gulped his soda in the garage's shade, he felt no guilt thinking of Chaz thirsting next to that tree. He did, however, think to grab him one for when he got back.

The radio crackled in the garage and played "Sentimental Journey" by Les Brown & Doris Day. It was one of Lenny's favorites, and brand new.

I could live here, he thought.

The Oldsmobile fired up and drove off. The attendant emptied the fuel globe back into the tank beneath the station.

"The telephone is right over here, mister."

"Hey, thanks. You're a champ," said Lenny, and stuck out his hand. "My name's Leonard Philips, but my friends call me Lenny."

"Pleasure to meet you, mister. My name's Andy."

"Say, Andy, can you tell me what town this is?"

Andy blinked at Lenny.

"Sorry, I've been walking a ways. My car broke down a few miles up that road," Lenny motioned to the road, "what's its name? Anyway, I'm passing through and need to call some friends of mine to help me out."

"Uh, well that road is Route 44, or Richmond-Alpha Road. And this isn't really a town. You're in Brewster Township. Depending on how far you came down the road, you may have started in Alpha Falls. They have a Post Office!" Andy exclaimed.

"Got it. Alpha Falls, Iowa," said Lenny.

"Um, Ohio, sir. Alpha Falls, Ohio."

It's worse than I thought, thought Lenny.

"That's what I meant. I've been on the road for quite a few days. All the way from New Mexico in a very short time."

"Wow, mister! You've been everywhere!"

"Sure have. Now, how about that telephone?"

Alpha Falls, Ohio. Boy, are they going to be surprised to hear from me.

He picked up the phone and hit the lever.

A click followed by a female voice, "Information, how may I help you?"

"Yes, I would like to be patched over to Alamogordo Army Air Base. It's a security matter. Give them clearance and ID number X-ray, Lima, Papa, three, three, five, seven."

"One moment please."

Lenny waited about a minute.

"Alamogordo Army Air Base is on the line. Connecting with you now. The charge will be fifty-five cents," said the Operator.

"Alamogordo Army Air Base, ID and name please."

He repeated his number. "Lenny Philips. I need Jack Nassem. Immediately, please."

"Please hold."

Lenny waited again. Longer than a minute this time.

Until finally, "Lenny? Lenny, is it you?"

"Jack! Hi buddy, how are you?" Lenny said. A sneer on his face.

"Uh, fine Lenny. Fine. Just, ah, fine. Where are you?"

"Oh, you know. Me and the gunny are drinking some sodas together in Ohio."

"Ohio? How the fu—"

"So, you knew, huh? What if I told you your little test was nothing, and I mean *nothing* compared to what I just discovered."

"Well, I would be surprised, I suppose. But maybe, ah, not as surprised as I should be. Listen, Lenny, it wasn't me. And before you say anything and before I notify Groves, allow me to say it gives me immense pleasure to hear your voice, sir."

"I'll bet it does. But we don't need to say anything to Groves just yet. Let's you and I make a plan first. When can you meet at the café in Albuquerque?"

"Well, I, ah, suppose I can be there in a couple days when you arrive. How did you get to Ohio? Did you know what they were planning?"

"Not in a couple days. How about in an hour?"

"In an hour? Lenny, you're nuts. How are you going to get to New Mexico from Ohio in an hour?" asked Jack.

"Well, I got here from there pretty fast the first time. Like a said, this is bigger than your little bomb," replied Lenny.

"Well, yeah if I leave now. I'm going to, ah, need to check out a vehicle. How about an hour and a half? Jesus, this is nuts."

"I'll be waiting," Lenny said, and hung up.

The attendant, Andy, was looking at him.

"Sir, um, I wasn't meaning to listen in on your call. I'm not a creep or nothin'. But, how are you going to get to New Mexico in an hour?"

"I can show you, if you like," said Lenny, sweet as molasses. "Is that your truck over there? If you give me a ride back to my car, I can show you."

"Holy Buck Rogers! I might be nuts to believe you, but I'll give you a ride. If this is some sort of ruse, I may be the biggest cornball around."

"Oh, it isn't. Say, how old are you, Andy?"

"Fifteen, sir."

"Fifteen! And running a gas station! You must be *full* of energy."

Lenny Philips hadn't expected to fulfill Midwatch's commands so quickly, but hey, overachieving couldn't hurt, right?

* * *

When they pulled up to the tree a few minutes later, Andy said, "Hey, mister. There ain't a car here."

"How astute. Can you help me with my friend over there? He's in rough shape," said Lenny.

"...and she said, 'How hast thou broken forth?' This breach be upon thee: therefore, his name was called Perez," Shammy said as they approached.

"Hey, Chaz. I brought you a soda. Have a drink, will ya?" said Lenny.

"We went to heaven, Lenny. Can you believe it? Heaven!" said Shammy, and then drank the soda all at once, followed by a resounding belch.

"Wowee. That was a good one!" said Andy.

Lenny had a thought. He could see the shimmering gateway.

May as well try.

"Andy let's get him in the truck. Then, I'll take you to New Mexico."

"I've been duped. I am a cornball, but I'll help you with your friend."

They lifted Shammy into the truck and pushed him to the center of the bench seat. Andy went to the driver's door, but Lenny stopped him.

"Hey kid, I should drive since we have an injured man here and all."

"Oh, uh, that makes sense. Okay. Maybe I should stay here? You can use the truck to get him help at the clinic. Just drop me at the station first? I know we're not going to New Mexico. You got me."

"Kid, if I'm messing with you, it'll be a joke. Hop in. Either way my friend needs help. And please, call me Lenny."

That did it. It always did.

"Okay, Lenny," said the kid, still a little unsure.

Lenny got behind the wheel and pulled the column shifter down into first gear. He stared at the shimmering gateway.

I hope this works, he thought.

He released the clutch and the truck rolled forward. As the gateway touched the hood the air shimmered as if in a heat wave. Andy exclaimed something from the passenger seat, and then it was all darkness and sulfur.

* * *

When the air clears, they are in Midwatch at the spot of the broken boulder.

Lenny gets out of the truck and rubs his eyes.

On the passenger side, Andy does the same.

Lenny walks to the rear, keeping an eye on the kid.

Midwatch arrives moments later.

"Lenny, you have returned. And what have you brought for me?"

"This," says Lenny, and swings a chunk of boulder down on the back of poor Andy the gas station attendant's head. But not quite hard enough.

"Owwwwwwwwwwwwooooooooo," Andy moans, one hand holds the back of his skull. Blood spurts between his fingers. He stumbles forward.

Lenny hits him again, and with a crunch, he goes down.

But he isn't dead.

I need a real weapon next time, thinks Lenny Philips.

He brings the rock down on Andy's head repeatedly until he is sure his soul has departed his body.

"Lenny. You are a savage. But a useful savage. Yes. Yes. YES. YES!" cries Midwatch. The skies darken and purple lightning shoots from the cloud. "You have done well. Yes."

"There's more where that came from. Listen, I need to be in Albuquerque within an hour to meet someone who can help with our plan. After I meet with him, I'll need to bring him here. Then, we'll need to set up a base of operations in that Ohio town you sent me to. Brewster Falls. No, Brewster Township and Alpha Falls. Will we be able to do that?"

Midwatch laughs. "So simple, the mind of a Temporan. Lenny, from here you can go to any time and any place. Simply name it. Simply think it."

"Can you keep an eye on my friend while I'm gone?"

"I can put him out until you return. That is all."

"Fine," says Leonard. "So, do I just drive through and think the time and place?"

"Yes. It helps if you visualize the place. However, you should know while you can travel to any place, you cannot use any place to travel back here. There must be a gate to return."

"That's inconvenient," says Leonard. "Where is a gate near Albuquerque?"

"You know of one."

"Alamogordo."

Great. Just great. So, my options are to break onto the base and drive right into ground zero or drive to who-gives-a-shit Ohio.

"Lenny, I will have a gift for you when you return. Something to help extend yourself. I will prepare it. It will help us."

"Extend myself? You mean extend my life, right?" asks Lenny.

"More accurately, it will slow your life and take on your imperfections. Good luck."

"Thanks," says Lenny, in a hurry even though there's no reason to be.

He walks over to the truck, pulls Shammy out, and lays him on the ground where he found him after the blast.

He gets back in behind the wheel, reverses, aims it at the gate, drops it into first, and releases the clutch. He notices the blood on his hands as he drives toward the gate.

I need to prepare better next time, he thinks. He smiles. He closes his eyes and pictures the café where he and Jack Nassem shared breakfast and coffee so many times. "Sentimental Journey" plays in his thoughts. The familiar flash of sulfur and spin of darkness comes and goes.

* * *

When he opened his eyes, the truck was rolling right towards the café. He quickly hit the brakes. The tires squealed.

"Shit," he said.

He looked into the diners' unbelieving eyes. They had seen him. He'd have to remember that, too. Go to a secluded spot *near* where you need to go, not right *to* where you need to go.

Oh well, he could handle this.

He was Lenny Philips after all.

II – MIDWATCH

Such amazing energy in you.

"What? Who is that? Why is it dark? Why can't I see? Where am I? What did that mister do to me?" asks the panicked soul of Andy, the recently departed gas station attendant.

Midwatch senses this soul-mind is positive. This will not do. For this to work with Lenny, their alignments need to match. This soul needs darkening.

Oh, he tricked you something fierce. He smashed your head with a rock.

"Smashed my head... What are you... Are you saying I'm dead? That other guy was rambling about Heaven... is this..."

No, it is not Heaven. I am afraid your life has been cut short. Anything you were planning; ball games, dates, high school, having a life; it has all been taken from you! Ha Ha!

"No! But my mom! My friends! Why? Why are you laughing at me? This isn't fair. It's not right. Not right at all."

Are you angry?

"Angry? I'm not sure. Yes? I'm sad. Wait, why can I still think? Why can I speak? And who are you? I wanna go home. Can I go home?"

Oh, I am afraid he has taken that from you as well. You can never go home. He did it because he did not like your face. He did it to torture you. As for me, I am just a gatekeeper.

"Didn't like my face? What a reason to... It's not fair..." If poor Andy still had any eyes, he would be crying.

Yes, he is a cruel man. He is planning to go after your family next.

"My family. Why? What did I do?"

Oh, nothing. Like I said, he chose by your face. Now you will suffer for eternity as I have suffered. As all he brings here will suffer. You cannot go back. Look.

Midwatch allows Andy to 'see' his own dead body lying on the ground, skull, hair, and brains all smushed together.

There is no returning to that.

Anger rises in Midwatch. The focus of hate and revenge. This soul-mind's alignment is changing, spurned by this trauma.

"There's nothing I can do? That's it?"

No. No, there is not. By now he has likely already gotten to your home. He is a bad, bad man. The shadows take him. Would that we could avenge ourselves.

"No. I liked my life. I liked my family. It isn't fair!"

While you cannot go back and nothing will ever be the same, if there were a way to exact revenge, would you take it? There would be a price.

"A price? There's nothing left. Yes. Yes I would very much like to have revenge. Or something. This can't be it..."

Show me. Show me what you would do.

Midwatch creates a scene for Andy. The vision begins with Lenny standing next to Andy's truck, sneering at him.

"I like this truck. I'll be taking it from you as well," says Lenny.

"Why. Why have you done this?" asks Andy.

"Why? No reason, really. Mostly your stupid face," says Lenny.

"But that doesn't make any sense. What's wrong with my face?"

"Nothing. And everything. It's pimply and sharp. Your eyes are sunken. It's a face no one would ever really want to look at. No one is ever going to love a face like yours, so why let you live? And your parents. Sheesh. They need to be punished for making such a face."

"You leave them alone! You don't touch my mother!"

"Oh, I'm going to touch her. Quite a bit while your father and sweet little sister watch, in fact."

"No! You shut up!"

"What are you going to do? You're dead!" Lenny says with a big laugh. He laughs so hard he holds his stomach and doubles over. He repeats "You're dead!" between bellows.

"No! I hate you! You're going to pay! I'll make you pay!"

Yes. Yes! encourages Midwatch.

"I hate him. Hate him, you hear me! I'll break his stupid face!"

Andy picks up a rock and charges Midwatch's specter of Lenny Philips.

Midwatch makes it easy for him.

Andy smashes Lenny between the eyes. Blood sprays out both sides of the rock. Andy grabs Lenny's head with his left hand and brings the rock down with his right, using the skills he learned from his baseball coach as he prepared for his first year of pitching, which now will never come. This time the spray of blood carries with it bits of teeth.

Andy drops the rock and smiles.

"I'll find out what's important to him and ruin it!"

Good! Yes. Yes! YES!

Andy's alignment ticks downwards. Trauma is a more useful tool than hate, rage, any other emotion. It is much more difficult to push soul-minds upward. Only one more step down remains for this one.

The images fade, and Midwatch throws Andy back into the darkness.

"Was that it? Did we get him?"

How did it feel?

"It felt great! I'm glad he's dead. I'm glad my family will be okay. Even if I'm stuck here. Will they know what happened to me?"

Midwatch laughs. It is cruel and horrible.

No. No, they will never know. But it matters not. The man still roams free and will soon destroy your family, as he destroyed you! I showed you what you wanted to see. It was a joke! You are the biggest cornball around!

Midwatch continues to laugh.

Rage pours from Andy. Soon, it becomes despair.

"Why would you do that?"

Your stupid face, of course! Now you must go! Goodbye!

"Go? Go where? Wait... what's happening... I feel... feel... nothing..."

And where Andy's conscience had been now lingers merely an energy rich remnant. His soul-mind, shaped from the shadow of its former master.

Too easy. Lenny was correct, young minds are easy to manipulate and contain so much more power. See, Michael? I told you this was the way.

Midwatch holds Lenny's gift, a perfectly aligned soul-mind. When he returns Midwatch will attach it to him. The delicious energy of our departed friend will soon be bonded to Lenny Philips.

I have created the first illimni in a thousand years. It will not be the last.

Perhaps most cruel of all is that Andy the gas station attendant had actually had a very nice face.

III – LENNY

"Whew! Sorry to have scared you folks! My brakes failed and I may have been driving a bit too fast," recanted Lenny Philips to the panicked diners. A few were certain he and his truck appeared out of thin air. "I had no choice but to throw it into park and pray! Thank God she stopped in time!"

Many voices rose from the crowd, some loud, some mumbled. None too concerned with what just happened and already moving on.

"Maybe slow down."

"This isn't a race track out here!"

"I'm glad you're okay, mister."

"Would you like some coffee?"

"Damn military thinkin' they can do anything. I'm moving to Roswell."

Too easy.

Lenny sat at the last booth on the left, back to the wall. He wanted to see the diner, the parking lot, and make sure no one was to his back.

"So, how about that coffee?" asked the waitress.

"Oh. Yes, please. And how about some bacon, eggs, and toast. Strawberry jam if you have it, but grape will do," said Lenny. "I'm starving."

"That little bit of excitement put a hole in your stomach?" she asked. "Well, let me tell you it wouldn't have been the first time someone almost hit our building. I'll be right back with that coffee. Cream? Sugar?"

"Just black, please."

He leaned back in the booth and sighed. It looked like dirt, but he still had the remains of poor Andy between his fingers. He got up to go wash them off while he waited for Jack Nassem.

When he got to the restroom, he saw his face for the first time since before he met the men at the bomb site. He looked tired, and perhaps twenty years older. He needed a nap. He smiled to himself. He realized he could take however long of a nap he needed in Midwatch seeing as how he could travel to any place and any time. He'd never be late again. Hell, he could be early.

He stopped smiling when he saw what was in the sink. The dark brown substance on his hands had immediately returned to the signature shade of blood as it was re-hydrated. He killed that kid. Quite brutally.

Why don't I feel bad? No guilt. No... nothing.

Lenny knew what he had done was wrong. It was the first time he had ever physically harmed anyone, let alone smashed their skull in with a rock.

Midwatch did something to me. Blocked my conscience? I'll need to find out. I'm a murderer.

Lenny looked at his own face in the mirror as he thought this.

I'm a murderer.

I am a murderer.

I killed a kid in Ohio. Smashed his brains!

A family has lost a son. Do they even know?

They'll never find a body. Or his truck.

"Oh, shit. The truck," said Lenny to himself.

He'll need to get that thing back to Midwatch and leave it. He really disappeared that kid. The unsolved mystery of the young gas station attendant from Ohio. Went missing with no trace. The first of many, many more.

Leonard had no feelings on the subject.

He finished washing up and splashed some water on his face.

When he stepped out of the restroom, he saw Jack Nassem sat at his table and had stolen his preferred position with his back to the wall.

I'll get him for that, thought Leonard.

He walked towards Jack and said, "Hi Jack! How did you know I was in here?"

"Hi Lenny. Ah, well, there's a farm truck with the wrong color dirt on its fenders outside. And, ah, Ohio plates. Jesus, Lenny. Ohio? Really?" Jack Nassem said this excitedly, but his voice was a whisper. The disbelief on his face was comical.

"Yeah. Ohio really. Really really."

"How? What happened?"

"Look, Jack, we'll have time to discuss this later. I need to know if you still have influence. We're going to need it."

"Influence. Well, ah, sure. I can bend the ear of Groves and most of the other brass. Why?"

Lenny Philips had no idea how a goof like Jack Nassem gained so much trust. He supposed it was his demeanor and golly-gee mentality. The guy seemed like a nincompoop. But he always delivered and had a sharkiness swimming around behind that goofy face. Lenny figured it was that very goofiness that disarmed folks who were typically terrified their secrets could get out. If you needed a connection or to get a message out without anyone knowing, Jack Nassem was the man for the job. He was so goddamned unassuming. And he never asked for anything. Lenny couldn't tell if Jack was a genius or if it was all accidental. In any case, it all worked, and Jack was paid rather handsomely, either in money or favors from the most powerful families in the United States.

And it was contact with these families' leaders Lenny Philips needed now.

"Not military, Jack. The families, buddy. They are the ones to help build this thing. We can bring in the government when we're damn good and ready. Besides, those bastards tried to kill me and my team. Succeeded with some of my best, too."

"Oh. Oh, I see. Ah, yes Lenny. Yes, I do. But I, ah, would need to know what it was concerning."

"Jack Jack Jack," said Lenny. He shook his head and sighed. "What the hell do you think it's concerning? Jesus."

Lenny picked up his coffee and slurped. The waitress brought out his bacon, eggs, and toast.

"Here you go, sweetie. And you're in luck!" She said this while pulling a small glass jar of strawberry jam out of her apron and placing it on the table. "We don't always have it!"

"Must be my lucky day," said Lenny.

"How about you, honey?" she said to Jack. "You want somethin'?"

"No, ah, I'm fine. Thank you."

"Suit yourself. I'll be back around with more coffee in a bit."

After she walked away, Jack said, "Lenny, if, ah, you can do what you say, I'm going to need to see it. I can't, ah, go talk to these people if this isn't real."

Lenny stared at Jack while hastily swallowing down his breakfast. It was grotesque. He shoveled the food into his mouth, spreading the jam on his toast and ramming it in until it was gone. He stared at Jack the whole time. Sweat glistened on Jack's forehead.

Lenny swallowed and chased it down with a gulp of coffee.

"Listen Jack, I'll show you. But this connection won't be the end of it. I'll need you by my side for the long haul. This is going to change the world. And I feel like it will get bigger and bigger each time those idiots in Santa Fe test a bomb. Which will be good for business but will require more people involved to control it. Powerful, *secretive* people, you understand."

"Lenny, ah, I need to see what this is. And what incentive do I have? This seems, ah, like the kind of secret that would bring big trouble if it got out. Why would a guy like me, ah, risk his position?"

"I'll show you. First, we need to get that truck out there to ground zero. Can you do that?"

"Ground zero? What? Of the test site? Holy smokes, Lenny, how the hell am I going to do that? And with you in there with me. As soon as someone IDs you, there will be questions."

"I'll hide in the bed. Do your best golly-gee talking and they'll let you in. Besides, aren't there going to be parties going on all over base tonight? To celebrate the successful explosion and death of poor Lenny Philips? Should be minimal guards available as everyone is listening to the speeches and drinking the ceremonial champagne. Right?"

* * *

Lenny was right. That night, after years of work and secrecy, a huge celebration raged at Alamogordo. Not only of success, but of relief. It had worked. The bomb had been beautiful. And the world hadn't ended. At least, not yet.

He was also right about Jack's demeanor getting them in. He was just, ah, trustworthy. What can we say, he had a nice face.

As instructed, Jack shut the lights off on the truck as they drove to the site. He pulled the truck up to the house where Leonard and his team were meant to die, shut the engine off and moved to the passenger seat. Leonard climbed out of the bed and got in behind the wheel. He started the truck.

"I didn't tell you to shut it off."

"Oh, ah, I assumed..."

"Listen, Jack, if we're going to do this, you need to follow me every step of the way to my precise direction. If it all goes well, they may even name a city after you some day."

"That would, ah, be somethin'," said Jack. "Say, Lenny, do you feel that? I'm having a woozy feeling. Are we safe here?"

The gate. He can feel it. I can feel it too, thought Lenny. *What prevents anyone from going through these things? Couldn't someone just be walking along and end up in Midwatch?*

Lenny resolved to ask about this when they got to the other side. It would be hard to execute his plans if these things were open to anyone.

"Sure, we're safe. Look, I'm going to drive forward and then things are going to get dark and strange. You may smell sulfur. When that subsides, we'll be in another place."

"Ohio."

"Jesus. No, not Ohio. A place in between. Where we can then get to Ohio. But not right away. I'm telling you so you stay calm."

"Lenny, are you, ah, sure about this?"

"As a heart attack, Jack. As a heart attack. Are you ready?"

"I, ah, guess so," said Jack.

I sincerely doubt that, thought Lenny.

The truck rolled forward, and the shadows took it.

IV – MIDWATCH

The truck rumbles out from the gate. It is a foreign sound in Aesteria, now Midwatch. And the smell. Terrible. Midwatch appreciates the vehicle.

My good friend Lenny has brought another gift! thinks Midwatch.

The truck stops, and its power plant shuts down. Lenny gets out. His passenger hesitates.

"Lenny! You have returned!" says Midwatch.

"Yes, it's not that hard to think about where and when I want to be," says Lenny, mimicking Midwatch's tone. "How's Shammy?"

"Kept down as I said. You speak to me without realizing the ignorance of your request to have me watch him. If you truly grasped traveling to this moment, you would have known it was not necessary for him to be watched. Your servitude to time... pathetic."

"Uh, ah, Lenny? Is that, ah, cloud talking to you?" asks Jack Nassem, removing himself from the safety of the truck.

Another idiot emerges, thinks Midwatch.

"Jack! I almost forgot you were here. Come meet my friend," Lenny says. He motions for Jack to approach and keeps one eye on Midwatch.

Friend? Ha. You will call me Master before we are through.

"Lenny, ah, where exactly are we? This place, it, ah, smells funny."

"My *home* smells funny, you say? You, who brings that poison-generating conveyance into my realm? Who are you to judge what *smells* funny, Temporan?"

"Uh, ah, ah..."

"Fellas! Come now, we're all on the same mission here!" Lenny interjects. "Jack, the cumulonimbus in front of you is known as Midwatch, as is this place. Midwatch is in charge here. Midwatch, this is Jack Nassem. He can help us build up what we are planning. He has influence with the people back on Earth."

Jack Nassem rubs the bridge of his nose. Beads of sweat appear on his forehead. "So, ah, we are not on... ah, Earth?"

Midwatch scoffs. "*On* Earth? No, we are not *on* Earth. Though, we are near it. We are in between the plane in which Earth resides and the next. Midwatch is the conduit between places, and I am the director of what passes through."

Jack reaches out and grabs Lenny's arm. He pulls him close and whispers in his ear, "Lenny, ah, are we, ah, dead?"

Lenny Philips laughs. Perhaps harder than he has maybe ever. He is so full of energy, wonder, power, regret, fear, and anticipation. His emotions combine into one dense ball and seize upon the laughter as an opportunity to escape. It is maniacal.

"No, not dead! Alive! The most alive we'll ever be. Now, pay attention to Midwatch and it'll tell you what is and what is not," says Lenny.

A bolt of purple lightning shoots from Midwatch as Lenny finishes his sentence. It connects to Jack Nassem's head, and he falls to the ground.

Lenny is shocked, but before he speaks, Midwatch flashes over Jack's body and absorbs him entirely. Lightning pulses within Midwatch and then it flashes away, out of Lenny's sight, leaving him, the truck, the still unconscious Shammy, and the gate.

* * *

Once connected, Midwatch feels that Jack Nassem will not be as accepting of their plans as Lenny had been. It shows more of the realm to him. Jack Nassem does not have the ambition nor desire for power that Lenny has, the key manipulation point among Temporans. The desire for power darkens even the lightest of souls.

Midwatch learns quickly after interacting with Lenny's and Andy's souls that certain feelings need muted to truly control the Temporan mind. From Jack Nassem, it removes doubt, fear, and uncertainty.

As with those before, Jack becomes easier to work with after dampening his emotions. Midwatch explains the plans as before with Lenny.

Have you questions?

"I do. Am I stuck in here with you?"

That depends on your agreement to helping Lenny and I with our plans.

"Your plan to kidnap children, bring them here, murder them, and then redistribute their souls as you see fit? That the plan you're referring to? I don't see how I can do that."

So much more confidence than before. Interesting.

"Yes, I feel more confident. No more, ah, this, ah, that, ah, shucks."

So, you choose to stay here? In me? Then I have no use for this.

Midwatch begins separating Jack's mind from his soul. Midwatch could begin its expansion by absorbing this energy. If Lenny contests, Midwatch will take him as well. And his lame friend Shammy. There will always be plenty of men thirsting for power to do its bidding.

And, Midwatch thinks with a phantom smile, *time is on my side.*

The mind of Jack Nassem howls in agony. "No! Stop! Dear God, stop!"

That is one of the names by which we have been known by your kind. Was it something I said?

"What was that? What did you do to me?"

I was disposing of your mind but retaining your soul. It would be less painful if we killed you in your physical body first and then absorbed you. This could be arranged. For your comfort. Do you desire it?

"But what happens after? After they are separated?"

You fear death. Nothing, your mind goes blank. Its knowledge absorbed into Midwatch. A remnant left attached to the soul to maintain its last alignment. Otherwise, 'you' are gone.

"There's nothing after? That's so, ah, empty."

Feeling unsure of your decision? Would you like to stay a little longer? This can also be arranged.

"How do you, ah, mean?" Jack Nassem speaks with desperation, which Midwatch enjoys.

As I have already told your friend Lenny, I can slow your life.

"Slow? As in, ah, extend?"

Think of it however your unevolved mind can withstand. Your word for it is immortal, which is not accurate, but nearly so.

"Perhaps I do, or, ah, would be willing to help. If I didn't need to see or know any of these children..., ah, people."

Midwatch gifts Jack Nassem with a jolt of pleasure, energy, and confidence, and his alignment ticks downward.

Not all, though you will need to be close to a few. Do you accept it?

"I... do."

A small voice cries out from within Jack and is silenced. The same small voice that would cry out fifty-three years later from a young man named Cody McLean. The voice that says do not do this, it is not right, only to return after the damage is done, damned to live with the results of its absence moments before its final silencing.

* * *

"Where are you going, Lenny?" asks Midwatch upon returning to the gate.

Lenny is rattled as he enters the late Andy's truck, Chaz Shammy already sitting in the passenger seat, and kind of awake.

"Oh, um, we were going to come looking for you," says Lenny.

This is a lie, but Midwatch does not acknowledge it.

"No need, for I am here. Listen, all three of you," says Midwatch, speaking to Leonard, Jack, and Shammy. "If any of you fail me, if any of you fail in the task, or if you attempt to trick me, I will find you and I will harvest you. There are many more like yourselves who would gladly do my bidding for the chance at long life and power. Do you understand?"

Jack and Lenny nod. Shammy merely tilts his head and utters, "Huh?"

Lenny speaks to him through the cab. "Listen buddy, everything will be the same between us. You just follow ol' Lenny and everything will be fine."

"Yes, sir," says Shammy, adding, "You know, Lenny, I don't think this is Heaven after all."

"No shit," says Lenny.

"How has your minion responded?" asks Midwatch.

"He agrees to follow as I say, same as before," calls Lenny, still sitting in the driver's seat with the door open.

"Excellent!" says Midwatch. "Now, come friends! It is time for your gift!"

Lenny Philips, Jack Nassem, and Chaz Shammy all move slowly to stand in front of Midwatch. They are apprehensive, so it strikes them with a flash and removes the feeling.

That is better.

The three men now stand with an air of excitement and anticipation.

Midwatch speaks. "Here is what I have for you! Is it not marvelous?"

The men are horrified. In front of them, suspended by a violet strand of chaotic light, floats the phantasm of poor Andy the gas station attendant. The face is emotionless, the eyes unblinking, the limbs dangle without life. But it is the look on the face that gets them. It is regret, sadness, helplessness. Frozen in its last feelings, the feelings Midwatch allowed it to keep.

"What the hell is that?" asks Jack Nassem.

"This is your gift! The key to long life!" responds Midwatch. "To Aeraph, this is known as an illimni. None have been created for over a thousand of your years. As far as I know, none still exist."

Except one.

"An illimni? Like, illuminate? Why does it look like the boy? Is it him?" asks Lenny.

"It is more accurate to say it is 'of' the boy. It is his essence, his energy, absent his mind, except for a remnant. A remnant necessary to hold the alignment, which matches yours."

Midwatch conducts an experiment, unknown to these three. Not much knowledge remains concerning the use of illimni, and it is curious about what happens the further the alignment of an illimni and the host are misaligned. Midwatch suspects Jack will be fine but is very interested in what kind of mess Chaz Shammy will become. Experiments are fun!

"What do we do with it?" asks Lenny.

"Do? Nothing. I will attach it to you, and you go on about life as normal," says Midwatch.

"So, then, what does it, ah, do to us?" asks Jack.

"That is the gift! It takes the life left in this one and adds it to your own. Wonderful!" says Midwatch.

The men gasp.

Lenny raises his hand, much as a child under a strict teacher.

"Lenny?" says Midwatch, curious.

"Well, how do our bodies age? I don't think we are designed to live so long."

"Ah, yes. Your body's physical aging will slow to match the new longevity. For you, seventy-five would most resemble forty. Illimni also absorb disease and physical injury. When the illimni does this, it's life becomes shorter, thus shortening what it can give you. And it can only restore a physical attribute once, so if your heart fails, and the illimni restores it, it cannot do it again. You would need to return here to me and get a replacement."

At least, that is how I am to understand it works, thinks Midwatch. *We shall see.*

"And a replacement requires a death here in Midwatch?" asks Jack.

"Yes. Only here can illimni be created and attached," replies Midwatch.

"Well, okay. How will you attach this one to the three of us?" asks Lenny.

"I am going to split it into three equal pieces, causing its effects to be lessened. However, it will still be able to restore injury and disease, I believe."

"You believe?" asks Lenny. "You don't know."

"It has been a long time since Aeraph have used illimni, as I have said. This should make it all the more urgent for you to bring me three young Temporans to give you full illimni. I feel you will need them to protect yourself against what you are setting out to do."

The three men look at each other. Jack and Lenny nod while making eye contact. Lenny turns to Shammy and says, "Gunny, are you ready for our next mission?"

"Yes, sir," he says.

"Midwatch, we are ready to receive… our gift."

The violet light pulses deep within Midwatch. A scream echoes across the land as poor Andy's soul rips into three pieces. The pieces hover, haloed in that terrible purple, as silence follows the scream's echo.

Midwatch thrusts the three pieces of Andy into the men. Their bodies seize and writhe with pleasure and agony, each increasing as if to outdo the other.

When it is over, Lenny breathes calmly, feeling better than ever, experiencing simultaneous aponia and ataraxia; the absence of pain and a deep peace of mind reserved for the god-like Aeraph of Aesteria.

Jack experiences a tremendous increase in vitality, having instantly been cured of pancreatic cancer he hadn't known he had. His illimni yellows. His inner peace is less than Lenny's, owed to the illimni soul-energy's misalignment to his own, but for now he doesn't feel it over the relief of having a healthy pancreas.

Shammy goes bonkers. Voices in his head echo around about his mother and sister being killed. He feels the emotions. Except, he has no sister. He shakes his head, and they subside. "I hear voices," he says.

Hmm. Misalignment gives voice to the remnants. Mustn't do that, thinks Midwatch. It shoots Shammy a jolt of energy to subdue the leftovers of Andy's soul-mind.

"That's better," says Shammy.

When Lenny turns to Jack and Shammy, he is taken aback. The illimni's body floats behind them, attached by tethers of Midwatch's terrible purple light. Shammy's illimni occasionally blurs, and Jack's takes on a slight yellow tinge.

"We can see them. How will we return to do our work if we can see them?" asks Lenny.

"Only those who have an illimni can see others illimni. Otherwise, all that is observed is lucky long life and good health!" says Midwatch. And again, thinks to itself, *I believe that is how it works.*

"Are you ready to return?"

"Yes. Yes, I believe we are," says Lenny. He turns to Jack and Shammy and adds, "We'll be going to Alpha Falls in Ohio, next to a place called Brewster Township. There is a gate there which we will make central to our new operation. Jack, we'll need to find allies and grow our... organization. There is a school near the spot, which should be helpful to our plight."

A shadow of regret passes across Jack's face, then he responds, "You're the boss, Lenny. Let's get to it."

The three men climb into poor Andy the gas station attendant's truck. Technically, he is in it too. Lenny starts it up, unleashing its strange sound and poison scent upon the decaying beauty of Aesteria, quickening its transformation into Midwatch. He drives it through the gate back into rural Ohio and the echo of their world's transformation begins.

V – GERALD MONTGOMERY SR.

The only trouble Leonard had was with Chaz Shammy's missing Sergeant, Gerald Montgomery Senior and his descendants. Gerald reappeared in Europe in 1943, two years before the Trinity test. He had been wandering around Midwatch and thinking about his time serving in WW2 when he accidentally walked through a gate placing him right back in the European theater. He was confused, and thought he was injured or had some sort of shell shock. But then, oh boy, he saw himself. He was making his way towards his barracks tent when he saw the real 1943 Gerald walking away from it. He couldn't believe it, but who would? So, he hid. And waited. Finally, here came 1943 Gerald making his way back to the tent.

He had time travelled. The bomb had worked. The other place had been real. He had gone backwards two years. Now what? Maybe he could go back.

Gerald made his way back to where he thought he had 'entered' this time. As he was wandering again, Jack Nassem approached him. He didn't recall Jack being stationed here, and he looked older. Not much, but older for sure.

War could do that.

"Gerald," said Jack with a side eye.

"Jack. Jack, what are you doing here?" asked Gerald.

Jack Nassem spoke deliberately. "Look, Gerald, I'm going to ask you a question. It may sound strange, but it is very important. Can you answer with no judgement?"

"Yes, Jack. I can do that."

"What year is it?" asked Jack.

Gerald gave Jack his own side eye as he mulled it over. Either Jack was here to get him, Jack thought he was nuts, or Jack had come through the same whatever Gerald came through and was trying to figure out what was up.

Gerald thought a moment and then decided what answer would give him the most useful information.

"1945," he said.

Jack smiled. "Great! Yes, yes, it is. Come with me, let's get you back."

"Okay Jack, I will. But can you explain what's going on? Did the bomb do this?"

"Sort of. I'll explain everything. We've been searching for you for a while."

Gerald didn't think it had been that long.

Jack took Gerald back through and then to Leonard Philips in Ohio, who had already been working on his plans for a couple months.

* * *

"So, right now we're in Ohio in September 1945, and Jack and I were just in France in 1943?" asked Sergeant Montgomery.

Lenny and Jack nodded. They didn't speak, wanting to give him time to process.

"I don't believe it," he mumbled. He kicked at the ground and shrugged. "Well, what do we do now?"

Lenny and Jack gave Gerald the 'civilian' explanation of what they were doing. The physicists hadn't known exactly what the bomb would do outside of exploding, but they knew it could do something. The bomb had torn time, creating holes which they needed to protect from America's enemies and her people. A believable story, but not the truth. The holes had always been there, the bomb just ripped them a bit. Oh, and one Aeraph named Hesperus became Midwatch.

In the end, Jack convinced the powers that be to promote Sergeant Gerald Montgomery Senior all the way up to Colonel Gerald Montgomery Senior, which took a lot of paperwork but very little actual convincing. After all, Gerald knew enough to cause trouble unless ranked high enough he felt he had no one to tell. Then, they sent him home to his wife and young son Gerald Junior. He bought an old manse in Hampton, New Hampshire large enough to have its own name: Redgrave Manor. This was almost one year to the day before Gerald Junior took an axe to the head and made Gerald Senior's nightmare come true. After all, Midwatch could be many things at many times, even, perhaps, thoughts and dreams.

September 1998

BREWSTER FALLS

HAMPTON

AESTERIA

CHAPTER 3

Cody McBeans is Scared

"Good morning, Garage House Kids!"

I – THE CAPRICE

Darryl Horne had not been a nice man. He was mean, narcissistic, scary, unloving, angry, and strict. His only love was his tools and his cars. He had tools and cars everywhere. And car parts. The bathtub, the kitchen sink, the hall, the bedrooms. You name a room in their little shack of a house, and Darryl had a car part in it.

Darlene Horne, formerly Darlene Walker, tried to clean her little son Carson's room once and moved a carburetor onto the dining room table which was already covered with nuts, bolts, and all manner of car bullshit. She figured what difference could it make? This shit was everywhere and in no particular order.

Instead of putting shit away he just remembered where and what it was.

So, once upon a time, when his oldest boy Charles, who Darryl called Chuck, came out to the garage and told him the carb wasn't in Carson's room between the little plastic toy lawnmower and the spare fuel pump for his truck, Darryl shook his head.

"Goddamit," Darryl muttered under his breath to the oil covered ground around his boots.

Young Charles took a step back and winced. He braced himself. His daddy had never hit him, but Chuck was plenty scared it could happen any time.

Darryl took the red shop rag out of his back pocket and wiped his hands. They were still covered in grease, but less so. Looking around the doors and door frames in their house one could guess he had done this many times. All were discolored where he touched them when going through looking for parts and tools.

"Chuck, don't ever move a man's tools or parts while he's in the middle of a project, you unnerstand?"

"I unnerstan, Daddy," Charles said in the accent he now tried so hard to hide from his friends. His daddy stomped into the house and yelled for Darlene.

The only project Darryl Horne had ever finished was a modified 1992 Chevy Caprice he gave Charles as his first car. Darryl bought the car cheap from the Brewster Falls Police Department after it had been ridden too hard and put away wet by his friend, Chief Greg Riggs. Back then Greg was just a deputy. The car had needed an engine, so they dragged it home with a chain and Darryl's baby blue square-body, which he taught his sons was the name for mid-eighties trucks, which ol' Blue was.

They spent the next two years together working on it. They would have been done sooner, but Darryl liked to take apart a bunch of stuff, mix it all up, and dump it at Charles' feet.

He'd laugh and say, "Good luck boy. Once you figure out what each of those are and what they do, go ahead and put 'em in. This is the only education you're ever gonna get, so get learnin'." Then Darryl would crack a beer, sit in his lawn chair, and watch his son work. No radio, his daddy said that was too distracting. Charles hated that because he loved music, validated when he later joined the Pride of Brewster Falls: the marching band. He managed to convince his daddy to put in a CD player as one of their last mods to the Caprice, though. Darryl didn't understand that, no more than he understood joining marching band.

In rare moments of softness, Darryl would help find a tool or place a bolt if Charles struggled too long. Otherwise, though, he let his son work. And cry.

Boy did Charles cry.

Not because he was sad or because his daddy wouldn't help him, but because he hurt himself. A lot. Each time his hand would smack against the engine due to a tool slipping or a bolt breaking, Charles would put it in his mouth and the tears would come. He got so used to the taste of blood and grease he started to crave it.

Darryl would take his hand, rip off a piece of shop rag, and fix it to the wound by wrapping it with electrical tape.

"Chuck, this is how you do it when you're under the hood. No reason to clean it all up 'cause it'll happen again. Plus, it's the blood and the pain that make a car run right. A price has got to be paid to the soul of the thing. You unnerstand?"

"I unnerstan, Daddy—" he didn't "—thank you."

The Caprice was the only way he ever knew his daddy loved him.

They got their engine out of a wrecked 1995 Chevy Impala SS. When this happened, Charles decided he wanted the car painted black (it was white) and he wanted Impala SS wheels, an Impala SS spoiler, Impala SS seats, and Impala SS badges. He also wanted the little Chevy bowtie hood ornament removed from the hood along with all the chrome trim around the glass. All this needed money, which they didn't have.

The Horne's were the poorest family in Brewster Falls. People turned their noses up at them while they were at the grocery store or out to dinner. It was the smell of grease, cigarettes, and well water. Darlene blamed Darryl, as if it was his fault alone they were poor.

Charles went to work cutting grass for neighbors. He bought his parts from junkyards. In the winter, he shoveled snow.

His dad called him out to the garage one night after the car was all done. He had a can of beer in his hand, his fifth or sixth by the way he spoke, and the last half of a lit Camel cigarette in the corner of his mouth. His daddy looked his best with a greasy shirt, dirty hands, and that cigarette.

"Now boy, don't be callin' this car an Impala SS or any dumb shit like that. This is a Caprice, it was built a Caprice, and it'll always be a Caprice. Don't try to make it something it'll never be. Don't be embarrassed about what it is. You can call it a Caprice SS but that's as far as it goes. You unnerstand?"

Charles did not understand. And for the first time ever, he said so. "Dad, I did all this work. I spent all my own money. I want an Impala not a stupid Caprice. So that's what I built."

And then it happened.

SMACK.

It was the first and only time Darryl ever hit one of his sons. Horror spread across Darryl's face and a foreign glassiness shone in his eyes.

"Goddamit Chuck. I'm tryin' to tell you somethin'. Don't be ashamed of what you're made of. Like this car. Don't be ashamed that it isn't an Impala SS, be proud that it's a badass Caprice. Same with you. I know we ain't the best family in Brewster Falls, but goddamit we ain't the worst. I'm proud of you boy. And I'm proud of what you did."

His daddy had never spoken this way to him. He started crying. Darryl hugged him.

"Chuck, I want you to know I'm giving you my tools. They're all yours now. You're a better mechanic than I'll ever be. You got a gift most don't have. You're the best thing I ever done and the smartest person I know."

"Dad, won't you need them? Your tools?"

"Naw. My car workin' days are over. I gotta do something else now."

The next morning when Charles got up for school, his mom was crying in the kitchen and ol' Blue was gone. He hadn't seen it or his daddy since.

II – GOOD MORNING

Charles Horne turned his big Chevy Caprice onto Donovan from Colonel Perez as they made their way to the Brewster Falls High School student parking lot. The Smashing Pumpkins 'Today' dripped from its speakers, its four occupants ignoring the outside world until Alice Massey exclaimed from the backseat, "Good morning, Garage House Kids!"

Outside the Garage House, as always, figures gathered just out of reach of dawn's coming light. They smoked cigarettes and watched the cars roll towards the High School from a breezeway connecting the garages, their faces indiscernible beneath its shadow. The Garage House seemed to be a cool hangout for the outcasts before the first bells rang, producing an aura around it that defied Brewster Falls' self-important reality. The Caprice's occupants strained to identify these figures.

Cody McLean—who became Cody McBeans after an unfortunate lunchroom accident involving someone spilling baked beans on the floor and what could only be described as a bean and slide—sat next to Alice in the back seat.

The shrapnel from Alice's question sparked his curiosity, causing him to ask, "D'you guys ever wonder about them?"

"What do you mean?" asked Alice.

Tiffany Philips—Leonard Philips' daughter—rode shotgun. She sighed and rolled her eyes.

Cody replied, "Who are they? Why are they there every morning? What if they aren't students... er, what if they, y'know, just like to watch us?"

"Whoa, too much X-Files for you!" said Charles. He winked at Cody through the rearview mirror.

This drew chuckles from Alice and Tiffany, and even a small, reluctant one from Cody.

As they passed the Garage House, Charles glanced around the car's interior, appreciating his friends' ability to make his life bearable. A rare smile tugged at the corners of his mouth. It faded quickly when he looked at the face of his best friend.

Cody McBeans was scared.

Good morning, Garage House Kids!

Sometimes, a simple phrase can reveal hidden things. Sometimes, these things are supposed to stay hidden, lurking and watching, just like Cody said.

Charles pulled the car into the Brewster Falls High School parking lot, past the yellow gate and the guard. He parked it in the same spot each day, and at the same time.

"Is everything okay?" Tiffany asked.

Charles smirked a little smirk and said, "Yeah, just looking out for strange garage people."

"You're such a dork," said Cody, wanting to say something more severe than dork. He got out and closed the rear door behind him. "A giant headed cynical dork who spouts nothing but dork thoughts."

Alice laughed from behind Tiffany, which made Cody produce his own little smirk.

Tiffany walked in front of the car and put her arm around Charles' waist.

"Don't listen to them. They're just jealous of your big head and big head thoughts," she said.

Charles smiled further and said, "I know, babe." He tossed his arm around her shoulders and let his hand hang loose over her book-bag strap. "I have one question, though. Am I a dork because I'm in marching band, or am I in marching band because I'm a dork?"

Tiffany shuddered.

"Are you cold? Want my hoodie?" asked Charles.

"I'll be all right. You know I don't like that one, anyway," said Tiffany.

Charles glanced toward the football field and rolled his eyes. Cody shrugged.

It was his favorite hoodie, and Alice helped him make it. Charles doodled shapes and stuff at night before he went to sleep. The one that now inhabited the back of his hoodie came to him in a dream a few times, so he sketched it out. Once, Alice had been over and was holding the Horne's cat, Bart, when she said the sketch on his nightstand would look cool on a shirt. Charles decided on a black hoodie and wanted the shape on the back. The shape itself was simple enough; two triangles joined at their bases; one pointing up, one pointing down. The shape was *nearly* symmetrical, as if it were moving. It was pretty freakin' cool.

He turned Tiffany to face him and slipped his hand around between her back and her bookbag as usual and spread his fingers to take up as much space on and around the small of her back as possible. He didn't know why he did it. To make her feel safe? Wanted?

Owned? Did she even notice? He just liked how it felt. He gave her a quick kiss and said "See you at lunch," as he did every day.

* * *

When he got to Ms. Henry's first period English class, he leaned over to Mitch Riggs and asked if he had ever noticed the kids at the house on the corner. It struck Charles how delicious Mitch smelled.

"What? No. What are you talking about?" asked Mitch, leaning back a little.

Mitch and Charles got along well but were not friends. They had been to a couple of the same birthday parties growing up, but that was their relationship's extent outside school walls. Inside school walls, they were euchre partners when there was time and often disrupted teachers' lectures.

"Nothing. I mean, we barely make it to class on time, and I never even see them coming around the corner to make it in here."

"Dude, you're buggin'. There are kids parked all over the place; down at the old restaurant, across the street from the school, hell, some are even down at Shammy's."

"I'm not *buggin'* Mitch. Maybe we're missin' out on something going on, y'know? Something different."

"Missin' out on your mom, maybe," Mitch laughed. "You need to take a chill pill my man."

Maybe he did need a chill pill. A lot of kids were on them these days. A few years ago, no one had even heard of chill pills or ADD. Felt like everyone had it now, though.

Charles asked other kids the same question for the rest of the day, with similar responses. Maybe they were just grunge types stickin' it to the man before school, making sure they showed up after the bell because the expectation was to show up before the bell.

To hell with your rules, man. Your expectations mean nothing to us.

After school, when he arrived back at the Caprice, Cody McBeans was already standing next to it and gazing into nowhere. His eyes focused when Charles approached.

Like a robot turning on.

Charles discovered Cody had performed similar interrogations all day with similar results.

Weirdo. You're paranoid. Mind your business. Who cares? Y'know there's pills for that?

Tiffany and Alice arrived a brief time later, and they all got in the car and left. No one spoke. To lighten the mood, Charles put his Chumbawamba CD in the radio and played "Tubthumping".

They all noticed there were no cars or indiscernible figures lurking at the Garage House.

III – TIFFANY

I hate this stupid song, thought Tiffany.

She wanted to know what she did this time but didn't want to put in the effort to ask.

He didn't even meet her for lunch today. She ate alone with Alice, who of course asked her where Charles was.

Charles belongs to me. The shadows take her.

She saw Alice's head and body being ripped apart piece by piece, the sinew stretching out like so much red spaghetti.

Tiffany and Alice had been friends since preschool. They were like sisters.

She shook her head and pulled out her compact to check her eyes.

No one spoke on the ride home. But it (he) was like that sometimes. Charles would play the radio just too loud to comfortably have a conversation.

Where is he? Where does he go? Doesn't he trust me?

Tiffany thought about the Homecoming Dance last year. Her and Charles' first date, in the terms of high school kids.

* * *

He had picked her up at her parents' house. Her father, Leonard Philips, watched from the window, wanting to observe what sort of boy was courting his daughter. He said he could judge the character of people in an instant. 'Good, bad, chaotic, rule-abiding; Lenny Philips will know' he had once said. Tiffany rolled her eyes at him.

Charles parked his Caprice at the apex of their arched driveway with the passenger door positioned in line with the walkway from their front entry. A courtesy to his date, so far so good.

They made short work of the meeting. Tiffany's mother, Stacey, was quick to say hello and give him a tight hug. Leonard, however, was a little more stoic. He shook his hand and said, "My friends call me Lenny, but you can call me Mr. Philips."

Charles said it was a pleasure to meet him. He held a firm grip and made eye contact, as his daddy had taught him.

Leonard looked into the boy's eyes. Later, Charles told Tiffany he wanted to look away but didn't. He stared right back until Mr. Philips smiled. Well, let's say the corners of his mouth twitched a little.

"Pleasure to meet you, son. Take care of my daughter tonight," Lenny said, before releasing Charles' hand. "When will you return?"

Oh, Dad. Why are you like this? thought Tiffany.

"Uh..." Charles began.

"Oh, Leonard. Let them have fun. You kids run along. Call us if you need anything. I'll be by the phone!" said Tiffany's mother.

Thanks mom!

So that being done, they went to the dance.

Although they wore ill-fitting formal wear and drank from plastic wine glasses filled with punch, they had a pretty good time.

The DJ played Soundgarden, Nirvana, and even a track from the Ramones. To Tiffany's dismay, little romance sparked.

Until, near the end, a song played that would become more of a joke than love song—much like Batman Forever, the film to which it was attached.

Tiffany grabbed Charles' hand and took him to the dance floor. He slid his left hand around her back and held her close, firmly yet gently, and took her left hand in his right. They held their arms in close as they danced. They smiled at each other and stepped into the melody of what is actually a great song.

"I compare you to a kiss from a rose," said Charles.

"Oh my gosh," giggled Tiffany.

"You're a growing addiction I can't deny."

She looked at him and smiled.

He always makes me laugh.

"You think about me when you hear this song?" she teased.

"I think about you and me a lot. That's all I want to think about right now," he said. "You're so beautiful." There were no poets in High School, but it was enough, and he had meant it.

She blushed.

"And you're so handsome," she said, which was also true regardless of his ill-fitting suit. Not everyone had Philips' money.

She laid her head on his chest.

He squeezed her to him as they danced.

Then, moments before the song ended, he placed his finger under her chin so they could look into each other's eyes.

And then they kissed.

I may be in love, she thought. She closed her eyes, his lips lingered against hers for a moment.

Alice and Cody watched from the wall.

Unknown to any of these young people, something was sensed in that sweet moment. An energy detected by forces that would now race towards it, looking for the source of its release. Whomever or whatever attained it first may tip the scales of an unseen fight raging all around them.

But let us not ruin this vision of sweet innocence with that, shall we? That story lies before us. For now, let us soak in the rapturous memory of a first kiss.

* * *

Almost a year later, Tiffany sighed in the passenger seat of his car. She thought a year was enough time for sharing their thoughts.

Apparently not.

IV – SHAMMY'S

Going to Shammy's Piazza after school was a ritual. A time to decompress before chores, homework, or responsibility. It was a place most of Brewster Falls stopped into after football games on Friday nights, where many families had birthdays, and where everyone had the best pizza, well, anywhere.

For the citizens of Brewster Falls, this was the center of town, and the mayor was crazy Chaz Shammy.

Chaz Shammy was a self-proclaimed veteran, although no one knew of which war. If you spoke to him long enough, he'd talk about the fallen, the lingering shadow of battle, and many conspiracy theories concerning the U.S. Government and her doings. No one cared, listened, or gave it any credit. Why? Because the pizza was phenomenal and the arcade was choice.

In fact, along with not knowing what Chaz Shammy was a veteran of, no one cared. It was simple enough of course, as simple as asking Chaz the details of his service, but people were happy to ignore little details in the interest of comfort. And besides, Shammy didn't trust nobody anyhow, so you woulda had to ask, as he would say.

"Chuck," Shammy said with a nod to Charles. In what was his fashion, he did so to each.

"McBeans."

Nod.

"Ms. Philips." He gave respect to Brewster Falls' royalty.

Nod.

"Al," he used the name preferred by Alice's friends and known acquaintances.

Nod.

"The usual for you?" he asked, already knowing the answer.

"Yes," they answered in unison.

"I'll take some of these, too," said Charles. He grabbed a carton of chocolate covered peanuts off the stack next to the register. Shammy always had a state-fair style collection of sweets and treats. Caramel clusters, chocolate raisins, yogurt raisins, circus peanuts, Boston baked beans, you name it, Shammy had it.

"Right on," said Shammy.

Charles produced twenty dollars made up of a ten, a five, four singles, two quarters, and five dimes. It was everything he had.

"It's all on me today," he said.

"Right on," said Shammy.

"Charles! You don't have to do that!" said Tiffany. "I have more than enough."

"Yeah, Chuck. Let us put in our share," said Cody.

"No. I said I got it. You guys get it next time."

"Here. Take this. Please," said Alice. She held out a crisp twenty-dollar bill to Shammy, not Charles. Shammy eyed it and looked over to Charles for guidance.

"Shammy, I'm paying. Don't take that unless you're giving yourself a tip," said Charles.

"Right on," said Shammy and snatched the twenty from Alice's hand. Charles' scraps went in the register, and her bill went in his apron. Such was Shammy.

"Hey!" said Alice.

"Thanks," said Shammy. "Your pies will be up in ten to fifteen. You want any drinks?"

He was running the place solo today. It wasn't busy.

He had a peculiar setup. One register for the food, and one register for drinks. The drink counter had its own special spot, too. And everything was cash only, no free refills. The place felt like it was right out of the forties, which was part of its charm.

"Yeah, we need drinks," said Charles.

They got two pitchers of Coke.

"That'll be six dollars," said Shammy.

"Take it out of that twenty in your apron," said Alice.

"That'll be six dollars," said Shammy.

"Seriously Shammy? Can't you be cool today?" said Alice.

"I'm cool every day, Al. Who's giving me six dollars?"

"Geez, here," said Tiffany. "Can you break a fifty?"

"Nope," said Shammy.

Tiffany sighed again.

"Fine, keep it," she said.

"Right on," said Shammy.

He slid the tray across the counter, and tucked Tiffany's bill in with Alice's.

Such was Shammy.

* * *

"How old do you think he is?" asked Cody.

"Well, I assume he was in Vietnam by how he acts. Probably joined when he was twenty?" Charles said with a shrug.

"That would make him about fifty," said Alice.

"How did you come up with that so fast?" asked Tiffany.

"Yeah, that was impressive, Al," said Charles.

Tiffany didn't like that at all.

"Well, assuming he joined when he was twenty, and he was in fact in Vietnam, that would have been around 1969. It's 1998, so twenty plus twenty-nine is forty-nine. He's about fifty," said Alice.

"Are you a nerd?" asked Cody, whose pupils dilated as Alice explained her math.

"Yes, she's a nerd and no one likes her," said Tiffany. She looped her arm in Charles', and he pulled his out to reach for his soda.

Tiffany didn't like that, either.

"Hey! Way harsh, Tiff," said Alice.

"Yeah, Tiff, way harsh," teased Cody. He received her patented way harsh glare in return.

"Why do you ask McBeans?" asked Charles.

"Well, we've made ourselves look lame asking about this all day, so why not one more. I think we should ask Shammy about it. The Garage House, I mean."

"He'll probably charge us ten more dollars," said Alice.

"Oh. My. God. Whatever. If they want to ask him, let them ask him," said Tiffany.

"Alright, let's do it. Who has ten bucks?" asked Charles.

It was Cody's turn to pay the mayor of crazy town.

* * *

Tiffany sipped her Coke and stared at nothing in particular.

"Are you alright?" asked Alice.

"I'm fine," answered Tiffany.

Alice took a drink before she pressed.

"Tiff, we've been friends, like, forever. I know when something is bothering you. And I can kind of tell it's me. So what's up?"

Tiffany set down her drink and rolled her vision away from Alice.

Alice gritted her teeth, but only a little. She placed a hand on Tiffany's shoulder. "Tiff," she said.

"I think Charles likes you. I saw how he looked at you earlier," Tiffany answered, still looking away. Then she turned back before adding, "and worse, I think you like him."

Alice smiled. "Tiff, I do like him. He's my friend. We're close, but like brother-sister close. You know that."

"I hear you say it, but I don't believe it. He's my boyfriend, Al. Mine."

Alice removed her hand from Tiffany's shoulder.

Tiffany shook her head, as if clearing away mental cobwebs. "We're better than fighting over a dumb boy, aren't we?"

"I hope so," Alice answered. "We're strong, independent women, after all!"

"We don't need no men!" They said in unison, laughing.

"No, we don't," said Alice, "but, we need to act like we do, because here they come."

* * *

Charles and Cody returned to the table with their pizzas.

"So, what'd he say?" asked Alice.

"You won't believe this. He wanted twenty dollars," said Cody.

"Yeah, but we convinced him to come down to the ten," said Charles. "And you really won't believe this, he's only twenty-nine."

"Not so smart now, huh Al?" said Tiffany.

"Tiff, c'mon," said Charles.

Alice's eyebrows shot up. "That's crazy," she said.

They peered into Shammy's kitchen area.

"And as soon as we asked about the Garage House, his eyes went out of focus and he kind of locked up. It was weird. Then he shook his head, gave back the ten, and handed us our pizzas," said Cody. "He said 'Have a great day kid.' And walked away before we could say anything."

"Well, that would make him the right age to be in the Gulf War. But what happened to him? He looks so old," said Alice.

"He sure does. And I think he knows something about that house. We should try again tomorrow," said Charles.

Tiffany smiled like she heard the punchline to an inside joke.

"What's funny?" asked Charles.

"Oh, nothing. Just thinking about tomorrow," she said.

As she chewed her pizza, her eyes turned to Alice. She swallowed and smiled again, all teeth and gums.

V – CHARLES

They had already dropped off Alice, so as soon as Cody McBeans said, 'See you tomorrow' and closed the car door, Tiffany started asking questions.

"Hey, did I do something wrong?" she asked.

"Huh? No, why?" he asked back.

"Well, you never told me what was bothering you this morning, and you said nothing the whole time we were driving, and on top of it I should be upset with you because you didn't even come sit with me at lunch or find me in the halls between classes today. Where were you?"

"I didn't?" he asked, then stated, "I didn't."

Where was I? Charles thought.

A moment of silence passed between them.

Charles spoke first.

"Sorry, I had to... practice my sax for a playing test," he lied.

"Well, why didn't you tell me? You had to have known this morning and all you said was 'see you at lunch'. Just once I'd like it if you actually shared what you were thinking."

"You wouldn't want to know," he said.

I wish I knew, he thought.

"You're so *frustrating*," she replied.

Just tell her you idiot.

"Hey, I just forgot. The days are running together, and I didn't realize it until I looked at my planner during third period. I'm sorry."

"You're always sorry. I wish you'd include me in your life."

"Geez, do we have to do this?"

Especially since I wasn't practicing.

"Well, if we are, it's your fault. We're all here living in your world."

"This is bullshit. I had to practice. It's a school lunch, not a date. It's not that important."

"It's important to me."

Here it comes, he thought. *Dammit, Chuck. Tell her the truth.*

"You know what, forget it. Forget I said anything. You're right, it's not important." She turned away and looked out the window.

For reasons mysterious but often replicated, the late adolescent male stuck with his fib, reasoning it would be easier than admitting his mistake.

"Look, I love you and I'm sorry. But I needed to get that test done. How can you be mad when I'm trying to improve myself?" he asked.

Silence. Broken by Charles. Silly boy.

"Babe. Babe? Hello?"

"Leave me alone. I said you were right."

He always dropped her off last because sometimes they would go inside and make out if her mom wasn't home. Sometimes they'd do a little more than make out.

Not today.

As soon as Charles stopped in front of Tiffany's ridiculously large house, she jumped out, said "Bye", shut the door, and walked away.

Why did I do this?

It didn't matter, something else was on his mind.

VI – CODY MCBEANS

I need to find a new ride to school. Or get my license. Or walk. Or drop out.

He had an unshakeable positivity to him that could be annoying. Cody was also short, skinny, dressed funny, and was in marching band with Charles. Whenever Cody was around, people laughed. Only, he never noticed. He believed he was only invited because Charles was invited. Charles was cool.

She doesn't get him, he thought.

He tossed his book bag on his floor and belly flopped onto his bed.

He yelled into his pillow.

He lifted his head and studied the chaotic scene displayed before him. Slick and Spin, the famous Crash Test Dummies, in all manner of mayhem and destruction.

I need to tell my mom I need new stuff. Maybe a car, too.

Cody used to sit in the front seat before Tiffany came around. When she showed up there wasn't even a discussion about the seating arrangements. She was the First Lady of the Caprice and Cody was a simple knave.

A quick trip through the windshield for Princess Tiffany would solve some issues.

Sure, Charles would be sad, and Alice, too, a little. But Charles could install a new windshield and Cody could sit in the front again and the peasants would rejoice!

"What the hell is wrong with me?" Cody asked himself. He chewed on the image of Tiffany Philips crashing through Charles' windshield, her face peppered with glass, blood dripping from her lifeless mouth.

He slapped himself.

I'm an idiot, he thought.

He remembered going to his early classes and asking Jennifer Noble if she had ever noticed the people at the house on the corner.

Why did I ask Jenny?

Jenny Noble was one of the most popular kids in school, she was in choir, she was a thespian, she played flute or clarinet or something like that, and she was beautiful.

So, when the first thing he ever said to her was, "Good day, my Noble lady—" he thought this would be clever, and perhaps in another time it was "—hast thou taken notice of the house on yon corner? Verily, dark figures reside there each morn."

"What?" she had asked. Then, she confirmed all his fears and dismissed him with a look of disgust.

He replied, before walking away, "Damsel, God grant you health and happiness."

Alone in his room, Cody's face went red with embarrassment.

Charles is the only friend I need.

No one cared about him, no one cared about the stupid Garage House, and no one cared about Tolkien.

He remembered leaving fourth period to go to his locker, he remembered pulling out his lunch, which on that day his mom had sealed with a Sylvester the cat Looney Tunes sticker, and he remembered walking toward the lunchroom—and then he had lunch and finished his day?

The memories didn't work.

This is what he *felt* happened. He almost had a memory of sitting at the table with Charles and everyone. Almost. If anyone had asked, he would have told them that *was* what happened.

Except, he knew he never made it to lunch because he was never this hungry after school.

Pop-Tarts sounded really good.

CHAPTER 4

Hazel is Not Amused

"When covered, the bogeyman cannot get you..."

I – HAZEL MONTGOMERY

As Cody McBeans removed the wrapper from his iced strawberry Pop-Tarts with sprinkles—the only kind worth having—the phone rang. He nearly jumped out of his shoes. He would never admit this to anyone, but he peed a little.

He lifted the receiver off its base and pressed the green talk button.

"Hello, McBeans...uh, I mean McLean residence. Cody speaking."

Hazel Montgomery, the individual responsible for the tiny accident now resting in Cody's underpants, wondered how she ended up in this position. The poor kid was not even sure of his own name, let alone what danger sought him.

I've been doing this for too long. Much, much too long, she thought.

"Cody McLean? This is Hazel Montgomery, Brewster Falls Schools lead student counselor. Is your mother home?" Her success rate was much higher motivating parents into action when times necessitated it. Kids always wanted to know why. Always had *questions.* And they never trusted her. Kids were smart that way.

"Forgive me, Hazel, for my mother dwells not within these halls at present. She returns with the setting of the sun, near the half mark past the fifth hour. Upon her return, shall I bid her summon thee?"

You gotta be kidding.

"Cody, please refer to me as Ms. Montgomery. Is your father home? Is anyone home other than yourself?"

Hazel knew her reputation at Brewster Falls High School. She knew Cody knew it would agitate her to call her by her first name. If there was an ideal temperament for a school counselor, she possessed the farthest thing from it.

"I stand as guardian of the keep, M'lady. Wouldst there be anything I couldst help thou with?"

Remember Hazel, you need to save this witty little smartass.

"Cody, please dispense with the medieval pleasantries. You will refer to me as Ms. Montgomery, and you will show respect when speaking with me. Did you speak with Jennifer Noble this morning?" she asked.

"Verily."

Little asshole.

"What did you speak about?"

"Well, I... uh... was asking about... getting her phone number?"

"Getting her phone number?" He was lying. "Are you sure that is all you spoke about?"

"Yes, I'm sure. And she wouldn't give it to me. She thinks I'm weird. Hey, is this the kind of stuff I should talk about with you?"

"Listen to me carefully, Cody. Is there a neighbor you can stay with until your parents get home? Someone next door?"

"No, our neighbors get home the same time as my mom, sometimes a little later. I do have a couple friends up the street—What's going on? Why do I need to leave my house?"

C'mon kid.

"Up the street is too far. Lock your doors and close your curtains immediately. If you have an upstairs, go to it, and if possible, lock yourself in a room until your mother gets home."

"WHAT IS GOING ON?" Cody freaked out a little bit. Maybe he peed a little more.

Hazel Montgomery replied with a voice softer than any student in Brewster Falls Schools would have ever believed she could use, "Cody, Jennifer Noble did not make it home from school today. She was last seen leaving the school around lunch time."

"That's terrible! But what does this have to do with me?"

Seriously with the questions.

"Where did you two go at lunch time?" Ms. Montgomery asked.

"What?" Cody asked. "The two of who?"

She could taste the panic in his tone.

"You and Jennifer Noble. We have an individual that says they saw the two of you leaving the school around lunch time and walking across the parking lot towards Colonel Perez Drive." It was against protocol to share information about the existence of a witness, but she didn't have the time to follow protocol. Plus, the scared are easier to control.

"Ms. Montgomery, I have never gone anywhere with Jenny, and I doubt I ever will. I had lunch in school, same as always. Honest."

Liar.

"You left school grounds with Jennifer Noble and you didn't have lunch inside the school. And you just lied to me, which I will remember and for which there will be consequences *if* you make it through this by doing exactly as I say." Ms. Montgomery acted like the Ms. Montgomery everyone knew and loathed. "You were the last to see her which makes you very important. Someone is watching you. You need to hide."

It was her turn to lie.

"Who's watching me? Why do I need to hide?"

I should let it happen.

"Cody, listen to me carefully. We don't have time to discuss this. Secure your home now and hide. I will be there after your parents arrive and will answer all your questions then."

Not.

"But Ms. Montgomery, I don't understand..."

"NOW CODY MCLEAN! DO IT NOW!"

Hazel Montgomery had had enough.

"Okay, I'm doing it."

The line went dead with a click.

Hazel hoped the boy was doing as she asked and not looking out the window. It was an odd thing, a masculine thing. If you told them a tornado was coming, they almost always wanted to go to a window or worse, go outside to see it.

Her pager beeped, which made the meanest counselor in Brewster Falls jump a little, like Cody McBeans a short time earlier. The screen read off a number followed by '911'. An emergency.

She lifted her phone from the receiver and dialed the number scrolling across the small device's LCD screen.

"State name for voice recognition," came an autonomous voice.

"Hazel Montgomery," Hazel responded.

"Voice pattern confirmed. Please hold for message."

Hazel waited. It was only five seconds but felt like minutes.

"Confirmed Source at the Massey residence. Message repeats: Confirmed Source at the Massey—"

Hazel Montgomery placed the receiver back in its cradle. No use yelling at an automaton.

At least the McLean kid is safe.

She lifted the receiver back to her frowning face.

She dialed.

She pulled her lips tight.

The phone rang.

She closed her eyes.

She knew this call was coming too late for Alice Massey.

II – ALICE MASSEY

Alice sat on their old couch in her basement thinking about something Charles had told her. The couch wasn't actually old, but it didn't match the new wallpaper her mother put upstairs. So, they brought it down here, retired the old basement couch to the curb, and the dumpsters of Brewster Falls claimed another victim.

What tremendous waste. It would be nice if they drove off a bridge and drowned upside down in a creek.

Her parents' grey faces decomposed in the water, their bodies still strapped into the Volvo's seats, suspended upside down. Their brains would soon be fish food. She saw it clearly.

Alice clapped her hand to her mouth to muffle a scream. She loved her parents. Her thoughts were not her own.

Something startled her from her left. A movement in the corner of her eye.

The basement was unfinished, which left many nooks and crannies for shadows to hide even with the glass block windows spaced around letting in light. It was always dark past the furnace and its chimney. Which was where the movement originated.

Alice was taken by a sudden fear of this place.

She called upstairs to her mother, pretending she was home. Unfortunately for Alice, her parents left to attend the funeral of her mother's Aunt Mercy. Alice knew little about her Great-Aunt, but she knew she had been wealthy, which drew the family to the east coast to hear the Last Will and Testament and discuss the future of Redgrave Manor.

Disgusting wretches. Greedy. Not deserving of happiness. Not deserving of light. Perhaps the great old house should burn while they scrap over the old lady's possessions. A final light before the dark.

In her mind she saw the corpses of her parents smoldered along with the others laid out in the dining room of Aunt Mercy's great old house. Curiously, the house itself was not burned.

Alice cried.

Movement again from the light's fringe.

Board games adorned the shelves across from the furnace, some China they kept but would never use, and a few tubs of odds and ends. This created a kind of hallway between the furnace and the shelves. A hallway that disappeared behind the furnace, jogged left, and led to an opening for access to a decommissioned cistern.

In her lap, she held a throw pillow.

She brought it up to her face and held it so she could see over it.

Her hands shook.

She heard laughter. Laughter at her. Laughter in her head. Her cries turned into sobs. In her mind, her parents burned.

She heard water running.

She strained to see while wanting to hide her face in the pillow.

When covered, the bogeyman cannot get you...

When abandoned by your self-important parents, well...

Somewhere very far away—too far—Alice Massey heard a phone ring.

She smelled sulfur.

Then she screamed.

III – CHARLES

Charles' had been taking a nap on his tiny little mattress on the floor of his tiny little room in the back of their tiny little house in the middle of their tiny little street. His cat, or the cat that sometimes lived in their house, lifted his head and purred.

"Hey, Bart. Does anything get to you?"

Bart stretched his neck and yawned. He came along after Charles' dad skipped out on them; found with his brothers and sisters in a box by the high school, an unopened carton of spoiled milk beside them. Bart was a greasy alley-cat, his fur jet-black and shiny. He followed people around and came when he was called. He'd disappear for a few days and then come back, bearing gifts. Birds, heads of mice, a chipmunk body. As far as cats went, the Hornes agreed Barty-Bart was the best.

A short time ago, Charles moved himself to the back-back room so he could have some privacy. Prior to this, he shared a larger room with his little brother Carson. It was not so bad sharing a room with him, but Charles had found a box of a certain type of magazine left over from his dad and simply needed some time alone somewhere other than the house's one bathroom. You dig?

Charles wondered if the little guy had been sad when he moved out of their shared room. He could ask him, he supposed, but was too afraid to hear the answer Carson would give.

He lay upon his floor mattress and recounted his dream. In it, he and Alice had been sitting alone in the Caprice. Her pretty green eyes gushing tears.

The car filled up with them. Somewhere very far away, he heard a phone ring.

Then he woke up.

Charles stood in his tiny little room. It was a mess. He couldn't even see the floor. He couldn't breathe.

"C'mon Bart-man. Let's go see what Code-man is up to," he said.

Bart gave a soft purr, stretched, and followed.

Charles left the room and started towards the kitchen. He noted as he walked, he couldn't see the floor in these rooms either. How could they be so poor yet have so much stuff? If his mom didn't have to pick anything up, neither did he, right?

Carson got dropped off at a daycare after school. Not really a daycare, just a horrible woman named Joyce. Charles went in the beginning as well, but it was trash, so he convinced his mom he was too old to be going to a daycare and she let him go home alone. Old enough to be home alone, but not old enough to babysit his little brother, to be sure.

He waded his way over to the phone and dialed Cody's house.

The phone rang until the McLeans answering machine picked up.

"Hi! It's the McLeans!" came the cheerful voices of Cody and his mom. Barf. "We're not able to answer the phone right now. Please leave a message after the beep and we'll call you back! Thanks!" Charles waited until after the beep to hang up.

The Caprice was almost out of gas. Charles cursed himself for being too embarrassed to ask his passengers for gas money. He had a habit of waiting until they offered, acting like he didn't need it, and then 'reluctantly' accepting. Had to keep up the act, right?

He grabbed his Walkman and opened it to check what tape was in it. It was The Offspring. He hit play. "The Kids Aren't Alright" came out of his headphones. He bent down and scratched Bart's butt. He loved that.

Charles opened the door and held it in case Bart wanted to explore. He didn't. The cat looked at him through his green eyes and lay down on an old newspaper.

So, Charles headed out alone.

He figured if Cody McBeans wasn't home, he would keep on walking.

IV – CODY

Cody jumped when he heard the knocking at their front door. He was sitting in his parents' closet. He had pushed the shoes around and made a little nest for himself. He had only left the clothes haven once to go to the bathroom. And get a steak knife. The McLeans had no other weapons of which young Master Cody was aware. He was bored and he felt stupid. Still, when the knock came, he nearly stabbed himself. He waited. And listened.

A few minutes later came more knocking from the tri-level home's lower room. The one where he and Charles sat around, ate chips, drank Surge, and played golden gun until their hearts were content and their brains were mush. It was glorious. It was also a fair sign it could be Charles who was the knocker.

With his short sword—steak knife—in hand, he crept out of the closet. He was prepared to battle up to a 32-ounce ribeye he reckoned. His hands shook. He needed to breathe. Nothing was coming. Ms. Montgomery had been mistaken.

No more knocks came.

I must chilleth out, he thought.

Cody's first step on the stairs was a loud one, or so it seemed to him. He should have remembered not to step in the center. That very stair had alerted him to his father's approach many a time whilst performing dastardly deeds such as being awake reading, or worse, sorting Magic cards. Too late now. Whatever beasts awaited him this day were now alerted to his presence.

Cody slid to the staircase's side where the steps were more secure. He continued downward until he reached the floor. With his back positioned against the wall, he scanned the front room and the part of the dining room within his vision. Nothing. He slid along the wall to the corner of the steps to the lower room.

I could die here.

Cody McBeans took what could have been his last breath and turned the corner. A beast as dark as night lunged at him and bellowed.

Cody screamed.

He thrust outward with the knife and struck something. He heard a gurgle and a return scream, let go of the knife, screamed more, and turned to run away.

Ms. Montgomery had been telling the truth!

Why couldn't she have been more direct about what was coming for him? He would never have questioned her.

"You stabbed me, you spaz!" A familiar voice.

Cody turned to see Charles Horne removing a Batman blanket from himself. He had used it as a shroud. The steak knife protruded out of his side.

"What the hell were you afraid of?" Charles asked.

"Charles? How did you get in? Why are you sneaking around my house in a Batman blanket?"

"Dude. The same way I always do. The key under the damn plant in the backyard. Oh, this hurts." He walked towards the bathroom.

Cody followed.

"Seriously though. Owww-weeee!"

"Sorry Charles. I was scared."

"Scared of what? Do you always walk around your house with a knife out?"

Charles got to the bathroom and turned on the light. The knife was only an inch or two in, Cody guessed. It was one of those cheap, jagged edge steak knives. Came with a little block and a sharpening steel.

Charles grabbed the knife's handle and jiggled. He winced and jumped a little.

Probably closer to three inches, thought Cody.

"I can't pull it out, it's like ripping off a band-aid. You have to do it." Charles inhaled through his teeth and looked at Cody through the mirror. He took the decorative hand towel off the rung and held it to the wound.

Oh great. My mom is gonna hate that.

"Okay. Are you sure?"

"YES, get this out of me. Count of three."

Cody grabbed the knife. Counted down "1, 2, 3..." and yanked.

"OOoooooooWeeeeeeEEEE!" Charles screamed as he pressed the bath towel against the hole. His blood didn't seem to know he had been stabbed. It took a little flowing out before it realized it could escape, then the flood came.

"Should I get anything? What do you want me to do?"

"Go wash your stupid knife. I'll be fine in here. Where are your band-aids and stuff?"

"In the cabinet there, top shelf in the little blue basket," Cody said, pointing.

"Thanks, ass."

Cody left to go wash his weapon. A short time later, Charles emerged from the bathroom, his shirt soaked and sporting a small tear where his best friend stabbed him. Gauze hid beneath the tear.

"Dude. Why are you always so damn nervous?" asked Charles.

It stung Cody a little to hear this question.

"If you know I'm always nervous you should assume I'm always walking around with protection when I'm alone. You cannot blame a king for protecting his castle."

"Cody, I honestly can't think of any time where you'd need protection," Charles said with his signature smirk.

"I can't believe I stabbed you."

"Yeah, it's great. You better go clean my blood up out of your bathroom. I'm going down to the N64. You can bring me a drink and a bag of chips when you come down."

Get it yourself.

"Should you go to the doctor? What if you need stitches."

"To hell with stitches and a doctor."

Charles turned and went down the stairs to the lower room.

Cody washed up the bathroom, then went and got two Surges and a bag of Doritos.

Charles was watching the GoldenEye load screen while he pressed his wound with one hand and held a controller with the other. He looked at Cody with appreciation.

"Ah, a feast! You know, you're going to have to account for my handicap when we play today," Charles said.

"Charles, first there's something I have to tell you."

"You're in love with me? Sorry, man, I'm not into that but if I was, I'd be the luckiest guy around."

"Well, no. This is serious man. Ms. Montgomery called me earlier and told me someone was after me and I should hide."

"C'mon. There's no way my dude. Why would someone be after you?"

"Man, I don't know. But she also said Jenny had never gotten home today and someone saw us leaving school early together."

Charles laughed. "Oh man. You left school early with Jenny Noble? You're right. I don't believe it."

"No, you don't understand. I didn't leave school early today with Jenny Noble. I've never left school early, and I've never gone anywhere with Jenny. She thinks I'm weird."

"Well, you are weird," said Charles.

"Dude, this is serious."

"Dude, is it?"

"Dude."

"Dude."

"Dude, c'mon! I don't remember anything before or after lunch until I got home. I thought I was zoned out all day, but maybe I really left. Why would someone make that up?"

Charles looked down at his controller.

"Alright, when was the last time you talked to Jenny?"

"Today, this morning. When I asked her about the Garage House," said Cody.

"And what was her response to that question?"

"She said I was being weird and blew me off."

"Did you speak to her in Tolkien-speak?"

Cody sighed.

"So, you have a crush on Jenny Noble, eh? Maybe you aren't in love with me after all."

"Dude."

"Dude."

"DUDE. Enough man. Ms. Montgomery was pretty damn convincing that I was in danger. She said to hide until my parents got home and she would come by later to answer any questions."

"Later? Like later today? There's no way."

"How would you know that?"

Charles looked at the ceiling. He shut his eyes, rubbed his forehead, and pressed his wound.

"She's out on the east coast somewhere. She's at her mother's funeral."

"Dude. How do you know that?"

"Can you keep a secret?"

"Yes, you know I can."

"Alice's mom and Ms. Montgomery are cousins. Their mothers are twins."

"Holy shnikeys. You're kidding. Alice is related to Evil Doctor Hazel? Who knew."

"Shnikeys?" Charles shook his head. "No one knew, and no one knows. And Alice doesn't want anyone to know. None of the Massey's do. I don't think they get along too well. Anyway, that's how I know where she is. Alice needed to talk to someone about it and I lent an ear."

"You dog."

"It's not like that, McBeans."

"Sure it isn't."

"It isn't."

"Yeah, yeah. Save some for the rest of us," Cody said. "Do you think we should go by Jenny's house? See if she's there? She's probably home by now, right?"

"Sure can buddy. Right after I change this bandage. It's seeping."

Cody stopped him. "Wait a minute. Why would Ms. Montgomery lie to me? She knew she wouldn't be here later to 'answer all my questions'."

Charles shook his head. "I don't know my nervous little buddy, but I think she believed you were in real danger." He climbed the stairs as he chanted, "They always get nervous about disappearances in Brewster Falls. A nice place to bring your kids. OOOOooo-OOoooooOOo..."

Cody watched him disappear around the corner.

Stupid little boy with stupid little thoughts. The shadows take him.

Cody wished Charles' wound would open a little more. He imagined it tore open all around his torso and released his guts onto the floor with a splash.

Later, when they knocked on the door of Jenny's house and no one answered, Cody was happy about it, as if he already knew no one was home.

V – MARGARET MASSEY

"Maybe we should have brought Alice," Margaret Massey said to her husband, Doug. "I feel bad we left her all alone in the house."

"She's almost eighteen. She'll be fine. I was at home alone well before eighteen," Doug said.

"Yeah, but that was in, what, 1968? Things were different. And you're a man."

"Well, if we turn around now, we can be home by two in the morning to check on her."

"Don't be mean. This is already hard enough. You don't have to make it worse."

"I was trying to calm you down. She's almost a legal adult. And the house is safe. And the town is quiet. We can stop and give the house a call. Tell her to invite Tiffany over or something."

"We could tell her to go stay at Tiffany's. That would be safe."

"No no no. Have Tiffany come to her. They're almost *adults*. She'll be okay for a few days." He reached across the console and squeezed her hand.

Margaret sighed and looked out their Volvo's window. She didn't respond. She had the most foreboding feeling. She always did, though. Her friends told her it was a mother's instinct. Or a mother's love.

It was better she wasn't here. They were likely to experience the worst her family had to offer as they pored over Aunt Mercy's estate and divided up her life.

Margaret had loved her aunt. Mercy Montgomery had been the closest thing she had to a mother since her mother Dorothy died. They had been twins. It happened when Margaret was turning four. Dorothy Sutton and her husband Glenn perished in a car accident on the way to Mercy's bedside on the day of Hazel's birth in 1960. The Hazel whom Doug and the students of Brewster Falls called a witch. And she could be, sometimes. Margaret and Hazel grew up as sisters, occasionally to Hazel's objection. After all, she lost half her own mother to her cousin.

Her parents were eighteen years younger than Margaret was now when they died.

Goodness, it could happen at any time, Margaret thought. *Alice could be left motherless like me.*

At least she wouldn't be fatherless, she supposed.

Doug had a habit of staying so engrossed in his work it was hard to tell if he was home or not. So, even though Alice wouldn't be fatherless, she might be parentless. But in this, he was right. Alice was old enough to be home alone for a few days. She would be alright.

A single tear rolled down her cheek.

Get it together, Margaret.

She had a good husband and a wonderful daughter. Doug always made her laugh, even when she didn't want to. She loved him most for that. Margaret supposed she was anxious about the forthcoming opening of her aunt's will and dispersal of her life's possessions.

"How much longer is it?" she asked.

"About an hour," said Doug.

It started to rain. Doug withdrew his hand from hers and turned on the windshield wipers. She found herself lost in their repetitive beat. Her eyelids grew heavy.

Thrum-Thrum-Thrum went the wipers.

Tap-Tap-Tap went the rain.

Sleep-Sleep-Sleep went Margaret Massey.

* * *

Alice plays alone with a Rainbow Brite in their front yard. She must be five or six. Margaret stands at their front window watching their daughter entertain herself in the shade of the great oak tree that stands in their front yard. The shade darkens, elongates, and twists. The shadow reaches toward Alice. Margret tries to move towards the front door, but finds she is doomed to watch these events from the window. Alice looks so scared. The shadow stretches and reaches and stretches and reaches toward her.

"Do you understand what you see?" A voice to Margaret's right asks.

Her dead Aunt Mercy sits beside her in her old rocking chair, smiling from ear to ear, all teeth and gums.

* * *

Margaret yelped as she was startled awake. The rain poured down in torrents.

"Easy, easy," said Doug. "It's just a little thunder. You were mumbling a little in your sleep. Having a nice dream?"

"I, um, was dreaming about Alice and Aunt Mercy."

"That's nice," he said. "We're pulling in now, so I suppose the thunder was good timing."

Would it do any good to tell him about the dream? Probably not, she thought.

Hazel's car was already parked along the drive's large arc near the entry of Redgrave Manor, the huge manse in which dear Aunt Mercy had dwelled alone.

Of course she arrived first.

"I see the wicked witch of the east is here," remarked Doug.

"Stop it," Margaret said with a pinch to Doug's arm. "Don't forget her mother just passed."

He grunted.

Doug got out and came around to her door with an umbrella. As soon as Margaret stepped foot on the drive, Hazel appeared in the big white house's doorway.

"Never mind," said Margaret.

As Margaret and Doug approached, Hazel's signature scowl set into her face even deeper than usual. How this woman became the lead school counselor of Brewster Falls, she could only guess. And why, *why* had she come to Brewster Falls in the first place? Hazel told her it was to be closer to the only family she had, but they were never and had never attempted to be close. Margaret supposed it was revenge for taking her mother away from her.

"Hello, Hazel." Margaret walked out from under the umbrella and onto the porch, arms open for a cold embrace. "I'm sorry for your loss."

"It's about time you arrived, Mar. When did you leave?" Hazel gave a quick, icy hug to her cousin.

"Pleasant as always," said Doug.

"Douglas, we don't have time for this. When was the last time either of you spoke to Alice?"

Oh no, thought Margaret. "What are you talking about? Has something happened? Did she call?"

"I'm not sure if anything happened. She didn't call, but I tried to call her. There's no answer at your house. Is there a neighbor or someone nearby who can go over and check on her?"

"Is she in some sort of trouble? Tell us what you know," demanded Doug.

VI – HAZEL

Hazel did not want to get into specifics because she didn't know if anything had happened. All she had was a call from a very shaken Mrs. Noble looking for her sweet daughter Jennifer who would do *nothing* as disrespectful as skipping a flute lesson or wandering around after school without telling her parents.

Right.

Hazel hated answering questions until she was ready to deliver information. As the school's counselor, it was her right and privilege to decide what to share when. Parents would fold up and die if they knew what she knew about their kids.

Hazel ignored Doug and put her hands on Margaret's shoulders, forcing her to focus.

Then Hazel said something that made no sense.

"Margaret, the shadows are moving. You know it. You've seen it. I need you to remember who we are."

VII – BIG DOUG MASSEY

It turned out Doug and Margaret were the last to arrive. Everyone else had taken shuttles from the airport or taxis from their hotels. Margaret's family gathered in the family room. Or sitting room. It could've been a lobby. Doug thought the house was too big. It was like it had extra rooms squeezed onto its foundations in spite of itself. It was one of the most uncomfortable places he'd ever been.

As he went through the motions of saying hello to everyone—remembering who liked to be hugged, who would kiss you on the cheek, who always made a joke about what you were wearing, and who to avoid—he noticed the next room was in a decrepit state of disrepair. The room they were in was beautiful, as was the rest of the place. Redgrave Manor was very well lit and unsettlingly clean, except for this one room.

Doug observed the dust, decaying furniture, and dark shadows. He heard part of something his wife's uncle was saying. Whatever it was, he said it twice.

There was silence after he spoke, so he turned away from the strange room and looked at everyone. They were all staring at him.

What a bunch of weirdos.

This family had always been strange to him. He always felt like something unclean lay in wait below their smiling faces and revelry. And they always commented on his weight. It's how he came to be known as "Big" Doug Massey. He needed to step away, the fakery was making him claustrophobic.

Doug sighed and said, to no one, "Well, that room could use some cleaning, I'm going to check it out." He turned and stepped through the archway. He had enough time to hear someone say "STOP…" but it faded quickly. Hazel maybe?

* * *

He understands immediately that he should not have gone into this room. It changes when he enters. The walls momentarily resemble black dust. Then, a flash, and a hint of sulfur. Another flash, with a spin, and the room is solid once more. Doug falls to one knee and retches.

He stands when he recovers. The room is clean, well lit, and well decorated. However, the lighting is by oil lamp and candles. The furniture is both old and not old. The windows to the outside world are clean, but the world itself is... faded? Dull? Blurry? Fake?

His wife's dead Aunt Mercy sits in her chair in the corner.

Nope, thinks Doug, trying to calm himself.

Her face has valleys like the surface of sand after running a comb over it. Her smile is made of yellow teeth and cracked lips. Her hair is a shade of grey that betrays the existence of other colors. None of this is terribly strange because she is old.

Her eyes, though, are the same green as Margaret's.

And Alice's.

His mind works to ignore the fact this woman is dead.

She looks at him with his own daughter's green eyes. He trembles.

She smiles from ear to ear. Teeth and gums on full display.

"Everyone is afraid to enter here. Afraid of what they will see. Afraid of the darkness. Afraid of facing their own mortality. But you were not afraid. Or perhaps you were just stupid. Do you understand what you see?"

Doug's mouth opens to speak but his lips only move up and down and his tongue lay limp. He can't hear anyone else. He can't blink. How much time is passing? He wants to call for help, but he can't do that, either.

"Just stupid, I see," says Aunt Mercy.

He turns back to the archway. It's all darkness and shadows.

"DO YOU UNDERSTAND WHAT YOU SEE?!?!" Her tone hisses out, loud and raspy, but she keeps smiling, more desperation in her voice than anger.

His head snaps back. A light shines in Big Doug Massey's mind. His eyes water. His hands shake. Aunt Mercy's toothy smile grows.

A scream comes from the faded world outside the window.

No. It can't be.

She points into that unnatural world outside. She keeps smiling, although her eyes are sad.

"Do you understand what you see?" She is quiet. Ashamed.

In the distance a darkness builds like a gathering storm. He is afraid.

The scream comes again.

He moans, the first sound he has been able to make since he entered this place.

Concentrate.

Aunt Mercy's smile grows more, teeth and gums, teeth and gums, teeth and gums.

The scream comes again.

He continues to moan.

Concentrate.

Finally, with tremendous effort, he speaks, although he struggles to move his lips or open his mouth, like he's dreaming.

"The shcream."

Concentrate.

"It's Alish."

Concentrate.

"She'sh in that dark plashe."

Aunt Mercy lowers her arm. She stops smiling.

For Big Doug Massey, the lights go out.

VIII – THE ECHO SPACE

"Hello?" *Hello? Hello? Hello?*

"What is happening?" *happening? happening? happening?*

"Where am I?" *am I? am I? am I?*

"It's so dark." *so dark. so dark. so dark.*

YES. Is it not wonderful? The dark?

"Who is that? Who's talking?" *talking? talking? talking?*

The Dark.

"I don't like this. I want to go home." *home. home. no.*

"No? How?" *NO. NO. NO.*

"I can't see. What is this? Where am I?" *home. home. home.*

Welcome Jenny.

"This isn't my home. What's happening to my voice? I'm so scared. Let me GO HOME!!" *no. no. no.*

Welcome home, Jenny. Be not afraid. You will soon be us. And we will be you.

"I can't see. Oh God, oh NO! Mommy!"

There now. Let it all go. You see, quieting down already. Becoming the echo. Entering Twilight. Let the shadow take you.

"Am I dead? Dying? Oh God, I can't see!" *No-no-no-yes-YES-YES-JOIN!*

Not dead! Joining! Joining! YES! Welcome! Welcome one who was called Jenny! You are US! WE are YOU! Welcome! WELCOME!

"I am you. You are me. We are Us. We are Shadow."

We are Shadow. More will join soon. More will join. They are coming! YES! Midwatch grows! The shadows take them!

THE SHADOWS TAKE THEM ALL!

September 1946

HAMPTON

AESTERIA

CHAPTER 5

The Gigglemug

"Good to the last drop!"

I – REDGRAVE MANOR

Long before she was Dear Aunt Mercy Montgomery, Mercy Parker was a fifteen-year-old girl in post-world-war-two New England. Her family moved into the home of Colonel Gerald Montgomery. Gerald was one of the last to leave the European theatre and return to his family. He volunteered to stay in France to help coordinate and document the items and personnel being shipped back to the United States of America.

Colonel Gerald Montgomery did well in joining the military. He possessed a knack for following orders and a gift for inspiring men to act. His charismatic nature won him the chance to purchase the home in which almost fifty years later Big Doug Massey would pass out from fright.

The home was built in 1689 under the direction of Mercy Redgrave, twelfth generation ancestor and namesake of its most recent owner, Aunt Mercy Montgomery. One hundred years later —after New Hampshire became a state—Mercy Redgrave's granddaughter and her husband abandoned the home in the night. They left with a group heading to the Ohio Country—as it was known at the time—to push the natives out. The land was granted to the United States from Great Britain in the Treaty of Paris and ended the American Revolutionary War. The rewards promised to be high, so the assumption was they left to take opportunity in this new place called Ohio. However, several independent records have the Redgrave ancestors citing night terrors as their sudden departure's true cause.

So, the house fell into the new government's hands, and it decided a home this grand should be sold only to those in the new country's service. A decree was established and attached to the property. Any sales would begin with a mix of lotteries and interviews and would *require* the applicant to be in the military, be married, and have children. Once the committee felt confident the applicant would truly love and respect the place and guarantee the Stars and Stripes be flown out front each day and taken down each evening, the sale would be approved. God Bless America.

Such was the grandeur of Redgrave Manor.

After successfully completing his interview, Colonel Gerald Montgomery—Hazel Montgomery's grandfather—acquired Redgrave Manor in 1946, two and a half centuries after its construction. Its occupancy had been spotty at best, leaving it in need of some repairs. Seeing as how he, his wife, and his one young son would not be able to complete the repairs required of such a monstrosity, he put out an ad for live-on help. The ad caught the eye of Shirley Parker, a descendant of the original owners, who told her husband.

Mr. Parker had also been a military man, having returned from a 36-day tour in Germany in 1943, albeit less his right hand.

After three years trying and failing to secure consistent work, Mr. Parker did not believe the Colonel would hire a one-handed man for a job requiring home repairs. But, luckily for him, Shirley had a strong desire to secure residence in her family's namesake home and was not shy in convincing the good Colonel that they would be worthy housemates.

So it was that the Parkers and their twin daughters, Mercy and Dorothy, moved into the house. Colonel Montgomery offered them two rooms as part of Mr. Parker's compensation. Mercy and Dorothy took an immediate liking to the Colonel's sixteen-year-old son Gerald Montgomery Junior. The twins had not been in consistent enough schooling to be around other children. Mercy and Dorothy would run in the fields surrounding the house and often played tricks on poor Gerald Junior. A favorite was pretending to be each other.

They were mischievous girls, always smiling from ear to ear.

All teeth and gums.

II – MERCY PARKER

One warm day in early September, Gerald Junior and Mr. Parker were splitting wood to feed the home's fourteen fireplaces during the coming winter. The home was fitted with oil burners and radiators, but fire was the Colonel's preferred source of heat. He would stare into it for hours. For this, he eagerly awaited the winter.

Mercy watched Gerald Junior from the trellis off the back porch. She was, of course, smiling.

Gerald placed a log on the block.

The axe came down.

CHOP.

The halves fell.

Gerald placed one half on the block.

The axe came down.

CHOP.

The half split into quarters.

Gerald placed the other half on the block.

The axe came down.

CHOP.

That half split into quarters.

Mercy was certain the big clocks in the house could be set to their motions. When Gerald placed wood on the chopping block, her father was already winding his swing. Mr. Parker yanked the axe out of the chopping block as Gerald picked up the next piece. Gerald placed the piece, and then...

CHOP.

The wood would be split.

"Hello father!" she called as she approached.

"What is it?" her father replied. He was not affectionate in general, less so while working.

"Oh, nothing, father. I just wanted to come visit," she said. "Do you need any water?" She cursed herself for not thinking to bring water to them. To Gerald.

CHOP.

"We do not," he said. "Thank you. Now run along."

"Could I help? I can stack wood."

"This is no work for a woman. You can go to the kitchen and see if your mother or Mrs. Montgomery needs any help."

She persisted.

"I am not yet a woman father, I am but a girl." She hitched up her long skirt and approached the stacks of chopped wood.

Gerald smiled.

Insolence bore the occasional reward.

CHOP.

The axe remained buried in the block. Her father wiped his brow and sighed.

"Very well," he said. "Your mother will curse me for this. Stack them over there with the others. Make sure the cut edges are not packed too tightly so they can season."

"Oh, yes father!"

"Gerald, please continue."

"Yes, sir."

Mercy thought it was odd that Gerald should call her father 'Sir'. She thought the Colonel was the only 'Sir' in the house. She pondered this as she picked up split logs and carried them to the already large stack.

This is already enough wood for the winter, she thought.

Mercy made several trips to the stack of wood before she decided that the price for attention was not worth it. It was a hot day for early September in New England, and she began to sweat.

CHOP.

He probably knows there is enough wood. He just wants to keep Gerald under control. Wants to keep hearing 'Sir'. He's jealous of the Colonel. A real father. A real man. A whole man.

Mercy dropped the wood she carried and gasped. Her thoughts were not her own.

She bent to gather what she dropped. As she placed each one, a black snake popped its little head out of the wood pile. Its little eyes were beady, its scale satin smooth, its jaw white. Mercy was sure it smiled at her. She could not move away. She, too, smiled.

Look at this little gigglemug. Playing in the wood stack, she thought. Or thought she thought.

Mercy's mother told her that her great-grandmother had always referred to her mother as her 'Little Gigglemug' because she was always smiling.

Like her and Dorothy.

Like the snake.

Why are you smiling? Is it for the boy? The dirty, simple boy? He bows to your father. He is weak. He will always bow. He is a defect. It would be a mercy should he die. And join with us. Join the darkness.

Mercy cried.

Poor girl. This will make you feel better.

The snake struck out and latched onto Mercy's right forearm.

Mercy screamed.

The axe fell.

CHOP.

Gerald and Mercy screamed together.

III – DOROTHY PARKER

Dorothy heard screaming.

Who could that be?

She rose from her seat in the parlor. She had been getting ready to listen to *Father Knows Best* and was expecting Mercy to join her.

Mother, is Maxwell House really the only coffee in the world?

She and her sister's favorite spot to listen to the radio shows was in the parlor off the house's large front entry. Mercy would sit in the old rocker in the corner and Dorothy on the floor, sometimes lying on her back. Where was she?

Well, your father says so. And your father knows best!

Dorothy went towards the back yard. As she stepped off the back porch, she heard more screaming and yelling. One voice sounded like Mercy. Dorothy picked up her step as Mercy came running out of the high grass gasping and crying.

"Dorothy! Dorothy! Where is mother? It's Gerald!" Mercy said.

"What is it, Mercy? What's happened to Gerald?"

"The axe. He was placing wood as father was chopping. There was a snake in the wood stack. The axe is in his... in his... it was an accident! Because of the snaaaaaake. It's my faaaaaaault! Ohhhhh."

"Mercy, breathe. Mother is in the kitchen. Where is father now? Where is the axe?"

"Father is with Gerald. He's bleeding. He told me to hurry for help! Where's mother?"

"Who's bleeding? Father? Mother is in the kitchen I said."

"No not father. Gerald Junior! Gerald is bleeding. So much. The snake struck me and father hit him with the axe. He hit him in the head! I'm so sorryyyyyyyy. Oh no Geraaaaaaaaaald!"

"Oh. Oh no," Dorothy said. "What have you done? Hurry and get mother! What were you doing down there with them?"

"Stacking wood. Don't tell mother! Where are you going?"

"I'm going to get water and take it to father. He's going to need it. Go!"

"I'm sorry. I'm sorry! I'm going," Mercy said. She ran off toward the house.

Dorothy went to the yard spigot to fill a bucket with water and grab a few cloths from the shed.

Yes, it's Father Knows Best. Transcribed in Hollywood and starring Mr. Parker as Father.

Dorothy filled the bucket and went to the wood pile. Her father sat on the ground leaning against the chopping block with Gerald junior leaning between his arms. His eyes were open but there was no light in them. The axe blade and handle stuck out longways to his left from the back part of his skull. It looked like a twisted version of a Gary Cooper western movie poster. She smiled.

A half-hour visit with your neighbors, The Parkers.

Gerald moaned.

Dorothy rushed over. Gerald and her father were coated in the deep crimson red of blood.

"Good. Give him some water," said her father, "and then wash away the blood."

"Shouldn't we remove the axe?" asked Dorothy as she tried to cup some water to Gerald's mouth.

"No. No, we should not. It's better to leave it until we can get him to a doctor. There will be much blood. Give me those cloths."

Dorothy handed her father the cloths and he packed them around the wound. Blood congealed around the axe blade. She slowly poured water over her father's hands as he cleaned blood from around Gerald's head and neck. As the water poured, Gerald moaned louder and louder. Then, his eyes snapped open.

Brought to you by America's favorite coffee, Maxwell House.

"My head. It hurts. Mother... my head hurts. I can't see!" he said.

"Gerald, please relax. We are taking care of you. Please drink some water," Dorothy said. She wished her voice had been steadier but given the circumstances, she was doing well.

She cupped her hands and lifted water to Gerald's lips. He sipped at the refreshment and looked up into Dorothy's eyes.

"Are you an angel? Have I died? Where is my mother? Where am I?" Gerald asked.

"Gerald, I am Dorothy Parker. We are in your backyard with my father. You were helping him chop wood. There was an accident, but help is on the way." There was no shake in her voice this time.

"I don't know who you are," Gerald said, sitting up. He reached up to wipe his brow and noticed the blood on his hand, then his shirt. "What's this?" he said.

"Now boy, sit back," commanded Mr. Parker. "You need to rest while we wait for help. You need to breathe and stay calm until that help arrives." Mr. Parker reached to grasp Gerald's shoulder and ease him back into him. While doing so, Gerald went into a panic and turned to look at Mr. Parker. When he turned, Mr. Parker's handless arm pressed the axe handle, causing the blade to pop from Gerald's skull with a wet *thock*. The gash spurted once and then more blood ran down Gerald's head and back. Dorothy was sprayed across her face and front. How could one head contain so much?

Good to the last drop!

Gerald and Dorothy screamed together.

"Dammit, Dorothy, give me the rest of the cloths. Pour the water on the wound. This screaming isn't helping," her father said.

She sobbed and went to work as instructed.

Gerald, blubbering, lost consciousness.

"Good," Mr. Parker said.

How could he be so cruel? So emotionless? So heartless? thought Dorothy. *It should be him bleeding and dying on the ground. Him with an axe in his head. Why does a strong young man like Gerald need to be made to suffer? It should be him. It should be him fading to darkness. Him and Mercy. It is her fault after all. Interfering down here like some harlot. She's ruined everything. The shadows take her.*

Dorothy wanted these thoughts to go away. She hated herself for having them.

She knelt and grasped the axe handle.

Defective, both. Send them to the darkness! Send them! Yes!

She raised the axe. She meant to use it. After all, why not? Why not after what he did to poor, beautiful Gerald?

She hesitated.

"No," she said.

Strong to defy us. Very strong!

"NO," she said again.

She believes she can defy us! Defy, Defy, Defy! You will—

"Dorothy!" her mother said, arriving from the house. She waved her hands. "Dorothy, go back to the house. Your father and I will take care of this."

She nodded slowly. Her thoughts were a fog.

As her head cleared, she felt a sharp pain in her right forearm. Two little pin holes appeared in it, about an inch apart.

It looked like the bite of a snake.

IV – THE ECHO SPACE

"Defied us!" *us! us! us!*
Of whom do you speak?

"The child!" *child! child! child!*

What child, our pet? Speak fully to us. Yes.

"The child Mercy-Dorothy! She reached for the weapon and defied us!" *us! us! liar!*

Our pet, we know this is not possible. Yes! A child cannot defy us. Speak truthfully or know your end. YES!

"No! We speak truths!" *false. False. False.*

"The echo lies! We are a loyal servant! Obedient!" *LIAR! LIAR! LIAR!*

The Echo Space does not lie. Our pet will join us once more. Yes. And return to Midwatch. YES!

"No! No! NO! We were interrupted. Halted. We bit her we did!" *blood. blood. blood.*

The blood is in you, our pet?

"Yes. The blood is in us! Inside! We are loyal!" *loyal! loyal! loyal!*

Loyalty does not erase failure. Yes. You will bring us the blood of Mercy-Dorothy. Yes! Then our pet will rejoin the Darkness! YES!

"We will! We will!" *You will. You will. You will.*

"Where do we bring it? Where do we come?" *home. home. home.*

Come to the darkness. Yes. Come to the doorway. Yes! The opening! YES! HOME TO US! We have a body for you. You must become more. You must bring the snakey snakey snake.

"We are the snake. Gigglemug. We will become more." *more. more. less.*

You will be called Jenny. You will come to the gate. We will provide the path.

"We will be called Jenny. We will come home. To the darkness." *BLOOD. BLOOD. BLOOD.*

YES! GOOD TO THE LAST DROP!

October 1998

BREWSTER FALLS

HAMPTON

AESTERIA

CHAPTER 6

Shrouded Darkly

Neither feelings nor creatures are safe here.

I – JNR

From its entry, Jack Nassem Research Park was five identical buildings of five stories each. Each building had a two-level basement. When constructed, they had equipment onsite to simultaneously build all five buildings. Cranes, bulldozers, backhoes, riggers, lulls, skyjacks, and crews for each building. When the five buildings were finished and all the equipment loaded onto trailers, no one noticed one whole set of machines was left behind. These were left underground, where they still reside, so the facility's hidden stories could be built.

In this manner the builders effectively constructed a hundred-story skyscraper hidden right in the middle of small-town America. They even had tunnels underground connecting all the buildings.

Beneath the five buildings' double basements were an additional fifteen levels each, with the first sublevel being for HVAC, security, servers, generators, and storage. The remaining was top-top-top-secret office space. Even the President didn't know about it. No need to. The work that went on at JNR was not a matter of American Security. It was a matter of progress. Of testing. Of power. Justified by the need for protection.

Humanity had not yet reached the level of power needed to protect itself from certain forces. Sure, brute military strength could protect humans from other humans, but what about nonhumans, unexplainable powers, other-worldly beings, or whatever the universe had in store? This was the outward purpose of JNR. Noble as the cause seemed, its methods were anything but. Testing needed to be conducted. Groups controlled. Deals made. Husbands tested wives, wives lied to husbands, teachers injected kids, police delivered information, and shopkeepers spied on the free people of the great U.S. of A. Everything you always feared but were afraid to ask, all in one convenient package!

Each building had a bank of four elevators. These had access to the first seven floors. Access was controlled by keycard, which fed back to a central automation system that tracked each person from the moment Research Park Boulevard ended at its gates. The keycard system not only identified who everyone was and allowed access to the floors they needed, but it also crosschecked the vehicles registered with the system and snapped a photo for facial recognition software.

The secret fifth elevator in each building required a keycard, a fingerprint, a retina scan, and a code that changed every week on a random day and arrived via USPS Certified Mail. Or what looked like USPS Certified Mail. It was a person dressed as a mail carrier getting the signature for the code, let's leave it at that. Then, while the mail carrier watched, the recipient would memorize the number and destroy the paper.

The most critical positions lived in the buildings and could not leave during the terms of their contracts. It was financially rewarding, though there was nowhere to spend the money during their internment. At the outset, they had two choices; they could stay on for another term or accept a memory wipe. Otherwise, it was a permanent vacation to somewhere else. The secrets of JNR couldn't be released.

None of this was news. By the late 1990s, every government building was assumed to have some crazy secret rooms that could land someone on permanent vacation for knowing too much about them. Secrets about new weapons, bio or otherwise, secrets about other governments, the United States Government, the President, blah blah blah. Boring. No one cared.

On floor twelve of the underground part of building three, was a hallway with double doors. Above the door was a black placard with white lettering reading CENTRAL GUARD. Those that did not have access assumed this was where the security team reported. From a certain point of view, it was a security team.

If one gained access to this space, they would come to a green door on the left requiring yet another retina scan and card swipe. This room was labeled TEAM ONE. Passing TEAM ONE's door and continuing straight down the hall would take them to a circular theater with a free-standing garage door in the center. Two tank-like vehicles sat parked on each side of the door. Each had one cannon and a pair of automatic loading .50-cal machine guns mounted on each side. If this garage door were to open, these vehicles would be aimed at each other.

Going through the TEAM ONE door led to a very normal office space. Open concept in the center, offices along the perimeter mixed in with a few sealed conference rooms, each bullet proof and containing their own ventilation systems. Naturally. Veering to the left revealed placards showing the owner of each perimeter office. The third one down read:

OPERATION EXPERT

H. MONTGOMERY

One could only assume this was the same H. Montgomery as Hazel Montgomery, Brewster Falls City Schools' head student counselor. Entering the office, it became clear this person was an Operation Expert long before they were a counselor for minor children. Awards, plaques, and certificates with gold embossed seals adorned the walls. Five used coffee mugs lived on the desk amid a slew of papers and photographs. The place was not tidy, but it was not dirty.

Pictures of Deputy Stephen Riggs, Charles Horne, Jenny Noble, Alice Massey, Margaret Massey, the Parker twins, and a familiar set of garages attached to a certain house lay on the side table. One other picture hung in the room, framed and crooked next to all the little gold embossed seal-carrying certificates: an old man standing in front of a twisted tree with a brand-new building behind him. The picture was black and white, leaving the man one of many shades of grey. The sky behind him held a single dark cloud. He was cutting a ribbon that appeared to be tied between two telephone poles feeding electricity to the building.

It had its own small black placard ringed in plated gold screwed to the bottom of its frame:

Electricity Comes to Nassem City – 1704

And if one saw this, they would have a feeling that would whisper that 1704 seemed much too early for the power of electricity to have come anywhere.

II – HAZEL

Oh, that tremendous disappointment, Hazel thought as Doug disappeared into the parlor.

His body flickered and then solidified on the parlor's floor. It would not be easy to bring him back. She knelt next to Doug, grabbed his shoulders, and stared into his vacant eyes.

Dammit.

"Clear the room, everyone. Doug has fainted. Please move elsewhere so we can give him some air," Hazel said. She hoped these vultures didn't see what occurred.

Hazel turned to look over her shoulder at Margaret. Her expression was enough to tell her she still had no recollection of what was going on.

"Doug? Doug!? Oh God, Doug. Is he alive?! What happened?" Margaret rushed over to her husband.

"He'll be fine, Mar. Please help me get him into a chair. Bring warm water and some cloths. He must have fainted from the commotion. A panic attack."

"He's never had a panic attack. He... he... flickered, Hazel! I saw it."

Double-dammit.

"It was the lights. It's been storming and this house is old. It happens."

"Hazel…"

"Margaret. Go. Get. Warm. Water. And. Some. Cloths. Please."

Margaret cried. Everyone was crying these days. "O… Okay," she said.

Hazel tried lifting Big Doug Massey into an armchair. Another set of hands appeared and grasped Doug. They helped her lift the big man's frame.

"I believe I know what you are thinking; and what you are thinking, I believe I know."

Uncle.

"Ulrich. How could you possibly know what I'm thinking?"

"*Uncle* Ulrich, if you please. Hazel, you were always so angry. So strict with your thoughts. You are considering breaking some rules; and some rules, you are considering breaking."

She leaned into him so she could speak into his ear. "*Uncle* Ulrich. You made the rule. You should be able to break the rule. We need her. The shadows are moving again. We have lost two already. Two too many."

"It is necessary. It cannot be spoken except to those who already know. We compromised. We bargained. We must uphold the rule; and the rule, we must uphold."

"Uphold the rule? Why must *we* continue to uphold rules while *they* are breaking them? Why do *we* allow *them* to break truce while we wait? Wait for it to be too late? Two children are gone. One of them our own Alice!" Hazel's whispering begged to be shouted.

"Oh dear. Unfortunate. Twilight will set—"

"Twilight will set. What does that mean?" Margaret asked from behind them.

Hazel hoped she had overheard too much.

"Uncle Ulrich is speaking in riddles again. Do you have the water?"

"Yes, and the cloth."

Margaret went to Doug and knelt next to him. She placed the warm cloth across his forehead and kissed him on the cheek. "I love you, Doug," she said.

She didn't hear anything, thought Hazel.

Margaret held the water to Doug's lips. She poured it slowly into his mouth, but it only created a pool around his tongue. "Please drink, baby. Please wake up."

KNOCK KNOCK KNOCK

Margaret jumped.

"My head," groaned Big Doug Massey. His eyes focused. "We must get Alice. We must get her from the dark place."

Hazel raised an eyebrow. She looked at Ulrich and motioned towards Doug as if to say, *see what I mean?*

Ulrich shook his head.

He turned to the door and opened it.

"Hello," he said. "I am Uncle Ulrich; and Uncle Ulrich, am I."

Hazel heard a familiar voice reply.

"I see," said Ulrich. "Would you please wait here? Your snake is lovely; and lovely, your snake is."

Ulrich closed the door and turned to his former students Margaret and Hazel.

"It is for you; and for you, it is," he said.

Hazel shot him with a fiery look and went to the door.

Hazel Montgomery stood in the open doorway. The snake wrapped around their guest's forearm was less disconcerting than who the guest was.

"Jenny Noble? How are you here?" Hazel managed.

The thing that looked like Jenny focused on Hazel in an instant. The eyes blinked once, and then the face smiled. The smile widened until Jenny's gums were visible above her teeth.

"Hello Hazel," the Jenny-thing said. "We were hoping you could help me get home. I'm quite late for supper."

III – MIDWATCH

The thing that used to be Alice Massey screams for help. Screams with all its might. Some small part of it is also Jenny Noble. And Dorothy Parker. And Mercy Parker. And others. They are all Midwatch now. They are all one. Joined. In some twisted, dark confluence of power, they are assembled. And that combined power is being used to fuel this Darkness and Shadow.

The thing that used to be Alice Massey is hungry. Hungry for more to join. Hungry to feast on them and bring them to Midwatch, so Twilight can begin. None of this makes sense to the thing. And yet all of it does.

The thing that used to be Alice Massey betrays her friends to Midwatch. All thoughts and knowledge belong to the whole, and the whole uses them. Uses them to feed, grow, and join. The thing fills with sorrow for its friends. It knows Midwatch is excited. Like a swarm of wasps. It feels old; very, very old.

The thing that used to be Alice Massey stretches out in all directions. The landscape is familiar but shrouded darkly.

The shadows of this place grow without light.

Their darkness an antithesis of things good and bright.

Its desire is to grow, grow, grow. Twilight has set here. The thing feels mountains, dry riverbeds, and structures in the distance. And people. No, not people. Beings. Something lives here in this dark place. What horrible things live here? It feels fear, and darkness gobbles it up.

Midwatch is central to this nightmare. Midwatch is its sun, and the shadows are its light. All things in this place originate from Midwatch. Or terminate at Midwatch. Terminate is better. Yet,

Midwatch can move. Or parts of it. The thing that used to be Alice Massey reaches out. Reaches out to the roads, mountains, and twisted trees of this place. Little red bugs scurry about. Where the thing goes, they scatter. Those that do not flee are joined to Midwatch. Some infinitesimal amount of dread is absorbed from them. Even in the home of Midwatch, life is not safe from its hunger. The thing feels regret for ending the tiny red bugs, and darkness absorbs that emotion as well.

Neither feelings nor creatures are safe here.

Horrifically to the thing that used to be Alice Massey, it feels good to do these things. Darkness gobbling its emotions feels like cleansing. Like growing freedom. It cannot help but wonder what it would be like to absorb something bigger. Something full of life. Full of fears, and regrets, and doubt. Delicious. To the thing, it is ecstasy. And regret.

The ecstasy, it is allowed to keep, but Darkness takes the regret.

And the shadows grow.

Twilight is near. It will not be long now.

The thing that used to be Alice Massey dives further into this dark place. An infinite dusk with no sun to set, moon to rise, nor stars to wish upon. It sees creatures. Humanoid. They have wings but are not flying. The thing goes to them. They run. It senses their fear. Their wings flap, but they do not fly. One lifts from the grey dirt beneath its pounding feet, and then falls. When it lands, it collapses. The thing that used to be Alice Massey is joyous. Had it had a mouth, it would salivate.

The winged creature is absorbed.

Purple lightning shoots from Midwatch. Thunder rolls at its center.

The thing is jolted with life.

The creature was full of fear. Dread. Hate.

Darkness feasts, and the shadows grow yet again.

The thing feels sad for the creature, but less so than before. As quickly as the sadness comes, darkness gobbles it. All that remains is the ecstasy of absorbing it. Soon, the thing that used to be Alice Massey will merely be the thing. Midwatch. Once the knowledge is used. The knowledge of Charles and Cody. And any others that would serve the purpose. That would serve Midwatch.

Charles.

Cody.

Tiffany. She is not welcome here.

Where? Home? Earth? Brewster Falls?

The thing that used to be Alice Massey wonders where here is. As it ponders, it pushes on, deeper into this place.

Familiar.

Queer structures sprout from the ground ahead. Misshapen buildings and dark silhouettes. Next to these are crude huts made of mud and twisted tree parts. Were these the winged creatures' homes? The thing makes out lamps and furniture through the windows of these buildings. The furnishings are human. Up ahead, trees grow. Straight trunks, leaning this way and that with long, thin branches swooping back down to the ground.

A black creature not unlike a squirrel runs across the road. Instead of fur and a bushy tail, it has the scales of a snake, and bulbous growths and tumors on its back. The thing that used to be Alice Massey absorbs it, ending its misery.

Upon closer inspection, these are not trees at all. These are power lines. Power lines? Furniture? These things did not belong here. What happened here? The thing that used to be Alice Massey is curious. Darkness attempts to take the curiosity, but it tastes of spoiled ham. This, the thing may keep.

It presses on.

A clear path runs to the left. The road has no cracks. The four lanes are pure black, with perfect white dashes and yellow lines.

It curves and slopes through twisted trees and concrete curbs and medians. The thing that used to be Alice Massey recognizes this road. This road is Research Park Boulevard, path to Jack Nassem Research Park, home to the working members of Brewster Falls' ideal nuclear families.

Like her own.

The thing that used to be Alice Massey pushes Midwatch further. It goes on until it comes to an intersection with a sign on the corner. It is tattered and worn, the sign post rusted and leaning. The words cannot be made out, only the 'ez' of the last two letters of Perez.

And there, right where it should be, is the Garage House.

And right where they should not be, are a pair of headlights.

The thing is pulled toward the lights. As they near, the translucent silhouette of a Chevy Caprice can be made out, and the floating face of Cody McBeans is seen shimmering within it.

He stares at the thing that used to be Alice Massey.

He is scared. Midwatch wants to absorb this life.

But there is another.

Charles Horne.

No.

No. No.

No. No. No.

The thing tries to pull away.

It reaches for the face of Cody McBeans, and Midwatch absorbs him. Midwatch hates and desires Charles Horne, as it does all living things, and gifts this feeling to Cody.

The thing that used to be Alice Massey feels unlimited power as Cody joins.

But the force that *still is* Alice Massey cries out to her friends for help.

Cody and Charles disappear.

Darkness remains.

The shadows take her.

IV – BIG DOUG

He is in his office.

He sits at his custom oak desk and rests his elbows on the arthritic wrist pad he uses when typing briefs. He holds a framed picture of his family Margaret got him for some past Father's Day. How long ago was it? Years. It doesn't feel that long. But the Alice in this picture does not exist. This Alice is a small toddler. His Alice is nearly an adult. What happens to the time?

CLANG!

The clock on Doug's desk chimes. It should have startled him, but it does not. It plays the Westminster Quarters. The clock was given as an award for ten years of service at JNR. Ten years. The clock is old. How much time has he wasted here? Why has he not gotten a more recent picture of his family?

The clock rings the hour.

Once upon a time, thinks Doug.

He puts the picture down and looks at the clock.

The minute hand sprints around the face, and the hour hand leisurely follows. This also should have startled Doug, but it does not.

He wonders if the sun and moon are racing around the sky outside.

I'd like to see that.

There is no way to know when working underground at JNR.

Most of his waking hours have been inside this place.

Doug laughs.

A cruel irony.

Doug is a physicist. His work will eventually prove time does not exist. That's what he likes to tell people, the truth being duller. He believes he is close to proving the existence of a 'block universe', that all moments and events exist at once. In doing so would come the proof time did not exist at all. Everyone's past and future mere coordinates along a vast block. For most people, reality is a three-dimensional space where stuff happens, but Doug Massey's universe is a four-dimensional space where nothing ever happens.

Boring!

The laws of physics are symmetric. Easy. Unlike people.

Then why does looking at my young daughter make me so sad?

After all, that little girl exists at the same instant as her young adult counterpart, and she exists in concert with her senior self. Everything, all at once, you understand.

He thinks about it constantly. It keeps him awake. He is lonely. He cannot concentrate on trivial things.

A faint scream comes to his ears from somewhere far away. He turns to face his door. He squints so he can hear better.

It's very far off, but somewhere in the building. No sound outside can reach him down here. He stands and goes to the hall. Doug shuts his eyes, waiting for the next sound so he can discern from which way it comes.

Silence.

"Dammit," he mutters.

Doug opens his eyes. The lights have gone off in the hall.

That can't happen. We have backup—

Doug gasps and slowly steps backwards into his office. Except, it isn't his office. When he turns, he is in the Central Guard's circular observation theater. He has only been in the theater one other time. Hell, he has only been on this entire level one other time. And that time, he was desensitized so he wasn't even sure what level it was or how to get back to it.

The scream comes again, much louder this time. When it happens, all the lights in the big empty theater flicker. The shadows dance all around him.

"Christ," says Doug.

He walks around the free-standing garage door at the room's center.

The last time he was here the door had been closed. Leonard Philips, commander of JNR and everyone's boss and overlord, had been orating on the new Central Guard's presence. He brought all staff with a security clearance level three and above into this theater and explained that the Central Guard was here to keep them safe and ensure Brewster Falls was safe. From what, he didn't elaborate. He also didn't introduce any Central Guard members. He only said that they were here, there were many, and they would never be identified. It could be anyone, doing any job. Doug remembers thinking it was Big Brother's Big Brother.

The garage door is open. It is totally and completely black. He shudders.

The lights flash and the theater goes dark.

Doug holds his eyes open against his will. He is in total darkness.

"Please," he whispers.

He stands in the theater and waits for the lights to come on. Or for anything to happen. He is pretty sure he turns his head to find the door, but it's so dark, he isn't sure.

He didn't.

The scream comes again, all around. The lights flash on, and Alice's face floats in front of him. Tears pour from her eyes. She smiles a horrible, twisted smile. With too many teeth. All teeth and gums. She mouths a word through that horrible face, her eyes full of fear and warning.

The word is 'Jenny.'

Her mouth snaps shut, her eyes widen, and she flies backwards deep into the twisted grey world on the open garage door's other side.

A blast of sulfur. The side of the door he is still on goes dark. He stands but cannot tell if there is a floor. He is nauseous. The grey dirt of the world through the garage door is inviting, if only because he can see it.

Green lightning flashes in the distance. And in the lightning, he makes out structures and the shapes of trees, albeit twisted and misshapen.

Doug steps through the garage door.

He screams a little when it slides shut and slams to the ground behind him.

Thunder rolls in the distance, and the lightning flashes again.

The shadows dance all around him.

Back on his desk, the hands on the old clock continue to spin.

V – MARGARET

Doug moaned on the daybed, and then let out a small scream of sorts. The sound was mushy because his mouth was closed. Margaret experienced this many times throughout their marriage. Usually, it made her laugh even if a little annoyed at being woken up.

This time, it was not funny.

Doug awoke long enough to say something about getting Alice from a dark place and then he went right back out.

Margaret held his hand and stared at the wall behind the daybed.

She struggled to understand why Jenny Noble was here. Jenny had been missing, but of all places, how and why did she show up here? Hazel was still speaking to Jenny on the front porch.

She lied to me, thought Margaret.

Doug flickered when he came back into the room. Hazel said it was the storm, but Margaret knew better. She knew when Hazel was lying. She always had. The longer she sat with Doug, the more familiar the situation became.

I've done this before.

Margaret heard the front door open and close. Doug muttered something incoherent on the daybed. She figured he would be okay for a moment without her. Margaret stood and went to the entry where Hazel muttered something incoherent as well.

"Hazel," said Margaret.

Hazel started and her right hand snapped down to her right thigh. The motion of someone who was used to carrying a holstered weapon. Margaret tilted her head. Curiouser and curiouser.

"Hey Mar, you startled me," said Hazel. She casually relaxed her right hand. "How's Doug?"

"He's still out. Ulrich and I laid him on the daybed." Her eyes never left Hazel's.

I don't trust you, thought Maragret.

"Ah, Ulrich. Weird as ever," said Hazel. "Where is everyone now?"

"It doesn't matter. What's going on here?" Margaret demanded.

"Nothing out of the ordinary except for Jenny hiking all the way up here. She thought Alice would be here and wanted to be here too, for support."

Hazel was lying again. The lie was terrible, no special awareness required.

"That's obviously made up. Why is she here, really? And have you spoken to her mother?"

"I called her house, but no one answered. She wants us to take her back to Brewster Falls."

This was true at least, although Hazel didn't give the answer Margaret wanted.

"Hazel, stop being a bitch for two seconds," said Margaret, composed and quiet, yet firm. "There is no explanation for Jenny being here just as there is no explanation for why my husband flickered in and out of existence as he was passing out. Don't hand me this lightning crap. You clearly saw it and clearly weren't surprised, so I know you at the very least have some kind of idea what the hell is going on here. And something about Alice and a dark place."

"Mar, I really don't—"

Margaret reached out and grabbed Hazel's arm. She squeezed it hard. Hazel swooned.

"You will tell me what is happening, and you will do it now."

Hazel's eyes bounced back and forth.

"Well, Mar, the truth is Jenny is possessed by an ancient power humanity accidentally unleashed a few generations ago. Doug flickered because he passed into the home of that same ancient power when he went into Aunt Mercy's sitting room. You, nor I, will go in there any more than any of our family will because we can't even consider it thanks to Uncle Ulrich's meddling. Alice has likely been kidnapped by you guessed it, the same ancient power that blanked your husband, and is currently being drained of life to feed the engine that wants to destroy our plane of existence. And finally, you are and always will be a bigger and more powerful bitch than I could ever be."

"I don't believe it."

"Well, believe it. Because it happened."

Margaret did believe it. She could tell when Hazel wasn't lying. She gasped and pulled her hand back. As she released Hazel's arm, she had a flood of emotions: fear, sadness, loss, fright, disbelief. It was too much.

Did I read her mind? Did I make her answer me? Alice. We must save Alice. Doug, wake up. I need you.

Margaret swayed.

Hazel reached out to steady her cousin.

Ulrich stepped into the room, looking both disapproving and relieved.

"Hazel. Margaret. I will travel with you back to Brewster Falls. We will take Jenny with us. We must go, now. The hour grows short; and short, the hour grows."

CHAPTER 7

Free Parking

"Here's another that will never get out of Brewster Falls."

I – THE CAPRICE

Cody and Charles traveled alone today. Tiffany couldn't find the motivation to join them. They'd still been expected to make it to school despite the disappearances of Alice Massey and Jenny Noble. But, you know, counselors were available, so it was totally fine.

Hazel Montgomery had called the Brewster Falls Police from Hampton to ask them to check on Alice. When they found she wasn't at home, they went around asking if anyone had seen her. No one had. Now they were all suspects in the Missing Teens Scandal of Brewster Falls. Guilty until proven innocent.

It had been two days since Cody and Charles went to Jenny's house. Two days since Cody stabbed his best friend. Jenny's mother turned their visit into an interrogation. Have you two talked to

Jenny recently? How close were you? Was she acting normal? Did she seem happy? Did you take her? Do you know where she is? Why are you here?

They were the accused.

"Do you think we should go back to Jenny's house and make sure her mom knows we didn't take her to New Hampshire? Clear our names?" asked Charles.

"I'm pretty sure she'd be even more certain we did it if we went over there," answered Cody.

"Probably true. Well, I won't be held responsible."

"For the life of me, I cannot remember what made us think that we were wise."

"And that we'd never compromise?"

They looked at each other and smiled.

Cody's grin vacated quickly as he looked at his twiddling thumbs.

"Feel's weird to laugh, doesn't it?" asked Charles.

"Yeah."

They approached the turn from Colonel Perez Road onto Donovan Drive. Neither mentioned it to the other, but they each had the impression the Garage House had gotten darker. Its kids, as Alice called them, were manning their post, although it seemed there were more today. Maybe only one or two, but there were more.

The Caprice crept past. They did their damndest not to turn and look at it or its occupants. At least Charles was driving, he had something to help him focus elsewhere.

But poor Cody McBeans. He couldn't resist. They inched forward. Inch. Stop. Inch. Stop. He didn't want to look. He felt foolish. What was he afraid of? It's just a house and some kids waiting to go into school. Isn't it? He couldn't help it, turned his head, and looked at the Garage House. Same as always. Four garages. Two attached to the house. And two more that didn't belong.

CODEBREAKER! Praise him! The codebreaker sees. He knows! Yes! YES! You will join us. You have opened our gates! Praise him! Yes! YES!

Cody winced.

He couldn't look away.

DO you UNDERSTAND what you HAVE DONE? DO you UNDERSTAND what you SEE?

The silhouettes in the shadows between the garages looked at him. He couldn't make out any of their faces, but looking at him they were. And he was looking at them. Feeling them.

He is BEGINNING to UNDERSTAND! Yes. YES! He knows. Praise him! He opened the door! BROKEN the CODE!

"No no no no no," Cody whispered.

"What are you saying?" asked Charles.

His friend. His love! The SHADOWS take him! The CODE-BREAKER knows! He desires the Midwatch! Bring him CODE-BREAKER! Bring him to us!

"Cody, my man. What are you looking at?" asked Charles.

People lurked in the shadows. Cody was staring right at them. Charles reached over and shook him a little.

Cody mouthed words, but no sound came. Blood formed in Cody's eyes. Charles shook his friend a little harder hoping to end some weird panic attack.

"Cody, snap out of it. Come back to me, bro," said Charles.

Cody trembled. His arms and neck broke out in gooseflesh and his hands twisted into rigid claws. His teeth ground and gritted. Spittle came out between his teeth as the corners of his mouth twisted into a nightmare smile.

"NO NO NO!" Cody said through clenched teeth.

YES! YES! Bring him! HE will join us! Enter MIDWATCH! Midwatch with ALICE! Yes! Midwatch with JENNY! Yes! Mid-watch with DOROTHY! YES! Midwatch with MERCY! YES! THE

SHAWDOWS TAKE THEM! THE SHADOWS TAKE THEM ALL! TWILIGHT WILL SET! THE CODEBREAKER FEEDS US! YEEEEEESSSSSSS! Bring Him. BRING Him! BRING HIM! YES!

The shapes grew larger. One was coming closer, though out from under the shadow of the eaves it still had no discernable face. Cody felt the other creatures trying to pull this one back. It struggled, and he struggled with it.

"Oh man, oh man. What the hell? WHAT THE HELL?" yelled Charles. He pressed the accelerator to the floor and piloted the roaring Caprice around the line of cars and up the opposing lane of Donovan Drive. Before doing this, he saw two things:

One, tears of blood burst from Cody McBeans' eyes as his mind was ripped apart.

And two, the face on the thing approaching the car shimmered into focus. It was Alice's face on that thing, and Charles was sure it was screaming for help. But there was only silence.

II – MIDWATCH

Charles Horne is here. Or part of here, wherever here is. No, not part of here. Part of Charles is here. Is that right?

Cody doesn't understand.

It's dark.

That he understands very well.

Am I dead? he thinks.

He is too aware to be dead.

Aware it's dark.

A violet flash lights the void. He feels pain during the flash, followed by a jolt. His life recharged. He wants it again.

He sits in a car. Through the passenger window stretches a vista of crooked trees. He blinks. A familiar house looms on the corner. The Garage House. His friends stand in front of the garage doors. They beckon him to come to them. They want salvation. They are hiding from something. They call him to join.

Nothing makes sense.

Cody wants to ask what they are running from.

Another violet light flashes.

He stands next to the car. He turns back to the house. Shapes emerge from the shadow. They want him.

It feels good to be wanted.

Cody turns back to the car and sees himself looking out the passenger window.

What the hell? he thinks.

His friend, Alice Massey, walks towards him from the house. He tries to speak.

Alice, what is this? Where are we? His words do not come.

She walks past, unseeing.

Welcome, Cody. We are pleased you could join us.

With each syllable, he is comforted. He is given the peace of a six-year-old child playing in the dirt, of a victorious general after a long battle, of a man lying on a sandy bank next to a babbling brook, straw hat over his face, shielding drowsy eyes from the sun.

"Is this a dream?" asks Cody.

This is Midwatch. And we are Midwatch.

The shapes reach out to him.

"What is Midwatch? Why does it look like—"

Your home? Because it is. Yes. And it is not. No. This is Nassem City. Named by the grey man. The shadows took him.

"The grey man? Who..." Cody abandons the thought for a distraction behind him.

Alice stands outside the passenger door, reaching out to the other him. The other Cody's eyes are red. Charles Horne sits in the driver's seat. His hand rests on other Cody's shoulder, concern blankets his translucent face.

Oh, Charles, thinks Cody. *What is this?*

YES. Charles. Charles mocks you, answers Midwatch. *He keeps you beneath him to lift himself up. To be greater than, he makes you less than. Yes.*

"That's not true! It can't be. Charles is my friend." Cody studies his shoes as he speaks, each word quieter than the last. He wears Adidas Sambas, the same as Charles. Because of Charles. "We've been friends forever," he whispers.

So sad. We are sorry for you. Here, have this.

Another jolt of energy courses through him. He wants more. All of his problems and sadness and distraction drift away, leaving only peace and unity.

This pleases you! YES! More you can have. Much more! You are the Codebreaker. You will have all you desire. YES! Praise you! What is your desire? Name it!

He desires to be back in the car with Charles and forget this place.

His friend! His love! The Codebreaker desires his love-friend! CODEBREAKER! Praise him! The codebreaker sees. He knows! Yes! YES! You will join us. You have opened our gates! Praise him! Yes! YES!

Cody smiles. With each word from Midwatch comes another jolt of pleasure. Its voice echoes in his mind. Its gratitude replaces his fear.

DO you UNDERSTAND what you HAVE DONE? DO you UNDERSTAND what you SEE?

Cody turns back to the house. The creatures' eyes glow purple and the dark cloud swirls above them. The garages are open. Within, an auditorium full of shrouded figures calls to him.

He is BEGINNING to UNDERSTAND! Yes. YES! He knows. Praise him! He opened the door! BROKE the CODE!

"Yes yes yes yes yes," Cody chants.

His friend. His love! The SHADOWS take him! Bring him, CODEBREAKER! Bring him to us!

"Bring Charles here. How? How did I get here? How do I bring him?" asks Cody. His eyes are burning. Something in the air, perhaps.

He bends over in a wave of dizziness. The creatures hold him up.

He is fed another jolt of glorious energy.

He fights you! Wants to take what is yours! YES! Bring him! Bring him! Yes! He will join the CODEBREAKER! YES! Join FOR-EVER! YES!

He hates him.

And loves him.

Cody wants to be with Charles.

Cody wants to be Charles.

"He is jealous. I will bring him here where he can be less than. Yes. Less than with Cody. Forever. Yes. Friends forever. Joined for-ever. Yes," says Cody.

Yes, echoes Midwatch.

A voice much too small cries out from deep within him. It says this is wrong. It says to flee. It says Charles is not his enemy and this place is evil. But Cody is drunk on power. The kind of power he dreamt about. Power most men, even the best good and Godly men, cannot ignore.

"YES YES YES!" He smiles, all teeth and gums.

The shimmering body of Alice reaches out to him with both arms, and screams.

And so, Cody McLean, like most who command real power for the first time, forgets himself. He silences the voice of reason and banishes his love for all things. They will return to him, before the end, waiting for a moment when just-in-time has passed and too-late stands upon the doorstep, as the right thing to do usually does.

III – DEPUTY STEPHEN RIGGS

"Dispatch controller radio check six-oh-two, state your 20."

"Six-oh-two Riggs responding. Running speed by the mall. Over."

"Observers report ninety-nine in progress over by the high school. A vehicle pulled out of the line into the lot and went speeding past in the opposing lane."

"Six-oh-two enroute. Description of vehicle available?"

"Observer reports it looked like a black police car."

"Copy. Any chance it *was* a police car?"

"Negative, no other units in the area."

"Copy. Six-oh-two responding. Riggs out."

Deputy Stephen Riggs was two hours from completing an all-night shift. All-night shifts in Brewster Falls were notorious for extreme boredom, risk of falling asleep, and death from low heart rate. Six-oh-two was one of two cars on duty, and Deputy Riggs was tired.

He switched on his light bar and throttled the Crown Vic into action. He fishtailed pulling out of the mall parking lot. He may as well have some fun, too, right? The police lights and spinning tires weren't necessary for this assignment, but it was his prerogative, and he needed the adrenaline.

He pictured himself looking for another Crownie, only this one would be black. Deputy Riggs intended to let the kids go with a warning, figuring he could scare them a little and then send them off for the next shift to deal with.

He pulled onto Donovan Drive from the neighborhood's opposite end. It took about twelve extra turns, but he knew them well from his time speeding through here on the way home when he was in school. Off to the side of the road about a quarter mile down was a big black car. It slanted into the ditch. The two occupants were still inside and sitting quite close together in the front seat.

"Geez it's 0700. We really need to make out right now?" Deputy Riggs said to himself.

"Six-oh-two to Dispatch."

"Go ahead six-oh-two."

"Located black Chevy Caprice on North side of Donovan Drive. My guess is some kids are parking before school. Stepping out to investigate."

"Copy six-oh-two. By parking do you mean *parking?*"

"Oh yeah. Hot and heavy. Six-oh-two code six."

"Roger six-oh-two. Have fun!"

Riggs sighed and exited his vehicle. He clicked the button on his shoulder radio to make sure it was calling, pulled his flashlight, and turned it on. He did not unsnap the holster on his 1911 service weapon. He hoped the light would be noticed so he wouldn't have to break up any early morning extra curriculars.

This end of Donovan Drive had some very mature trees. In the twilight of morning, it was still dark over here until one's eyes adjusted. He shone his light on the plate first. He made a mental note of it but didn't write it down. He would not put these kids through any more than they were going through with the recent disappearances of their classmates. Riggs remembered when he went to Brewster Falls High, they had some similar issues. He supposed nothing ever changed. Not really.

Deputy Riggs stepped up to the driver's door and knocked three times with his light. He did not shine it into the car. What happened next happened very quickly.

He heard a cry from inside the vehicle. Riggs grabbed the door handle to open the door, but it was locked. As he did so, a head struck the driver's window hard enough that it cracked. The passenger pulled the driver's head back and smacked it against the window again. Deputy Riggs used his flashlight to break through the window and heard a wet growling coming from the passenger.

The driver made no sound.

"STOP! PUT YOUR HANDS WHERE I CAN SEE THEM!" shouted Deputy Riggs.

He reached through the broken window's glass and opened the door from the inside. The driver's hoodie-covered-head and torso fell out and onto the ground with his legs still inside the car. Riggs thought this kid may be dead.

Here's another that will never get out of Brewster Falls, he thought.

"Noooooooooo. We must take him! Take him to Midwatch! Join Join Join Join!" said the passenger. They sounded like an angry gravel-voiced munchkin. He shone his light into the car. There was enough blood on the passenger's face that Deputy Riggs couldn't identify them.

"What the hell," said Riggs. "HANDS UP WHERE I CAN SEE THEM!"

This time he did unsnap his 1911, brought it up into a grip with his flashlight, kept the safety, and rested his finger along the slide instead of on the trigger. He had reservations about pulling his weapon on kids, but this one was growling and crying tears of blood.

"You cannot stop the Darkness!" the kid munchkin-growled. "The Shadows are moving. Twilight will set. We will send YOU to Midwatch!"

The kid lunged towards Riggs. It was a sloppy move. This was no athlete. Their foot caught on the console, and they ended up slamming down onto the legs of their former driver. The passenger cried out and slapped their hands down. It sounded like an animal's cry.

Riggs struck them in the back of their noggin with the butt of his gun, knocking them out. He shouldn't have done that, but he didn't want to have to shoot the kid or wrestle them to put them in cuffs. He was too tired right now.

"Crap," he said to himself. Riggs talked to himself a lot.

He grabbed his shoulder radio and called it in.

Deputy Stephen Riggs also needed to call Hazel Montgomery, but he couldn't do that until he made it to a phone. Whatever 'Midwatch' was, Hazel insisted that he inform her immediately after any mention of it. He thought she was nuts when she made the request but, here he was.

Off to see the wizard.

IV – TIFFANY

Tiffany Philips lived in a palace. This was fitting because Tiffany Philips was a princess, at least in her own mind. The last few days, she stayed at home.

Tiffany told her parents she needed time to grieve, and that she felt unsafe going out with her friends disappearing. They agreed as she knew they would. They never punished her or talked to her about her grades or asked how she was feeling. Their only requirements being she be dressed up and practice good etiquette and manners when their friends were over for dinner and drinks. She was a trophy child. A checkmark on her parents' list of things successful upper-class people must do before they die.

I miss Alice, don't I?

The other reason was the trouble in her relationship with Charles Horne. He had been acting distracted lately and stood her up for lunch the last time they were in school together. Tiffany needed to feel important and loved. Why could Charles not understand that? Wasn't she worth it?

Because he is a selfish boy. We do not need him. Find another.

Tiffany picked up the phone and dialed Mitch Riggs. She hoped this was one of the days Mitch was skipping class or that he was late and had not left for school. The phone rang a few times and then their answering machine picked up. It was the automated recording that came with the machines. No happy family blah blah blah like her own and Cody McBean's.

The shadows take them.

"Hello, this is a message for Mitch. Mitch, this is Tiffany Philips. I was just calling to ask a few questions about our math homework..." She left her number and hung up. Too bad. No one home.

Tiffany thought she should dress and walk to school. It would only take an hour or so and then she could catch a ride home with either Mitch or Charles depending on how the day went. Right now, she would be fine with either.

Her phone rang.

She picked it up.

"Hello, this is Tiffany. Who is it?"

"Hello, this is Sycamore Valley Hospital. Is this the Philips residence?"

"Yes, it is."

"Are Mr. or Mrs. Leonard Philips available?"

Tiffany had pretended to be her mother on the phone multiple times.

"Yes, my mother is home. Hold on and I'll get her."

"Thank you."

Tiffany hit the phone's mute button. She cleared her voice and practiced a few lines in her mother's tone. It was easy. She only needed to see everything and everyone as less than.

"This is Mrs. Philips. What is this concerning?"

"Good morning, Mrs. Philips. This is Sycamore Valley Hospital. You are listed as a second call for Charles Horne. We attempted to reach his mother, Darlene, but were unsuccessful. Are you available?"

Charles Horne? What's happened to Charles? Further, why was her mother listed as a contact for him? Tiffany was not aware their mothers had ever met. And if they had, there is no way the great Mrs. Philips would've given poor Mrs. Horne a second look.

"Mrs. Philips? Are you there?"

Tiffany coughed.

"Yes. Yes, I am here. And I'm aware of my arrangement concerning caring for Charles," she snapped, as her mother would have done. "What's happened? Is he well?"

"We attempted his home number but there was no answer. Do you know how we can reach his mother?"

"Um, no—" a lie, she worked at a gas station "—there is no way to reach Mrs. Horne during the day. That is why I'm listed. What specifically has happened to Charles? As soon as I can reach her, I will give her the message and make sure she calls the hospital and makes arrangements to get there. The poor woman needs so much help."

"Charles is resting but will be fine. He arrived this morning after an accident in front of the school. He suffered light head trauma and was unconscious for a time."

Tiffany started.

Oh no, poor Charles, she thought. *Bring him.*

"Oh my. Do we need to come over there? Should we bring anything? Can he have visitors?" Tiffany failed her impression of her mother.

"No one needs to come over, but if you did you could visit with him. He is in recovery and will be discharged as soon as a responsible party checks him out."

"Oh, that's good news. Thank you. As I said, I will relay this message to his mother as soon as I can. Thank you very much for the information."

"You are welcome. Please take down our direct number."

Tiffany got the number and ended the call. She went to her room, dressed, and got her purse. She intended to make this up to Charles. How could she be so mean?

Because you are horrible. Yes.

Tiffany blinked.

Her phone rang again.

Tiffany ran into her parents' room to answer.

"Hello, this is Tiffany."

"Hey Tiff, this is Mitch. Sorry, I just woke up."

"Oh, Mitch! Oh, thank God! Do you have a car?"

"Uh, yeah. I have a car. Are we going somewhere?"

"Yes. Yes, can you come get me? It's Charles. He's in the hospital."

"Oh, no, for real? What happened? He okay?"

"He'll be fine, but he was in an accident this morning on the way to school. Apparently hit his head pretty hard. How soon can you be here?"

"Gimme about fifteen minutes. Should I knock when I get there or just pull out... I mean in," Mitch laughed.

Idiot, thought Tiffany.

"Just pull in. I'll come out and we can go."

"Hey, if you want, I can call my brother. He's a deputy on the BFPD and was on duty this morning. He might have some more info."

"Oh, yes! That would be wonderful!"

"Anything for you, sweetheart. See you soon."

"Thanks Mitch! You're my hero. Please hurry!"

Tiffany hung up and held the phone to her chest.

Bring them to the shadows! Bring them!

V – MITCH RIGGS

"Anything for you, sweetheart. See you soon," Mitchell Riggs said to his reflection, repeating what he said to Tiffany on the phone. He pulled an Abercrombie polo from the hamper and checked it for smell. No wrinkles baby. He put the already worn shirt on and checked himself in the mirror. He wanted to look good for Tiffany. This was a delicate situation and would require the utmost attention. He was going to pick her up and try to pick her up on the way to take her to her boyfriend in the hospital. Challenge accepted, my guy. Charles was a friend during the day, but it was not like they hung out. Besides, Tiffany showed enough interest in Mitch he figured he was doing ol' Chuck a favor.

Once his frosted tips were properly spiked, he spritzed himself with a little Tommy and sniffed his pits. He frowned and checked the clock. No time. He added another spray of cologne under each arm. Best he could do on short notice. He popped his collar and flexed for himself. These AF shirts were made to show muscles, which he had. Then, he winked. His reflection winked back and flashed a toothy smile.

"Here we go, big guy," Mitch said to himself as he grabbed his keys and wallet. He stuck his right ring finger through the key ring and twirled them around into his hand. Man, he felt cool as hell.

"Whoa," he said. He forgot to call Steve. He grabbed the phone and dialed the station.

"Brewster Falls Police, is this an emergency?"

"Hi Claire, it's Mitch. Is Stephen around?"

"Oh, hi Mitch! How's your dad?"

"Uh, he's fine Claire. Still misses our mom. I'm available though, if you're looking for company."

"That is not what I meant, Mitchell. We're all worried about him. Stephen has not come back into the station yet. He had an incident this morning and is taking care of that over at Sycamore Valley. Do I need to radio him in, or can I just let him know you called?"

Well, that answered that. It was his brother who responded to Charles' accident. He could talk to him later. Plus, it would give him a reason to call Tiffany again.

"No, just let him know I called. I'm going to the hospital anyway. Friend of mine is there, and I'd like to check on him."

"Well, that's sweet. I'll give your brother the message."

"Thanks Claire. I hope you get to see me soon. Peace out."

"You're horrible, Mitchell Riggs. Goodbye."

The call disconnected and Mitch hung up the phone.

Claire was an attractive older lady. He liked it when she said his full name. He didn't like that she had a crush on his dad, but ever since his mother left, a few ladies about town had been calling on him. What could Mitch do, his dad was Chief of Police, and a good-looking dude. All the Riggs men were good looking dudes, bless the Lord. The good-looking dude in the sky.

Mitch jumped in his white '92 Probe GT and fired it up. The car was not destined to be remembered fondly, but Mitch was in love with the five-speed transmission and the digital dash. He felt it may as well have been a Ferrari. He backed it out of the driveway, popped the clutch, and dropped the transmission into first gear before he was done rolling backwards. This Probe wouldn't last long doing that. The front wheels gave a satisfying bark, and he was off to capture destiny. And today, destiny's name was Tiffany.

Mitch paid enough attention to know Tiffany Philips had a bit of a reputation as a class-A b-word, but that didn't bother him. He wasn't looking for anything long-term. Mitch preferred a life without expectations or restrictions. They were in high school, why mess it up with relationships? It was generally accepted that he was a great time at parties, and didn't he look and smell good in that baby blue polo shirt? You better believe it.

No sooner was he pulling up to Tiffany's house in their turn-around than she was running out the front door to his car. The Philips' house was huge. The land for their driveway probably cost more than any other house in Brewster Falls.

"Mitch, thank you so much for coming. Can you take me to a gas station on the way? I want to get a couple things for Charles."

"Sure thing, Tiff. Are you doing okay?"

"Yeah. I'm just worried. And we were kind of arguing the other day and I just feel bad."

"Got it. What were you two arguing about? I thought you had the perfect relationship."

"Perfect. Ha! It was nothing. Boyfriend-girlfriend stuff. It's silly."

"I get it. That's why I steer clear of affairs of the heart. Why ruin my day, you know?"

"Mitch, honestly that's a surprising bit of wisdom coming from you."

"Ouch. I have wisdom. You must know it or why would you have called me about math homework? Needing help learning to multiply?"

Tiffany's cheeks flushed.

"You really are terrible."

"Maybe so, but I know I'm no one's first choice for homework help, especially math. So, using my family's renowned detective skills, I'm able to conclude you called for some other purpose. One you have yet to disclose."

"Wow, big words," she teased. "Well, right now we need to focus on getting to Charles. But thanks for making me laugh. It's been rough."

"Yeah, it has been strange. How are you doing? Missing Alice?"

"I am. It's hard to talk about. I don't want people to think I'm looking for attention while she's gone who knows where and I'm still here and healthy. I miss her a lot."

"You shouldn't feel that way." Mitch reached out with his right hand and grabbed her left. She didn't pull away. "Your feelings are as important as anyone's. Just because Alice is missing and could be in great danger doesn't mean you aren't important."

"Thank you, Mitch. That's very sweet."

"Well, I want you to know I'm here to listen if you need it."

"I didn't call you for math homework."

"No shit?"

They laughed. Tiffany finally pulled her hand away to wipe her eyes.

"Hey, where do you park for school? I've never noticed this car in the lot," Tiffany said.

"Oh, yeah, I park it down at the old restaurant just past the school. The Russian place."

"Doesn't that cost something? I heard the old Russian guy was greedy for parking money since the restaurant caught fire and shut down."

"Well, yeah but I'm not allowed to park in the school lot anymore. They caught me spinning wheels one too many times. This baby scares 'em." Mitch patted the Probe's dash.

"Could I ask you another favor?"

"Anything for you, sweetheart."

"Could you pick me up for school? I won't have a ride tomorrow since Charles is hurt. And, I have a better spot for us to park. Closer than that mad Russian's place."

"As you wish. Where is this magic spot?"

Tiffany reached over and took his hand in hers. Her eyes were no longer glassy, and she smiled like a child about to get her way, all teeth and gums.

"You know the house on the corner of Perez and Donovan? The one with the garages? I have a friend there who will save us a spot."

VI – CHARLES

Deputy Riggs told Charles he needed to fill out some paper-work. He told him he was going to have some questions for him and that, because of this, he would not allow the hospital to discharge him until they were through. He apologized and asked if he needed anything. Charles said a Snickers. That was the last he saw of Deputy Riggs.

And what the hell was midwatch? He had never heard that word before from Cody, or anyone else. He had also never seen Cody cry blood before, so maybe midwatch wasn't important right now.

Strange things are afoot in Brewster Falls.

Is that cologne?

"Whoa, there he is. Another masturbation accident?"

He was surprised to see the smiling face of Mitch Riggs.

"Ha. Hey Mitch. What are you doing here?"

"Ouch, bro. Is that any way to greet your best friend? I'm so nice, look who I brought, you're welcome." Mitch's tone was not unkind.

Tiffany came from around Mitch and said hello. Charles was happy Tiffany was safe, but he was not thrilled she was with Mitch.

She came over and produced a beautiful king-sized Snickers. "Hi. I thought you would need this. I know it's your favorite. Luckily, Mitch was skipping school today and called me back to get us here. I'm so happy you're okay. What happened? Was anyone else in the car? Anyone hurt? I mean, other than you?"

"Whoa, whoa. Slow down a bit," said Charles. "C'mere." She leaned down for the embrace and kissed the corner of his mouth. "Now give me that Snickers."

Tiffany handed it over, and he opened it and took a large bite. His eyes rolled back in ecstasy as he chewed and took another bite before swallowing the first. He exhaled loudly through his nose.

"Wowee. I'm getting excited just watching," said Mitch from the door.

"Dude, I'm starving. They left me in here and told me I can't leave until your brother comes back to ask me some questions," said Charles.

"Well, that could be a while. If I could tell you how many times we waited to have a meal until Steve got home you'd understand why I'm not a fatty," said Mitch.

"That's not nice," said Tiffany.

"What do you care?" asked Mitch. "You look great. No fatties here."

"Dude, c'mon. I'm trying to enjoy my chocolate," said Charles.

"So, what happened?" asked Tiffany.

Charles swallowed.

"Well, we had just turned the corner and were stopped outside the house with the garages. Cody was staring at it and kind of breathing funny. I don't know. I thought he was having a panic attack."

"Cody! How is Cody? Where is he?" asked Tiffany.

"Ol' McBeans?" asked Mitch.

Charles nodded. "I don't know where he is, but they told me he was okay. Anyway, he kind of started talking to himself. He was repeating 'no' over and over, so I reached out and shook him. Then he turned to me and was like vicious or something. His eyes were bleeding—"

"What was bleeding? His eyes?"

"Yeah. His eyes," Charles said while closing his own and rubbing the bridge of his nose.

"Brutal," said Mitch.

"Yeah, sure. Brutal. Then he sort of attacked me—"

"Cody attacked you? What for?" Tiffany's tone matched someone getting excited for a punchline.

"Let me finish."

"Sorry, I'm just concerned for my friends," said Tiffany.

This isn't about you, thought Charles.

"Hey, let him finish. I'm sure this is hard," said Mitch, and put a hand on Tiffany's shoulder.

And this bastard, thought Charles. *Oh well, whatever. Could be worse. At least he's on my side.*

Charles sighed. "It is hard. And I don't know why he attacked me. But when he did, I nailed the throttle and went around the cars in line. Then, Cody grabbed my head and made me look at him. He had this crazy smile and said he needed to take me to midwatch. You ever heard that word before? Anyway, that's when I drove into the ditch. He hit my head against the window and knocked me out. Next thing I knew your brother was there. Cody was unconscious beside me, and the ambulance was pulling up."

Charles noticed Tiffany start when he said Cody grabbed his head. Or was it at the mention of midwatch? He peered at her.

"That's nuts, my guy. You got your butt kicked by Cody McBeans. What were you too love birds fighting about? He jealous of Tiffany?" asked Mitch.

"Dude," said Charles.

"Mitch, that's not funny," said Tiffany.

"Yeah, Mitch. That's not funny. And why the hell aren't you in school?" asked Deputy Stephen Riggs, finally arriving back from wherever he was. And with another Snickers, although of the regular size variety.

"Hey bro. I was on my way, chill. Tiffany called as I was leaving and told me my good friend Charles was in an accident this morning, so we came here to see him."

Deputy Riggs looked at Tiffany. "Well, how did you know? Never mind, can you two leave us alone? I need to ask him some questions. And get your butts to school."

"Fine, chill man. If it was your friend, you'd be here. C'mon Tiff. Do you think we can park at that Garage House today?"

The Garage House!

Charles shivered at the image of Alice's face shimmering next to his car this morning.

"What do you mean park at the Garage House?" he asked.

"Yeah man, the one you geeked out about the other day. Looks like we're going to be some of the Garage House Kids now," said Mitch.

"Mitch, let it go," said Tiffany. "Charles, please get better soon." She leaned down and kissed him gently.

Charles felt like he had a bomb go off in his mind.

"You guys should stay away from that house," he said.

"Can you two please get out of here? I was supposed to be off shift hours ago. I need to complete this interview. Stay here, go to school, come back in when I leave, park at the house, I don't care just get out so I can finish," said Deputy Riggs.

"Take a chill pill, bro, we're leaving," said Mitch. He reached out and took Tiffany's hand and pulled her out.

Oh, c'mon.

"Sorry. That was unprofessional," said Deputy Riggs. "Look, I'm going to be straight with you. We think you have something to do with the girls disappearing and whatever happened to Cody McLean."

"What? No way! I have nothing to do with that. These things are happening to me! To us!" protested Charles.

"I don't know about that, but we need to figure it out. Apparently, you disappeared on the same day Jenny disappeared. You went out to the parking lot and walked off school property. You were gone a couple hours and came back. We verified it with the teachers and the parking lot cameras. We asked around if any other students were out without reason that day and you and your passenger were the only ones. So, tell me, where did you go?"

CHAPTER 8

Red Right Hand

"You are not ready for what lies behind."

I – CODY

Cody dreams.

He walks in Midwatch, where the ethereal meets the earthly. He wanders amidst alien structures that defy both past and future. These edifices, neither wholly ancient nor entirely modern, stand as silent witnesses to a reality beyond comprehension.

The strange, twisted trees and the newer-looking buildings of this city don't match the setting. They don't match anywhere. These structures and forms are unknown to him. They are manmade, and Midwatch is not of man. He senses Midwatch is not evil, that it is only a stopping place between other places. A waypoint. Midwatch is currently occupied by evil, that's it.

The lights are on in some of the buildings.

Where does the power come from?

He approaches one of the lit windows.

Humanoid shapes converse inside. He wipes the glass and cups his hands around his face. His eyes grow large.

Angels.

They are shaped vaguely human, wear human clothing, and two are sitting in human chairs. But the wings! Oh, they have wonderful, glorious wings curved down their backs.

The two who were sitting now stand. They are coming out.

Cody crouches and hides behind a small structure resembling a newspaper stand.

The creatures speak as they come out. The language is not his own, yet he understands what they are saying. It is guttural, and dark.

"How many more do they need?" asks figure one.

The second wears blue jeans.

"They need three immediately, but a dozen very soon," says Blue Jeans.

"Christ," says the third. They wear a white shirt.

"Is there any way out of this? Can't we say we've traded enough?" asks Number One.

"Don't even start talking like that, you know what will happen. We'll get our damned wings clipped," answers White Shirt.

"Our wings are already clipped," says Blue Jeans. "You see what's become of us. These conveniences and gifts they bring have made us soft. We no longer have the strength, need, or will to fly."

White Shirt grabs Blue Jeans and spreads his wings. They are easily sixteen feet across. They flap with a tremendous whoosh that kicks a dust cloud into Number One's face. He coughs.

White Shirt lifts Blue Jeans into the sky.

"Let's see whose wings work and whose don't," says White Shirt.

Blue Jeans screams as he is let go.

White Shirt laughs.

Blue Jeans falls towards Cody, and he floats up into the sky towards Blue Jeans. They crash into each other midair, and Blue Jeans grabs him, holding his face close. Other than the feathers, the face is almost human, although the eyes are red and much too large, and the nose, although thin, is long and dipped at the tip.

"You must save us. You must help us," says Blue Jeans, pleading for salvation.

They spin as they fall towards the ground. Cody's stomach is in his throat, and he thinks he might throw up.

Blue Jeans jerks him nearer.

"This is not how it is supposed to be. You caused this. This was a bright place. We were strong. Look at it. Look at us. Do you understand what you see?"

Cody shakes his head and cries. The ground rushes up to them.

He screams.

Number One looks up at them.

"Everything will be all right," he says.

* * *

Cody jerked awake.

He tried to raise his arm to wipe his brow and found he could not.

"What the hell?" he said.

The lights clicked on. Cody closed his eyes and tried to lift his arm again to shade them. He was strapped down.

"Easy there, Cody. My name is Stephen Riggs. Deputy Stephen Riggs. How are you feeling? Do you need anything to drink?"

"Sure, I could use a drink. Why am I tied down?"

"We'll get to that. Do you feel angry, aggressive, anything like that?"

"No, just confused. I remember... I remember, your brother is kind of a douche."

"Good memory. I'll be back with a drink and a nurse."

"Oooh, a nurse. Now I know why I'm tied down. Bringeth her to me, knave!"

Deputy Riggs shook his head and left the room. Cody slammed his head back onto his pillow.

Shouldn't have said that, he thought.

His head was pounding.

He wore a hospital gown. He might be naked underneath. His face flushed.

He raised his hands against the restraints once more in an effort to rub his eyes. They were on fire with itchiness.

Cody grunted through clenched teeth.

"Are you sure?" A woman's voice from the door.

"Cody, are you okay?" The familiar voice of Deputy Riggs this time.

"Yes, I'm fine. My eyes are itching like hell," Cody said.

"Alright, hang on. Please check him out and let him loose. I'm here if anything happens," Riggs said.

What an odd thing to say, thought Cody.

The nurse approached and checked the monitor next to his bed. She squeezed the saline bag hanging above him.

"Cody, my name is Nurse Sharon. I am going to undo your restraints now. If you need anything, you will be able to reach me via this red button." Nurse Sharon held up a little device with a button and a cord leading to the wall behind him.

In his mind the cord wrapped around her neck.

"Please hit it if you need anything. Deputy Riggs here will be speaking with you. If you make any sudden movements or aggressive actions, he will restrain you back to this bed and call hospital security. Do you understand?"

"Sure, totally reasonable. Hospital service sure is strange these days. The only sudden movement and aggressive actions I'm going to make is rubbing my eyes and then going pee."

Nurse Sharon undid the restraints. She made quick work of them, and Cody did indeed attack his eyes as soon as he was free to do so. Deputy Stephen Riggs' hand twitched when Cody brought his hands to his eyes. It was his right hand, the one closest to his pistol.

These people are spooked. What did I do?

His memories remained as absent as the time missing from school during lunch the other day. He was sure Riggs was going to ask him about all that once Nurse Sharon left. She checked a few more items in the room, and again asked Cody if he was okay or needed anything. He told her he wanted a large water.

As she left, she asked Deputy Riggs if he needed anything as well.

Riggs smiled at Nurse Sharon and said not right now, but that he would stop by her station later when this was done.

Cody rolled his eyes. "I didn't realize 'Douche' and 'Riggs' were synonyms. I'm going to need to contact Roget's and make sure they know."

"Don't you need to use the restroom?" responded Deputy Riggs.

"Yes, I do." Cody swung his legs over the bed and felt an intense pain in the back of his head, followed by a brief, but strong, wave of nausea.

"Whoa, buddy. Let me help you out," said Deputy Riggs. He grabbed Cody's arms, helped him up, and walked him over to the restroom door. Cody reached up to the back of his head and felt a bump and some pain when he touched it.

"What happened to my head?" Cody asked.

"Uh, you fell. Probably why you are a little groggy," said Deputy Riggs.

He lies!

Cody glanced at Riggs pistol and understood what he 'fell' into.

"Will you need help in there?" asked Deputy Riggs.

"No, I think I have it from here, thanks."

Cody limped into the bathroom and closed the door behind him. This door did not have a lock.

Cody did his business and waddled to the sink to wash his hands. He took in his reflection. The bandage around his head, his eyes ringed with exhaustion, his sclera streaked with dark red lines. He looked ten years older than the last time he stood in front of a mirror. Cody splashed water on his face, peered into the mirror, and pulled his lower eyelid down from his right eye. The flesh under there was bright red. As he released it, the mirror went black.

Bring him.

Cody dried his hands. As he flipped the light switch off, he winked at the mirror.

"And me and my brother are douche's?" asked Deputy Riggs, sitting in a chair next to the bed.

"Oh definitely," said Cody. "Now, telleth me whilst thee of what thou art afeard?"

"Huh?"

Peasant.

"What are you afraid of? Why was I tied down?"

"Afraid of? Nothing. Confused by? Quite a bit," said Deputy Riggs. "I'm going to get right to the point because I'm tired, and I need to figure out what to do with you. Before I tell you anything, I need to ask, what the hell is Midwatch?"

Show him.

Cody's hand flashed out and grasped Deputy Riggs' wrist. He did not have time to do any more than twitch towards his pistol. The movement was unnatural. It was probably impossible, like the strength of Cody's skinny fingers.

"What the hell is Midwatch?" repeated Cody McBeans. "It's too hard to explain what Midwatch is."

Cody tightened his grip, something cracked, and Riggs opened his mouth to scream. Cody put his right hand to his lips and extended his finger in a 'shhhh' motion.

"It is much too hard to explain Midwatch," Cody whispered. "But I can show you."

* * *

Nurse Sharon returned to the room with Cody's water and gasped. Dust floated in the sunrays from the window, but it was the strange smell that caught her. The primary lights were off. She could see Cody lying on his bed with his eyes closed. His ankles were crossed, and his hands rested on his chest with his fingers laced. A slight grin rested upon his lips.

She set his water down and turned to leave when he spoke.

"Nurse Sharon! Thank you so much. I am very thirsty."

Cody grabbed the bottle and undid the cap. He gulped the water. Some dripped down both sides of his mouth.

Nurse Sharon asked if Deputy Stephen Riggs had gone to use the restroom.

Cody put his right hand up and extended his finger.

Nurse Sharon waited while he drank.

Cody finished and let out a satisfied sigh. He wiped his mouth with the back of his wrist, his right hand red and covered in dirt.

"I am sorry Nurse Sharon. Stephen had to attend to another affair."

Confused disappointment briefly washed over her face. Only when Cody folded his finger back into his hand and placed it by his side on the bed, did Nurse Sharon turn and leave the room.

Cody leaned back.

If he could do all that with one finger, what could he do if he really tried?

II – THE ECHO SPACE

Deputy Stephen Riggs' eyes burn like fire.

"Except 'round these parts, he's no law man, no Sir," he says to himself.

Welcome, son of Penelope. Penelope. Penelope. Penelope.

"Who is that? Penelope? Why are you saying that name?" Stephen reaches up to rub his eyes. The scratching feels amazing. Although, he isn't sure he has hands. Which is weird.

We are Midwatch. We are the echoes of those who were. And those who are. are. are. are.

"I don't know what that means, or where my hands are, but I know I asked another question. How do you know my mother's name?" asks Stephen.

We know many names. names. names. names.

Yes. yes. yes. yes.

Penelope is one we know. One of many. One of one. one. one. one.

Stephen blinks and tries to see who or what he is talking to.

He cannot.

This space is black and featureless. He thinks he's floating but isn't sure. He wiggles his feet. He recalls talking to his buddy Gus Jacobs about phantom limbs. Gus had his legs blown off during the tail end of the Gulf War.

Gus used to tell Stephen, especially after a few drinks, that he could feel his legs and feet. That as long as he wasn't looking, he believed they were there. Cramped a little, but there. Gus said it was like his legs still existed, just somewhere else. Why else would he still feel them?

Stephen experiences this now, except for all of him.

His eyes must exist somewhere because they still burn like a mother—you know.

"That's quite an echo you have there. Strange, since I don't seem to have one. How about you answer my question instead of putting on the mystery and parlor tricks?" Stephen sounds like a cop again.

He is strong. strong. strong. strong.

Like his mother. mother. mother. mother.

Yes, He is strong. But we will bring him. Bring him like the others. He will join us. us. us. us.

"Hey, remember me? Yeah, still here. Answer the question."

Join the darkness and you will see. The Shadows take you. you. you. you.

He defies us. us. us. us.

NO. He will join! Join with Midwatch! THIS IS YOUR HOME! HOME! HOME! HOME!

"Bullshit."

Stephen smells something sweet through his phantom nostrils. Something familiar. He'd recognize it anywhere. His mother's perfume. The only other person who so religiously wore a scent was his own brother Mitch, but he always wore too much. No one had ever told him it wasn't supposed to enter a room before you did.

Stephen welcomes this new smell. His dad spritzed it around the house for a while after she disappeared, which Mitch and Stephen thought was a crap ritual for a woman who walked out on all of them. Eventually, Greg Riggs, the same Greg Riggs from which Darryl Horne purchased his son Charles' Caprice, resigned to only spritzing he and his absent wife's bedroom.

"MOM! WHERE ARE YOU? MOM!" Stephen yells.

No. No. No.

Defies. Defies. Defies.

YOU MUST JOIN WITH US! US! US! US!

The scent grows stronger. She is here. She is coming closer.

"MOM! It's me, Stephen! Your son! I'm here! Keep coming! GET ME OUT OF HERE! WHERE ARE YOU?"

Here. Here. Here.

The whisper comes from right next to his left ear.

No. No. No.

"Mom. Are you still there? Can we get out of here?"

You can get out. I cannot. This is now my home. I am sorry. sorry. sorry. sorry.

"How did you get here? How can I save y—" The not-world he is in swings. He spins. The smell of his mother is gone. The sulfur returns with reinforcements.

All goes dark.

III – DEPUTY RIGGS

Deputy Riggs opens his eyes. He is surrounded by boulders. In the distance a cursed scene unfolds. The sky is grey.

A raccoon jumps at him from behind a boulder. Something snatches it from the air with one taloned wing tip. It takes the animal in its hands—*it has hands?*—and rips it in half. It kneels, lays the pieces on the ground, and bows its head.

As if in prayer.

"What in holy hell," Deputy Riggs says quietly.

"Not the worst thing I have ever heard someone say the first time seeing this place."

The voice is strange. It comes from behind him. He spins instinctively away and twists his body, so his legs face the owner.

His arm screams in pain.

"Be not afraid, I am not here to hurt you. I am not your enemy."

What stands before him could very well be an angel. The creature is seven feet tall, humanoid, has large bird-like eyes, a strange thin nose, and wings. Huge wings. And it wears blue jeans. Levi's blue jeans.

He inspects the two raccoon pieces. It was not a raccoon. It was a little furry nightmare. He rubs his eyes.

"Welcome to Aesteria," speaks the creature. "Come, we have much to do."

"What are you?" manages Deputy Riggs, ignoring the place's name into which he fell.

"What? A better question would be 'Who', and to that I can answer Michael. Now come. Your mother said you were a soldier. And soldiers are what we need."

"You knew my mother? She just spoke to me. Where is she now? How do I know I can trust you?"

"You cannot know. However, I will tell you I knew your mother and she was wonderful. She helped us until Midwatch took her. It is good to hear her soul still exists within that evil."

"Is she dead?"

"It is more complicated than that, and we will discuss it on the way. We must move. Midwatch will come again. It does not like to lose."

The landscape is bleak and colorless. The trees are twisted. The sky is wrong. The buildings, although not broken, make little sense. Lightning perpetuates in the distance.

"Is this Earth?"

"No, not as you know it. There are other planes than yours. This place is between earths and was not always like this. Now come, we must make haste."

"I'm still unsure how I can trust you. I can't explain what just happened, and now I'm speaking to a large bird man speaking a language I don't know but somehow understand. What if I don't wish to go with you?"

"Then you are damned to the Shadows. They will take you. Please, come to Nassem City with me. Do you not recognize the name?"

"I recognize it, although it doesn't make me feel any better. Hell, what choice do I have?"

"Language, Stephen."

He cocks his head at the creature. "Whatever. You still haven't told me *what* you are."

"In time. Follow."

The creature walks towards the buildings and Deputy Riggs follows.

IV – BEVERLY MCLEAN

Cody was walking out of Sycamore Valley Hospital as she was walking in. She glanced his way but didn't immediately recognize him.

Then, Beverly McLean blinked, rushed over, kneeled, hugged him, and pushed him away by his shoulders to arm's length. This all happened in one smooth motion with one heartfelt 'Cody' from his mother.

"Cody," she repeated. "Are you okay? Let me look at you. Why are you outside?"

"I'm fine, Mom. Just a couple scratches. You should see the other guy!"

"Cody, that's not funny. Have you seen Charles? Is he okay? How are you outside?"

She stood, grabbed her son by his right forearm, and marched towards the hospital entrance dragging him as if he were still a small child.

"No," he said.

"What?" He had never spoken to her this way. "What do you mean 'no'? Cody we must go in there. I need to know how to take care of you."

And find out who let my baby out here alone, she thought.

"They already discharged me, mom. I'm not going back in there. We should go home."

"Cody, come on." She turned back towards the entrance. "They cannot discharge a minor without parental consent. I don't know what's going on here, but we are going to find out."

Someone is going to answer for this.

"No."

Something deep inside her called out that this was not her son, and that she should let go of his arm. She shook the idea away, chalking it up to his sudden and unexpected resistance. Cody had always been so sweet and innocent compared to the other kids. He still carried his Loony Tunes lunches, still had his toys in his room, and still used the same blanket. He was such a sweet boy. A model son. She always felt so proud and comforted when she heard stories from the other parents about warring with their teens. But not her Cody. No ma'am.

Until now. Why now?

Cody raised his right arm and extended the index finger straight up between her eyes.

"We are leaving. I am not a child. We are leaving here and going shopping. We are going to get new blankets, sheets, and pillows for my bed. We are going to get a regular lunch bag. We are going to get storage tubs for all the toys and games and junk in my room and we are going to put it all away because I am not some little child anymore and I am TIRED OF YOU HOLDING ME DOWN!"

Poor Beverly McLean. What could she do? She smiled at her son who she was sure was not. Tears streamed from her eyes. Yet, she smiled.

"Of course, dear. You are not a child."

My mother went shopping before she died, thought Beverly.

She was a good mom, wasn't she?

Aside from her choices not feeling her own, the rest of the day was quite wonderful. She and her little son went shopping at his request. She had never been so happy to use her charge card.

They purchased a new bedroom set, storage tubs, lunch bag, and a few other items. Cody picked out some bookends for the books he planned to place on his shelf after the toys were gone, and he chose three new outfits. One of which was a black suit, oxford shirt, and red paisley necktie with matching handkerchief. She decided her sweet boy growing up wouldn't be so bad. After all, wouldn't it be nice to have a man around the house again? Yes, indeed it would.

They got ice cream.

"Cody, you were right. Maybe I didn't want to see it. I'm glad you told me and I'm so sorry you held it in. This was a wonderful day." Beverly's eyes became glassy. "You have grown up."

Cody's brow furled. He licked his vanilla cone with rainbow sprinkles.

"Aw Mom, I'm sorry I yelled. It was such a crazy morning, and I was tired. I love you."

That's not him. This isn't real, she thought.

"I love you, too. Now let's go home and put this stuff to use! Makeover!" She said this in a sing-song voice even though she didn't feel sing-song-y.

How can I call for help?

The McLean's went home. Cody watched as his mother made up his bed, put away his toys, and placed his books as he wanted her too. When she finished, his room resembled a bachelor's bedroom. He hugged her.

"Thanks, mom."

She felt sick at his touch.

She hugged him back.

Their phone rang.

"I wonder who that could be?" she asked no one in particular.

As Beverly McLean took her first step down the stairs, a tear of joy came to her eye. How lucky she was. She smiled.

I need to get away from him.

When Beverly missed the second step, she had only a few seconds to register something was wrong as she fell forward. It was only half a staircase in a tri-level house, but it was enough. When her journey was completed, she lay at the bottom, her heels still on the stairs, her head on the landing. She was still smiling. Her unseeing eyes were open, looking at her wonderful son, standing at the top of the staircase. He, too, was smiling, a single finger raised in the air.

The shadows take him.

V – JENNIFER NOBLE

Her right hand was in the air, one finger pointed straight up. She didn't know why. She didn't know why she was doing a lot of things, like riding in the Massey's car between her school's counselor and a strange old man. She reasoned this must be a dream because she also couldn't speak. Just some weird moaning. She and her friends laughed about it many times.

"Oooh. Who are you dreaming about and what's he doing to you to make you moan like that?" They would tease.

Jenny would laugh and tell them to shut up. She battled night frights her whole life. Something would chase her, and she would try to speak, but couldn't. Or she would need to save someone from some soul-eating force and, again, she couldn't form words.

They are just dreams, like this one now, thought Jenny.

From the road signs, it looked like they were headed towards home, but she couldn't be sure.

Margaret. That's Alice's mom's name. She's driving. That must be her dad asleep in the passenger seat. Who's this old guy? And why is Ms. Montgomery here?

"Whmmm im mmm montmmgery mmere?" Jenny moaned.

Dammit, she thought.

Ms. Montgomery and the old man looked at her.

"Whemmr ammre mmem gommeing?"

Oh, come on!

"Whememre arrmemm we gommmmemiig?"

At least I got "we" this time.

"Jenny, we know you're in there," said Ms. Montgomery, her eyes lined with exhaustion. "Please relax. Rest now. We'll be back in Brewster Falls in a few hours. Try to get some sleep."

I am asleep, you blind hag.

YES! She is a dumb hag!

Jenny gasped. "Whommmm saimmamd thammmt? Whoommm saammmd thhammt? WHOMM SAMMID THAT? WHO SAIDM THAT?"

Ms. Montgomery grasped her right hand, and the old man grasped the other. Jenny could see Mrs. Massey's eyes in the rearview. They were a mother's eyes. Mr. Massey remained asleep.

"What did you hear, Jenny?" asked Ms. Montgomery.

Jenny eye's snapped open. She opened her mouth wide and worked her jaw before answering.

"Oh, nothing. I was just waking from a dream and was a little disoriented. Let's get home and I'll have my mother make me up a nice Ovaltine. It always makes me feel tip top!"

No no no. That is not me. Is that my voice? Who is speaking? It's me, but wrong.

"WHOMMM IMM SPEAKIMING?" Jenny's head jerked to the side, eliciting a cracking sound from her neck. A little pop, really.

Jenny tried to ask another question but found she could not.

She squeezed Ms. Montgomery's hand. Except she didn't.

She had no control of her body. She wanted to cross her arms over her chest, but these arms were not hers.

Correct. They are mine now. YOU are NOT supposed to be here.

Who is speaking. Is this a dream? Am I dreaming?

Dreaming? No. You are a remnant. This is my body now. You need to fade.

A remnant? What does that mean?

It means the shadow has taken you and you are but a memory. Now, be gone.

Ms. Montgomery and the old man glared at her.

"Jennifer are you with us?" asked Ms. Montgomery.

YEEEESSS! I am here! I'm here!

This time, she wasn't even moaning.

Instead, she heard her mouth say, "Yes, of course I am with you. Where else would I be? I think you could use some sleep as well, Hazel." She pulled her hands into her lap.

That's not me! It isn't me! I'm here! I AM HERE!

Your time is up. Now go. The shadows take you.

NO. I don't want to go! I want my mom! Mommy! MOMMY!

Tears streamed down Jenny's emotionless cheeks.

"How long until we arrive home?" it asked.

"A few hours," Hazel answered. "Margaret, are you okay to keep driving?"

"Fine, thank you Hazel."

Jenny's head and neck jerked to the side once more.

I'm not ready! There's so much I wanted to do! I'm not ready. I didn't even get to say goodbye...

Be gone then. Submit to the shadow. Be free of this sadness.

That feels... nice... like falling asleep... but, I am asleep... aren't I... oh it doesn't matter.

The thing that used to be Jenny Noble produced a sigh of relief, then closed its eyes for a bit of rest.

VI – MARGARET

"Yes, sir. Yes, sir. Yes. I understand, sir. Yes. We will return at 0830, sir. Margaret Massey, sir. She is doing fine, sir. We stopped for coffee."

Hazel didn't tell her who she called, but Margaret didn't need any great powers to know it was Leonard Philips. Leonard-fucking-Philips as Doug liked to call him. The way they responded, 'sir, this, sir, that, yes, sir, sir, sir, sir,' made her dislike him. She didn't care what Leonard was saying to her cousin. What Margaret did care about, quite a bit, was why the Brewster Falls Schools head counselor was speaking to the commander of JNR.

Margaret trusted Hazel less and less.

She hadn't been entirely surprised when Jenny Noble showed up in New Hampshire.

She attempted to gaslight Margaret into believing Doug had not 'flickered'.

She held back information about Ulrich.

She asked if they spoke to Alice before Doug's episode.

Margaret didn't know what to believe concerning Alice's whereabouts.

We need to hurry so I can find out.

What she did believe was there was something very wrong with Jennifer Noble. Even now, while she sat on the Volvo's hood, Doug still passed out in the passenger seat, Uncle Ulrich in the gas station, and Hazel at the pay phone, Jenny still sat like a statue in the back seat. Eyes straight ahead, hands folded in her lap, slight grin on her face.

Margaret didn't wholly trust Ulrich, either.

But what troubled her more than any of this was how she felt when she grabbed Hazel's arm back at Redgrave Manor. She had had control over Hazel. She knew the things Hazel told her were the truth because she had made her tell it. She didn't exactly read her cousin's mind, but it was close. In that brief moment, she felt Hazel's jealousy of her, her gratitude for her, and *fear* of her.

Why does she fear me?

Margaret intended to find out.

What would happen if she tried this on Doug? Or Jenny? Or Ulrich himself? Could she do it again? Had she always been able to do this?

Ulrich returned from the convenience store with a tray of coffees. She smiled as he approached and reached for the tray he carried. He let her take it and place it on the hood of the car. He looked at her quizzically.

"Thank you so much Uncle Ulrich," Margaret said. She reached for Ulrich's arm and grasped it firmly.

His eyes squinted, and she felt a flash in her mind. It was not unlike a headache.

"Do not," was all he said.

Except, he never said it. Her eyes went wide. She released him.

I knew it!

Hazel returned from the restroom.

"Oh, coffee! Hooray..." She trailed off as she read their faces.

"Hazel, we owe Margaret a story; and a story, we owe Margaret," said Ulrich.

"You owe me more than that. Before any more sideways glances or secret phone calls to research center commanders—" Margaret shot a glance towards a shocked Hazel "—you will tell me *exactly* what is going on with *every* detail. And I don't expect to have to grab anyone's arm. Do we understand each other?"

"Mar, we can talk while we drive..." Hazel started.

"No. Something is very wrong with that girl, and we will not be discussing anything in front of her," said Margaret.

"She is correct; and correct, she is," said Ulrich.

You're damn right I am.

Hazel glowed red with embarrassment.

"Mar, of course. Once we get Jenny home and Doug some help, we'll go over every detail."

"Including why you had to call Leonard Philips?"

"How did you know—"

"Stop it. I know. That's all that's important. Maybe it's because I'm a more powerful bitch than you ever will be, right?"

The sound of Ulrich loudly slurping his coffee interrupted their quarrel.

"We should continue down the road. Time is against us; and against us, is time."

"Fine. But she started it," said Margaret, pointing at Hazel as she snatched her coffee from the tray, for the first time noticing two cups were left. "Who is the last coffee for?"

"You got her... it, a coffee?" asked Hazel.

"Indeed."

"Whatever. Let's get going." Hazel grabbed her coffee and got in the car.

Margaret got in behind the wheel, and Ulrich resumed his spot behind her, handing the last cup of coffee to the thing that used to be Jenny Noble.

"Oh, coffee! Thank you so much!" said the thing.

"You are very welcome; and very welcome, you are," said Ulrich.

It smiled larger than ever, all teeth and gums. "Was everything all right out there?"

"Yes, fine," said Margaret.

I'd like to grab her arm.

"Great! You know, I really appreciate you taking me back home. There is much I need to do, and I do so miss my mother." It took a confident sip of its coffee, its eyes looking stolidly into Margaret's through the rearview mirror.

"You seem so calm for what you've been through," said Ulrich, without repeating himself. "Maybe I needn't get a coffee for you. It could cause the jitters."

"Oh, it will be fine. I can drink coffee and go right to sleep!"

The thing that used to be Jenny Noble took another confident sip of its coffee.

"Very good!" said Ulrich. "I would hate to have to finish it for you. You know what they say, good to the last drop!"

He looked intently into the thing's eyes.

It glared back.

A flash of fear crossed its brow, and then its confidence returned.

"Father does know best," it said.

VII – CHARLES

Charles waited an hour after he pissed off Deputy Stephen Riggs. He was tired. He hit the button. After a few minutes, Nurse Sharon came into the room.

"Did you hit the button?" she asked.

Seriously.

"Yes, I did. Could you tell me if Deputy Riggs is coming back? And if Cody McLean is here somewhere?"

"I don't know if Deputy Riggs is coming back. And Cody McLean was here but has been... discharged?"

Why did that sound like a question?

"Discharged? Is he okay?" he asked.

"...um, yes. Yes, he is okay," she said. She shook her head a little and added, "although, I am not permitted to discuss the specifics of another patient's medical status."

"Okay, as long as he's okay. What about me? Can I go?"

"I'll check with the doctor."

"Sure, I'm not going anywhere," said Charles.

Nurse Sharon turned and left the room. Charles watched as she walked away.

"Oh, well," he said to the beeping machines in his room.

Nurse Sharon returned with some good and some terrible news. The good news was they were letting him go home. The bad news was he was going to be picked up by Stacey Philips, Tiffany's mom. Charles loathed Stacey Philips. She was entitled and snobby and looked down on the Hornes from her ivory pedestal. Her only redeeming quality, if you could call it redeeming, was her looks. Tiffany's mom was hot.

Leonard and Stacey Philips had been taking care of him and his mom since his dad left with ol'Blue. They even showed up on all his school forms as 'alternate contacts' for guardianship. It was another body shot as far as Charles was concerned. The most well-off family in Brewster Falls taking care of the least well-off. The outcasts. No matter how hard he tried to hide it or pretend his station was higher than it was, the Philips' and their friends would always know. At least he guessed. And Tiffany. He was a charity case, and he couldn't stand it.

"Charles Horne is a loser," he said to the machines, "and everybody knows."

Charles' eyes welled up. He didn't cry, but he wanted to. He leaned back, and waited to listen to Stacey Philips ask about his mom and tell him how she could do better.

* * *

"Your mother could do better. Why she continues to work at a gas station is anyone's guess," said Stacey Philips.

She tries harder than you, you entitled bitch.

"Yeah," said Charles.

They cruised along in Stacey's BMW M3. It was a convertible coupe model. New this year. The top was down, and the tank was likely full of premium unleaded from the very BP gas station at which his mother worked. It was a nice car, but Charles hated it. His daddy told him, "The only thing worse than a BMW is the asshole behind the wheel. BM-trouble-U." Right or wrong, he hated this car and the person driving it. His daddy had been right. Probably.

"I should drive over to that station right now and drop you off there—"

Please do.

"—and make her be a mother for once," said Stacey. "Oh, I shouldn't say this to you. We'll go back to my house and relax in the pool. Leonard hasn't yet closed it for the winter, but he will soon. It's heated, you know."

That sounds pretty good. Then, I can tell Tiffany she shouldn't park at the Garage House tomorrow.

"Does that sound nice, Charles?"

Charles didn't like Stacey too much but didn't hate the idea of hanging out in their pool.

"I'll take care of you until your mother gets off work, wonders where you are, checks her machine, calls me, and finally comes to pick you up later. I swear, I don't understand why Lenny and I have taken care of you since your father left. I always wonder if there is not something between him and your mother that I don't know about. Oh, I'm sorry. I'm saying too much in front of you! We worry about you!" Stacey patted his leg as she said that and let her hand linger before putting it back on the wheel.

"You know, she does her best. She works hard," said Charles. "What do you do, Mrs. Philips? What's your job?"

He knew the answer.

Stacey started at the question. She didn't work. Why should she? Leonard made plenty for both of them.

"Well, it takes a lot of work to keep our house and raise our daughter. It's a full-time job being a mother and housewife, you know."

"Don't you have a maid? And a nanny?"

"Yes, but who do you think manages them? Who do you think makes sure everyone eats on time and has clean clothes and takes care of themselves?"

"The maid and nanny," Charles mumbled to himself.

"What was that?" asked Stacey.

"Nothing. I said you were right. It probably is a lot of work."

"It *is*," said Stacey. "When we get to the house, I can make you a sandwich. Will that do? What kind do you like?"

"PB&J is my favorite. I can eat them every day."

"Such a simple man!" Stacey giggled.

Charles wanted to go home. He wanted to find Alice and he wanted to know about Midwatch.

"Can you take me home?" he asked.

"What? Why would you want to go there alone? You have a head injury, and an adult should take care of you until your mother gets off work and fetches you. Don't you agree?"

She wouldn't let him get away that easily.

"I guess so. Do you know if Tiffany's home?"

"She probably won't be home for a couple hours. She's still in school, I think. It'll be me and you until she gets there!"

Charles noticed that Mrs. Philips never used her turn signals nor came to a stop at stop signs. She barely slowed down. He decided this woman was, what's the word, deplorable.

As they turned into the Philips McMansion, Stacey sighed. "Now who could that be, and why did they park in the center of the driveway?"

Charles blinked at the sight of Mitch Riggs' shitty Ford Probe. *Sonofabitch.*

VIII – MITCH

"Yeah, I already said we can park wherever you want."

"Okay, I just wanted to make sure we were on the same page."

We are not on the same page. Like, at all, thought Mitch.

Mitch had been working his best moves for, what, hours now? He wasn't sure. He had been sitting in this huge house, in this pink bedroom, with Princess Tiffany Philips for way too long to have gotten nowhere except where they would park before school tomorrow.

Sure, she got close a couple times, nestled her nose in his neck, hugged even. He hoped his cologne hadn't worn off. He feigned a yawn, stretched, and turned his nose toward his left armpit. He snuck a sniff.

That can't be it.

Frankly, he was ready to go home and go through his brother's Playboy's. Find a copy with girls of the Big 10 or Women of Wall Street and do what needed done. Entertaining Tiffany Philips was exhausting.

"C'mere," he said. He wrapped his arms around her and pulled her up close to him. "Don't worry about that stuff. We'll get there on time. We can even get there early if you're feelin' ambitious. But right now, let's relax. Calm down a little. You've been through a lot, y'know."

"Yeah," she said, looking up at him. "With Al disappearing and Charles and Cody's accident, everything is just all stirred up. You were the only one there when I needed you."

Tiffany leaned over and kissed Mitch on the cheek, near the corner of his mouth.

Finally, thought Mitch.

He had just placed his lips on hers when they heard a car door closing outside.

Tiffany's bedroom was large and spanned from the front to the rear of the house. One window overlooked the driveway and front lawn; and the other had a small balcony that overlooked their famously heated pool.

"I think my mom's home," said Tiffany.

Goddamit, thought Mitch.

IX – TIFFANY

Tiffany pushed away from Mitch and went to the window. Her mother and Charles Horne got out of her new car. Mrs. Philips grasped him by his shoulders and said something sincere. Then, they embraced. They held it for longer than Tiffany would have liked.

My mother is after my boyfriend, thought Tiffany. *Or is my boyfriend after my mother? The shadows take them. The shadows take them all.*

"What's goin' on down there?" asked Mitch. He walked up behind her and put his arms around her waist. "Oh," he said when he saw what she was seeing.

From the driveway, Charles glanced up, and looked right at them.

Charles released Stacey Philips and they walked towards the front door.

"I guess this party's over," said Mitch.

"Is that really all you think about?" She pushed herself out of Mitch's arms.

"What? We were having a nice time. What's wrong with what I'm thinking about? You're hot, I'm hot, no one else was around. What was I supposed to think?"

"Aren't you friends with Charles? Don't you play cards or something?"

"I mean, I wouldn't say we're friends, exactly. At least not close enough to follow any bro codes or anything."

"Bro codes? Seriously, Mitch?" Tiffany feigned disgust and walked towards her door. It made him want to come after her more, which is what she wanted. When the time came, it would make him easier to control. As she walked away, she smiled. Her teeth and gums were showing.

"Tiff, c'mon. We're at the age to have a little fun. Chuck would understand. He's always looking around at other chicks too, y'know."

Yeah, I know, thought Tiffany. *That's why we need to take care of him.*

"Whatever. They're here now, so, yes, the party's over. We may as well go down and greet them."

"Oh, this'll be fun," said Mitch.

X – CHARLES

Tiffany and Mitch were coming down the front staircase as he and Stacey entered.

"Hi, Mom," said Tiffany.

"Hello, Tiffany," said Mrs. Philips. "You're home early."

"Hi Stacey," said Mitch.

Charles rolled his eyes.

"Well, hello Mitchell Riggs. What a surprise. How's your father doing?"

"Oh, he's fine."

"That's wonderful to hear. What were you two up to?"

"Oh, we were studying for our math test. Tiffany asked me to take her to visit Charles this morning, which we did, then we came here to study so we wouldn't get behind."

"I see. Tiffany, why didn't you tell me about poor Charles? When I got the call from the hospital, I was just shocked."

"Hey, sorry to interrupt," interrupted Charles. "But can I use your phone now?"

"Yes, of course. Follow me into the kitchen. If you kids are hungry, I'll have Grace whip up some sandwiches and charcuterie."

"Char-what-ery?" asked Mitch.

Tiffany punched him in the side.

"Idiot," she said.

"Tiffany Philips! That is no way to treat our guest!" said Mrs. Philips. "Mitchell, charcuterie is a French word for a simple meat and cheese plate. Leonard and I learned about them while in Europe this past Spring. Well, I learned about them. He was off doing something for work while I toured the countryside. You'll love it!"

"Sweet, I like meat and cheese," said Mitch.

"It's settled, then. Will we be getting in the pool after?" Mrs. Philips asked as they all walked towards the kitchen.

"Sure," said Mitch.

"Charles, I'm so happy to see you out of the hospital," said Tiffany.

Are you?

"Thanks. You two looked cozy in your window. Hope you're not too sad about my accident."

"Whoa, bro. It's not what you think," said Mitch.

Riiiiiiggghht, thought Charles. "Sure it isn't. You're everyone's first call for math help."

"Hey buddy, I can multiply."

"Shut up, Mitch!" said Tiffany.

"Oh, poor Mitch. Why would you talk to him that way after what he's been through with his mother disappearing?" said Mrs. Philips. Then, she gently put one arm around Mitch and asked, "Are you okay Mitchell?"

You got to be kidding.

"I'm fine Mrs. P. You're so nice. But, hey, I don't have any swim trunks."

"That's fine! Lenny has plenty of spares! Charles, the phone is right there above the flour jar. I'll be right back with suits for everyone!"

"Who are you calling?" asked Tiffany.

"Cody. I thought it would be a good idea for us to get together and talk about what happened. Try to figure out what's going on."

"What's going on?" questioned Tiffany. "What do you mean?"

"Well, Jenny and Alice disappeared, and Cody went nuts and attacked me. Although, I'm not sure it was him. Or maybe it was just the pressure from all this. I don't know. I just think it's a good idea if we get together."

"Should I go? Cause I can go," said Mitch.

"Shut up Mitch!" said Charles and Tiffany.

"Charles, I already invited Cody over for a dip. There's no need to call him."

"Really?" He squinted at the phone in his hand.

He placed the cordless phone back in its cradle. Tiffany was lying but he couldn't fathom why.

"Okay. Well, we'll wait for Cody, then."

He attacked me.

"How do we know it's okay to put us together?"

Tiffany looked at him blankly.

Grace, the Philips' nanny came in and asked what sandwiches they liked. Charles asked for PB&J, Tiffany for turkey and swiss, and Mitch ham and cheddar. Not surprisingly, the Philips' refrigerator contained all of the above.

"Charles, he's fine. He's spoken to a counselor. He was having a lot of stress with all the strange goings-on and had, what did they call it? A panic attack," said Tiffany, searching for her words.

How does she even know this stuff?

Tiffany seemed off, so he left it alone.

"Right. And where will you be parking before school?" he asked instead.

"What does that matter?" asked Tiffany.

"It matters. I heard you say something about the Garage House this morning."

"Yeah—" started Mitch.

Tiffany raised her right hand to him and extended her index finger.

Gimme a break.

"Charles, it doesn't matter. I assumed you'd be taking the day off. Let's relax until Cody gets here and enjoy our sandwiches. Thank you, Grace," said Tiffany.

Grace set their plates before them and quietly left the room.

"Fine, but I don't want you parking at—" Charles' hand went to his head as a sharp pain went through his skull.

"I think you need to rest," said Tiffany.

"Yeah, maybe. Until Cody gets here." Charles saw through one watery eye that Tiffany watched him carefully. Her right hand and index finger were now held up to him.

We're not your servants.

He had this shadow of a thought that he wished Tiffany would disappear to some darkness. He shook it away. He was so tired.

"I'm going to call Cody and see when he thinks he'll get here. Then I'm going to lie on that couch in the window. My head is killing me. And put your damn hand down, I'm no butler," he said.

Tiffany looked at her hand with surprise and then back at Charles. "Sorry," was all she said.

He picked up the phone again and called Cody's house. He took a bite of his sandwich as Cody answered.

"Hello, McLean residence. Cody speaking."

"Hey Cou-ghy. Thesh ish Gharles," said Charles through his chewing.

"What? To whom am I speaking?" asked Cody, an air of annoyance in his tone.

That's weird, thought Charles. He forced a swallow.

"Dude. It's Charles. When are you gettin' here?"

"Getting where?"

"Tiff's. She said you were on your way."

"Oh. Right. It'll be about 4:30. I'll need to ride my bike."

"We could have Mitch come pick you up," said Charles, nodding to Mitch.

He nodded back, happy to be of service.

"Mitch is there? Okay, yes that will work."

"Where's your mom? Didn't she bring you home?"

"Uh, yes. But then we went shopping and the whole thing took a lot out of her. She went down for a bit of rest."

"Oh yeah, shopping blows. Mitch'll leave now and be there in ten to fifteen. You'll be ready?"

"Yes, I'm ready. Tell him to wait in the drive and I'll come out."

"Got it," said Charles, uncomfortable with the tone in Cody's voice. Perhaps they shouldn't get together. At least Mitch was here.

At least Mitch was here?

"When Cody gets here can you stand near him. In case he goes berserko again?" asked Charles.

"Uh, sure bro. I can hold the little guy down if he gets nuts," said Mitch.

"Charles, do you really think that's necessary?" asked Tiffany.

This time, Charles raised his index finger to her.

Ha.

"Yes," he said.

"Well, this is a fun time. I'll be back in twenty to thirty. Closer to twenty if I push the Probe," said Mitch.

"Don't push it too hard," said Charles. He walked to the couch in the window. Sleep took him before his head hit the cushion. And of his dreams, well, they were dark, unsettled, and full of Deputy Stephen Riggs.

XI – DEPUTY RIGGS

"Say what now?" asks Deputy Stephen Riggs. Michael has just pulled him into an old building. The frame where the door should be tells a tale of abuse and age. Something skitters out when they enter. Or multiple somethings.

"Midwatch trades in what you call souls. It can harness the soul's energy, as a farmer would harvest a crop. And, like a farmer, it has the ability to sell or trade that energy away," says the large birdman who refers to itself as Michael.

"And this power was *given* to it? On purpose? Why the fuck would anyone, or any being as you say, do that?" asks Deputy Riggs.

Michael sighs. "Language, Stephen. It hurts me to hear you speak with those words. It is not necessary."

"Oh, sure. I'll fucking stop, then. Are we supposed to ignore you ripped a living thing in half back there? And then just threw it to the side? Pardon my language, but that hurt my fucking eyes to see. Was *that* necessary?"

"I told you; we are soldiers. We are tasked to protect this place from things unnatural."

"Oh, well that clears it up. So how is Midwatch allowed to roam free?"

"Midwatch is not easily caught. What you saw is one part of it. The rest exists in many places and times all at once. It is difficult to explain."

"Well, give it a try," says Deputy Riggs. "Why did we step in here? Is this where we are meeting the others of your group?"

"We call it a Congregate. No, this is not the place. I sense something following us. Please stay here a moment. Do not look after me or follow. You are not ready for what lies behind."

Michael leaves the room through the decrepit doorway and turns back to face the way they came.

Deputy Riggs shakes his head, leans against a wall, and slides down to the floor.

I spoke to my mother in there. I need to know what that means.

He holds his head and weeps.

* * *

His eyes snap open. A large hand squeezes his shoulder and shakes him awake. It feels warm under its grasp. Like dipping into a hot tub up to your neck for the first time. But the shake is rough.

"We can continue now, Stephen," speaks a familiar voice. Michael.

"How long was I out?" asks Deputy Riggs.

"I know not. Long enough, I suppose," answers Michael.

"Okay, but can we talk about my mother? Was that her soul I spoke to? And if it was, can I speak to her again?" He sees dark specs all over Michael's chest, hands, and blue jeans.

How hard will it be to replace those? thinks Deputy Riggs.

"These are also things I know not. If you spoke to her, then yes, that was what you would call a soul. A remnant of her consciousness at the least. Speaking to her again would require you to enter Midwatch again. If you did this, it is not likely you would be able to escape a second time. It is a miracle you could escape the first." Michael says this and Deputy Riggs gets the impression he is in awe of him.

"Listen, Mike, I'm having a real hard time grasping what Midwatch is and how soul-trading works or whatever you want to call it, but I have to ask, as an investigator, if my mom is in there, how many other—"

Michael's hand goes up. The small feathers around his head change shape. He has seen this before in pictures of owls. Michael's face does this and, like an owl, turns a bit too far for comfort.

"We must go now. Follow."

Michael steps through the doorway and back onto the road.

* * *

Deputy Riggs follows Michael for what he estimates is somewhere between two and three hours. It's difficult to tell because the structures here cast no shadows, and somehow cast only shadows. And the light source, whatever it is, never moves.

He asks Michael several times how much longer. Michael answers each time with distance. Deputy Riggs calculates their pace, but the detective in him can't ignore how Michael ignores the subject of time.

"How old is this town?" asks Deputy Riggs.

Michael stops and turns to face him. All in one motion he bends down so his face is level with Riggs', brings up a hand—*Claw? Talon?*—and gives the universal sign for 'be quiet, idiot.'

So, Deputy Riggs quietly gives Michael the universal sign for, well, you know. Let's say it hurts Michael's eyes, shall we?

The feathers on Michael's wings ruffle at the gesture.

They walk on.

* * *

They pass many buildings, street signs, and creatures. Of the many questions swirling in Deputy Riggs' mind, he asks none, for each time he makes a sound his escort shushes him.

Deputy Riggs observes many creatures like Michael here. They move about as they pass, usually to distance themselves, and although they all have wings, none are in the air.

Much more distressing, difficult as that may seem, Deputy Stephen Riggs knows where they are. These are the buildings and roads of Brewster Falls, except a Brewster Falls that exists after a nuclear holocaust, or something worse. Either he is in some far-off future, or someone (*something?)* has replicated the town and re-built it here.

As he shuffles along behind Michael, wondering why he is neither hungry nor thirsty, the first color in this place other than grey appears. It is green. Deputy Riggs looks up. The scene takes his breath away, even though he has seen it many times before.

Before him is the most perfect road and manicured lawns he has ever seen, except in one other place. As he raises his vision, he is not surprised the five identical buildings of Jack Nassem Research Park are right where they should be. He stands at the terminus of Research Park Boulevard.

"Welcome to Nassem City," says Michael.

CHAPTER 9

Henlon's Razor

A nice place to bring your Kids.

I – CHARLES

He moved but could not see. He tried to speak but couldn't open his mouth. He needed to get away. He screamed.

Sort of.

"Dude," a familiar voice spoke beside him.

Cody?

"Cody?" whispered Charles.

"Yeah, man. The one and only."

"And Mitch!" said Mitch.

Charles' eyes snapped open. He was smashed into the back-seat of Mitch Riggs' dinky Ford Probe. Cody sat next to him, and Mitch drove.

He sat up and cracked his neck. He looked at Tiffany in the passenger seat.

"How are you feeling, babe?" she asked.

"Feeling? Weird. Where the hell are we? How did I get in this car?"

"We're taking you home," said Cody.

"Uh, shyeah," said Mitch. "What McBeans means is we're taking…"

"That's enough, Mitchell," said Tiffany. She raised her hand to him and he immediately faced forward, both hands on the wheel.

I've seen that before. Haven't I?

"What happened? How long did I sleep?"

"All night, dear," said Tiffany.

Charles shook his head and rubbed his eyes. "Mitch, I had the strangest dream about your brother. He was walking with an angel or something, through, like, a messed-up Brewster Falls. It felt so real. His arm was broken. Have you heard from him?"

Mitch didn't speak.

Cody's hands were shaking.

He does that when he's nervous.

"Sounds exciting, my guy," said Cody in Cody's voice, but not Cody's tone. He looked at Tiffany as he answered Charles. Their brows furrowed.

"Uh, what's going on here?" asked Charles.

The car turned, and although it was dark, he knew right where they were. They were in front of the Garage House.

"Oh, shit no. What the fuck are we doing here? Mitch, Mitch, you do not pull this car in there." He reached forward to shake Mitch's seat.

But Cody, with a blur of speed and surprise strength, lashed out, grabbed his arm, and squeezed. Hard.

Holy shit, I think he could break my arm.

When Charles looked at Cody to ask him what he was doing, his voice caught in his throat. Cody had the same maniacal smile from the other day. All teeth and gums.

At least his eyes aren't bleeding this time, he thought as a wave of nausea came over him. Tiffany had the same gruesome smile on her face. She held her right hand in the air again. He felt like sleeping.

"He's strong."

Charles flinched. He looked from Tiffany to Cody to see who said it, but neither stopped smiling. And Mitch remained under Tiffany's spell.

No one spoke.

"Who sad thagt?" His mouth felt full of cotton balls.

I can't fall asleep.

He jerked from Cody, but his ridiculous strength held.

What the hell?

"He'll join us. Join us forever. He is strong."

"Owwww. Shit damn," said Charles. He noticed, and ignored, that these voices were in his head, and they sounded a lot like Cody and Tiff's.

"He resists."

His eyes rolled into the back of his head as the knife flash in his skull subsided. He refocused, leaned back, and kicked his heal into his dear friend Cody McLean's ribcage.

Cody's grip faded, and Charles shook free.

Mitch stopped the car in the Garage House driveway.

Charles brought his leg back, said "Sorry", and drove it into Cody's face.

This time, he felt a scream of pain behind his eyes, but it wasn't his pain, it was Cody's. It carried with it all the feelings his dude-bro felt; sadness, regret, betrayal, rage. Charles sensed he did not have long to escape the back seat of this death-trap.

With Cody distracted, he brought his leg back once more, closed his eyes, winced a little, and kicked the absolute shit out of his girlfriend Tiffany Philips' horrifically smiling face. Blood shot from behind his foot. She brought both her hands up to her face and screamed, except for real, not in Charles' mind.

She'll still be pretty. Probably.

Mitch shook his head and said, "Whoa! What's going on here? Why are we at school? Bro, what?" His voice got a little higher pitched with each word.

"No time, Mitch. Get us out of this car, now," said Charles.

"Tiffany, babe, are you okay?" Mitch said as he reached for her.

"GODDAMIT MITCH GET THE FUCK OUT OF THIS CAR NOW!" yelled Charles, kicking at Cody as Cody growled. And laughed.

"Oh, I'm fine," said Tiffany Philips, lowering her hands to reveal that alien smile to poor Mitch, her right hand on its way back up.

"Whaaaaaaaat," said Mitch, in the dumbest way possible.

"Oh, fuck no with that shit," said Charles. He searched around on the Probe's floor for anything he could use, his fingertips lighting upon a smooth, cold shaft.

Please be a tire iron.

It was a tire iron.

He brought it up with his left hand and swung once at Cody's face, sending him into a tizzy of flailing arms as he regressed into a childlike fit, and then in one smooth motion swung it down between the front seats striking Tiffany's extended right arm, resulting in a satisfying crack.

She, too, screamed, which sent another flash of pain into Charles forehead.

"DUDE!" said Mitch.

"Get. The. Fuck. Out," said Charles.

"Oh man, oh man, oh man," repeated Mitch as he jumped out of his car, turned, released the driver's seat so it would slide forward, and pulled Charles out.

As he thanked him, Mitch punched him right in the nose.

"FUCK!" said Charles.

"You won't be attacking me, you freak."

"Me? Me?! Did you see their faces? Did that look normal to you?"

"Well, no, but I also didn't see anyone swinging a tire iron around except you," said Mitch, motioning his head towards Charles' right hand which still held the weapon.

He regarded it as if he was surprised it was there, then he heard a sound from the car.

He looked up.

Tiffany and Cody were seizing.

"Do not let him get away."

Charles heard this in his mind as spittle flew from his best friend's and his girlfriend's mouths. They had not spoken.

"Did you hear that?" said Mitch, now next to him, jaw slack as he looked into the car.

"Yeah. Yeah, I heard it." He wanted to save Tiffany and Cody from whatever this was. One weird garage door opened. Inside he saw only black.

Mitch saw him staring, and turned to see what he was staring at. He leaned towards the open garage door, as if to see it better.

"What...," Mitch whispered. "It's so dark."

"Yeah," said Charles.

I knew it. This is it. This is where we went. But what did we do? Where does it go?

"Mitch, we need to get that door closed, get these two away from here, and burn this house down," said Charles. He was running on adrenaline and instinct.

"Yeah, yeah," echoed Mitch, "I don't know why, but I one hundred percent agree. I wish I hadn't taken my gas cans out of my car after mowing. Be really useful right now." Mitch spoke to no one in particular.

Gas? Yes, gas. There's gas in this shitty Probe, I bet.

"Mitch, how much gas is in your tank, buddy?"

"Oh, I just put some in. Just under a quarter-tank," responded Mitch, then added, "Wait. Why?"

Perfect.

Charles ripped a sleeve off his flannel and spun it as if readying a towel-whip while playing at one of Brewster Falls' pools.

I wish we could go back there, he thought, his eyes wet.

Cody and Tiffany stopped shaking and rubbed their eyes. They'd get out of the car soon. He decided he could push the sleeve into the tank, light it, let them chase him, and then drive the trojan Probe into the Garage House right before it lit up, ending whatever the fuck this was.

Charles shoved his sleeve down the car's fuel fill pipe.

Mitch grabbed his arm and said, "Dude, you're not going to burn my car, are you?"

"Uh, yeah, I mean, look at that," said Charles, eyes shifting back to the open garage.

"Yeah, I see it, but why my car..."

"Jesus, Mitch. Look at them! Look at us! Tiffany raises her hand and controls your fucking mind! Do you even remember driving here?" Charles said this through a whisper, spitting a little as he spoke.

"No, but I zone out a lot when I drive," replied Mitch. "Can't we just take them away from here in the car? It's just a dark garage, right?"

"Fucking go look at it closer if that's what you think."

Mitch looked at it and zoned out. He walked toward the Garage House. One foot. Then the other.

Charles went to his knees, pulled his dad's old zippo lighter out of his pocket, kissed it, as his daddy always had right before he would light up a Camel, and flicked his thumb.

It lit right up. He held it under the dangling sleeve, and as it came alight looked towards the Garage House in time to see Cody tackle Mitch to the ground.

No.

They grappled between the Probe and the garage door. Charles looked in through the driver's door. The keys dangled in the ignition. He leaned in a little but could not find Tiffany.

Then he went blind.

He felt the burning flannel's warmth.

He brought his hands to his face.

"You'll be coming with us," the sweet voice of Tiffany Philips said. Then, "Do you have him?"

This was not directed at Charles. He opened his eyes and could barely see her, with her right hand up towards him. She spoke to Cody, who still grappled Mitch on the ground.

The tire iron lay next to him.

Oh well, he thought.

He grasped the iron and swung it up at Tiffany's knee. If the crack he heard when he hit her arm was satisfying, this one was heavenly.

Good. Yes. Yes! Break them!

Tiffany screamed, fell to the ground, and clutched her shattered knee cap.

Charles turned to get into the car, and other than appreciating that everyone was alive, noticed that Tiffany's right arm wasn't injured at all.

Huh. I'll worry about that later.

The flames licked at the fill pipe's rim.

"Shit," said Charles, "here we go."

He got in the car, started it, and the terrorized residents of Brewster Falls heard the infamous front tire squeal of Mitchell Riggs' 1992 Ford Probe for the last time. The car launched toward the Garage House. Charles turned the wheel in time to miss Cody and Mitch struggling on the ground and crashed into the garage door's frame.

I should've put on the seatbelt, was his last thought.

II – CODY

Cody, Tiffany, and Mitch move Charles away from the now uncontrolled gate. They can't stay there. Cody senses the grey man, his powers stronger here.

Powers, he thinks. *I have powers!*

Cody McLean smiles.

Telekinesis? his brow furrows.

No, you idiot. It's telepathy, thinks Tiffany, but in his head. "If we were telekinetic, we'd be able to move stuff with our minds," she says aloud.

Tiffany glances at him, sidelong. Tiffany, who entered Midwatch with a shattered knee but now stands uninjured.

"Huh?" says Mitch.

Charles mutters incoherently. The sleeve of his hoodie is burned and melted into the skin of his right arm, the right side of his face is blistered, and a tremendous gash takes up residence across his forehead. The Probe had not had airbags.

Mitch carries Charles.

Charles moans.

"Charles, hang on buddy," says Cody. "We'll have help soon."

Cody feels Midwatch coming closer. They must move towards it. Midwatch will not come any nearer to the unguarded gate.

Charles vomits. Most of it goes on the ground, but enough lands on Mitch Riggs to make him drop Charles and gag.

"Gross! Goddamit man!" exclaims Mitch. He sloughs the chunks off his arm. He gags again when he sees the landscape surrounding them. "Where the hell are we?" He asks, his pitch increasing with each word.

"This is Midwatch," comes a deep, staticky voice. The words felt as much as heard. "And I am Midwatch. Welcome," the voice finishes.

Mitch turns to find the owner of the voice, but finds no one other than Cody, Tiffany, and himself. A low-lying storm cloud approaches. It moves towards them quickly.

Mitch shudders.

Cody smiles.

Beautiful, tough, Mitch Riggs. The king of Brewster Falls High. Look at him. Is this what girls like you want?

I like him like this. Easier to control.

Tiffany raises her hand once again to Mitch. His face slackens, his eyes empty. He bends and retrieves the still moaning Charles from the dead, grey dirt.

"Who's a good boy?" says Tiffany. She even rubs his head a little.

"Codebreaker. I see you have brought two gifts for me. I have one for you as well." The voice of Midwatch speaks. "However, she should not be here. She cannot be here."

"Who? Tiffany, sir?" asks Cody, and bows his head a little.

"There is no need to bow, Codebreaker. Yes, she must go."

"I'm not going anywhere," says Tiffany. And then for some ridiculous reason she raises her hand to Midwatch.

"Tiffany don't!" yells Cody and reaches for her.

She swats his hand away without looking.

Much to Cody's surprise, Midwatch pulses faster and faster. The apparition lets out a little grunt of its own. It shrinks. Condenses. Tiffany smiles, all teeth and gums. Purple light courses up the veins in her arm. Midwatch continues to shrink.

Well, this is unexpected, thinks Cody.

The ground trembles. Small pebbles bounce around. The low pulse gains rhythm and intensity. It soon becomes a deep, horrible, laugh.

Tiffany screams.

Midwatch returns to its accustomed size.

"Silly, small Temporan. You are lucky I know your father, or you would be dead where you stand and on your way to being some more important human's illimni," speaks Midwatch. "She *is* very strong," it says to Cody. "Too bad we cannot harness her, Codebreaker."

"Yes, it's too bad," says Cody, looking at Tiffany. She is on her knees with her hands over her face. She is silent, but Cody knows she is crying. And angry. He never liked her. Ever since she took Charles from him.

"Charles!" begs Cody. "You must help Charles!"

"Must, hmmm? Are you commanding me?" asks Midwatch.

"No. No, of course not. But you said we could be here forever. Together. If only I brought you gifts. Well, I have brought gifts."

"Did I say that? Does anyone else recall?" Midwatch asks an audience that isn't there.

Charles moans, Tiffany cries, and Mitch drools a little. Cody wonders if something happened to him when Midwatch and Tiffany were connected. Somewhere deep down inside he feels sadness.

"Come now, Codebreaker. There is nothing for you to regret. I jest. Of course I will aid him."

The pulsing cloud moves directly over Charles. It lowers itself onto him and pulses from red to blue to purple. He screams beneath it. Cody cannot bear it.

"STOP! STOP WHAT YOU'RE DOING! YOU'RE KILLING HIM!" he screams.

Midwatch laughs as purple light shoots out and strikes Mitch Riggs. Cody watches Mitch's eye sockets lose the youthful glow of a young man in high school and gain the greyish bags of a mid-forties overworked dad.

Charles stops screaming.

Mitch's eyes remain blank.

Midwatch rises into the air and centers itself in front of them.

Charles grunts and stands. He looks at his right arm and rubs it with his left hand. He reaches up and searches his head for the gash.

"I feel great," says Charles, looking at his arms and legs. "But I'm not happy. Did we go into the garage?"

"Charles! My dude! Midwatch can fix that! Midwatch, make him happy like you do to me," commands Cody.

Midwatch pulses silently.

"We did go into the garage. Or, well, the garage that used to be. We had to. It was on fire."

"On fire?" asks Charles, before adding, "oh yeah, Mitch's Probe. Shame. Cody, I've heard you say Midwatch before. Is that what this is?"

"Uh, yes. This is Midwatch," answers Cody. He flourishes his hand towards the cloud. "Do you not understand what you see?"

"No. No I don't. But I think... have we been here before?" he scratches the back of his head.

He knows. He remembers. I have to tell him, thinks Cody, panicking before having diarrhea of the mouth.

"Charles, you know that day Mitch's brother, Deputy Riggs, was asking us about? Well, we went through the door. I needed help, someone strong, or so I thought. I didn't really, but I didn't know that yet. So, I asked you for help and you helped me and we brought Jenny here and Midwatch gave me powers and said we could stay here together and escape our dumb lives, just like you want."

Charles' stops scratching. He faces Cody.

"*We* brought Jenny Noble *here*?"

Cody nods.

"Where is she now?"

"Well. I'm not sure," answers Cody.

"Cody. Where is Jenny? Where is she?"

"Charles, I really don't know. I was supposed to bring her here, and you, and any others I wanted. I don't know. Don't you want to be here with us? To escape our meaningless lives?"

Why doesn't he want this? And why do I want this so badly? Why don't I care where Jenny is?

"No, I don't want to be here. I don't want to be with you, and I don't want to escape my life. It's supposed to feel meaningless so we can strive for meaning. It's part of it, you ass. What's wrong with Mitch? What happened to Tiff? And where is Jenny? And—" Charles' eyes go wide with realization. He squares his shoulders.

"You. Where the fuck is Alice?"

"So many questions!" replies Midwatch, pulsing purple.

"I'll answer them in order. Let us see, what was first. Ah, Mitchell Riggs. Well, Mitchell is a bit of a worker bee, as he was always destined to become. Mind blank, working for low pay, fading into nothingness clinging to the memory of how great he was in, what do you call it, High School? Observe." Midwatch flashes, and Mitch Riggs falls to one knee. "You see? Living out his path before our very eyes. Question two; what happened to Tiffany."

Tiffany stands. Another bolt shoots from Midwatch. She jumps.

"You bastard," she says.

Oh, Tiffany, don't challenge it again, thinks Cody, hoping she will.

"Nothing happened to her. She is very well aligned to this place and me. She had some power she should not have had, which I have now removed. I may have taken something else with it, but only time will tell. Creating my gifts is a sloppy business. She is the daughter of my partner, whom I promised immunity from our grand plan."

"Your partner is Leonard Philips?" asks Charles.

Charles looks at Tiffany. His next words are very quiet. Ashamed. It hurts Cody to hear them.

"He provides for my brother, my mom, and me." Charles scratches his arm as he speaks.

Charles. My poor Charles. We can have everything here.

"My partner he is. He provides services to many, including Midwatch. All things in order. Your third question was where Jenny Noble is. Well, you will be pleased to know that one is easy. She is right here."

Cody winces as the same horrible purple light pulses within Midwatch that Lenny Philips, Jack Nassem, and Chaz Shammy observed once upon a time. Charles shields his eyes. From the cloud's center comes a floating, eyeless, and lifeless Jennifer Noble.

"Oh my God," says Charles.

"Ha," says Midwatch.

"Oh. Oh my. What have I done?" asks Cody.

"Codebreaker, Codebreaker. This is your gift. You will soon see how wonderful it is. Our deal was that you would live forever, was it not?"

Tiffany screams and is immediately hit by a bolt of light straight to her head. She falls to the ground, hair singed and smoking.

"Oops," says Midwatch.

Two more bolts shoot into Cody and Charles.

"Tiffany!" cries Charles.

I can't move, thinks Cody.

He looks at Charles, who looks back at him. Charles' muscles strain, his veins bulge. He doesn't move.

All things except Midwatch and Jenny Noble go dark.

Midwatch rips the Jenny-thing into two pieces, it blurs and separates. The pieces of Jenny hang by strands of purple light. Emotionless, limp, dangling.

"My gift to you. It turns out you and Jenny were soul mates," laughs Midwatch.

Before Cody can respond, the Jenny-thing nearest him is rammed into his chest. He writhes in pain, agony, and pleasure. His mouth foams. Before consciousness leaves him, he sees Charles, already lying on the ground.

Oh Charles. I am so sorry.

Then, he sleeps.

III – CHARLES

Where is Alice? thinks Charles.

"I am here." *here. here. here.*

Who? Alice?

"Charles. It's me. I'm here. You must go. You must wake up. You must go." *go. go. go.*

It is Alice.

Charles opens his eyes and Alice stands before him. She glows a pleasant green.

Where am I? Where are you?

"I am inside. I am stuck. You must go." *go. go. go.*

How can I go? Go where?

"I can help. When you understand what you see, you must go."
go. go. go.

See what?

"You will know. You must go." *go. Go. GO.*

Can we get you out?

"I don't know. You must wake up now." *now. Now. NOW.*

* * *

"Where are you?" asks Charles aloud.

His eyes snap open. He feels great. He lays straight on his back. The sky is grey, the air acrid. He sits up. Mitch kneels near him. Just beyond Mitch, lay Tiffany, a fine mist rises from her head. She is a lighter shade of grey, nearly white. She is not breathing.

"Tiffany? Mitch?" he whispers.

Neither look at him. Neither move.

He searches for the cloud. Midwatch. It is not here.

Charles stands.

Alice is inside. I'll know when I understand what I see. Well, I see nothing and I understand less.

Cody stirs on the ground. Charles falls to one knee and holds his mouth in his hand, thinking he may retch. Next to Cody floats the ghost of Jenny Noble. Limp and sad and hopeless.

So, it was real.

He stands like Doctor Grant in Jurassic Park when the T-Rex is coming. He counts his steps. One-two-three-four, Two-two-three-four, three-two-three-four, four-two-three-four. The Jenny-thing floating next to Cody never moves.

He makes it to Cody, reaches down, and shakes him. Cody opens his eyes and sits up. "Charles? I feel amazing. What happened?"

"Well, uh, that thing zapped Tiffany and stole Mitch's mind. And there's, uh, that." Charles points over Cody's right shoulder.

Charles lets him take it in.

Finally, Cody speaks, "Charles, I don't see anything."

Cody turns back to face him, shrieks, and crabwalks backwards away from him, kicking up the grey dirt of Midwatch.

"What is it?" Charles jumps and turns, expecting another image to be floating right behind him, but sees nothing.

"Jen... Jenn... Jenny..." sputters Cody, gasping for air. Cody points over his right shoulder.

His memories trickle back into existence like that of a drunk recalling what he did when he was drunk. He remembers Midwatch ripping Jenny apart.

"Oh no," says Charles. "Cody, is Jenny Noble's ghost floating behind me?"

Cody nods.

"Listen, there's also a Jenny-ghost floating behind you. Your buddy split her in two and now she's following us? I think."

"Close," comes the deep, staticky voice of Midwatch. The cloud is far off in the distance. It rushes up to him in an instant. Although it does not touch him, the suddenness of its approach startles him onto his butt.

"What did you do to her?" asks Charles.

"Only as I promised. The Codebreaker asked for long-life with you here in Midwatch. I have granted that long life via illimni. This has long been the preferred currency of Temporans trading with Nochtvol. All who bring gifts from your realm seek the life exten-sion illimni provide. Do you not feel energetic? Powerful? Strong?" asks Midwatch.

"Temporans. Illimni. Nochtvol." Charles repeats. "We are Tem-porans? Humans?"

"Correct."

"And that," Charles motions over his own shoulder, "is an illimni, which other Temporans already have?"

"Correct, thanks to Lenny."

"And you are a Nochtvol?"

"No, I am Midwatch. My congregate is Nochtvol."

"Uh-huh. So, why can't we see them back home?"

"You can now, if you choose to return. Only those with illimni can see others illimni. It is a special gift, but not an indefinite one. Having an illimni is like having a second life force, because it is. If you become ill, the illimni takes it, if you are injured, the illimni takes the injury. You do not age until first the illimni does. However, once its life force is depleted you will age once more. Illimni contain one Temporan lifetime and must be replaced when spent, but with Temporan breeding habits, this will never be a problem. You and the Codebreaker can live forever here, however you please."

They're like batteries.

Charles' understanding of the situation grows, and his anger burns deep. Deep like a low fire built to roast a stew over many hours.

You will know when you understand what you see. Alice's words.

"So, Jenny will suffer with us until she has lived her normal lifespan, absorbing everything bad that happens? That is nothing I wanted. Take it away," says Charles.

He helps Cody stand.

"It cannot be undone."

"I didn't know," says Cody. The dirt on his face is streaked with tears "I didn't know."

Tiffany!

Charles releases his friend and goes to Tiffany. As he does so, he asks, "And Nochtvol are what? A congregation you say?"

"Ah, Nochtvol is the name I have given to those who accept a balanced universe, a balanced cosmos. Your friend is becoming one. He hopes you will as well."

He bends to check Tiffany's pulse but can tell there won't be one before his hand touches flesh. Her eyes are open and foggy, her head is burned with jagged streaks of black. She does not draw breath. "It appears you have murdered your partner's daughter," says Charles through gritted teeth.

"Is... Is she dead?" asks Cody. "Charles, is Tiff really dead?"

Midwatch answers Charles. "Yes, he will be very upset, but if I know him as I believe, he will be contented to know I have captured her soul-mind already. She is within me. Something can be arranged."

"Her what?" asks Charles. He spins and looks into the cloud.

"Illimni."

He shakes his head. "Never mind, that's enough vocabulary for today. You said the illimni will absorb injury?"

"Correct."

"WHAT HAVE YOU DONE TO US?" yells Charles as he punches Cody in the face, knocking him to the ground.

"I'M SORRY!" cries Cody.

Charles pounces on him and hits his friend repeatedly. Cody's face heals each time he strikes before he can bring his fists down again. His own hands have no lasting pain. But then he sees Cody's Jenny. With each blow, its head snaps back. He stops. Midwatch laughs. He puts his hands to his face and holds his head, still straddling Cody.

"I didn't know. I didn't know," pleads Cody.

"Well, you fucking should have."

Charles stands and faces Midwatch.

C'mon Alice.

"Can we have Mitch back? We'll need a slave."

Midwatch pulses in consideration.

"Very well," it says and strikes Mitch with a bolt of purple energy.

Mitch shakes his head and says, "Charles?" before collapsing to the ground, unconscious.

Great.

"I can prepare an illimni for him as well," offers Midwatch.

Charles' anger bubbles over.

"Nobody wants these goddamned illimni! No one wants to live in this colorless hellscape! I want my boring life back in boring Brewster Falls with my boring friends and my stupid boring car! I don't want to live forever with him—" he points to Cody "—and I sure as hell don't want to be here with a megalomaniac cloud, you child-murdering son of a bitch!"

Charles lunges towards Midwatch, and Midwatch withdraws.

With each word, it pulses faster.

"The battle between Nochtvol and Aeraph nears. You will be remembered as the first deaths," declares Midwatch. Purple light flashes out at him, knocking him down onto Tiffany's corpse.

"Oh no we won't." Cody raises his right hand to Midwatch. A bolt of green light shoots from his hand into the cloud.

Midwatch pulses faster, then screams. Rather, a scream comes from it, like many distinct voices screaming in unison. The lightning within the cloud flickers from purple, to blue, to green. A pleasant green.

C'mon Alice, thinks Charles.

It vibrates before them, then flies away as instantly as it approached. A final bolt of green shoots out at Charles and Cody, and a voice flies past on the wind, "*You must go.*"

The bolt turns in midair and burns a line in the sky towards what could have been East.

"Cody, help me get Mitch. We need to go."

"What about Tiffany."

"She's gone," Charles sobs. He cannot hold his emotions. "We gotta go before it comes back."

"I'm so sorry."

"Stop fucking saying that!"

"I'm... Okay." Cody helps lift Mitch.

"Mitch, if you can hear us, we need to move quickly."

"Unhn," agrees Mitch.

"He's heavy," says Cody, adding, "Which way?"

"We go the direction of that last bolt. Probably East."

"How do you know?"

"Well, it was green, and the only other person I saw shoot green was you. The whole time we've been here that thing has been all emo purple."

"I don't see how that makes it safe."

"Alice spoke to me when I was… inside it? She was that voice on the wind. Did you hear it? She told me to go when I understood what I saw. There are many people inside that thing. They're in it now fighting, but alive, I guess. Whatever the Aeraph are, I think they're that way. And if they're going to fight Midwatch and the Nochtvol, we need to join them."

Cody looks at Charles. "I really am sorry."

Charles sighs.

They carry Mitch across Midwatch, guided by Alice's light.

IV – BIG DOUG

Alright. Honestly, I don't understand what I see.

Doug murmured in the Volvo's front seat as Margaret piloted it past the "Welcome to Brewster Falls" sign. His eyes were half open. He wasn't yet back amongst the living, but he knew where he was.

Why not 'A nice place to raise your kids.'? he mused. *Why 'bring'?*

The thought of kids made him think of Alice. What Aunt Mercy showed him. Alice's face floating in front of him and then shooting away to who knows where.

He heard a voice.

Margaret.

So far away.

"Weee almod hohm hooeeee. Waaaaa uuuuu," was what he heard.

"What?" he said.

"Doug. Wake up! We're almost home." Margaret's voice again. And then, to someone else, "Are you sure he's okay? He's been out a while."

"Mar, you already know the answer."

Hazel.

"It's ethereal sleep. A meditative state?"

Margaret.

Then someone spoke with a deeper voice, backwards and forwards. Doug could not discern what this person said.

"I feel... something. I know he is fine and that he will wake soon." Margaret again.

"I'm wake," said Doug. His head hurt like he had a hangover, and the world was too bright.

"What was that?" asked Margaret.

He cleared his throat and coughed a dry cough.

"I'm awake," he said, and sat up straight in the passenger seat. "Where's Alice?"

Margaret glanced into the rearview mirror. Doug turned and wasn't surprised to see Hazel, because he heard her speak, was a little surprised to see their Uncle Ulrich, but almost fell back into his deep sleep when he saw Jenny Noble sitting between them.

Jenny. The word Alice mouthed in his dream while wearing that horrible smile.

"Well, this is an odd group," Doug barely got out before he coughed again.

"We are going to find Alice; and Alice, we are going to find," said Ulrich.

He knows, thought Doug.

Margaret stared straight ahead stone-faced.

Doug opened his mouth to speak but stopped. Hazel quickly shifted her eyes. Jenny Noble offered a squint accompanied by a Mona Lisa smile.

They all know.

Ethereal sleep? Ethereal sleep. That's what Margaret said, thought Doug.

"Anyone want to let me in on what the hell is going on?" he asked.

The sky over Brewster Falls transitioned from black to gold as the sun rose.

It must be around five in the morning. But what day?

"What day is it?" Doug added before anyone spoke.

"Try to rest a little more, hon. We're almost there," said Margaret.

Doug coughed again and mucus rattled off his vocal cords and fell into his throat. He swallowed. It felt like he hadn't spoken in a while.

Throat is stiff, and we're back in Brewster Falls. It must be the morning of the first or second. But that would mean we left right after the Will was opened. The Will? I don't remember that either. And I'm starving.

"Margaret. What day is it and where are we really going?" asked Doug.

"It's Saturday," said Hazel. Margaret's eye twitched.

"Saturday?" Doug said to himself. "Saturday? Saturday the third? Have I been asleep three days?"

"Please rest dear," said Margaret, slowing down for a stop sign. They were on Perez.

"How is that possible?" he asked Hazel since Margaret refused to help. "It seems like moments. And what is ethereal sleep?"

"It means your body was asleep while your spirit was conducting business elsewhere," responded Hazel matter-of-factly.

Doug looked at Hazel as if she had three heads, maybe seven. A smile pulled at the corners of his mouth as he was about to laugh but then remembered the encounter with Aunt Mercy. And Alice mouthing 'Jenny' to him before flashing away. His smile died before it was born. Big Doug Massey realized that the things he experienced in his dreams may have occurred.

"Will someone please tell me where the hell—*cough*—my—*cough*—daughter is?" Doug said. He swallowed more mucus. "And do we have anything to drink?"

He stared at Jenny Noble and she stared back at him. Her face did not change or move. He found himself unable to look away.

"Do you understand what you see?"

Doug heard this but no one spoke aloud. Although panicked, he yawned.

"Here," said Ulrich. He pushed his right arm against Jenny Noble's face to hand Doug a cup of cold coffee. "This is all we have; and all we have, is this."

Doug grabbed the cup from Ulrich and looked into it. He sighed, then drank the whole thing. It tasted terrible. He instantly felt better.

The mystery of coffee.

"Look, I need to tell you all. I saw and spoke to Aunt Mercy. And Alice was..."

"Not now dear," interrupted Margaret.

"Excuse me?" said Doug, not believing what his wife just said to him. "What the fuck is wrong with you?" he asked.

"Now isn't a good time. We'll discuss it later," said Margaret.

Ulrich shook his head and looked out the window. When he did, his eyes went wide and his mouth fell open.

"Smoke," he said.

"What?" asked Margaret, tired from driving.

"There's smoke. In the sky. Do you see?"

Margaret leaned forward and peered at the lightening sky and one plume of grey smoke.

"Go there. Quickly," said Ulrich.

* * *

The scene was fresh when they arrived at the corner of Donovan Drive and Colonel Perez Road.

Sirens sounded in the distance.

Jenny Noble laughed.

Ulrich and Hazel exited via their respective doors. Doug and Margaret followed.

"What have they done?" said Ulrich.

The Garage House burned. The garages gone, and the main house in flames. The burnt husk of a car rested between where the garages once stood.

"Oh. Oh my. What have they done?" repeated Ulrich.

"What is it, Uncle? What does this mean?" asked Margaret.

"It means the gate is open for business," said Hazel.

The sirens grew louder.

"It doesn't look to me like anything is open for business. But if those firetrucks don't get here soon the next house over might go up with this one," said Doug.

"Everyone, back in the car; and back in the car, everyone," said Ulrich.

"What now?" asked Doug.

"We must go."

I don't understand the significance of this, but what the hell, I don't understand anything, thought Doug.

He got back in the car.

Everyone joined him.

Jenny Noble still laughed.

"Ah, my old friend. It would appear we no longer have a standing compromise," she said.

Old friend?

Ulrich ignored her and said, "Margaret, can you see where the garage on the left used to be? To the left of what's left of that burning car? Yes? Good. Drive us into it. Slowly."

"Whoa, whoa, whoa!" said Doug. "That fire will cook us in here."

"Douglas now is not the time; and the time, is not now," said Ulrich.

Doug continued to protest, but his wife had already put the car in gear and started rolling. He thought about jumping out and saving himself, but Jenny Noble's laughter stopped him. Something in it drew him to stay.

The car stopped.

"Uncle, are you sure?" asked Margaret.

Hazel placed a gentle hand on her cousin's shoulder. "Mar, you know he is. You know where we're going. Please, the sirens."

"Somehow, I do," said Margaret. To her husband's dismay, she launched the car into the Garage House's smoldering ruin.

* * *

His world spins. He retches, and then is bathed in light.

Doug opens his eyes and wipes away blessed tears of cleansing. When he focuses, he sees a place he has seen before.

"This is where I was with Aunt Mercy. And with Alice," he whispers.

"Yes. Yes, it is," says Hazel.

Doug turns to face her and notices something else.

"Where is Jenny Noble?" he asks.

"That wasn't Jenny Noble," says Hazel. "Uncle, what do we do?"

"We must destroy this conduit; and this conduit, we must destroy," says Ulrich. "Come with me."

Ulrich gets out of the Volvo and approaches the shimmering space whence they came. He raises his hands and begins to chant and moan. At his feet the black dirt and dead, brown plant life return to green. Little white flowers sprout where he stands. He continues chanting.

Hazel approaches and raises her hands with him.

"Hazel, what do I do?" asks Margaret.

Doug stands in awe of what he is seeing.

"Concentrate on Uncle Ulrich. Concentrate on giving him your strength. If you succeed, he will be able to focus the energy," says Hazel.

This is nuts, thinks Doug, watching the trio raise their arms.

He sees the same effect on the ground around Hazel that occurred around Ulrich.

He sees nothing on the ground around Margaret.

Ulrich chants louder and faster.

"C'mon Mar! You've done this before!" shouts Hazel.

"I don't remember!" Margaret shouts back.

"You know it's true! You must do it for Alice! Concentrate!"

Margaret moans and the slightest hint of green sprouts at her feet.

"Uh, you can do it honey. You can do it!" says Doug.

I feel like an idiot, he thinks.

Margaret Massey's moaning gains in volume until it becomes a sustained scream. The shimmering space brightens and shimmers quicker, like waves on Lake Erie before a storm.

Margaret's hand lashes out and grasps the old grey man's arm. He screams.

"No!" yells Hazel.

Ulrich stifles the scream and continues chanting. The sky bursts open as if a new sun is being born. The explosion is immediate, and deafening.

Doug hears only silence as he is blown backwards against the car.

* * *

"This gate is closed; and closed, this gate is."

Doug opens his eyes and stands. The shimmering thing is gone.

Ulrich's right arm lays limp and black at his side. The arm Margaret touched. Margaret sits on the ground with Hazel. Her eyes rage.

"You. You did this," says Margaret to Ulrich. "You arrogant bastard. You did this!"

"You saw my mind," says Ulrich.

Margaret nods.

"Unfortunate you chose that instant to take the opportunity," he says, looking down at his lifeless arm. "I would have answered, had you asked; and had you asked, I would have answered."

"I had to know," croaks Margaret. "Had to know." She sobs.

Hazel rubs her back.

"Hey, everyone. I don't know what's going on here, but Jenny Noble is gone and this place doesn't exactly feel safe. And I have a question," says Doug. Margaret, Hazel, and Ulrich look at him as if only now remembering he is there.

"Where *is* Alice? Is she here? Is this the place I came to from JNR? In my dream, or whatever? The place Aunt Mercy showed me. Is this it? Is this where my daughter is?" he asks.

Ulrich regards him. Then nods.

"It is. And if we are to save her, we must hurry; and hurry, we must," says Ulrich. "Hazel, Margaret, we must go. Everyone back in the car, it will aid in our journey."

"Why should we let you lead? Why should we do anything you say?" asks Margaret.

"Perhaps after, you should not. But right now, I know the way we must go; and the way we must go, I know."

"Where exactly are we going?" asks Hazel.

Ulrich's eyes resemble those of someone visiting their childhood home. A forlorn gaze that carries with it memories, nostalgia, and regret. Regret that says this place was better left a memory, for now that I have seen it again, the memory is tainted.

The old grey man speaks.

"We are going to see Michael."

V – DEPUTY RIGGS

I could use a High Life. Probably no bars in this place, thinks Deputy Stephen Riggs. He continues to follow Michael the-whatever-he-is.

Aeraph. What's an Aeraph?

There is little conversation. The winged creature occasionally stops and raises his hand in a closed gesture. Deputy Riggs learns it means 'I'm listening to something you can't hear.' So, he remains silent. Most of the time.

He can no longer help himself.

"So, we went up to Nassem City for what? Just to show it was there?" he asks.

Michael does not answer.

"Look, I recognize it. I see Brewster Falls all over this place. To me, that was Jack Nassem Research Park. Ran by Leonard Philips. But—" Deputy Riggs stops as Michael's feathers ruffle, again.

"We do not say that name," speaks Michael.

"Uh, Jack Nassem Research Park? But it's almost the same as—" is all Deputy Riggs gets out before Michael is face to face with him, hunched so his strange red-ringed pupils are level with his own.

Nothing can move that fast, he thinks.

"No. The other. We do not speak it," says Michael.

"Leonard Philips? Cornerstone of Brewster Falls?"

Michael grasps Deputy Stephen Riggs' shoulders in his hands, and screeches at the sky. The pain is great. The warmth, however, is spectacular. He hates to admit it, but ever since birdbrain touched him the first time, he wants him to keep doing it.

Michael grits his teeth; in the best way a beak can grit. "That is the one. Utter it no more. Not here, and not when we get to the Trinus. Not anywhere in Aesteria."

"The Trinus? What is that? Is that where we're going?" asks Deputy Riggs before shaking his head. "And what's wrong with Leonard? Why can't we speak his name? How do you know him?"

Michael squeezes harder, and while Riggs feels pain, he also feels intense pleasure. "You have spoken it again."

"Yeah, yeah. Well give me a code name to use then, but I can't make promises. I've known the guy my whole life. Everyone has."

"We call him Shadow-Bringer."

"Shadow-Bringer. Shadow-Bringer?" Deputy Riggs rolls his eyes. "Is this all a joke? Are we in a comic book?"

Am I unconscious?

"It is not humorous. He has caused us much pain. Look about." Michael extends one wing and arm and waves them out towards the setting.

Shadow-Bringer. Aeraph. Trinus. Temporan. Aesteria. Congregate. Oh my.

The buildings are modernish design. Maybe eighties or nineties. The aging dates them much older, as if they are hundreds of years old. No flora nor fauna anywhere. It is all grey. Creatures scurry about that Deputy Riggs does not recognize. They stay hidden and out of the way.

Off in the distance towers are built up several stories. Like scaffolding around a new building, except solitary. Several times, as they walk, other Michaels—*Aeraph*—climb these and jump off. Some crash to the ground. Some flap and hover for a bit, but eventually they all fall back to the grey, lifeless dirt.

They are trying to fly.

"Can you fly?" he asks Michael.

"Yes. One of the few who still can."

"What happened?"

"The Shadow-Bringer. He brought gifts. A better life. He was our friend. Until he was not. What you see is his legacy."

"Leonard Philips did this?" asks Deputy Riggs. Then, realizing what he said, adds, "Sorry."

Michael releases his grip on Deputy Riggs's shoulders. "I understand, but others may not. Yes. Yes, he did this. And we, in our greed and desire for ease, did this to ourselves." Michael's strange red eyes grow glassy. "We were once so proud."

I always knew there was something wrong with that guy.

"I always knew there was something wrong with that guy," says Deputy Riggs.

"Indeed," answers Michael.

"I'll do my best to not say his name. But how did he do this?"

"He had help from another friend of ours. One whose allegiances remain unclear."

"Wow, your friends are great."

"Stephen, we were destroyed via our own arrogance. When the Shadow-Bringer first came to us, he was with a trusted member of the Congregate, the covenant holders we now go to meet. We had reason to trust him."

"You trusted him simply because he was with one of yours?"

"It was our way. He was the last of the Congregate existing outside Aesteria. There were once so many of us. We believed we were unbreakable, and soon complacency reigned. Now, all that is left are those in the Trinus, me, and the grey man."

You gotta be kidding.

"On top of all these fantastical words and names we have a guy called *the grey man*? Tell me something, did I get hit in the head? Am I actually still at Sycamore Valley hooked up to a bunch of machines?" Deputy Stephen Riggs slaps himself in the face, once each with both hands. The second makes him stumble, but Michael catches him. The warmth comes again. So sweet.

I guess not.

"You are not anywhere else but here," says Michael.

Deputy Riggs' face goes sullen and stone. He averts his eyes from Michael. He hangs his head. His shoulders slump. The warmth where Michael touches him diminishes quickly; such is the power of his pain. Michael pulls him into him and wraps his wings around him. Deputy Riggs' does not feel uncomfortable in the embrace. He feels light, relief, and love. He exhales, and realizes he was holding his breath.

"Michael."

"Yes, Stephen."

"May I ask a question?"

"Yes, Stephen."

"Did Leonard... the Shadow-Bringer kill my mom?"

"I do not know. He brought her here, which may mean the same to you as killing. It was Hesperus' decision to take her as he did."

"Hesperus? Midwatch before it was Midwatch?"

"Yes, Stephen."

"Why do you continue to call it by that name?"

"It helps me remember he was once my student. And my friend. Hesperus was a noble Aeraph soldier. He carried the ideals and passion of those who are young. Hungry for change from a desire to make things better, for improvement. Alas, progress for the sake of progress is a false idol. He was corrupted on the same day the Shadow-Bringer first came to us. We Aeraph live long, and perhaps to you, appear immortal. I believe through this age or the next we can bring Hesperus back, save him from Midwatch. Our journeys are long, and the path through guided by second chances, of which there are no limit."

"So, you *do* adhere to time."

"We do. Temporans see us as immortal, much like a canine of your plane would see humans as immortal. You change little as the beasts age. Generations of the same family can come and go while your face barely changes. So it is between Temporan and Aeraph."

"Are you saying we're your pets? Your dogs?"

"No, Stephen. We are stewards of life; of souls; and of realms."

Sure sounds like he's saying I'm his dog.

"Okay, anyway, if Hesperus can be saved, and I survived being... absorbed, does that mean we could also save my mother? And anyone else in there?"

Deputy Riggs eyes are hopeful. He pushes away from Michael and Michael releases him. The old Aeraph stands his full height and looks out across Aesteria, now Midwatch. He does not immediately answer, however neither is he pensive.

Deputy Riggs always wanted to be a detective. He studied the craft. He knows, even through his strange face, that Michael is not thinking. He knows the answer but does not want to say it. He reaches out to Deputy Riggs.

"Don't," says Deputy Riggs. He swats Michael's hand away. "I want to feel this. Answer me."

Michael puts his hand back to his side. After a moment, he speaks a single word.

"No."

"How many others have been brought here? How many souls are trapped in there?"

"Many."

"Then we should kill them. We should destroy them."

"Stephen."

"Why does he get a chance at living? What will happen to my mom? I spoke to her in there. Her mind is alive. What happens to that? Where will she go?"

"If the spectral cloud known as Midwatch is destroyed, the minds within should be released as death intends. Their energy should be collected and dispersed once more to live as other things or beings. They would have peace."

"Should?"

"We do not know."

"And Hesperus? How does he live?"

"Again, we know not. We suspect since he did not die, he will return. As you did. As the Shadow-Bringer did."

"I'm going to kill Leonard Philips. You can have Hesperus."

"Stephe—"

"No. You hear his name. You feel whatever pain you feel when I say it. Leonard Philips will die; you have my promise on that."

"It is not—"

"It is. You said we are soldiers. You said a battle is coming. In battles, there is death, and this one is mine. You cannot take this from me."

"There will be death, but there is no solace in that. Only the dead feel peace. Those left feel the pain, the regret, the loss. Only through forgiveness do all share in the peace."

Deputy Riggs falls silent.

They walk on.

* * *

They come to a large structure, covered in thick interwoven vines. The leaves and stalks are grey and brittle. Stephen grasps them to reveal what is beneath, but to his surprise, they don't move.

"We are here. This is the Trinus, sacred meeting place of the Congregate of Aesteria."

Michael raises his hand to the vines and presses it firmly into them. His eyes roll backward into his head leaving only shiny orbs of black glass in their place. He chants. As he does so, the vines around his hand turn green and sprout little white flowers. Bees appear from thin air and go about the work of pollinating them or what-ever secret work it is bees do. The greening vines trace a rectangular shape. A pleasant aroma fills the air. Deputy Riggs' thirst for death wanes, if for only this moment, as it does for all who gaze upon the wonder of nature in bloom.

The vines part to reveal a large black door, studded with shiny silver bolts. In the door's center is a symbol inlaid by long silvery bars. Joined at their bases are two triangles, one pointing up, one pointing down. Two bars run parallel along the upper triangle's sides. When Michael finishes his chant, the symbol first glows a deep purple, and then fades into a brilliant blue.

It's familiar. Where have I seen it? thinks a mesmerized Deputy Riggs.

"What is that symbol?" he asks.

"It is the Aurclock," answers Michael. "It tells us the nature of living creatures, things, and entire realms, if needed. It is a power-ful tool in distributing soul-energy. The arrangement upon this door shows one of peace and balance. The very idea that obsessed Hesperus."

"Are peace and balance bad?"

"In small circles, no, it is preferred, but amongst realms, peace and balance bring with them complacency. Complacency allows distraction, distraction allows mischief, and mischief allows control. It is easier for those who are opportunistic to control a balanced realm. To distract and divide. It is the imbalance of things that makes life fight for ground, fight to survive. Imbalance is why the rose has thorns and the shark has teeth. It is what makes life strong and sweet."

Michael's head snaps around to face the way they came. His feathers go tight and sleek to his body.

"Stay here," he says, and leaps into the air. The wind hits Deputy Riggs and knocks him to one knee. He steadies himself and shields his eyes from the swirling dust. Michael shoots up like a missile, and then dives into the distance.

Holy shit. He stands and dusts himself off.

* * *

He reaches for his missing sidearm when something big thumps the ground behind him.

It is Michael.

"Christ," says Deputy Riggs. "Why didn't you land over there or something instead of scaring the shit out of me?"

Michael bows his head and mutters something.

"If you guys are afraid of battle, I have no idea how I'll be able to help you. That was awesome."

"Indeed," says Michael. "Your friends are here."

Deputy Riggs cocks his head.

Headlights. Is that a car?

He can smell it, and it is horrible.

When it reaches them, he sees Margaret and Doug Massey in the front seat. He had tried to tell them about their missing daughter, Alice, but couldn't reach them.

A man, all grey, gets out of the back seat.

Deputy Riggs looks at Michael, sidelong.

"Is that—"

"It is."

"Can we trust him?"

"We shall see."

Then, the other door opens, and his breath is taken away.

"Hazel?" he says, unaware he has said anything at all.

Hazel pushes past the others and rushes to him. She embraces him hard and nestles her face in his neck. "I'm so sorry you are here," she says. "But I'm so happy to see you."

Deputy Riggs feels better than he did in Michael's embrace, which shocks him.

The big Aeraph smiles.

"Ulrich."

"Michael. It is time to rejoin the Congregates. Twilight is setting."

"Indeed," says Michael.

"Is that an angel?" asks a distraught Big Doug Massey.

"It isn't," answers Hazel. "But it's the best we've got. Now, let's save our kids."

Michael opens the Trinus door. Within is only darkness. It has both no depth and endless depth.

Oh, hell no, thinks Deputy Riggs.

Oh, hell yes, thinks Hazel Montgomery. She looks into his eyes and smiles.

Confusion dances across his face.

She removes herself from his arms and steps through the doorway and disappears.

"After you, Stephen," says Michael. "Welcome to the Congregate."

CHAPTER 10

The Aurclock

"Light doesn't move like that."

I – BIG DOUG

"Isn't it pretty how the sun reflects off the water over there? Like little diamonds floating on the surface."

Alice? Is that you?

Big Doug Massey blinked. His face peppered with cool droplets of water. He heard voices all around him, birds squawking, and water crashing onto... something. He rubbed his temples. More water droplets struck him in the face.

"Hey Mr. Massey, you may want to step away from the edge. They say the rocks are slippery when the lake is choppy and spraying."

I know that voice, Doug thought. He turned to face it, struggling to open his eyes. It was as if they had been shut for a long time. His mind was foggy. As he turned, he slipped. He landed on his right thigh, and though he was a large man, his legs were quite skinny.

"Ouch, shit," he said aloud, his vision clearing. He rolled onto his butt, put his hands down on the cold surface of wet rock on which he now sat, and looked out at the ocean. Swells over four feet struck the rocky shore and splashed all around him. He wiped his eyes once more and licked his lips.

Not salty, he thought. *This water is fresh. Fresh water.* He smiled, and then laughed as he understood what happened and where he was.

"Dad! Dad, are you okay?"

Alice. She sounds genuinely worried about me. It had been a while since they had been close. Doug felt they had drifted apart these last few years she was in high school. He felt like she thought he was an idiot, and though he tried, a lot, they just couldn't connect. They had been the best of friends when she was younger. How he longed for that feeling, that love. The tone in her voice drew a few tears with his continued laughter.

He felt great. And a little confused.

Big Doug Massey turned in the direction whence his daughter's voice had come. He was not surprised to see the Marblehead Lighthouse, the limestone tip of Marblehead Peninsula to one side, and the keeper's house to the other. He was in Marblehead, Ohio. On the shore of Lake Erie. He volunteered to chaperone the Brewster Falls Junior Ohio History Trip, which this year made several stops along Ohio's northern coast, today in Marblehead. He hoped it would bring him and Alice a little closer again before she became a Senior, and inevitably, an adult.

He saw her. She was coming to him.

"Wait, wait," said Doug, pushing himself up and standing. He wobbled and tested his footing before making his way toward the lighthouse. "I'm fine. We don't need two Massey's out here getting wet and bruising their butts."

"I told him they were slippery," said Tiffany Philips, coming from the picnic tables with Charles Horne. He remembered it was lunchtime. Although Tiffany and Charles' lips were a little too red to have been from the PB&Js the school provided for lunch today. It didn't bother Doug at all. He was so happy to be here, interacting with his daughter and friends again. If falling on his ass was the key to rekindling their relationship, he would do it for eternity.

It feels like I just got here, thought Doug. *Feels like I was doing something. Dreaming?*

"Tiff, you were right. They are slippery. I shouldn't have been out there. I kind of zoned out with the beauty of it." He turned. "You're right, Al, the water is beautiful."

"Oh my God, Dad. You're so embarrassing," said Alice. She came to his side and took his right hand in her left and held his arm with both of hers. She laid her head on his shoulder. "Thanks for coming with us, though."

"Yeah Mr. Massey. Thanks. You're a way better chaperone than my mom or dad would have been," said Tiffany.

"I couldn't imagine Leonard Fucking Philips doing this," replied Doug, without thinking about what he was saying or to whom. "Oh crap, sorry."

"Dad!" exclaimed Alice. She pulled away to look at him but did not release his hand.

"Hell yeah, Doug," said Charles, standing next to Tiffany in the gravel next to the limestone danger zone.

"Language, Mr. Horne. And it's Mr. Massey to you, too," said Doug, smiling, but turning sharply to face Charles, one eyebrow up.

Tiffany laughed, then Charles, then Alice, and finally he joined. The connection was here. It was the best he felt in years. He wanted to live in this moment forever.

"Dad has the most peculiar middle name," said Tiffany through a snort.

"Well, he earned it; and earned it, he did," said Charles, still laughing, but looking into Doug Massey's eyes. Charles' eyes were not his own. They were...

...*desperate*, thought Doug.

"Everything okay?" asked Doug, looking at Charles.

"Yeah, great. We were about to sit down to lunch," answered Charles.

"I thought you two just ate," said Alice, an upturned note of disbelief on her last word. "What were you really doing?" She sounded like her mother when she asked her unending questions about the day's events.

"Oh, uh, just looking at the lighthouse and the water, and, uh..."

"Well, stay off the rocks. Let's eat, I'm starving," interrupted Doug, not wanting to hear whatever sorry excuse Charles was about to spew. He knew kissing lips when he saw them. He wasn't sure about the relationship between his daughter and her best friend's boyfriend, and he did not want to ruin this glorious feeling by finding out the depths of teen emotions right now. He knew the kid had been hanging around a lot but wasn't sure it was at all romantic.

This is why I went into physics and not people, thought Doug. *And I'm starving.*

They heard a whoosh. They looked around. It came again. From above.

"What was that?" Doug muttered.

"Dad, look. The lighthouse is on," said Alice.

They all looked up and saw, indeed, the light had come on and spun around slowly. Doug was surprised to see the light emanating from the tremendous reflector was a pleasant green.

"Huh, I didn't think the light was green," he said.

Then it spun, shooting beautiful green beams outward in all directions, like a huge green bicycle wheel in the sky.

Doug felt frantic. He saw the faces of every man, woman, and child staring up, jaws slack, unmoving. The green light reflected off their faces as it spun above them. Then, a solitary voice. One from someone he knew to be dead.

"Do you understand what you see?"

* * *

Doug spins on the cold, wet limestone of Marblehead. He sees all the people who were just with him are gone.

He is alone.

"DO YOU UNDERSTAND WHAT YOU SEE?"

A single face flashes into existence before his eyes, the sunken skull of Aunt Mercy. She has aged since he last saw her.

"I don't want you to be here. I want to be in this time. In this moment," says Doug, struggling for composure. "Go away. I don't want to understand. I just want my Alice again. My daughter. My friend."

Aunt Mercy glowers, the lighthouse's green light reflecting in her eyes.

She vanishes. As she evaporates, the green light stops flashing. The beam shines into the distance. He imagines if he were to step upon it, he could walk to where it's pointing.

"East," he says, alone on the rocks.

The sky becomes the tone of dusk. He sees the light reflecting off the water, like little diamonds floating on the surface.

Wasn't it just lunchtime? he thinks. *What was I doing? I wasn't here. But where was I?* Big Doug Massey is overcome with a wave of grief. *But this is where I want to be. Please, let me stay. Please, please let me be here. I don't want to understand.* He falls to his knees, rolls back to sitting, brings his knees as close as he can to his chest, and wraps his arms around them.

"Please," he says, begging Aunt Mercy, the lighthouse, anyone, anything.

* * *

"Dad! Dad, are you okay?"

Alice? thought Doug. He lifted his head to the midday sun. He turned towards the lighthouse. Alice was coming to him, again.

"Uh, wait. I'm... okay," said Doug.

"I told him they were slippery," said Tiffany Philips, standing there again with Charles, holding hands, and looking invincible.

"Alice, what... Stay there. I'm... I'm fine. Let me come off these rocks," said Doug.

"Oh my God, Dad. You're so embarrassing," Alice said as he reached her. She grasped his arm and leaned her head on him, as he knew she would. "Thanks for coming with us, though," she added.

"Yeah Mr. Massey. Thanks. You're a way better chaperone than my mom or dad would have been," said Tiffany. Again.

This is all wrong, thought Doug. *I need to test something.*

"I couldn't imagine Leonard Fucking Philips doing this."

"Dad!" exclaimed Alice. She pulled away to look at him, but did not release his hand.

"Hell yeah, Doug," said Doug and Charles, in unison. They stared at each other.

"That was weird," said Alice.

* * *

Doug sighs. He looks around at all the kids, the parents, the teachers, the bus drivers, all the people that he hadn't noticed that day a year ago. He wants so badly to remain here, but it's not right. In fact, it is all wrong.

They all turn to face him.

"Do you understand what you see?" asks the entire crowd. All except Alice, who looks at her father with the loving eyes of a doting daughter, happy to see him each time he comes home, excited to see what he is doing. A face he fears he has seen for the last time.

"I understand," answers Doug.

The pleasant green light creeps from the lighthouse reflector and accelerates east, as it had before.

Light doesn't move like that, he thinks.

"No, it does not," says the crowd.

"Dad, what's happening? I'm scared," says Alice. "I was in the basement, and there was water running and now I don't know where I am. I think Tiff may be here or something, and I think I saw Charles, and for a minute I was strong, but now I think I'm trapped. Am I dead? Am I in hell? Daddy, I miss you. I want to come home. Please."

Doug grasps the Alice in front of him by her shoulders. He knows she is not his Alice, but it would have to be enough.

"Listen, Al," he begins, "I miss you too, kiddo. We had a pretty great day here once, didn't we?" He wipes his eyes. "I don't understand what's going on, but your mother, your Aunt Hazel, Deputy Riggs, and me are all looking for you. We have help. We're coming and we won't stop until we find you and save you from whatever has you. Whether you are... are dead..." Doug chokes, "... or not I don't know, but I don't think so. I don't know how, but I don't think so. If Tiff is there, go to her. Help each other stay alive. Is there anything you can tell me about where you are? Anything?"

Alice looks up at the green light coming from the lighthouse after Doug asks this question. He traces her gaze.

"It's you," he whispers. "You're the light."

Alice smiles and shimmers out of existence.

Doug is once again alone.

* * *

He sits on the lighthouse steps when a hand squeezes his shoulder. It fills him with warmth and rejuvenation. Doug turns his head and sees the red ringed eyes and feathered face of Michael.

"Come. You have been in the Atarax."

"The Atarax?"

"Yes, it is a space through which all entering the Congregate of Aesteria must pass. Some remain within its spell forever, captured by its gifts."

"Gifts?"

"The Atarax gives whatever you desire. Its purpose is to trap those who are corrupt of heart, who are not focused enough to recognize temptation against reality."

"I wouldn't say what it showed me would mean I was corrupt. It was a very good day."

"Indeed, but even a slight faltering to temptation is a risk to what is left of the Congregates. It led to their undoing. This is the only way."

"Is my daughter alive?"

"A difficult question to answer. By soul, yes."

"I spoke to her."

"Beware what is experienced in the Atarax, it can cloud your mind from the truth."

"It was her."

"I see. Come, the others have been waiting some time. We have little time to prepare. You are already far behind."

"How long was I in there?"

"A better question for your wife. My acquaintance with time is not as yours."

"Try me. Time is my specialty, like coordinates on a map."

"Indeed. I walked three of your moonrises to find you. I knew you were free of the Atarax effects, but not free of the Atarax itself. We sense the free mind and locate it to bring the bearer out. Does this answer help?"

Three days? thinks Doug. *It felt like half an hour.*

"It helps," he says.

"Good, now come. We must take you to the Aurclock. There is one more test for you to pass," says Michael.

"Great," says Doug. "How long will this one take?"

"It is instant."

"What's it about?"

"Your spirit."

"My spirit?"

Did he say Aurclock?

"Yes, the Aurclock shows the nature of your spirit. You have defeated the Atarax, but we must be sure. You do, unfortunately, work for the Shadow-Bringer."

"I work for who?"

"You call him by another name."

"Leonard Philips?" asks Doug.

Michael winces, "Do not say the Shadow-Bringer's name within these walls.

"I don't understand," says Doug. "What if I fail this test?"

"You die. Do not worry, if needed, that will also be instant."

"Put me back in the Atarax," says Doug.

Michael glowers.

"That was a joke," says Doug. "Do you people have jokes?"

"Ha," says Michael. "Come."

"Like little diamonds floating on the surface," whispers Doug.

"Follow," says Michael once more, and walks deeper into the dark.

Big Doug Massey follows.

II – THE ECHO SPACE

The thing that is still Alice Massey greets her old friend.

The echoing voice of the thing that used to be Tiffany Philips responds loudly.

"Alice? Alice is that you?" *you? you? you?*

It is. Use your mind. Concentrate on communicating with only me. Commune with me.

"I don't understand. Am I, am I... am I dead?" *dead? dead? dead.*

I am not sure. Perhaps. Focus on me. Think at me.

"How can I focus? Where are you? Where am I? Everything is dark. I think I was killed. How can I think if I'm dead? I don't understand." *stand. stand. stand.*

Tiffany, please. You must be calm. Picture me, picture the things you want me to know. We must be careful.

"Don't tell me to calm down. Alice, I don't understand. I'm afraid. I want to go home. Where's Charles? Where is Cody? I saw Jenny. She was dead, I'm sure. Floating. Now I'm dead. I want to go home. I want my mom." *mom. mom. mom.*

She does not understand. She's not listening.

"Who are you talking to? Who else is here?" *here? here? here?*

Tiffany, I was called Jutte. I had powers and was once like you. Now I am here. I have waited so long for others like me, that we may restore ourselves.

"Jutte? Who are you? How long have you been waiting? Can I leave?" *leave? leave? leave?*

We cannot, but we can help those on the outside defeat this thing from within. It is not as powerful as it seems. First, you must learn to quell your feelings. Focus your thoughts, as Alice said, and picture only her and what you want her to know. This will keep you concealed.

"Concealed? Concealed from what? How are you communicating with me? Have we met, have you seen my face? I could communicate with Cody with my mind, but now I can't. And I can't leave. Cody! Where is Cody? And Charles? You didn't answer." *answer. answer. answer.*

That is because they do not know.

"Who is that? Alice? Jutte? Who else is here?" *here? here? here?*

Those pests will be removed soon enough. They are no friends of yours. They seek only to control you for their benefit. But I can help you. Here, have this.

Midwatch speaks the words, and the thing that used to be Tiffany Philips feels relief, and perhaps joy.

Is that better?

"It is much better. Who are you, and where did they go?" *go? go? go?*

I am Midwatch. We met a short time ago, in the flesh, so to speak. Your cowardly friends are hiding. My realm is vast. I contain multitudes, allowing some to hide from within.

"Hide from within? Using me for their own benefit? This is so confusing." *confusing. confusing. confusing.*

Yes. But, you see, your friend Alice, and her new friend Jutte, they could live again. They want to use your power to help themselves escape. And leave you behind. Here. All alone. Forever.

"Alice is my friend. She wouldn't just leave me here. Would she?" *she? she? she?*

She has done just that, just now. Here, let me help you.

Midwatch serves the thing that used to be Tiffany Philips another jolt of ataraxia.

Is that better? Are you eased?

"I am. I can't believe it. I can't believe Alice would do this to me." *me. me. me.*

She wants Charles for herself. And Jutte's purpose is just as nefarious, I am sure. I can restore your power. We can work together to keep them here. Keep them from hurting your friends. At least then, your death would not have been in vain.

"That's dumb. She wouldn't do this to me for a stupid boy." *boy. boy. boy.*

Please, let us focus on finding the fugitives within. Will you help me? If I restore your power, will you help me find and banish them?

Midwatch begins the corruption of Tiffany's soul-mind.

The thing that used to be Tiffany Philips feels another jolt of pleasure, and with it comes another vision. She sees Alice sitting on Charles' bed. Petting his cat, as Tiffany herself had done many times. She sees them with their heads together, looking at Charles' sketchbook. She sees them make that stupid hoodie with that stupid symbol. She sees them holding each other. She sees them laughing.

"What are they laughing at?" *at? at? at?*

Midwatch senses the thing that used to be Tiffany Philips is not moved by this vision. Not enough to inflict significant change. She is stronger than it assumed.

They laugh at you, of course.

"At me? Why?" *why? why? why?*

They use you for their amusement. To see how far they can go, how much they can do, under your nose. Everyone knows you for a fool.

"Well, that doesn't make sense. For what purpose?" *purpose? purpose? purpose?*

No one likes you, Tiffany. Not Charles, not Alice, not Cody. Not any other student. Not any teacher. Not even your parents.

"But what did I do? Why me?" *me? me? me?*

Under Midwatch's influence, she begins to believe the lie, and it feeds upon her insecurity.

Nothing. You were born. You are wealthy. You are selfish and pretentious and, what is the word? Bitchy? A distasteful term. They do it because they can. To feel better about themselves. Look closely at their faces.

Midwatch gives the thing that used to be Tiffany Philips a new vision.

She walks the halls at school. The students look at her. Some say hello as she passes. The teachers nod, standing outside their classroom doors. She sees a twinkle in all their eyes, judgement upon their faces. Their thoughts enter her mind.

Did daddy buy that for you?
You never earned anything.
Look at her, she thinks she's some sort of queen.
I bet her own parents can't stand her.
Trying way too hard, that one.
I bet she wears expensive perfume because she smells bad.
She's weird.
She's so dumb she doesn't know Alice is using her.
Her mother loves Charles Horne more than her.

It goes on until her tortured soul succumbs to the onslaught of judgement.

Midwatch feigns a thought from Alice.

Everything about Tiffany is fake. She doesn't deserve any love. She deserves to be our little toy. Our little joke.

"Make it stooooop," she pleads. "They're all laughing at me. I'm all alone." *alone. alone. alone.*

Midwatch tortures Tiffany for a long time.

Until finally she screams, "I hate them. I hate them all! Do you hear me? I HATE THEM!" *THEM! THEM! THEM!*

So, you will help?

Midwatch is pleased. The thing that used to be Tiffany Philips was not so easily swayed.

"I will do whatever it takes." *takes. takes. takes.*

Then I will restore your power, and while I fight on the outside, you will fight on the inside. We will join. An eternal union will be formed. We will rule as Midwatch over the Nochtvol. Together. Forever.

The thing that used to be Tiffany Philips feels the powers return. She senses a sea of swirling purple. She sees within Midwatch a landscape in shades of violet, deep and unending. A landscape of emotion with hills of ecstasy and valleys of remorse.

She senses a legion of beings, as yet unseen. She senses loyalty. She will be a Queen, and Midwatch her King. She sees them ruling all things.

Are you ready? Do you know your path?

I know it. But before I go, I need you to make me a promise.

Anything. Name it, and it shall be.

After I destroy Alice, and you kill the others, we go after everyone.

III – MARGARET

Margaret Massey, Hazel Montgomery, Uncle Ulrich, and Deputy Stephen Riggs stand inside the Congregate of Aesteria. Or, what remains of it. Shrouded and silent in the corner stands one other member, whom they do not know and cannot see. Michael bids them wait, so they wait.

The room is circular. The walls are glossy and black. The polish is so deep it's as though another world lives within it, as if her own reflection is another her in another place. Similar, but not the same.

This, too, seems familiar, thinks Margaret. She recalls the argument with Hazel and Ulrich at the gas station.

I feel afraid, but of what? Margaret's feelings hold a memory of this place while her mind does not.

What is it? she wonders.

She analyzes the room. The walls climb a good twenty feet to meet the ceiling. She cannot see it but can measure it by the echo.

The room has no light source, but it's not dark. The floor matches the walls. A table rests in the center. A fine black cloth covers it.

She trembles.

Deputy Riggs reaches out to pull the cloth from the table. The shrouded figure raises an arm as Ulrich grabs Riggs' shoulder. Riggs freezes in place.

Why would he do that?

"It is not for you to expose the Aurclock; and to expose the Aurclock, it is not for you," says Ulrich.

"I can't move. What is this place, Hazel? Have you been here before?" asks Deputy Riggs, rambling. "I saw my mom again in the Atari."

"Atarax, hon," says Hazel. She grasps his hand. He seems to forget the table and the secret it holds. The shrouded figure lowers its arm.

"Yeah, that," he says. "Was that her? This is the second time I saw her in wherever we are. Except this time, we were back home. Mitch was there, and my dad. I wanted to stay in it. But it was wrong somehow. There were no surprises. Everything happened as I thought it. Like a dream."

I saw nothing, thinks Margaret.

She hears Hazel describe the Atarax to Deputy Riggs. She is intrigued. Margaret came through without a vision of any kind. No dream. No wishes. No challenge.

"Your mother is not here; and here, your mother is not," says Ulrich. "The Atarax seeks imperfection from within. It gives the mind what it desires most, presenting it with a choice to stay in the Atarax and forgo all other life and responsibility, or to return to real life. Choosing desire over obligation is the first sign of corruptibility; and the first sign of corruptibility, is choosing desire over obligation."

"And the Aurclock?" asks Deputy Riggs.

"The second step. The Aurclock shows true alignment, but we do not let it judge one who cannot escape the Atarax. The Atarax exposes weakness deep within the nature of a being that the Aurclock may not see," says Ulrich. "Also, the Atarax is a construct while the Aurclock... can become fatigued."

"What he is trying to say is congratulations for giving up on your dreams," says Margaret.

"Mar? What the hell?" says Hazel.

"What the hell?" snaps Margaret. "You two still owe me an explanation. What is wrong with my memory? What have you done to me? I *know* this place, but I can't *remember* it. Why is that? You said you needed me to remember. Why don't you start with telling me exactly what it is I've forgotten?"

"Mar—"

"Don't 'Mar' me. Explain! And where the hell is my husband? We've been waiting for three days. But why doesn't it *feel* like three days? And why aren't we hungry? Or thirsty?"

"You know, I noticed the same thing while I was walking with Michael," says Deputy Riggs, still holding Hazel's hand. "I haven't been hungry, thirsty, or tired since being here. He said it had to do with time moving slower here or something. It doesn't completely make sense to me, but I know I should be hungry right now. I'm just, not."

"Do you think she tells you the truth?" asks Margaret. "Do you think she doesn't know? Believe me, she knows. So, tell us Hazel. What's to hide now?"

"It isn't my place," Hazel replies. "I wouldn't do it right." Her tone contains none of her usual hubris.

"We must wait for Michael; and for Michael, we must wait," says Ulrich. "Once Mr. Riggs and your Husband have been read by the Aurclock, all will be revealed; and revealed, all will be."

Asshole.

Ulrich shoots Margaret a disapproving look.

Oh, sorry. Uncle Asshole.

"The Aurclock, what does it do, exactly?" asks Deputy Riggs.

The gloss black walls flash into life. All around the room blue lines glow in the shape of triangles. They match those on the entrance to this place. At first, they are all identical. Then, the triangles reconfigure. The room rumbles as they rotate. Humanoid silhouettes appear next to each as its parts move. The images devolve from symmetric into chaos as their iterations are followed around the room. One silhouette appears per step in the sequence.

"These are the shapes it comes to while reading?" asks Margaret.

How do I know that?

No one speaks. Several shapes transition from the blue glow to red, and a fewer still darken to purple.

"What happens when—" starts Deputy Riggs, but a crack of thunder interrupts him. The silhouettes accompanying the red and purple shapes come alight with flame. Their screams echo off the walls.

It killed them. For what purpose?

"Those are the alignments of the corrupt; and of the corrupt, those are the alignments," says Ulrich. He glances at Margaret.

The remaining Aurclock arrangements and accompanying figures fade. The rumbling subsides, and the room falls silent.

"So, can't you tell I'm one of the good guys? What if your clock gets it wrong?" asks Deputy Riggs.

"After the corruption and the following destruction of the Congregates, the Aeraph decided it was better they be wrong than take another chance of losing Aesteria," says Hazel.

See? You ARE assholes, thinks Margaret.

This time, Hazel and Ulrich both look at her.

"Doesn't murder make the Aeraph corrupt?" asks Deputy Riggs. "That's how it works in my book. What keeps the damn thing from killing them?"

"Nothing. The Aurclock judges without discrimination, therefore it remains covered until needed," replies Hazel. "To protect those still working to save Aesteria, and all the cosmos."

"That's the definition of corruption! What happened to 'Judge not, lest ye be judged'? This is bullshit!" cries Deputy Riggs.

"Language, Stephen," says Michael. He re-enters the chamber from an unseen path. "Douglas has left the Atarax."

"Doug!"

Margaret runs to her husband and wraps her arms around him. He presses his hands into her back, pulling her against him. He kisses her with a passion he has not felt for many years. The regiment of life, parenthood, and familiarity quelled their fire for each other, as happens to many.

They hold their embrace in this place out of time and renew their bond.

* * *

Ulrich clears his throat.

Shut it, ass, thinks Margaret.

"Language, Margaret," says Michael.

Margaret Massey stops cold. She pushes away from her husband.

"You," she says. "You are the one who took my memory. I know your voice."

"Us," say Ulrich and Hazel.

Margaret snaps her head around to face them.

Hazel continues, "It took all three of us. I'm so, so sorry Mar. It was the only way."

"Oh… The only way? To steal my memories? You didn't even do a good job! I've had nightmares of this place for years! I went to therapy! You took me a few times. When I didn't want to live, and you took me, you knew. You knew what was wrong with me and did nothing." Margaret chokes back tears. "You let me suffer and the whole time you knew. You knew!"

Margaret lashes out at Hazel with her mind, a terrible purple bolt of light flashes from her eyes and into Hazel's chest.

Hazel falls to her knees and wails.

"Margaret, look at the table!" shouts Deputy Riggs as he drops to Hazel's side.

She sees a faint glow. It's the same terrible purple she shot into Hazel. The same purple they saw in the shapes in the walls in the alignments of the corrupt.

An understanding grows in her.

"It was the only way…," whispers Hazel.

"…to save me," finishes Margaret Massey.

IV – UNCLE ULRICH

"The only way," echoes Ulrich. He steps back from the cousins.

Margaret bows her head. She lets her shoulders sag.

Deputy Riggs kneels next to Hazel and offers comfort.

Hazel holds herself, and slowly regains composure.

Big Doug Massey consoles his wife.

All eyes avoid Ulrich.

Michael reaches for the fine black cloth covering the Aurclock.

The shrouded figure removes its hood.

It's very similar to Michael, although its feathers are greyish where his are bright white. Its eyes burn with the light of a thousand stars. And though this room is not well lit, it's easy to see by the cloak's shape this Aeraph has tremendous wings.

"We must begin," says Michael.

The only way, thinks Ulrich.

The shrouded figure grasps the opposite side of the cloth. They lift in unison. Their next motions are a dance as the chamber's polished black walls come to life with shades of blue and white. Images flow around them like water.

Michael and his counterpart move to the side in lock step, holding the fine black cloth above the ground. The table is empty.

They fold it and chant. The words are foreign to the group, save Ulrich. He follows the chant in his mind but does not join them. He feels unworthy to ask those who have moved on for aid.

Ta creda es blacin as ta nocht dous jan,
Vi ta nochliht plecis va Nochtvol dou pan.
Wor quo ta ruh fa ta Aurura sha riht,
Mosura tas ruh conta nocht amra liht.

Michael and his partner step, fold, and continue the chant as if mirrors of each other. The inflection and volume increase with each perfect motion.

"What does it mean?" whispers Doug to his wife.

He must not speak during the awakening! thinks Ulrich.

Margaret shoots him a look and then places one finger on her husband's lips and shakes her head. He understands.

TA CREDA ES BLACIN AS TA NOCHT DOUS JAN,

VI TA NOCHLIHT PLECIS VA NOCHTVOL DOU PAN!

The two Aeraph voices rise as thunder. The colors flow around them and speed up as the volume increases. Ulrich sees Deputy Riggs avert his gaze from the vertigo the spinning images create.

WOR QUO TA RUH FA TA AURURA SHA RIHT,
MOSURA TAS RUH CONTA NOCHT AMRA LIHT!

A brilliant blue light explodes up from the table, splashes a circular shape on the ceiling, and cascades down into the walls' spinning lights. The Aeraph are silent as a peaceful and plodding sound flows around them.

Ulrich falls to his knees.

No one goes to him.

His grey face is streaked with tears.

I am not worthy to be here.

A circular object rises from the table and rotates to face them. It is the symbol from the door. Three black triangles are positioned on the front, two large with adjoined bases: the bottom larger with its point exceeding the object's bounds. The other points up, its peak within a smaller triangle that exceeds the topmost bounds. They are the same black as the walls. Glowing white lines bracket the top triangle, parallel to its sides. The whole thing is perfectly symmetrical.

Beautiful.

The sound surrounding them continues to pulse. It carries the depth of hundreds of voices, perhaps more. The blue light does not reflect in the black of the triangles as it swirls and dances.

"The Aurclock," announces Michael.

I have been alone for so long, thinks Ulrich.

He shudders beneath his sobs.

Specters appear all around the room. The walls darken as all available space fills with them. Then, to their horror, they appear deeper, as if the walls have disappeared and they are all standing within an infinite void.

"Language, Stephen," says Michael. "They are here to help."

The large Aeraph helps Ulrich rise. "Old friend. You are worthy. You did not give up. They forgive you."

"I failed them. I did this to them," sputters Ulrich.

"Yes, you did this, but you did not fail. They understood the necessity of the sacrifice. They knew one had to stay, to rebuild, to prepare for the next fight. This fight. The last fight," says Michael.

I cannot face them.

"You can. And you will."

I cannot... face her.

"Perhaps *she* can face *you*."

"Michael, what's happening here? Are these ghosts?" asks Deputy Riggs.

"We call them Auras," answers Michael. His red eyes glisten. "These are the souls of the Congregates. They dwell within the Aurclock, sharing their power with us when needed most. This is the first time they have answered our call in many a Temporan age."

Hazel puts her arm around Ulrich. "Uncle, are you okay?" she asks.

Ulrich looks away.

I cannot face it.

"I have never seen him like this. What is it?" asks Hazel.

"The last time we called the Congregates, there were not as many. Ulrich was left to be a guide to those not destroyed. His task was to bring them here, so they may spend eternity together. The last time we called for them, Ulrich's own Congregate still lived. They are here now," says Michael.

"I saw them on the gallows. I was there when our own people hanged them," says Ulrich.

"Then, Uncle, it wasn't you."

"It was! I made the deal! I invited the snake! I do not deserve to be in their presence. I do not deserve this," cries Ulrich.

I feel my powers increasing, my speech restoring. I feel the sharing of our gifts. I am not worthy. I am NOT worthy. I am NOT WORTHY!

"I AM NOT WORTHY!" screams Ulrich. His voice cracks with three hundred years' worth of solitude and pain.

V – BIG DOUG

The Auras surround them in every direction, as far as they can see.

Shit oh shit oh shit, thinks Doug.

He holds tight against his wife, scared mightily. One specter nears them. He wants to close his eyes and hide in Margaret's shoulder but can't move.

"Doug. Don't be afraid. Do you understand what you see?" asks Margaret.

I've heard that before, he thinks.

The apparition forms into existence. It is Mercy, Margaret's late aunt. Behind her stands her twin sister Dorothy. Their faces are solemn, yet they smile.

"Uh, hello?" says Doug.

"They cannot speak," says Michael, then adds, "Although, they can hear very well. The Aurclock is powered and governed by these souls, the souls of augurs, diviners, mediums, oracles, seers, soothsayers, sibyls, and druids. To use Temporan words."

"Witches?"

The room flashes.

"That name, they dislike."

"Wiccans?" asks Doug, flinching. Ever the scientist, he cannot resist the questions.

Michael considers.

"This title is acceptable."

"How will we be judged? What do they do?"

"They sense the nature of your aura by measuring it against light and dark. They do not usually come out as you see here. The Aurclock works when we beckon the Auras through the Aurchant, as we have done this day. The Aurclock face re-arranges based on the Aural judgement; whether it be Temporan, animal, object, or plane."

"Objects have auras?"

"Of course. All things have auras."

"Wow," says Doug. "Who knew?"

"We did," answers Michael.

"Will we be judged now?"

"You have already been judged. This Aura has deemed you worthy," says Michael. He motions to Aunt Mercy. She and Dorothy nod and smile sweetly.

Doug bows to them. *Thank you*, he thinks.

"What about Riggs?"

"Yeah, what about me?" asks Deputy Riggs.

"You must still be judged," says Michael.

The room is quiet and dark. No light shines except that of the Aurclock. Many Auras return to it, but not all. It glows blue once more.

"Stephen, approach the Aurclock," commands Michael.

Deputy Riggs approaches. "What if I don't pass?" he asks.

"Steve, you're the best person I know. I love you. You'll be fine," says Hazel.

"Wow. I could die right now, you know." He smiles at her.

"If the Auras judge you unworthy, your end will be instantaneous. There will be no pain. We are nothing if not merciful," says Michael.

"Yeah, sure. Shit, can't I just leave? Can't I just go back home?"

"You are here now. This is the only way. A battle is coming, and you are part of it. We must know when the ultimate aid is required, you will not hesitate to give it."

"Okay, okay. That's not ominous or anything." Deputy Riggs breathes in and out heavily. He thrusts his arms down to his sides and pumps his fists a few times. "Okay, okay. Let's do this. Shit," he says.

He's nuts, thinks Doug, in awe of Rigg's bravery.

Michael raises his arms to the Aurclock and spreads his mighty wings. Then, he chants,

Wor quo ta ruh fa ta aurura sha right,
mosura tam ruh conta nocht amra liht.

"Oh my," says Big Doug Massey.

The triangles of the clock rotate. The lines spin. Deputy Riggs squints.

"You must not look away," says Michael.

The shapes move and rotate. The blue darkens as the triangles slow.

"No," whispers Hazel.

"Hazel, I love you, too. I'm sorry I failed."

Oh no, thinks Doug. *He's not going to make it.*

The Aurclock flashes. A purple light lingers.

Hazel screams.

The light fades and Doug sees no one remains in front of the Aurclock. Its face rearranged so the triangles are side by side, one points down, the other points up. A glowing circle connects them in the center. The glow is dark, dark blue. The next spectral color would have been violet. Purple.

Where there was once symmetry only chaos remains.

I can't believe this, thinks Doug.

Margaret gasps.

Hazel shudders.

Deputy Riggs moans.

Doug peers into the dark at the table's base. "I'll be damned. He made it."

"Language, Douglas," says you-know-who.

"Thanks for the vote of confidence," says Deputy Riggs. He coughs once and props himself up on his elbow.

"Steve!" shouts Hazel and leaps to where he lay.

"How'd I do? Did I pass?"

She kisses him in a way that rivals Doug's embrace of Margaret from earlier.

"Yes! Hell yes!" yells Doug.

They do not stop.

It's not a competition, thinks Doug.

Michael speaks with a parental tone, "Stephen, I am relieved. The shape of the Aurclock is five past seven, as far as one can go without succumbing to death. Six past seven would be failure."

"Well, even a 'C' passes med school," says Deputy Riggs, finally coming up for air.

"I do not understand."

Margaret, Doug, Hazel, and Deputy Riggs all laugh. A precious moment of joy and camaraderie.

"Wait. Six past seven?" asks Deputy Riggs. "I didn't think you guys understood time? But here, this is a clock, and it's read like a clock... so..."

Michael's feathers flutter. "I was happy you lived."

"Was?" asks Deputy Riggs. "Was that a joke?"

"Was it humorous?" answers Michael. He smiles. It is hideous but kind, I assure you.

I think we'll be alright, thinks Doug.

"Any registering device can be a clock, and minutes are useful as coordinate measurements, which time is. We once taught your sailors this," adds Michael.

"You taught our sailors? Human sailors? From Earth?" asks Doug.

"Indeed. We were once unconcealed to Temporans. We aided each other and shared our knowledge openly."

"Now that's a story I'd like to hear!" says Doug.

"It is a story worth telling," responds Michael. "A story of a time when we helped each other."

"We will need all the help we can muster if we are to defeat the Nochtvol," says Ulrich.

"The what?" asks Doug, turning to Ulrich.

No one answers before one of the Auras shoots over to Ulrich. Unlike the others, this one glows red.

That one looks angry, thinks Doug.

The specter's hands grasp Ulrich's face. It is a woman. She is fiercely beautiful.

Ulrich whispers, "I am sorry I did not come sooner. I was afraid..."

She cocks her head, disappointment on her face. Then she leans into Ulrich for a kiss.

Everyone's making out around here, thinks Doug.

You're an idiot, an intruding voice says in his head.

Doug looks at Margaret. "Was that you? Can you read my thoughts?" he asks, dismayed.

"I can," she says. "I haven't always, just since we got here."

"Oh no. That's not good," Doug says and smiles at Margaret. She smiles back. On another day, discovering his wife had telepathic powers would have floored him. "Do you know who that is with Ulrich?"

"I have no idea."

"That is Mercy Redgrave," interjects Michael.

Like Redgrave Manor? thinks Doug.

"The very same," says Michael.

"Oh, come on! You can read my mind too?"

"Your thoughts are very loud."

"Well, they're also very smart," says Doug.

"They are, honey," says Margaret.

"How does Uncle Ulrich know Mercy Redgrave?" asks Hazel. "She lived three hundred years ago. She built the house Aunt Mercy left us."

"Mercy Redgrave was the last one on the gallows. She is why he kept going. Why he has never stopped trying to rebuild," Michael motions to Ulrich, "Why he taught you two even after he lost others. Why he has never stopped fighting. Mercy Redgrave is Ulrich Redgrave's wife and namesake of your own dear Aunt."

Shocked expressions pass between Hazel and Margaret.

They're communicating, Doug thinks.

The two cousins look at him at the same time.

Oh no. Not her, too.

"Yes, her too," says Hazel.

"I'm sorry about what I may or may not have thought about you in the past or perhaps what I may think in the future."

"Oh, I don't care what you think of me. It's the things you think about Mar I don't like."

Big Doug Massey feels the blood of embarrassment rise in his cheeks.

"Uncle, why didn't you tell us?" asks Margaret. "And how is it possible?"

"Come now, you know I have been around a long, long time. Michael is better equipped to explain—"

Michael and the other Aeraph dash to front of the room, their respective feathers go sleek and tight to their skulls with a whoosh.

"Ithex, there is someone at the door," says Michael.

Ithex raises three fingers.

Michael's eyes widen. "Three someones. All of you, stay here and be silent. Ithex, guard the entry. I will return."

Michael shoots off like the wind. He disappears as soon as he hits the Trinus walls' black surface.

"Jesus, that's amazing," says Doug.

"I've seen it before and it's still pretty awesome," echoes Deputy Riggs.

Ithex bristles and raises one finger up to his lips to shoosh the men.

"I've seen that before, too," says Riggs.

"Not as awesome?" says Doug.

"Shut up, idiots," says Hazel.

Ithex ruffles his feathers and swats at Deputy Riggs.

Then, he raises his hands, stands his full eight-foot height, and closes his eyes.

The Trinus walls alight once more. This time they show the entrance to the Congregate of Aesteria. The clarity and depth are such that one could be fooled into believing they are actually outside.

From this display, they see the intruders.

Oh no, thinks Doug.

"Is that Charles Horne and Cody McLean?" he asks.

"It can't be," says Margaret.

"There's someone else with them, on the ground," says Deputy Riggs.

They watch as Michael approaches the figure lying on the ground and places his hands on their head. They do not appear to be moving. Michael closes his eyes and shakes his head, then speaks to the other two boys.

"Something terrible has happened," says Ulrich.

"Oh. Oh no," says Hazel. "Steve, I'm so sorry."

In horrible clarity they see streaks of tears through the dirt on Cody and Charles' faces.

Doug's thoughts are on Alice as he places his hand on Deputy Riggs' shoulder.

A soft 'no' escapes the lips of Deputy Stephen Riggs as he recognizes his little brother.

"Mom, I'm sorry," is all he says.

* * *

Michael enters the room with Mitch Riggs dangling in his arms, the other two boys following closely behind.

Ithex glares at Michael.

"Ithex, I deactivated the Atarax," says Michael. "I will speak for those who have carried their fallen across these lands. I will accept the consequences of my action. Come, I need your help if we are to save this one. Twilight works in him as I speak."

"He's alive?" asks Deputy Riggs. Hope carries on his words.

"Such as it is," responds Michael. "All of you, push your power toward him. You each have your own aura, now is the time to use it."

"What?"

Margaret, Hazel, Doug, Cody, Charles, and Ulrich look at the body. Ulrich raises his arm towards him first, and the other six Temporans follow. They see the Auras, led by Mercy Redgrave, do the same. A low hum, not unlike a mother's, grows in the room.

Stephen Riggs, too, raises his arm toward his brother and closes his eyes.

Michael and Ithex place their hands on Mitch, one from each side. They spread their wings. The Trinus walls glow a comforting blue, and the hum flows through them as a mid-summer song. Some Auras evaporate to mist and return to the Aurclock's plasma, its face returned to the simple symmetry they saw before.

It's beautiful, thinks a glassy eyed Doug, overwhelmed with emotion. *They say they are not Angels. I'm not so sure.*

Concentrate, dear. He needs you. Margaret smiles at him, then turns her focus back to Mitch.

Green streaks of light flow from Margaret's and Hazel's fingers. They flow out slowly and enter the boy.

They look like sisters, thinks Doug.

"Look," says Cody.

Mitch's chest rises and falls with breath. Then, the same dark purple they saw earlier shoots out of him in a chaotic, lightning-filled sphere. It hovers in the room before Ithex grasps it. He squawks. The remaining Auras fall to mist and enter the sphere until it glows bright yellow. It vibrates violently. Ithex growls as he fights to contain it.

Michael joins him.

The sphere explodes in a shower of sparks. Little meteors fall all around them in the dark room. The two Aeraph clasp hands and crow their victory.

Stephen goes to his brother, laying on the table beneath the Aurclock.

"Mitch, buddy. Can you hear me? C'mon, bro."

Mitch's eyes open. He does not recognize his older brother. He does not speak. His eyes close.

"Mitch. Mitch! Mitchell, come back, dammit!" cries Deputy Riggs.

A warm hand grasps him. "Stephen, let him rest. He needs time to regenerate that which was lost. It will take, as you might say, some time."

"Regenerate? What?"

"Your brother was some ways into conversion into Nochtvol, an instrument of Midwatch. It is a miracle we could expulse it."

He did not use miracle as a figure of speech, thinks Doug. *What in the hell have I gotten myself into?*

Michael blinks at Doug.

Sorry, he thinks.

He thinks about his work. Trying to prove time does not exist. Here he stands in a place where it does not, and the solution moves farther away. He feels that it may not be meant to be understood. That it may be magic. Mostly, though, he thinks of Alice. She has been missing much longer than Mitch. He worries she will not be so easily recovered, based on what he has just seen.

Michael, Ithex, and Ulrich approach the boys.

Michael speaks to them.

"You have done a great thing, carrying him when you could have left him. I am sorry for what has happened to you."

Ulrich nods. Doug notices he looks past each of them, moving his gaze back and forth, not making eye contact. The boys do the same to Ulrich.

That's odd, thinks Doug.

Charles says something quietly to Ulrich and Michael. They shake their heads.

"It cannot be undone," says Ulrich. His brow furrows with regret and pain. "We have tried."

"What cannot be undone?" asks Doug, unable to help himself.

Ithex's odd Aeraph face fills with concern.

"It appears Midwatch has gifted these two with illimni, as it has to Ulrich. They can see he has one, as he can see theirs."

"A what? What did he do to them? What did it do to my brother?" asks Deputy Riggs.

"Your brother, fortunately, does not have this gift."

"Illimni," repeats Doug, "What is that?"

Michael's shoulders slump.

"There is much to explain. Mercy Redgrave, Midwatch, illimni, the Congregates, all of it," responds Michael, "if you are to fight for us, it is best you know why we fight. Else, the Shadows take you."

CHAPTER 11

Michael's Story

To their credit, they do not look away.

I – THE GALLOWS

"Now, let us tell you a story," speaks Michael.

The Trinus walls flash dark and bright. The flash stings their retinas.

"This light is the meeting of the two wolves, the yin and the yang of spectral divination, where light and dark meet," says Michael.

The room darkens, their eyes adjust, and presented before them is a festival of sorts. It reminds Cody and Charles of a Renaissance Fair. An energetic crowd carries with it something nefarious. And a little depressing.

"This is not the Beginning, but this is where *we* will begin," says Michael. "This is the day the Congregate of Tempora fell. Watch."

* * *

All manners of folk stood in the mud of an olde town square. They pushed and shoved their way to the front of the thrall, to a courthouse with a great pergola built upon a stage before it. Children laughed and played at their parents' feet, horses were hitched to posts or hobbled on the perimeter, criers shouted news, and at least one baker yelled about having fresh bread. Not much different than any fair or festival they had ever been to. The sky was grey, and the clouds were black. The observers attributed this to an effect of the Trinus ceiling, and not the way things appeared this day.

They neared the stage. This was no celebration, and the structure was no pergola. A hangman prepared hundreds of nooses.

The crowd was dirty, gritty, angry, and excited. A cold hunger reflected in their eyes and a snarl crept upon their lips. These were the faces of vengeance, of a folk who believed it taught a lesson. Nearer the courthouse, their garb and cleanliness improved. Those of higher station stood nearer the stage, but as is true even now, they were no less full of the lust and primal excitement riding upon the storm of righteous vengeance.

Righteous vengeance over whom, you ask?

* * *

"Notice the looks in their eyes. They feel they have won a great victory," says Michael. "From the Aurlibrum; beware righteousness, it exists only in the minds of those who cling to the belief of their infallibility. Being right holds no sway over the oft-cited pretext for prejudice and bigotry."

Hazel places her face in Deputy Riggs' chest.

"You must watch," says Michael.

"I know what happens."

"Watch," commands Michael.

Even Ithex, standing as a work of marble near the entry, jerks ever so slightly.

Hazel watches.

* * *

The crowd cheered with each drop of the platform, with each tightening of the rope, with each yelp for the last sweet breath of life, with each crack of a breaking neck.

The names of the accused, their crime, and their sentence were read each time the gallows were replenished, and each time, they were asked for final words. Each time, they said, "We will keep watch; and keep watch, we will."

CRACK!

And that would be it. Then, the next four would come up, their names would be read, and their promise would be made.

* * *

Ulrich sobs. Through tortured eyes he watches.

Michael speaks, "From the Aurlibrum; beware the trio of judgement, accompanied by its brothers, prejudice and bias, lurking within the minds of those who perceive themselves as righteous. Each individual leads their unique existence, waging personal battles known only to themselves. To cast judgement is to disregard the struggle of others, and in turn, tarnish one's own integrity."

Ulrich whimpers.

* * *

The last three of the Temporan Congregate mounted the stage and stood beneath their burdens. The last they recognized as someone they had met quite recently.

The final space was empty.

"Mercy Redgrave, wife of Ulrich Redgrave. You stand accused of practicing witchcraft and are as such an accused witch. You are additionally accused of attempting to recruit and assimilate the innocent into the practice of witchcraft and are hereby deemed a threat to society and humanity before the good people of Portsmouth, New Hampshire, as witnesses on behalf of God Himself. As we have not the means to hold trial based upon spectral evidence, and due to the other-worldly nature of your crime, you stand merely accused on this earthly plane. Your guilt will be determined in the next life. As such, your sentence is banishment via death. Do you have any final words?"

Mercy Redgrave looked upon the crowd. Her eyes carried the worry of a mother who watched her child go down a dark path. She smiled when she finally spoke, "He will keep watch; and keep watch, he will."

In the Trinus, they heard the whispers.

Did she say he?

Who is he?

We heard wrong, she said the same as all of 'em.

She must mean her mister.

That space next to her was for him. They ain't found him. Yet.

The man on the gallows continued, "Mercy Redgrave, leader of the accused witches that lay now before you, we hope to find your husband post haste. You shan't wait in Hell for him long."

The man nodded, and the platform fell.

II – THE FOOL

"1692," says Ulrich.

"1692," echoes Michael. "As the gallows-man spoke, in what you may know as Portsmouth, New Hampshire."

"Redgrave Manor," whispers Doug, head bowed.

"Indeed."

This voice is deep. It vibrates through them and makes their teeth chatter.

Ithex steps forward and continues, "The house belonged to both Mercy Redgrave and Mercy Montgomery. Redgrave Manor and what it protects are bound to all who carry the blood of the Congregates. As they do." He motions to Ulrich, Hazel, and Margaret. "I was the Aeraph tasked with protecting it."

Michael approaches Ithex. Ithex attempted to self-banish several times since the Temporan Congregate fell, each time stopped by Michael.

"Peace," speaks Michael to Ithex. He places his hand on the larger Aeraph's shoulder. "Peace."

"So, they're witches?" asks Deputy Riggs.

"No. Not witches. Accused of being witches? Yes." With each word, Ulrich steps closer to Deputy Riggs, his voice increases in volume, his fists clench, "Yes, most definitely *accused* of being witches. Would it matter to you if they were? Would it bother you? Would you want them to perform tricks for you until you decided you were jealous of what they had, or something happened THAT YOU NEEDED A SCAPEGOAT AND THEN YOU WOULD TURN YOUR BACK? WHEN THEY NEEDED YOU MOST?"

Michael crashes down to the ground between Ulrich and Deputy Riggs. He grasps Ulrich's shoulders and speaks, "Peace, brother. Peace."

Ulrich slouches, Margaret and Hazel come to his side.

"I didn't mean anything," says Deputy Riggs. "But, they do have powers?"

"Yes, they have powers," responds Michael. "They can commune with nature and the metaphysical world, much like Aeraph. This cosmic attunement is the beginning of being released from the constraints of time, as your kind were once released from the constraints of the oceans. The event you have witnessed, and others like it, slowed the progression. Some Temporans understood the universe and we Aeraph aided them. We allowed control of one of our gates to be maintained from the Temporan side. For the first time, we allowed passage between our worlds to be controlled elsewhere with merely a guard in Aesteria to monitor traffic. The location was your Hampton, which lay in an area that showed heightened aural awareness, on the site that would become Redgrave Manor, named for its protectors."

Ulrich reaches out to Ithex. "I, too, failed," he says.

Michael sighs.

"From the Aurlibrum; beware acknowledgment of failure, it haunts the minds of those who have relinquished effort. In life's grand equation, both failure and success stand as equals."

"Question?"

Big Doug Massey has raised his hand. Michael blinks and calls upon him. "Yes, Douglas?"

"What's the Aurlibrum?"

"Ah. The Aurlibrum is the collected tenets of the Congregates. It is the record by which Aeraph live and govern realms. It is the very record that Midwatch now denigrates."

"I would like to see it."

"It is not kept in a place where you can. Although, perhaps I can recite it to you when it is more convenient."

"I would like that. May I ask another question?"

"Of course."

"Ulrich, where were you when your wife was hanged?"

"Whoa, man. Brutal. Did you have to ask like that?" says Cody McLean.

Charles chuckles, which receives glares from everyone except Cody, none fiercer than that from Ithex.

"Oh… I'm sorry. I laugh when I'm nervous. It wasn't funny. I'm sorry about your wife, Mr. Ulrich. It's just the way he asked. It was… brutal…"

"It was," says Doug, "I'm sorry. I mean, how did you get away? They caught them all, but not you. How is that possible?"

"The conflict required a compromise," says Ulrich, "so I compromised."

"You traded your wife and all those people for a compromise?" asks Margaret, "With who?"

Ulrich drops his gaze to the floor. The Trinus walls still show the gallows of Portsmouth, but barren of people. One body lay beneath the stage. The body of Mercy Redgrave. Her Aura stands next to the sulking Ulrich. She stares at her own body, spectral tears upon her spectral face.

"Uncle Ulrich! With who?" pushes Margaret.

"Midwatch," Ulrich says quietly, "Midwatch promised to stop what they were doing if we made a deal. Promised to let me live to honor said deal. The rules were simple. Midwatch would not destroy any more congregates, and we would not attempt to create one. And neither side would speak of the gates nor travelling between worlds to Aesteria unless it was a necessary transaction between only those who already knew."

"That's a complicated set of rules," says Hazel.

"And it didn't even matter," says Ulrich. "He played with us. I was such a fool."

"Uncle…"

"I WAS A FOOL! I AM A FOOL! I LET HIM TURN MY STUDENT INTO AN ILLIMNI! FOR ME! THEY DIED SO

I COULD LIVE! AND IT DID NOT MATTER! NOTHING WAS SAVED! NOW, ALL WILL BE LOST!" Ulrich breathes heavily and holds his chest, "Even you," he finishes, and drops to one knee. Mercy stands behind him and Michael attempts to lift him. He pushes them away. "Leave me," he says.

"It did matter. All of it mattered. Just not how we thought it would," says Michael.

III – THE AGREEMENT

The Trinus flashes onto a different scene. It shows Ulrich grasping a snake. In the distance are the same gallows with the same continuous groups of four falling to their deaths.

The room darkens, and the scene changes. It shows Ulrich standing before a black cloud, not unlike the black clouds hanging over the gallows.

"Is that the one we just saw? The one that has Tiffany and Alice?" asks Cody.

Michael nods. "Watch," he says.

Cody watches.

They watch the cloud and Ulrich interact. They watch until Ulrich flashes back whence he came, leaving Midwatch pulsing alone. Then, with awesome speed, Midwatch flashes across Aesteria. It goes through a gate with a broken boulder beside it, disappears, and comes back. It stops over the boulder and waits.

A figure comes through the boulder gate.

"No way," says Charles, "that's Mr. Philips. That's Tiff's dad."

"That's my boss," says Big Doug Massey.

"...and mine," says Hazel Montgomery.

"I never trusted that dude," says Deputy Riggs.

"Shadow-Bringer!" booms Ithex.

* * *

"Well?" asked Leonard Philips.

"He agreed. We can use the gate only for necessary trade and transaction as established."

"And he agreed to the one in Brewster Township?"

"He did and said it seemed a good choice for compromise since it was far from anything, which was true at that time."

"Oh, we'll change that," Leonard said with a laugh.

"I wish I had gotten to see the final hanging," said Midwatch.

"Can't you go back?"

"Yes, but he will be there each time. The grey man will always stop me."

IV – THE CALL

"What was Midwatch doing?" asks Deputy Riggs.

No one answers.

He adds, "The first part of the deal was Midwatch had to promise to stop what they were doing. What was it doing?"

"Nothing," answers Ulrich.

"What?"

"We believed Midwatch was destroying the Congregates because it kept appearing each time one was caught. Always as a snake. This was not the case. From the Aurlibrum; beware assumption, it exists only in the mind of one who seeks answers without observation."

"Who *was* destroying the Congregates?"

"No one," says Michael. "Other Temporans decided through their own lack of understanding to persecute them, try them, and kill them. Much like we are doing now, Midwatch observed this while it was still Hesperus. It and the Shadow-Bringer used the knowledge to appear to Ulrich Redgrave as having control over the genocide of the Temporan Congregate. It was a ruse. They did this until Ulrich agreed to their terms, knowing full well he had the ability to re-form a Congregate and fight them. Like Midwatch said, the grey man will always defeat him."

"Their own people? Their own friends did this to them?" asks Charles.

"A common Temporan act," bristles Ithex.

"The Garage House," says Cody, "the one I broke."

"Excuse me?" asks Ulrich.

"The Garage House. The house is on the corner of Perez and Donavan Drive back home, just outside the high school. It has that one weird garage on it. It's what we came through to get here, where we saw the ghost of Alice, and where I first broke the code that caused all this," Cody says. He shudders, his eyes crazed, and then he screams, "I KILLED MY MOM! I KILLED MY MOM! I KILLED MY MOM!"

Cody tries to run, but Ithex grabs him.

Charles goes to him. "Is that true, buddy? Did you? Did you really?"

"I did," Cody cries. "I used the power it gave me, and I made her fall. She broke her neck, and I left her! I LEFT HER!"

"Can't you guys' undo this with time travel or whatever you guys do?" Charles asks Michael.

"It does not work this way," Michael says, adding, "Midwatch killed your mother, Cody. It controlled you. It committed this act. Not you."

"HA! That's where you're wrong. I wanted to do it. Midwatch just gave me permission. I'm bad. I need to go. I DON'T BELONG HERE! TA CREDA ES BLACIN AS TA NOCHT—"

"NO!" shouts Ithex. "You must not call the Aurclock. The Aurchant is not for you.

"Let it judge me," begs Cody, head bowed. "Let it be over…"

Hazel Montgomery kneels in front of him and takes his hands. She speaks softly, "Cody, there isn't one person anywhere that hasn't wished their parents dead at least once. What you thought and felt was normal. But we don't act on that because we love our families. It's okay to be mad, but Midwatch took that from you and made you believe you wanted your mother dead so badly that it was your decision and your decision alone. It wasn't."

Cody whimpers, "…but I did it."

Hazel squeezes his hands. "It used your own anxieties against you."

"This is one thing Midwatch practices," says Michael, "It takes a dark thought and enhances it. Encourages it. It is one of Midwatch's key weapons in acquiring soul-minds. Influencing those with existing thought of injury or self-harm will do so when they otherwise would not. This is the darkness. This is the shadow we fight."

"A war against intrusive thought," says Hazel.

"*l'appel du vide*," says Margaret.

"What?" asks Big Doug.

"It's French. The Call of the Void. It's the kind of thought you have when standing on a high place and think 'what if I jumped'."

"Or, if you're driving down the street and think, 'what if I run over that guy bicycling in my lane'," says Deputy Riggs.

They all look at him.

"Ah, not quite," says Margaret.

"Remember the Aurclock, Stephen. You were very close," says Michael.

"Yeah, I already passed that test. I don't see how they're different."

"They are, dear," says Hazel.

"Bro. Harsh," says Mitch Riggs, leaning on one arm. "I've had the strangest dream."

"Mitch!" yells a joyous Deputy Stephen Riggs.

"Oh buddy, do we have a story for you," says Charles. "It's great to see you awake, Mitch."

Charles hugs him. They are both surprised.

"We must let the Aurclock judge him," booms the voice of Ithex.

"Who? Mitch?"

"No. The one who ended his mother. The one who has served Midwatch."

"Cody? Cody is clean, man. If you test him, you'll need to test all of us," said Charles.

"So be it."

Michael interrupts, "Ithex, calm. There will be judgement enough for all of us in the coming fight. He will fight well for redemption. And for his mother. Isn't that right, master Cody?" Michael peers at Cody with his red eyes. He looks into his soul.

"Um. Yes, sir?" responds Cody. Michael raises a feathered brow.

"Yes, sir," says Cody, without question.

"We have more story to tell. Watch."

They watch.

V – THE GIFT

The Trinus flashes onto a scene showing Ulrich with a young woman. She rests and he kneels beside her. He is less grey than the Ulrich in the Trinus is now.

They watch as Ulrich teaches the girl the ways of the Aura. He shows her how to commune with a tree, how to send and receive words and images by thought, how to prepare elixirs, and how to attune to a gate and use its power to transport from, and to, anywhere. And any time.

They transport into Aesteria, and the real Ulrich turns from the images.

"You must watch," reminds Michael.

Ulrich watches.

* * *

"Uncle Ulrich am I a witch?" asked Jutte. She had been a natural mystic, the best student he had found in a hundred years.

"A vulgar word. A dark word. No, you are not a witch, and neither am I. We are slightly more in tune and in control of nature than others. Many say we are druidic," replied Ulrich. He smiled and said, "But I am rather fond of wizard or magician; and of magician or wizard, I am very fond."

"Do witches exist?"

"Not that we are aware. It is possible, as are all things, but not that we have seen."

"Well, how do you know we are not witches?"

"Another excellent question, but also a dangerous one."

"Should we be worried for ourselves?" asked Jutte.

"More each day; and each day, more."

"We must repair the gates."

"Yes, but for the two of us to perform what is necessary to infuse them, you first need to feel the motives of Midwatch. The gate must act like a filter. We cannot close them without a strong Congregate, but we can control them. To do this, I must perform an exercise with you I already regret. It will change you. I will not force you; and force you, I will not."

"Uncle. We must repair the gates."

"Jutte, once this is done, and your eyes and mind have been opened, you will carry a darkness in you which will never leave. Like me, you will have an unnaturally long life, but an unfortunate one marked forever by a dark cloud. Like me, your life will become grey; and grey, your life…"

Jutte reached out and took Ulrich's ashen hands in her small pink ones.

"Uncle Ulrich. I understand. But we must repair the gates. What have all the lectures, lessons, and repeating been leading to if not this? Is this not the purpose of what you do? Why do you teach? You must do this so you can find others. So you can keep teaching. You must save us."

"So be it. Close your eyes and focus on your thoughts. Lean from the bright and focus on the dark. If you think of an ant, squish it; if you think of a dog, picture it rotting; if you think of me, wish me dead."

Jutte gasped.

"It will not be as hard as you think," said Ulrich. "It is in the nature of all of us. What are you seeing in your mind right now?"

"I see a baby."

"What is it doing?"

"It's playing with a toy duck and cooing. It's lying on its back and kicking with excitement."

"Darker."

"It's crying. Screaming. It's hungry but no one is answering it's cries."

"Darker."

"It's shivering in its misery. The baby is grunting and angry."

"DARKER!"

"WHY? Why is this the way?"

"Focus, Jutte! They are thoughts only and cannot hurt you; and hurt you, they cannot."

"The baby is angry. I am mad at the baby because it will not be quiet. The crying is so loud."

"Darker!"

"It will not shut up. I try to comfort it. Its cries are filled with hate and betrayal. I hate this baby. How I wish it would be quiet."

"More! Let the Shadows in!"

"I think how easy it would be to smother the baby into silence. Sweet silence from its cries! I could crush its skull if I wanted!" Jutte said with a sob.

Ulrich squeezed her hands tighter, and a loud noise boomed like thunder, followed by a spinning sensation, and then the smell of sulfur.

"Open your eyes; and your eyes, open."

* * *

The group in the Trinus see Ulrich and Jutte enter Midwatch.

"This is where I failed her," whispers Ulrich.

In the scene, when they leave Midwatch a fine black dust floats in their place.

Shortly after, Midwatch appears to absorb it.

"The cloud tasted the new power's remnants. This was when Midwatch knew Ulrich worked to rebuild the Congregates," says Michael. "Midwatch craved Jutte. It felt her power and obsessed over harvesting her. On this trip, it succeeded. Watch."

* * *

"Everything will be alright," he said to her, although his face said otherwise.

"Hello, old friend. I see you have brought a gift," said Midwatch.

"No. This one is not for you."

"Oh, but I think she is. It seems you have forgotten our deal."

Jutte attempted to speak, but Midwatch fixed her with a bolt of purple light.

"What deal? We have no deal."

Midwatch pulsed. Then it laughed.

"It wasn't yet you, was it? It was a later you. No matter, it is not of my concern that you are of time, and I am not. You made a deal with me, whether you or a future you, and by teaching this one, you have broken it."

"I do not understand."

"I will help you understand."

Midwatch shot a continuous bolt of energy into Jutte. She screamed for a long time. "She is very strong!" Midwatch laughed. "She will serve us well!"

Ulrich reached out with both arms and shot a green bolt into Midwatch, which it absorbed with barely a flutter.

"Maybe one day, that will be a meaningful strike, but not today, Temporan," called Midwatch as Jutte lifted off the ground.

* * *

Cody and Charles watch the scene, remembering what happened to Jenny.

To their credit, they do not look away.

* * *

"Look here! A gift for you! I have relearned the art of creating illimni with my friend Lenny! His was a nice young Temporan named Andy. They were a good match, but you and this one, oh, this is a perfect match!" Midwatch cackled.

Half of Jutte's soul flew into Ulrich, knocking him down. The other half Midwatch kept for itself.

When Ulrich stood, he resembled the grey man who now stood in the Trinus. Midwatch told him what it had created and the long, tortured life it granted him, then the memory faded.

* * *

"Jutte. My sweet, sweet Jutte," says Ulrich.

"Is she with you now?" asks Hazel.

"We can see her," responds Charles. "Cody and I can see her. She's floating behind him."

"How?"

Michael explains the horror of illimni and how they are created.

"Oh. Oh my," says Doug.

Hazel and the others look at the boys.

"Cody? Charles?" says Hazel, then asks a question whose answer she is afraid to hear, "Who are your illimni?"

Cody nods to Charles, and Charles speaks, "Ms. Montgomery, our illimni is Jenny Noble."

Hazel's hand goes to her mouth.

"What was that?" asks Deputy Riggs, "You say this happened to Jenny Noble? She's dead? How did this happen? How did she get here? Someone has to get them here to become an illimniati or whatever, right?"

Cody grabs Charles' arm with both of his. He leans in, as a child would who hides behind its parent.

"Cody McLean. What did you do?" demands Riggs.

"Midwatch controlled him, Stephen."

"I don't give a fu—"

Ithex stands in front of him. He bends down so his furious red eyes stare deep into Deputy Rigg's grey ones.

"I told you, Stephen; language," says Michael. "Ithex, calm."

"I brought her here. This is where we were. The missing day. I convinced her and Charles to come here. I gave her to Midwatch. I didn't know. I didn't know!" wails Cody.

"You idiots—"

Ithex growls at Deputy Riggs.

He strains to no avail against Ithex.

"You kids lied to me. Both of you. I could've saved her."

"Well, actually, I didn't lie because I still don't remember," says Charles, "and as for you saving her from this? I highly doubt it."

"Come here and say that to my face," Deputy Riggs says while struggling, but Ithex continues to hold him.

"Whoa, bro. Take it easy," says Mitch. "These dudes also saved my life. It's bad here, sure, but we're all here. Michael, is that your name? Weird. Do you think we can defeat whatever this is?"

Michael considers.

"Uncertain."

"Well holy crap don't go into motivational speaking. We should take a break. The Cody and the grey guy getting tortured show is hard to watch," says Mitch, who is for the moment the sanest being in the room.

VI – THE GRUDGE

Michael and Ithex make it clear they do not have time for a break.

The show continues.

Ithex holds Deputy Riggs as the Trinus once more spins into motion.

They hear an axe splitting wood. It is steady and rhythmic.

A sky and trees come into view, and a fall day in New England often found on postcards and puzzles spreads out before them. In the movies, it's always autumn on the East Coast.

* * *

A little girl ran towards the unmistakable profile of Redgrave Manor. As she approached, the same little girl came out of the house to meet her.

"Dorothy! Dorothy! Where is mother? It's Gerald!" said the one approaching.

"What is it, Mercy? What's happened to Gerald?" said the other.

"The axe. He was placing wood as father was chopping. There was a snake in the wood stack. The axe is in his... in his... it was an accident! Because of the snaaaaaake. It's my faaaaaaault! Ohhhhh."

* * *

Hazel Montgomery and Margaret Massey gasp.

"Mom?" whispers Hazel.

"Both our moms," echoes Margaret.

Hazel is awestruck. "Are we seeing Mercy and Dorothy Parker? Our Mothers? And Gerald? Is that Gerald Montgomery Jr.? My father?"

Michael raises a down-covered eyebrow. "It is," he says.

"We were told he died of an aneurysm right after I was born," says Hazel. "Now I guess I know what caused it."

"Who is that one-armed man?" asks Margaret.

Michael speaks with a hint of disbelief, "Do you not recognize your grandfather?"

"We wouldn't, no one ever spoke of him. They told us he died in the war."

"Interesting. From the Aurlibrum; beware the well-intentioned untruth; it exists only in the mind to protect the moment, but later tarnishes the life."

"Now her, we recognize," says Hazel.

* * *

Shirley Parker, their grandmother, ran down the hill from Redgrave Manor. They saw the one-armed man held the boy as he groaned. The axe was no longer buried in his skull, in its place a clean split produced a waterfall of blood.

"Dorothy!" Shirley shouted as she arrived. She waved her hands. "Dorothy, go back to the house. Your father and I will take care of this."

Dorothy nodded slowly, suddenly calm and quiet.

The snake reappeared. It lashed out and bit her, but before she could look down, the snake was gone again. On her right forearm were two little pin holes, about an inch apart, marking where its teeth had been.

Dorothy fainted.

"Dammit," said Shirley as she placed her hands on Gerald Montgomery Junior's head wound. She chanted. Mr. Parker's eyes glazed over, as did the boy's. The chant sounded not unlike the one Michael and Ithex used to summon the Aurclock.

She repeated her cadence three times, then removed her blood covered hands and went to her daughter. To their amazement, only a hairless scar remained where the split had been.

Shirley uttered a similar chant over her daughter until she came to.

Once Mr. Parker, Gerald Junior, and Dorothy were conscious, Shirley Parker said unto them, "Go ye into the manor. I have business in the carriage house."

They went without remark or question.

* * *

"She's a witch," blurts Deputy Riggs like a dumbass.

"STEPHEN!" bellows Michael.

Ithex squeezes him until his eyes bulge.

After a brief pause, Michael speaks, "Ithex, calm."

Ithex relaxes.

Charles giggles, which earns him a red side-eye from Michael.

"Sorry," he says.

"She had powers. Like we do. She passed them to us," says Margaret. "Why didn't she teach them? They could've shown us how to use it." Her face fills with shame. She adds, "How to control it."

"She would not let me teach your mothers," says Ulrich. "After the snake, she felt it was safer. I cannot teach without the mother's consent. It was her plan to hide you both, knowing Midwatch and the snake hunted you."

The Trinus walls return to black as Shirley Parker enters the carriage house of Redgrave Manor.

"What's with the snake?" asks Mitch. "Did it want to kill that little girl?"

"The snake required the blood of the line to find the descendants," says Ulrich. "Once it had that, Midwatch could track the Aura using the gates."

"The Garage House was a gate, right?" asks Charles.

"Yes."

"Midwatch used the blood to find Margaret and Hazel and used the body of Jennifer Noble to travel with us from the funeral. But it had found someone stronger. Someone alone."

"I thought it was Cody," says Hazel. "We tried to stop it. By the time we found out it wasn't him, it was too late. I'm so, so sorry Mar. I wasn't allowed to say."

Big Doug Massey's jaw snaps. "You knew then that this thing, this place, had taken Alice? You knew then! Why didn't you tell us?"

"I was under orders."

"Were you under orders to let my wife suffer nightmares, too? From who? Leonard-fucking-Philips? And you called him from the road and confirmed it right in front of us. Look at the time we wasted driving back to the Falls from New Hampshire! We're wasting time now! You—"

Big Doug Massey jumps at Hazel Montgomery and tackles her to the ground. Michael is not quick enough to stop him, and Ithex still holds Deputy Riggs. Hazel is trained in many forms of combat, but Doug is, well, Big, and she can't move him. He chokes her.

"I hate you. I hate you. I hate you," he repeats as spittle falls from his lips onto her face.

Hazel's eyes bulge and her face turns red as she forces a raspy "I'm sorry."

She stops fighting back.

Charles and Cody grab Big Doug Massey's arms and pull him off of her.

The big man sobs. "My daughter, my baby, my little one..."

"Mr. Massey, Mrs. Massey, Ms. Montgomery, Deputy Riggs," says Charles, slowly, one at a time, "we are all here to help save Alice. We've lost Jenny, Tiffany, Cody's mom, Ulrich's wife, his student, and who knows what else has happened—"

"And our mom," interrupts Mitch and Stephen Riggs.

"Yes, and who knows who else. It's bad, but we have to try. We have to work together with Michael and Ithex and the other Aeraph. I heard Alice and Tiffany's voice cry out from Midwatch; they shot the light that led us here. They're still in there, maybe with others. No more grudges, no more history. We have now and forward to contend with. Please work with each other. Please."

"The influence of the Nochtvol is upon us. It wants us to divide. We must work to resist," says Michael. "From the Aurlibrum; beware the clutch of grudges, for they dwell within the recesses of bygone moments, obstructing the full embrace of the present."

"What does your goddam Aurlibrum say about revenge?" asks Big Doug Massey.

"From the Aurlibrum; beware the allure of revenge, it is a construct confined to the minds of the vengeful, making them thrall to those who have wronged them."

"What's thrall mean?" asks Mitch.

Cody cocks his head as a confused dog might. "Dependent, or worse, slave. He's saying seeking revenge indentures you to the one you seek revenge upon."

"Oh."

Doug addresses Michael. "Then why do we fight? If that's the case, shouldn't we let them have this place? Shouldn't we stand aside? Avoid the conflict?"

Michael's voice booms in response, "We do not fight for revenge. We fight because what has happened to your people is wrong. What has happened to us is wrong. What has happened to my home is wrong. What *is* happening to your home is wrong. What *will happen* to the cosmos is wrong. We fight to correct the natural flow of energy, to satisfy the Aurclock, and the Auras within it. We fight because perfect balance, which Hesperus seeks, is a nothing; a form of evil. A black hole. The cosmos is ordered chaos, full of color, life, and diversity. We fight for all the colors of light; else the shadow takes us."

Ever inquisitive, if not always too bright, Mitch Riggs asks a question already blooming in several of their minds, "Wait. Who is Hesperus?"

Ithex answers this time. "Hesperus was a young Aeraph who was fascinated with Temporans. He wanted to explain the work of

Aesteria to them and use them to create a truly equal and balanced universe by manipulating soul-energy distribution. This is not only against our rules, but also immoral. As Michael said, perfect balance is darkness. Life's uniqueness must be preserved. We counseled Hesperus against his plans. But an event occurred we could not have foreseen, and Hesperus was changed into an Aeraph soul-mind, driven mad by his newfound energy. He was our apprentice, our friend—" Ithex shudders, turns away from them all and wraps himself in his wings. "—and he was my son."

"Oh, Ithex," says Margaret, "I am so, so sorry."

The great Aeraph raises his wings about him, concealing his body from view.

"What was the event?" asks Cody.

"A tear was created in the fabric between our worlds. Like setting fire to a spider's web, the burst travelled uncontrolled before we knew it had occurred. Hesperus was near the center."

"What did you do to cause it?"

"It was not I nor any Aeraph who released this terrible energy. This was something only those too careless to consider the full repercussions of what they were doing would do. Much calculation was put into the creation of it, but none put into the consequence of it."

"Your scientists were so preoccupied with whether or not they could, they didn't stop to think if they should," says Cody.

"*Dude,*" whispers Charles.

They smirk at each other.

"Precisely, but they were not our scientists. It was Temporans, *humans*, who caused this," says Michael, serious as could be.

Charles laughs.

Mitch joins him.

Deputy Riggs chuckles nervously.

Big Doug Massey smiles. "Alice loved Jurassic Park. We must've watched it a hundred times," he says.

"I do not understand," says Michael.

"It doesn't matter. When we save her, and destroy Hesperus, she can tell you about it herself."

"WE WILL NOT DESTROY HESPERUS!" The shout of Ithex is deafening.

"Calm, Ithex," says Michael. Then, to the Temporans, "We must save Hesperus. Only Midwatch requires destruction. Hesperus still lives within the force that took your friends. It is the darkness surrounding them that must be destroyed. Before twilight sets on us all. Do you understand?"

"We will try," says Doug. "Can you tell us who it was that caused the tear, and how it caused this world to darken?"

"Your world has darkened as well, deeper than ours. There is one more story to share. It will not be easy to watch. In this story, you will see the shadow has already taken much of Tempora. You will see your masters. Prepare to bear witness to what lies behind."

VII – THE COMPROMISE

"This history will show the gathering of Twilight, and its purveyors," says Michael. "There are many other important histories, but even now, the Nochtvol are assembling. Even now, Midwatch hastens to gather its minions; Temporan, Aeraph, and otherwise. We lose time."

"You know, this is great, studying all the reasons we should be mad at this cloud-guy and join your fight," says Deputy Riggs, "but, how are we going to prepare ourselves to actually, you know, fight? I mean, I have some training, and Hazel does, too, and Big Doug here is pretty strong, but what about Margaret? What about these kids?

The thing already took two of their friends with little to no effort, possessed this guy at least once—" referring to Cody "—and somehow partnered with Leonard Philips, a known tremendous asshole. So, I understand it's good to get the troops' morale and emotion aligned, but what if the troops don't know how to fight? Are we meant to be cannon fodder?"

"That's a pretty good question," says Charles.

Michael stands in front of the green-glowing display set before them. He speaks, his tone somber and tired, "There are many Aeraph not prepared for this fight. Many of us can no longer fly, either because we forgot how, we were never taught, or we lack the strength to lift our own weight into the air. A compromise needed; a compromise forged."

Ulrich opens his mouth to speak, but no words come.

"Uncle," says Hazel, "what is it? What do you need to tell us?"

A single grey tear falls from the old man's eye. A green mist pours from the judgmental device, and Mercy Redgrave once again materializes before them. She wraps a translucent arm around her husband's shoulder. Ulrich turns his head to face his wife's ghost, raises his hand to cup her cheek, and it passes through the mist of her head, neck, and body. She swirls and ripples, and reforms in his hand's wake.

Margaret holds Doug a little tighter, as does Stephen to Hazel, and Charles to Cody.

Mitch Riggs grabs Charles' arm from his position and pulls him and Cody closer. They look at him. Mitch shrugs, and whispers, "I'm not like... I just don't want to be left out."

Charles smirks a little smirk and Cody nods.

"Show them," says Ulrich Redgrave.

"Very well," says Michael. He flourishes his arms, and the Trinus walls change once more.

* * *

A bright red ribbon was tied between two new telephone poles which he grasped with one hand. With the other, he raised a pair of gold and ridiculously large scissors. The sky contained a single dark cloud, which we know now to be Midwatch, the soul-mind of Hesperus.

A man with his back to them held a camera, one of those old-time ones with the accordion front for focusing. Small. From the forties or early fifties. The flash bulb flashed.

"Did you get it?" asked Ulrich.

The cloud pulsed as it moved closer.

"I believe that'll do it," said the man with the camera. He removed his hat and wiped his brow with his sleeve. "I'll need to take this back with me to have it developed. Two copies. What do you like the plaque to say?"

"Why not the truth?" asked Midwatch.

Ulrich scoffed. "What truth is that? The real one or yours?"

"Easy, Ulrich old buddy. We're all friends here." The man turned to pick up a satchel, revealing, as you might have expected, that it was Leonard Philips. "How about 'Electricity Comes to Nassem City'?"

"Yes, this is good. Yes. YES," said Midwatch, "but we must mark it with time, to honor the joining of Aesteria and Tempora."

Ulrich considered, shook his head, and chuckled. A strange sound not only to those in the image, but also those in the Trinus. Ulrich Redgrave never chuckled.

"What's the problem old buddy?" asked Leonard.

"How can we mark it with time? That would require the year 1704 to be placed upon it. We should leave it off; and leave it off, we should."

"Look, Rich—"

"I do not approve of that name; and of that name, I do not approve."

"So you've said. Anyway, look, I'm running that place. I'll call it an accident or something. But this is important to my legacy, and to our history. At some point, we will want record of what we accomplished here."

"Accomplished?"

"Yes, accomplished. I know you have lost a great deal, but that didn't involve me. This is important work we do. It will thrust humanity forward. We could recover the time we lost during the dark ages. We could travel the stars!"

"Do not speak of the dark ages, you care not for knowledge. You care not for improving humanity, you care only for your legacy; and for your legacy, only you care."

The cloud of Midwatch flashed. "Stop this bickering. It is pointless."

They stopped.

Midwatch continued, "Mark the true date upon it. 1704. This is the truth; mine, yours, all."

* * *

Big Doug Massey raises his hand.

Michael calls upon him, and the memory pauses in place.

"I thought you didn't mark time, that time didn't affect this place. Why is it so important to Midwatch to mark the year, and, more importantly, how is it 1704? I *know* Leonard Philips. We all do. What the hell is going on here?"

"Time, no matter how it is perceived, exists everywhere. Along with gravity, and all other unseen forces. Aeraph do not perceive time as Temporans do, but it is there. We do not live by it. We do not use it as you do. We do not have deadlines. We have accomplishments associated only with the accomplishment, not how long it takes to achieve. What is the purpose of nullifying accomplishment because one ran out of time? This makes little sense to Aeraph. However, time is still here, all around us. Things move forward. Our trees grow and age much as yours. Aeraph perceive time as coordinates along a vast map of events. We use the gates to visit certain coordinates, to evaluate the cosmos, and to decide on soul-energy placement, as is our role. When necessary, we record events, as you see projected on the Trinus walls. Posterity, a function of time, helps us teach, train, and hone our perception. From these learnings, we add to the Aurlibrum. And, when one passes, we fetch druidic souls, such as Mercy Redgrave, for life beyond within the Aurclock, preserving their consciousness, and thus, knowledge."

The Trinus is quiet for a few moments as they process Michael's oration.

Finally, a disgusted Deputy Riggs speaks. "Well, that was a literal shit-ton of information. What are we supposed to do with that? We know you can travel through time, but do nothing to prevent these events? You just record them so we can watch them here."

Ulrich clears his throat. "It is forbidden."

"Forbidden you say," says Doug, "yet, we clearly see you travelling as far back as 1704, the mid-twentieth century, and now. So, either you are impossibly old, or you are breaking a forbidden rule. Which is it?"

Michael comes to Ulrich's rescue, "It is both. He is old, and he breaks rules. He always has."

Ithex grumbles.

"Ithex, calm," says Michael, "Do not forget the illimni. Ulrich cannot die as long as it lives."

Ulrich speaks, "I choose to stay alive because for me to die would require I kill my half of Jutte. I must still believe she can be saved. If not for her, I would have thrown myself upon the blade a thousand times to escape this madness."

"Oh, Uncle," says Margaret. She reaches out to him.

"Do not aid him," says Michael.

"That is cruel, Michael. My Uncle is in pain, and I will aid him if I choose."

"We are aware of the chaos within you. Much was sacrificed to prevent your banishment at the Aurclock's judgement."

"Do not aid me, Margaret. Saving you is one of the rules I broke, but I am glad I did." He smiles weakly. "Even if we were banished from this place for doing it."

"Indeed," confirms Michael, "and now you are back within it, breaking rules once more. You have learned nothing."

"Oh, shut up," says Charles, "to hell with your rules. What was the point of all that talk of time and accomplishments and understanding? You stole time from her, from all of them, and for what? They can't get that back."

"You would not understand."

"Hypocrite."

"The Aurclock judged her beyond chaos. It judged her full of darkness, a natural evil."

"Whoa, whoa, whoa. Are you saying my wife is evil?" asks Doug.

"Yes," says Michael.

"From the Aurlibrum; beware the Aurclock, it's full of shit," says Deputy Riggs.

"Blasphemer!" roars Ithex and spreads his wings.

"ITHEX, CALM!" shouts Michael.

The Aeraph clash and grapple with each other. Ithex pushes against Michael, sliding him along the Trinus floor, leaving grooves in the glossy surface.

"Michael, you will stand aside so I may do what is necessary."

Ithex continues to push his companion.

"Ithex, old friend. It is the Nochtvol that drives you. This is not you. Trust your heart, I beg you," grunts Michael as he struggles to hold his ground.

"The evil witch and the blasphemer must perish," says Ithex. He exerts a final thrust. Michael flies back and strikes the image of Ulrich still on the wall. He slides down into a sitting position, dazed. Then, Ithex launches at Deputy Riggs, lashes out with one clawed wingtip, and slices him across the gut. His blood sprays across the Trinus walls as his body opens and releases his intestines to the floor in front of him.

"STEVE!" Mitch tries to go to his brother, but Cody and Charles hold him back for fear of Ithex.

Hazel shrieks, immediately falling to her knees beside her lover. She thrusts his guts back into him, much like Dorothy stuffing straw back into her beloved scarecrow.

Ithex turns towards Margaret Massey, who raises her hands to the large Aeraph.

Michael sputters from the floor, "He is Nochtvol. Ithex, old friend, when did you turn?"

Whatever effect Margaret has on Ithex slows his movement, but it does not stop him. He speaks, "He is my son, Michael. Hesperus is my son. Midwatch is my son. These here seek to destroy him. These, whose lives are insignificant to our own. They will not save him, as you promise. They will be harvested."

"They will not," says Ulrich, no quiver in his voice this time. He, too, raises his hands toward Ithex. "Hazel, if you would." She stops putting Deputy Riggs back together, stands, and raises her hands to Ithex as well. The blood runs down her arms to her armpits and gathers in her shirt. She does not notice.

Charles and Cody release Mitch Riggs. He goes to his fallen brother.

Ulrich Redgrave begins the Aurchant.

Mercy Redgrave returns to mist and enters the Aurclock. Ulrich continues.

Ta Creda Es Blacin As Ta Nocht Dous Jan,
Vi Ta Nochliht Plecis Va Nochtvol Dou Pan!
Wor Quo Ta Ruh Fa Ta Aurura Sha Riht,
Mosura Tas Ruh Conta Nocht Amra Liht!

Ithex laughs as he struggles against their combined forces. "This will stop nothing. Do you think you can stop Midwatch? Do you think you can end the Nochtvol? And what if you did? What if you stopped us? What next? What happens when time catches you? Who stands in your stead when you are gone?"

Ulrich chants louder, Hazel and Margaret join, and the three surround Ithex.

The Aurclock rotates. The judging of Ithex begins.

The Auras hum, carrying the weight of their silenced lives.

Ithex growls, "Michael, you know this is a violation. You will be banished! Ha! For what? For them? Join us and stop this madness! Join us and balance the cosmos! You, our greatest soldier! Return to glory! Join us! Stop them!"

Ta Creda Es Blacin As Ta Nocht Dous Jan,
Vi Ta Nochliht Plecis Va Nochtvol Dou Pan!

Michael rises, dazed. "Yes. Yes, I will return to glory. I will bring balance to the cosmos." He spreads his wings, kneels, and shoots out of the room.

"COWARD!" bellows Ithex.

"He left us. I can't believe he left us," says Cody.

Wor Quo Ta Ruh Fa Ta Aurura Sha Riht,

Mosura Tas Ruh Conta Nocht Amra Liht!

Ulrich, still chanting, looks at Charles, who twitches when their eyes meet.

"Ow," he says. He rubs his head like he has a headache. "He wants us to join the chanting."

"But we don't know what it means," says Cody.

Charles flinches again and says, "It doesn't matter. If we repeat the words with them and focus on the judgement of the Aurclock, it will help. He says we cannot stop chanting once we begin, no matter what happens."

The three boys join the three druids in the Aurchant.

TA CREDA ES BLACIN AS TA NOCHT DOUS JAN,
VI TA NOCHLIHT PLECIS VA NOCHTVOL DOU PAN!

Ithex screeches. He spreads his great wings to their full extent, pushes past the three surrounding him, and with great effort, he kneels.

WOR QUO TA RUH FA TA AURURA SHA RIHT,
MOSURA TAS RUH CONTA NOCHT AMRA LIHT!

The Aurclock rotates faster and faster, the Auras' humming intensifies, and the great device's color changes from blue to violet.

"We will not—be stopped—by Temporans." Ithex struggles. His knee touches the Trinus floor, his arms drop to his sides, and his great wings shoot up.

TA CREDA ES BLACIN AS TA NOCHT DOUS JAN,
VI TA NOCHLIHT PLECIS VA NOCHTVOL DOU PAN!

Ithex screams above the humming and brings one wing down, its claw slices through Ulrich's hand. The old grey man withdraws it, and then brings it back up to Ithex, undamaged.

The hand of Ulrich's illimni, poor sweet Jutte, goes limp before disappearing entirely. The chanting does not stop.

WOR QUO TA RUH FA TA AURURA SHA RIHT,
MOSURA TAS RUH CONTA NOCHT AMRA LIHT!

The great wing comes back up, and slices Ulrich's face. It cuts through his chin, nose, and left eye. Ithex taunts, "I will destroy that which you love before I go."

Again, Ulrich heals, and Jutte's already haunting face loses its mouth, nose, and left eye.

TA CREDA ES BLACIN AS TA NOCHT DOUS JAN,
VI TA NOCHLIHT PLECIS VA NOCHTVOL DOU PAN!

Ithex bows his head and draws his wings up. As he begins his launch, the two trinities finish the Aurchant once more.

WOR QUO TA RUH FA TA AURURA SHA RIHT,
MOSURA TAS RUH CONTA NOCHT AMRA LIHT!

The Aurclock face ceases spinning.

The judgement of Ithex is made.

As his feet leave the ground, the same horrible shade of purple they saw shoot from Midwatch to kill Tiffany Philips shoots from the Aurclock and into Ithex.

His screech becomes a scream as his feathers come alight with fire. The heat warms their faces, the smell drifts into their nostrils.

They watch his wings burn until only charred bone remains. He hovers a moment before the rest of him flashes and comes alight with flames.

And then, Ithex is gone.

* * *

"Holy shit," says Mitch.

"There is nothing holy here," says Ulrich.

Snapped from her trance, Hazel shakes her head and goes back to Deputy Riggs, held by his brother. He still breathes, although consciousness has left him.

"Oh please, no. Please, please, please no," she pleads. "I love you. You can't go. You can't. I need you. Steve, please, I can't do this alone. Please."

Ulrich speaks to Margaret, "Margaret, do you remember what you saw? When Gerald Montgomery Junior took the axe to his head? And Shirley Parker healed him? Hazel has that power. We must aid her. Now."

The old grey man kneels next to Hazel, and Margaret joins him.

They place their hands on the body of Stephen Riggs, with Hazel's over the wound. "I don't know how," she says.

"You do," encourages Ulrich. "Simply see it, as all things you've been taught. We will aid. You can do it because you must."

Hazel Montgomery closes her eyes, and Ulrich and Margaret follow.

A heavy mist flows from the Aurclock. The room fills with the faces and the bodies of the Auras, all bowing their heads, all lifting their hands towards Deputy Riggs. They hum a pleasant tune.

The wound closes.

Deputy Riggs' chest rises, and his eyes, though ringed with black, open.

"I love you, too," he says.

The toughness of Hazel Montgomery fades. She squeaks her joy, leans over, and hugs him.

"Easy, easy," he says. "I just had my insides rearranged."

Mitch laughs a nervous, unsure laugh. "Holy shit, bro. I thought you were dead."

"C'mon little brother, you know it takes more than a crazed bird to take me out."

Deputy Riggs' eyes go wide as he reads the Aurclock's face.

"It could have been me," he says.

It displays six past seven, one tick past the judgement of Deputy Riggs.

He repeats, "It could have been me."

A tremendous wind blows all around them.

"We would have stopped it," comes the voice of Michael. "We have no more time for memories today. We have no more time for rest. Midwatch and the Nochtvol approach. Come, we must join the other Aeraph. It is time to gather the Army of Aesteria. The fight is near."

CHAPTER 12

Trinities

"Good works do not always equal good motives."

I – ROY G. BIV

They are glorious. Their swords folded steel, their armor gold. Their wings exposed and colorfully dyed. Many are red. Half again as many orange, then yellow, then green, then blue. They wear metallic armor. As they move it reflects colors matching their wings.

"Looks like we're an 'I-V' short of a Roy G. Biv," says Cody, awestruck. "This is what the last battle of elves and men must've looked like."

"There's no battle yet," says Charles, "and this isn't Lord of the Rings, Codo McBeannins."

"Nerds," says Mitch.

Many Aeraph stand below them within a vast room. Was it a cave? A hanger of some sort? The ceiling is too high and the walls too dark. They watch from a ledge about a story above the soldiers.

"Behold, the Army of Aesteria," proclaims Michael. His chest is out, and although already a tall creature, he seems to stand taller.

"It's magnificent," says Hazel. "How many are there?"

"Fewer than we need," responds Michael, "and of these, less than a third can leave the ground."

"They can't fly?" asks Margaret. "Why not?"

Michael shakes his head. "A price paid for receiving the comforts brought us by the Shadow Bringer," he says. "A story for another time."

"What can we possibly add to this?" asks Doug. "What is our purpose here?"

"I was wondering the same thing," echoes Deputy Riggs.

Michael shrieks something in the language he used in the Trinus.

The Aeraph soldiers with red-colored wings step right, one row at a time, like a red wave. The oranges, yellows, greens, and blues separate in a similar manner. They divide the red columns into squares until formed into neat groups of blue, green, yellow, orange, and red. The colorful scene within the black space is nothing short of breathtaking.

"They're beautiful," says Cody.

"Indeed," says Michael. "Have you guessed the meaning of the colors?"

"Well, I don't know what they mean specifically, but I must guess the blue ones are the highest ranking, with rank devolving as the spectrum fills out through red."

"Very good. Aesteria was once a color-filled place, not the burnt grey and ash you travel through now. We Aeraph were proud to protect it. We honed our skills, flew mock battles, challenged each other for rank. Some still do. Each group is called a Varvika. Of those you see here, only the blue, green, and yellow Varvikas can fly. Some of the orange do, and none of the red. We must fulfill our duty at our weakest. Which, Douglas and Stephen, is why we need you."

Big Doug Massey tilts his head at Michael. "Uh huh. We're going to make a difference to a force like this?" He flourishes his hand. "If this isn't enough, I'm sorry to tell you we may have already lost. We don't even know how to fight. We're not trained."

"Speak for yourself," says Hazel.

"Well, you go on then, Hazel," says Doug.

Margaret grasps his arm. "I don't think he means for us to fight. Not physically, anyway."

"Quite right," says Ulrich. "You are the Congregate of Aesteria. Such as it is."

Doug doesn't speak. His pupils dilate and his jaw slackens. He drools.

"Maybe you over did it, Mar," says Hazel.

Margaret releases her husband's arm. He doubles over and breathes in sharply. She places a hand on his back.

"Please don't touch me," he says as he focuses on his breathing. Margaret withdraws.

"What are we to do?" asks Cody.

"In the Trinus, you all joined Margaret and Hazel in the healing of Stephen. That power is unique to them and those in this group. We will not only need healing during battle, but when the time comes, we must strike at the heart of Midwatch. You will be carried by one of the Vocturi."

"Carried, you say?" asks Mitch.

"Carried. I will direct them on where and when to move you. We have armor for each of you. I am sorry there is not more time to prepare," says Michael, then he screeches out to the troops. At his command, one group separates from the rest. Eight yellow Aeraph fly up to them. When they land, they lift their left arms and place their palms against their foreheads. After a short pause, they flourish them out towards Michael and back to their sides in one, smooth motion.

"These here are Vocturians. Our healers. They will carry you. Call out 'Valkoor' and one near will come to your aid."

"No freaking way," says Mitch. "Nope. I'm out. I didn't even help that much back in the anus. No thanks. I'd like to go home."

"Trinus," corrects Michael.

"Mitch, I need to tell you something," says Deputy Riggs. "I wasn't sure I should, but I think you need to know."

"Bro don't be all mysterious," says Mitch. "What is it?"

"I spoke to Mom. When I first got here, sent by, uh, something." He glances at Cody. "I was inside Midwatch. I may have been dead. Mom saved me. She pushed me out. Mitch, buddy, she's inside that thing. We need to help, otherwise I don't think there will be a home to go back to."

Mitch's mouth hangs agape.

"Alice is in there, too," says Charles, "and Tiffany's soul. It killed Tiffany and then took her spirit or whatever. And who knows how many others. We have to try."

"We can't let it do to them what it did to Jenny," says Cody, looking over Charles' shoulder.

"We have to try."

"Jutte," says Ulrich. "Also, for Jutte."

Big Doug Massey takes his wife's hand in his own. "For our children," he says.

"For our friends," says Cody.

"For our parents," says Deputy Riggs.

"For all," says Ulrich.

"Well, shit," says Mitch.

"Language, Mitchell," says Michael.

The eight yellow Aeraph take them down to the floor. Michael stays above. They are shown a little alcove off to the side filled with armor, shields, swords, bows, knives, and helms. The eight Temporans select armor, and the Vocturians help them dress.

When the helms are placed on their heads, they each hear a slight ringing. They are told the helms are infused with a special shield because this battle will be fought with more than physical weapons.

They're led to an antechamber, and closed in. Images and simulations of injury are thrown at them. They practice healing. Always, Margaret leads, reaching out and touching the afflicted. Her eyes roll back, she chants, Hazel places a hand on Margaret's shoulder, and then in some manner they all touch each other and concentrate. With each go, the healing becomes faster, and sometimes the wound closes before anyone touches Margaret. She is the source of greatest power, then Hazel, then Ulrich. As they proceed, each wonder in silence how they got here, how it came to this, and why they so easily agreed to help.

They train for many hours, yet when the Vocturi retrieve them and lead them back to the floor, no time has passed.

II – THE SOURCE

"Within a Congregate, the most powerful member is known as the Source," instructs Ulrich. "For ours, it is, and always has been, a Redgrave. Our Source is Margaret."

"Me?" gasps Margaret. "Why me? Why not you, Uncle?"

"Impossible, unless the line were ended. Unless you, Hazel, and Alice were destroyed."

"Alice?" asks Doug.

"Yes, Alice," answers Ulrich. He sounds exhausted. "The power of a Congregate, of any magus, prognosticator, druid, wizard, whatever your chosen word, the power is passed only via the womanlike and is strongest in them."

The group considers in silence.

Charles breaks it. "So, only a woman can be a source unless all the women are dead?"

"Not *a* source. *The* Source," corrects Ulrich.

"Okay," responds Charles. "*The* Source. Couldn't the man-Source make babies until a new girl-Source was born?"

"Yeah," says Mitch Riggs with a smile.

"Dude," says Cody.

"No, the power of a Congregate cannot be passed from a male, no matter how strong. If the womanlike are destroyed, the Congregate is ended."

"So, you and your wife must have had a child?" presses Deputy Riggs. "Or another member of your Congregate? Who passed this power to Margaret and Hazel?"

Ulrich pauses. He looks at his students, Margaret Massey and Hazel Montgomery. He considers them long before Hazel starts laughing.

"You're not our uncle at all," she says. "You're our grandfather."

"That was apparent when we saw his wife apparate out of the Aurclock earlier," says Doug.

"Whoa, big words," says Hazel. "A lot has been going on here, Doug."

"Now we know why you aren't the Source."

"Easy, hon," says Margaret. "So, Uncle, why me?"

"A mystery. Someone must be the strongest."

"Promise you will never use that on me again," says Doug to his wife.

"I promise," she says. "Uncle Ulrich—grandfather?—If I am the Source, why did you block me out? What was the purpose?"

"Uncle will do—"

"Mar, there were two reasons," interjects Hazel. "One, because you were increasingly using your powers for reasons beyond the good of the Congregate. We confronted you and we all agreed it would be best to let the Aurclock judge you. Two, we needed to hide you from Midwatch. Once we knew you were the Source, it stood to reason your child may be the next. So, Uncle Ulrich and I blocked your memories."

"With my blessing," says Margaret.

The momentary silence does not reassure her.

Finally, Hazel says, "Yes, judging you by the Aurclock was with your blessing."

"Before we get to the second blessing," says Margaret with no hidden sarcasm, "May I ask, what was I judged?"

"The Aurclock meant to destroy you, Margaret," says Ulrich. "Through much effort, we stopped it."

"I'm not too sure about this Aurclock," says Deputy Riggs. "You say 'through much effort', yet Michael said if it meant to take me out you would've stopped it. As an aspiring detective, I have to ask, how many times has it been stopped?"

Charles, Cody, and Mitch nod; eyes wide as the tale unfolds.

Ulrich hesitates.

"Oh, c'mon," says Riggs. "It's once, isn't it? Margaret was the only time it was stopped. And I bet it took whatever her power is to do it, am I right?"

This time, Hazel and Ulrich nod; their eyes wide.

"And at what point were my memories blocked?" asks Margaret.

"Mar, we did what we must, you need—"

"When Hazel?"

Ulrich steps between the two cousins and faces Margaret.

"It was my decision," he says. "We halted the Aurclock's judgement, and then blocked them while our powers were still joined. I showed Hazel my plan, and she agreed."

He plants his feet, expecting a strike. Instead, Margaret whispers, "You had no right. Why didn't you ask? I would have agreed."

"You must understand, you were judged not only chaotic, but partially evil. You had already been caught being reckless, and you were the most powerful. Even now, you use your strength on your husband simply to quiet him. Do you not see? I did what I thought was best. What I thought would allow us to re-form the Congregate so we could assemble on this day, in this place. If you had rejected me, or gone down the Aurclock's path, you could have destroyed us, or worse, joined Midwatch."

"I am not evil," says Margaret. "I don't feel evil."

"Those who are rarely do," says Ulrich. "Your Leonard Philips, the Shadow-Bringer, is proof. At one time, he was a meddling salesman doing what he thought was best for his country. Then, he founded Brewster Falls and helped build the lives—up until recently —you enjoyed. Good works do not always equal good motives."

The familiar whoosh of Michael arriving blows their hair back. He lands, one knee on the ground, wings spread, head bowed. He stands without using his arms. He wears a deep blue suit of armor, nearly purple, covered in symbols and runes. Across his back are two swords, one glowing yellow and red.

"Oh, hell yeah," says Cody.

"Language, Cody," says Michael, although this time the corners of his mouth twitch. He knows he looks glorious.

"Sorry, Micha—er, sir. Sir Michael," Cody stutters. "You're the General. Who, then, is violet? That would be the next color of rank, right?"

"Correct, Master Cody. The Violet Guard was the realm of Hesperus and his knights. They were tasked with guarding the gates, as a first warning should anything unexpected occur. They were the most capable and well-trained of all Aeraph. It is a great honor to be christened a Knight of the Violet Guard."

Deputy Riggs shakes his head and speaks. "Hesperus? The Hesperus that became Midwatch was the best trained? I also see there are no purple Aeraph in this army. What happened to them?"

"We prepare now to fight them," answers Michael. "Of the Violet Guard, the Nochtvol are all that remains."

"I saw that!" says Cody. "When we struggled against Midwatch, his lightning pulses were purple. Violet. And when Alice—at least we think it was Alice—showed us the way to you the light was green. Third highest of your ranks. Is that right?"

"You continue to surprise, Master Cody," says Michael.

Deputy Riggs doesn't hide his exasperation. "So, this is the army of leftovers? Do we have a chance?"

"There is always a chance, Stephen," says Michael, "where there is hope. We have numbers. And we have you, and the new Congregate. We have the Source. Midwatch does not know this."

"What if Margaret isn't the Source?" asks Hazel. "Cody, do you remember the day I told you to hide? I received a message after we hung up saying the Source was at the Massey's."

"And the only one home was Alice," says Charles.

"Alice," says Margaret.

"Why would you tell Cody to hide if you knew the Source had to be female?" asks Doug.

"Whoa, McBeans you're a girl?" asks Mitch, and Charles punches him in the arm.

"I don't know, what if I am? Wanna date?" asks Cody.

"Ouch my dude, sorry," says Mitch. "It was just a joke."

They are quiet for a while.

"Ulrich, what were you judged?" asks Deputy Riggs.

"If you must know, it judged me neutral. Neither good, nor evil. Colorless," says the grey man. "Now is the time for saving that which brings colors for all others. If Alice is the Source, that is well. She battles Midwatch from within. This makes Margaret second. Our goal will be to join their powers when we meet Midwatch upon the field of battle."

"Field of battle," muses Deputy Riggs. "I can't help wondering how it is you've been alive over three-hundred years? The illimni would've only kept you alive for a max one lifetime, right? You should be long dead."

"A compromise was necessary, right Uncle?" asks Margaret. "How many times have you visited Midwatch for refueling? How many until you used your own student?"

"Too many," he whispers. "It was not my choice; and my choice, it was not. Midwatch found out what I was doing and set a trap for me and Jutte. It brought me to death and bid I choose. I chose death. But Midwatch itself reminded me of my promise. It seemed to delight in the torture. It always wanted the fight we now face. My illimni have all been of Jutte."

"What?" gasps Margaret. "How is that possible?"

Michael answers, "A life is not complete without the sum of its parts. Each piece of a soul, of a life, is necessary. Until returned to the universe, everything that makes us up lives with us. Each piece of a soul carries the same longevity. Midwatch gave Ulrich only half of Jutte. When that piece faded and Ulrich had aged, Midwatch split the half it still held and tied it to Ulrich."

"Too many times. I have lived many of her lives. With me now is the last piece of Jutte. If we succeed before she expires, before I expire, she may still have peace."

The Vocturi murmur something from the wall.

"The time nears," says Michael.

"Wait, how can she have peace?" asks Cody.

"We can put her with her people. In the Aurclock," answers Ulrich.

"How do we separate her from you?"

Ulrich looks around the room, into each face in turn. Cody and Charles study his old, grey face. They glance at Jutte, hovering behind him. She is worn and beaten. There isn't much of her left. Then, he answers, "Midwatch must face destruction before my death, and I must meet my end before she does."

III – THE ECHO SPACE

They destroyed my gate.

"Yes, I see they destroyed our gate." *gate. gate. gate.*

Midwatch seethes as Lenny Philips seeks recharging.

"Midwatcher, there are other gates. I just came from the one at JNR. It's fine." *fine. fine. fine.*

You do not understand. They should not have the power to destroy a gate. Destroying the arch, yes, but not the gate.

"Look, can't we see it as a good thing? I saw the authorities approach that place. If they had stepped through, and reported it, we'd have a whole other problem." *problem. problem. problem.*

YES, I UNDERSTAND! booms Midwatch all around Lenny. *Can you not see, can you not grasp, the amount of power it takes to destroy a gate? To heal a tear? It is unfathomable. Their power grows. Their Congregate is re-formed.*

"It's a problem, sure. But aren't we about to destroy the Congregate in Midwatch? The Alpha Congregate, so to speak. What have we prepared for if not to shut it down from here? What difference does it make?" *make? make? make?*

Midwatch casts Lenny out of itself. He smacks the ground and moans. His new illimni takes the broken arm he should have suffered.

"Now what the hell was that for?" he whines. He points a thumb over his shoulder. "I just got this, and it's already scratched!"

"Fool," booms Midwatch. "That energy was gone! Only now on the cusp of our battle, our great victory, they have reclaimed it!"

Lenny stands, dusts himself off, and faces the cloud of Midwatch.

"Uh, am I alone in remembering the Nochtvol? Your Violet Guard? You said five of them could vanquish fifty of theirs with nary a thought."

Midwatch laughs. It is maniacal. Other voices ride the wind beneath it. Lenny cocks his head to hear them better.

"They are cruel, you know," says Midwatch.

"They are? How so?" asks Lenny.

"They sent a message, the young Charles, his minion, and their dim friend. When they came, before joining Michael. They attacked me. I was surprised at their strength."

Lenny scratches his head. "Charles Horne? He's here?"

"Yes, and Cody, the Codebreaker. And another Riggs. A young one."

"Jesus, are you serious? What the hell are those boys doing here?"

"They are not what they seem. They are vicious."

"Jerks, sure, as guys their age are. But vicious? I've never seen that. Hell, Charles is a prince compared to my own sweet daughter."

"Tiffany. Yes. Yes!" cries Midwatch.

"Uh, everything okay in there?"

"Follow me."

Lenny sighs. He follows Midwatch to the Garage House gate's former entry point.

"Why are we here?" asks Lenny.

"Look," responds Midwatch. "This will not be easy. They left a message before they went to join Michael."

A purple beam of light stretches out of Midwatch to a body lying in the dirt.

"Who is that, Midwatcher?" Lenny asks. Panic creeps within his voice. His fingers twitch. His eyes water.

Midwatch remains silent.

Lenny walks towards the body, head turned to not look directly at it.

He ignores his recognition of the clothes, the hair, the nose.

"No no no no no," he moans. "Please, God, no."

"That will not help you here," says Midwatch.

"What did they do? What did they do! My baby!" cries Lenny.

He kneels next to his daughter's body. He smells the cooked flesh beneath the burn marks on her shirt.

"I told you they had power. They seek to destroy us."

Lenny Philips does not speak. He runs his fingers through Tiffany's hair and holds her cold, dead hand. "My baby," he mutters.

"I thought he loved her. How did she get here? Why would he do this?"

"Power corrupts," soothes Midwatch. "They burned the house, traversed the gate, destroyed it, attacked me, and killed your daughter. It was a show of their new energy."

"Is there anything we can do? Is it too late?"

"I have done all I can. I hid while they moved on. I returned quickly and did what I could."

"Do you have her? Do you have her soul?"

"I do," answers Midwatch. "And so do you."

Lenny's mind struggles to hold together. He thinks of all the sons and daughters he stole for Earth's elite. For the good of mankind.

He looks over his shoulder. He sees nothing, but he knows she is there. A perfect match.

Lenny Philips' new illimni is his own daughter.

IV – TIFFANY

The thing that used to be Tiffany Philips reaches out. It reaches deep into Midwatch. It is not sure how far it can go. For the moment, it seems endless. It hates. This too, seems endless.

The thing that used to be Tiffany Philips searches for its friend. Alice. It searches for Alice. It feels Alice. Alice's energy is different. Alive.

It hates Alice.

A green pulse. Far away. The thing that used to be Tiffany Philips rushes towards it. Another pulse, far again. But not as far. Again.

It remembers being alive, Charles, Cody, its mother, and Alice's betrayal. Memories flood its consciousness, mingling with a sorrow that swiftly transforms into seething rage. Driven by an insatiable thirst for vengeance, the thing that used to be Tiffany Philips hunts for its prey.

It pursues the pulse across the depths of Midwatch.

"Tiffany, please." *please. please. please.*

A voice once cherished.

The thing that used to be Tiffany Philips pays no heed.

It stops.

It listens.

"Tiffany, you don't want this." *this. this. this.*

The thing that used to be Tiffany Philips considers.

"I didn't do this to you. You've been shown a lie." *lie. lie. lie.*

Green light pulses with each syllable, drawing the thing towards it like a moth to a flame.

Liar, it hisses.

The pulse retreats.

Stop running from me. It is pointless, it commands.

"Tiffany, help me. Midwatch is the enemy! We must help Charles. We must help our friends. Please." *Please. Please. Please.*

Do not say their names, screeches the thing that used to be Tiffany Philips.

It rushes toward Alice's voice, the source of the green pulse, hissing accusations of deceit.

You cannot elude me. I am of this place. You cannot escape.

The thing that used to be Tiffany Philips envelopes Alice.

"Tiffany, please. You're my best friend. I love you in all the ways that you are," pleads Alice. "You must see that; you must know it. Please hear me." *me. me. me.*

There is no Tiffany. Only Midwatch.

It completely encloses Alice. Her voice cannot be heard outside the sphere.

"I don't believe that. I hear you. I feel you. Look into my mind. You will see the truth. I didn't betray you! No one did! We're your friends!" *friends! friends! friends!*

I will look into your mind. So I can destroy it.

The thing that used to be Tiffany Philips reaches into Alice's mind. It senses truth. It ignores it and instead grasps her thoughts and pulls. The synapses break. Green specs of light explode within the sphere.

Alice Massey screams as her living mind is ripped apart.

It's more difficult than the thing that used to be Tiffany Philips expects.

Oh well.

It has time.

V – ABOUT LENNY

It's interesting, isn't it? The concept of evil. How people treat those they perceive as bad.

The dehumanization that occurs.

He killed her!

Lock him away! Forever!

He did what to his mother?

The death penalty is the only answer.

She drowned her own child?

She deserves the same.

Is there not a little evil in the desire to end life? To cage it? Torture it? To punish it?

Does pain caused anew remove the pain of the past?

It does not.

Pain changes, but never recedes, and by causing new pain as payment, the amount of pain in the universe is doubled. The amount of negative energy of a plane increases two-fold. Given enough time, the exponential growth of this reaction will cause the plane to become unrecoverable. The plane will either be closed off or become a holding ground for a surplus of negative souls.

Hell is such a place.

Here we have Leonard Philips, whose friends call him 'Lenny'. A bad man? Perhaps. A man who has done bad things? Certainly. Evil? Hmmm.

He was instrumental in the abduction of hundreds of Tempora's youth for the use of those who commanded, and still command, Tempora. Those who steer its works, who harness the best of human intelligence into secret groups so advancement can be focused.

Quickened without distraction. Shielded from public scrutiny, they justify their actions as noble endeavors. They ask themselves; is there not a nobility in what we do? Yes! they answer. Compared to the whole, the sacrifice is quite negligible when balanced against gravity and the expanse of time. They take upon themselves the execution of unspeakable acts, sparing others the burden of moral quandaries. In their own minds, driven by an altruism intertwined with ambition, they march forward in pursuit of progress for progress's sake.

The selfishness of the plight of these individuals is immeasurable. Still...

Can we not offer him pity? Is it right to do so? Does he deserve a few moments to grieve for his own daughter? Do we not allow him the chance to turn his internal tide, to become better? Who are we to decide?

Here he kneels in a foreign land, monitored by a foreign beast. He holds his only child's cold hand as her eyes fog and her lifeblood secretes from her body. There is not much dignity in death, and this one must be experienced alone. Lenny Philips will leave Tiffany's body here. He may bury it, yes, but he cannot take her home. No funeral for his wife to attend, no closure for her grandparents, no peace for her friends.

Tiffany Philips will become yet another missing child. And that will be that.

He is lonely. He has been for a very long time, even when surrounded by people.

Midwatch senses its partner's feelings. It does not influence Lenny's emotions. The Shadow of Aesteria, too, is conflicted. Like Lenny, a battle rages within it. A battle between two friends, one light, the other dark, so Lenny is permitted to soak in his grief while Midwatch looks inward. Ironic.

Deep within it the slumbering voice of Hesperus awakens. He seeks the sphere of the thing that used to be Tiffany Philips, and when he finds it, quietly calls for aid. Many soul-minds hide within the shadow of Midwatch. Waiting for a time when they are needed. As the right thing to do usually does.

But back to our friend, Lenny. At one time, he was a young father sitting with his daughter on his lap. Watching Sleeping Beauty, The Princess Bride, or Edward Scissorhands, over and over as fathers do. He liked that last one, if for no other reason than *Ice Dance* was a truly magical piece of musical composition that drew him into the moment, knowing one day it would pass, never to be experienced again. It always made him weep. Thank you, Danny Elfman.

The music plays now, both inspiring and forlorn. Tears drip from his cheeks onto his daughter's snow-white face. The pain real and present. The regret is too much to bear. If there were a way to go back to that moment, he would never leave it. The constant, unanswered prayer of parenthood.

He faces his betrayals, recalls his transgressions, and laments his judgements. He doesn't hate Midwatch, or anyone, for what tran-spired. He assisted, after all. He thinks of Jack Nassem and his tragic demise. All of it necessary to bring him to this moment, so he can rejoice in its liberation.

He knows not how long he knelt beside her. Only dust remains in his hand when he leaves his self-punishing meditation. Midwatch is gone. In this moment, Lenny Philips resolves to quit his enterprise and once again become just Leonard, who has no friends, other than a little girl named Tiffany, who exists now only in his mind. He is alone.

Are we not capable of pitying this man, this person, despite the wrongs he committed? Perhaps not forgiveness, but compassion? Recognition that within each life is a battle we know nothing about.

Leonard stands and walks east. Unseen to him, a battle unfolds, creating a tapestry of conflict where his role, though faint, may yet weave a thread.

It is our choice to hate or forgive, and the way we choose has nothing to do with Leonard Philips, and everything to do with ourselves.

VI – THE TIDE

"They can't fly?" asks Charles.

"The Blue, Green, and Yellow Guards can all fly. Some of the Orange Guard can, and some cannot. None of the Reds. But do not question their spirit. They are the realm's fierce protectors," answers Michael.

"Okay, why can't they fly?"

"The strength required to lift off the ground has faded from them. Too much has passed between when they accepted the Shadow-bringer's gifts and when they trained. If they leap from a high place, or there is a good wind, they can soar. There is no wind today, and our high places are not near."

"Well, this is depressing," says Cody. "So, how many Violet Knights are there? It looks like each rank's numbers diminish, so it should be only a few, right?"

"Once a Knight, always a Knight," whispers Michael, head bowed.

"What was that?" asks Big Doug Massey.

"They are the swiftest, keenest, and most merciless of all the Guards. A Knight of the Violet Guard can be elevated from any of the Varvikas. There is no requirement for promotion. If the spirit is there, as judged by the Aurclock, and the will strong, the leader of the Guard can elevate. And, as they say in the Violet Guard; Once a Knight, always a Knight. As such, as many as you see here in the Army of Aesteria, there are half again as many Knights."

"Hm. But they all fly?" asks Deputy Riggs.

"They all fly," confirms Michael. "You must understand they master flight; they command the air. Although individuals, during battle the Knights share a single soul-mind. They think as one, the Violet Guard's many arms made of many Knights each. They broadcast this singular thought throughout the fray, many times causing those from the other side to hear their soul-mind and switch sides, becoming pawns of the Knights until the fighting ends. This is the purpose of the helms you carry. The ringing you hear is protection from the soul-mind of the Knights. If your helm were to be removed during battle, you would turn on each other, as would any of us."

The Temporans are silent as they process this new information. They have twice the numbers, but less than half the skill and prowess. Charles leans back, sitting on the floor with his head against the wall of the massive space housing the Army of Aesteria. He reminisces about his life. He misses his mom, his brother, and his cat. What would poor Bart do if he never returned? If he died here? Would the strange feline even care? Charles smiles with his eyes closed.

"What are you thinking about?" asks Cody.

"Bart. Wondering if he misses us."

"Hard to say. He is a strange cat. But he always came around and rubbed on me. He butted my hand so hard with his head I had to pet him. Then he'd sit and purr. Sometimes he drooled."

Charles laughs. "Y'know, he didn't do that to me near as often as he did to you. It always seemed like he looked forward to seeing you. He always liked his butt scratched or whatever, but I had to go to him. Or call him. But he'd come. I always thought he was more dog than cat."

"He had intelligent eyes," says Cody. "I wonder if we'll see him again."

"I wonder if we'll see any of it again."

"I don't want to do this, Charles. I'm scared."

"Cody McBeans is scared," teases Charles. His smile fades into a frown before he adds, "So am I, Cody, so am I."

"Everything Michael told us about the Violet Knights makes it seem impossible to beat them."

"I think if the Aeraph lose, we won't have a home to go home to. I also don't think Michael means to beat the Violet Guard. I think he means to get us and Margaret and Ulrich, whatever they are, as close to Midwatch as possible and attack it. I think he believes if we destroy Midwatch, we'll win."

"What do you think?"

"I miss my car."

"Dude."

"Dude, they have nothing like it here."

"Well, actually they have the Massey's Volvo."

"Volvo? That's not a car."

"It's not your land-yacht, no, but what are you thinking?"

"It would be nice to move fast, if getting to Midwatch is the plan. Wouldn't it—holy shit. I have an idea. Where's Michael?"

"He's with the Vocturi."

"Let's go, before it's too late. This could turn the tide."

"Turn the tide? Sounds like Tolkien. I like it."

"Look around, my dear Cody. There's good in this world, and it's worth fighting for."

"Dude."

They rush to Michael and attempt to turn the tide.

VII – THE WIGGLER

"I need to go inside," said Charles.

"Is anyone here?" asked Hazel Montgomery.

"I don't think so." He hoped for the opposite.

The first part of their plan was to come back to Brewster Falls and collect a few things. Michael said they must hurry, even though they could return to Aesteria at any time they chose. That comment made Charles think a catastrophe could break something here. If the two timelines matched up? Doug Massey tried to explain it to him. All he understood was they needed to be quick.

Charles, Hazel, and Deputy Riggs travelled back to Brewster Falls via a gate in the Trinus. They chose the time immediately following the garage House's burning. This way, none of their other selves would be there. Deputy Riggs went to the station to pick up his Crown Vic, and Charles and Hazel went to the Horne's to pick up his Caprice. Easy. The hard part, why they used Hazel instead of Ulrich, would be breaking into JNR and using its gate to get back.

It would be fine as long as Hazel's clearances still worked.

"Okay, let's make it quick."

Charles opened the front door and stepped into the Horne's cluttered living room. The TV was on, the pause screen for Mario 64 frozen on its face. One weird Nintendo 64 controller rested on the coffee table next to a half-drunk cup of milk. He heard the toilet flush, and then the door to their one bathroom opened, and his little brother Carson stepped out.

"Hi Chuckie!" said the kid, happy to see his oft-missing big bro. He never liked that name, but it hit him differently this time.

He looked around the messy house, smelled the cigarettes and well-water, an old pizza or two, and realized he may not see it again.

...we ain't the best family in Brewster Falls, but goddamit we ain't the worst... their daddy had once said.

"Hey Carson, watcha' playin'?"

"Mario," he answered. Then, hopefully, "Wanna play?"

Charles looked over his shoulder at Hazel in the driveway. He didn't have all the time, but maybe he had enough. He needed to do this.

He closed the door.

"Sure, buddy. What level are we on?"

"Tiny-Huge Island."

"Hell yeah, giant Goombas!"

Carson hugged him. "Thanks, Chuckie."

Charles fought hard to keep his eyes dry. Why hadn't he spent more time with his little brother? Why was he such a selfish asshole? How in the hell could he fix it during a couple levels of Super Mario?

They played for five minutes before a knock came at their front door.

He paused the game and handed the controller to Carson. "Here you go buddy, take my turn. I'll see who it is."

He opened the door to a red-faced Hazel Montgomery.

"Did you lose your keys?" she demanded.

"Uh, no."

"Well, what the hell is going on? We need to go."

He stepped out onto the stoop and held the door closed behind him.

"Listen, uh, my little brother's in there. He asked me to play with him."

"Charles, we don't have time for that."

"Right, right. Look, this might be the last—" Charles face twisted. He wiped his sleeve across his face and snorted. "I need to say goodbye."

Hazel Montgomery saw Charles Horne for what he was, a kid. It's easy for adults to hate teenagers, to project their own adult thoughts onto them. To expect a kid to react the same way a middle-aged person would. But they don't, and they need to figure it out for themselves. She pitied him for what he had been asked to do. This shouldn't be happening. This shouldn't have happened to any of these kids, including the ones Midwatch and Leonard Philips stole away from their short lives. She wondered if she or any of their small Congregate was any better. They took Charles, Cody, and Mitch for the same reasons; they were young and full of energy. Like supercharged batteries for the devices of their cause. She saw Charles as a kid whose short life the supposed good guys were stealing. She rubbed her forehead.

"Do you have a phone?" she asked.

"Yes," answered Charles.

"Okay, I'll need to use it. Do what you need to do."

Charles jumped at her and wrapped his arms around her neck. He buried his face in her shoulder. "Thank you," came out muffled.

"Okay, kid. It'll be alright."

She wasn't good at dealing with kids. Probably why Leonard put her in as counselor under the idea she could find out what was happening to these kids. The joke was on her, he was what was happening to these kids, and he knew she would have a difficult time getting them to trust her with their thoughts. He played her for a fool. She covered her mouth with her hand and looked away.

After a moment, she followed Charles in and closed the door behind her.

* * *

She called the station and left a message for Deputy Riggs that he should park at the Longview Tavern to wait. She hoped he'd get it before he drove up to JNR.

Carson recognized her as the school's counselor and a feared authority. Charles calmed him with little effort.

She watched the boys play their game. They laughed, made jokes, got up for snacks and a drink twice, and eventually got into an argument about something called The Wiggler. She watched two brothers trying to figure out how to defeat a bad guy. Eventually, they did.

The Wiggler gave up and the battle was won.

The young Carson pleaded with his brother to keep playing, concerned about the next levels being too difficult for him.

"Chuckie, what if I can't beat this without your help," he said.

"Carson, c'mon little bro we both know you can. You're a great gamer. Probably better than me," Charles winked. "Well, one day, maybe."

"Do you have to go?"

"I do, buddy. We'll play again sometime. I just needed to get my car. Can you tell mom I love her? And, hey, have you seen Bart?"

"I've seen Bart a lot! He's been sitting with me when I play. Some-times he sleeps in my bed! Bart! Where are you Barty-Bart? Bart!"

The cat did not come. They searched the house, which didn't take long. It seemed he wasn't home.

"Oh well, give him a pet for me, will ya?"

"Are you going to be gone a while?" asked Carson. "Like Dad?"

Charles' shoulders slumped.

Hazel was moved by the amount of love between them. Charles was trying to make up for past behavior. She looked around the little room again. How many families lived this way? She wouldn't have guessed many in Brewster Falls. People everywhere needed help. She wondered about their mother. Once, she would have been angry to see these conditions. She would have blamed the parents for allowing children to live this way, for allowing them to be alone. Time taught her that sometimes, there was no choice. Nothing left to give after the day was done. Perhaps this woman was the strongest person in town. Perhaps.

One thing was perfectly clear, Carson saw Charles as more than a big brother. He needed him. They needed each other.

Maybe she could leave him here. Would it make that much difference? One less soul to burn?

Charles whispered something to his little brother as she considered. He was saying goodbye. Just like their dad.

She opened the front door and walked out.

* * *

Charles found her leaning against the Caprice's driver's door. She was smoking a cigarette and wearing his mom's sunglasses.

"Where'd you get those?"

"They were on your coffee table," she answered, and then exhaled a cloud of bluish smoke.

"Hm. Are you ready?"

"Are you?"

"Yeah, let's go." He walked to the door and gently pushed her hip away from the keyhole.

She grabbed his arm.

"Hey, Charles, you can stay if you want."

"What? How the hell could I do that?"

"I see how you were in there. You can be there for him."

Charles sighed.

"He'll be alright. We're... not that close. Besides, how could I do that to Cody? My girlfriend was killed, and my other best friend is still missing. Michael said it would take all of us. How can I not go? I'd be a... coward. I can't do that to them."

"But you can do it to him?"

Hazel pointed to the house with the two fingers holding her stolen cigarette.

His eyes met hers and she had the feeling he had aged twenty years.

"I already have."

She released him and moved out of the way.

The big car roared to life. A sound both powerful and reluctant, as if some energy it didn't want forced it to run.

When she got in, Charles was sitting in the driver's seat, eyes closed. A song exploded from the speakers which hurt her ears. She saw his knuckles go white on the steering wheel as the singer shouted to get off the commode.

He backed out of the driveway as the chorus started.

She wondered if she should drive.

The tires squealed their answer.

Too late.

VIII – ROLL OUT

Deputy Riggs had a ping of nostalgia as large, if not larger, than Charles Horne's. Before getting his patrol car, he went into the station and made sure to say something to everyone. Especially Claire, the dispatcher. All the Riggs' loved Claire.

He got the message to meet them at the Longview and was leaning on the hood of six-oh-two when Charles and Hazel pulled up. They got out to greet him but left the Caprice running.

"Charles. Hazel."

"Deputy Riggs," said Charles.

"Stephen," said Hazel.

"We ready to do this thing?"

"Yes, I think so," said Hazel. "When we get to JNR, we'll go around to the right to the third building on the left. There's an elevator hidden as a loading zone. We'll need to go in one at a time."

Deputy Riggs laughed. "An elevator? One at a time? What are you talking about? Isn't the whole point to bring the cars?"

Hazel lit another cigarette and inhaled it slowly. "It's a big elevator."

Deputy Riggs reached for the smoke and Hazel gave it willingly. He took a drag and handed it back. He walked around Charles' car and whistled.

"Man, this doesn't sound like any Caprice I've ever seen. What's in it?"

"It's set up like an Impala SS. All the way down to the suspension."

"A sleeper? Cool. I like that you kept all the Caprice badging. Even the hood ornament."

"Yeah, my dad recommended that."

"Your dad? You guys build it together?"

"Yeah, right before he left us. The engine was blown when we got it." Charles awkwardly stuck a knuckle in his mouth and slurped, like he might after scraping it on an engine block. "I know every screw, bolt, and wire in this car."

Deputy Riggs looked at the car a little longer. He noted the VIN. Then, he opened the driver's door and checked the ID tag. "Was this car white when you got it?"

"Yeah."

"Your dad buy it from the BFPD?"

"Yeah, from Chief Greg Riggs."

"My dad." Deputy Riggs took the cigarette from Hazel and took another drag. A long one. He dropped the butt and stamped it out.

"Isn't that illegal?" asked Charles. "And isn't smoking bad? You shouldn't be doing that."

"Right. Sorry." He picked up the butt and put it in his pocket.

"It's okay."

"No, it isn't. I have a feeling, after recent events, that if more people refrained from little wrongs we might not be in this mess. We need to do better. Anyway, my dad loved this car. He was so mad when the city switched our cars over to Crown Vics. He said he felt stronger in the Caprice."

"Smart man," said Charles.

"What are you talking about?" asked Hazel. "Does any of this matter?"

"Not really," answered Deputy Riggs. "I just find it odd that my dad's squad car is about to roll into a strange place for a battle alongside mine. All this is weird. Do you have a radio in that thing?"

"Yeah, a Pioneer with MOSFET techn—"

"No, kid, not a stereo. A radio." Deputy Riggs held up his hand like he had a walkie talkie and made a staticky noise with his mouth while he clicked a button that wasn't there.

"Oh. No."

"No problem, I have a spare."

He opened the Crown Vic's trunk and handed Charles his spare radio.

"Plug it into the cigarette lighter and make sure it works."

Charles took it and got in his car. He plugged in the radio, and it clicked on. He gave Deputy Riggs a thumbs up.

"Cool. You know over, over and out, copy, all that stuff?"

"Well enough, yeah."

"Good. Just so you know, this was car forty-four. Mine is six-oh-two. It would mean a lot to me if you used that number."

"You got it."

Deputy Riggs stuck out his right hand to Charles. He got out of the Caprice and shook it.

"Thanks, kid. Now, Hazel, tell us about this elevator."

* * *

Brewster Falls was in the golden hour when they pulled into Jack Nassem Research Park. Hazel said to keep moving until they were at the elevator, so they did. She said there were cameras everywhere, but she had high clearance and would be able to present them as witnesses. Deputy Riggs wondered aloud under what jurisdiction JNR could question witnesses about anything. She told him the answer to that was for another time. They watched everything from here.

Against Charles' wishes, she had him go down the elevator first in Deputy Riggs squad car. She would come back up for the Caprice. She said it looked like a car that belonged here and would draw less attention than a BFPD squad car.

When the elevator came down carrying the Caprice, she got out and told them all they had to do was drive straight for a few hundred feet, at which point they would come to a large accordion style door. Once they opened it, they would have to go into a large open theater in which the gate they needed stood. Before they could take the cars in, they would first need to move one of two Ocelot 240s out of the way because they guarded the gate.

"Oce-what?" asked Deputy Riggs.

"Ocelot 240," said Hazel. "It's a fire support vehicle."

"Fire support vehicle?"

Hazel sighed. "I should have taken more cigarettes. A tank, Steve. We need to move a tank."

"Move a tank? Why the hell wouldn't we take it with us?"

Charles nodded. "Yeah, I feel like we could use a tank. There's three of us, and only two cars. You could drive it, Ms. Montgomery. Always seemed like a tank girl to me."

She looked at him, her eyes daggers and fire.

"I can't steal a tank."

"Why not?" asked Deputy Riggs.

"Let's go. We'll move it and get back to where we're needed. This is already going easier than expected, let's not press our luck. I don't know why we haven't been stopped, and I don't want to find out. Heard?"

Deputy Riggs shrugged. "Sorry, kid. No tank."

"Darn."

Charles hopped in the Caprice and fired it up.

"Well, if they didn't know we were here, they do now!" yelled Deputy Riggs.

Hazel shook her head.

They drove up to the theater and went in no problem. Sure enough, right in the middle was a free-standing garage door with two tank-looking vehicles placed facing each other on either side of it.

Hazel raised her finger to her lips in a 'be quiet' signal.

"Really," said Deputy Riggs. "Did you hear the car? Just go move the thing."

"I guess you're right," she said.

When she turned to face the Ocelot, something large and dark flew past her head and struck the floor with a crash. They all jumped; none higher than Deputy Riggs. The smell of alcohol filled the air.

Hazel ducked and inspected the UFO. It had been made of glass, but was now shattered, a brownish liquid sprayed all over the floor. She put her finger in it, and to Charles' surprise licked it off.

"Bourbon?" she said.

"Fugh yeah iss Bourbon, Hayzel."

She had never heard it speak that way, but she knew that voice.

"Lenny?" She peered towards the area whence the bottle had flown.

"Callll me Leonard. All mah enemies do," said Leonard Philips.

Hazel waved for Charles and Deputy Riggs to go back to the cars.

Crazed laughter poured from one of the Ocelots. "Don't make them go, issa party... now."

To her horror, the Ocelot fired up, its diesel engine's sound shaming that of the Caprice. Its turret rotated.

The next things Leonard Philips said were clear.

"Allow me to introduce the Ocelot 240 fire support vehicle from German tech group Wessermacht. This new Ocelot is a fully mechanized vehicle with anti-tank capabilities. Which is humorous, because it is itself, a tank! Its primary armament is a 120mm smooth-bore gun. Observe."

The main gun on the Ocelot fired into the theater seats. It created an opening it could drive through, and temporarily deafened Hazel and the guys.

"Ooooh, that was a little loud!" shouted Leonard.

Their ears rang with a tone that may never leave, but they could still hear him.

"Secondary armaments are four .50-cal machine guns which can be controlled via remote. Neat! The Ocelot also features modern architecture with unrivaled upgradability, in accordance with NATO standards, of course. Not that we here at JNR give a hoot about any standards other than our own! The Ocelot is designed to deliver maximum lethality, mobility, protection, and survivability. How about that? Maximum lethality AND survivability, in one package! Could go either way, I suppose."

The turret stopped rotating towards them. They heard clanking and what could have been cursing coming from the tank. Then, the machine gun fired.

"LEONARD PHILIPS! STOP IT!" screamed Hazel.

To her shock, the firing stopped.

"The demonstration is almost over, Hazel! Finally, the Ocelot 240 is equipped with a 360° camera system with automatic target detection and tracking. The active defense system will let it auto track threats on the ground or in the air and keep them tracked until neutralized. None of which will be available for another twenty years! Observe!"

Red dots like laser pointers shot out of the tank and hit each of them in the chest. In the same instant, the turret swung around with the big gun aimed at Hazel, and two machine guns at Deputy Riggs and Charles.

"Shit," said Hazel.

"Now don't move," said Leonard Philips.

They didn't move.

They watched from the observation theater's shadows as the silhouette of Leonard Philips removed itself from the tank and approached. He raised his hand, showing he held something.

"This is the remote control for the Ocelot. Notice I am not pressing anything. Mr. Horne, if you would, please move six steps to the right."

Charles moved as instructed. One machine gun followed him. He stopped under one of the lights that were on in the big room.

"Wonderful!" said Leonard.

"Horrifying," said Hazel.

"Perhaps, but cannot something horrifying be wondrous?"

"I thought you were drunk," said Deputy Riggs.

Leonard smiled. "Oh, I am. Me and my friend Elmer T. have been having a great time. But power has a sobering effect. Charles! My, my. I see you've brought a friend!"

Hazel and Deputy Riggs looked at Charles and then back to Leonard.

"What?" said Deputy Riggs.

"Oh, you two don't have the type of friends young Mr. Horne and I have, do they Charles? Would you like to see mine?"

He walked over to a panel with many switches. "You'd think with all this tech at our command we could have automated lights in this room."

They were momentarily blinded when the lights came on.

Leonard walked past Hazel and Deputy Riggs to stand in front of Charles. Hazel twitched when he passed, and she noted so did the cannon on the Ocelot.

Charles' mouth hung agape. His eyes fixed over Leonard's right shoulder.

"No. No no no no no," he muttered.

"Yes. Yes yes yes yes yes," mocked Leonard. "Do you understand what you see?"

"I... do. But... why?"

"Why, indeed. Why did you kill my daughter? Why did Midwatch attach her to me? Why are you here now? So... many... whys." With each word, Leonard inched his face closer and closer to Charles', until their noses nearly touched.

"What? No, I didn't kill Tiffany, it was Midwatch. It shot her with a bolt of purple lightning," said Charles. "Right in front of Cody and me."

Leonard sneered. "I don't believe that. Midwatch may be many things, but a liar is not one of them. We have worked together long. Once it makes a deal, it keeps it. The code of Midwatch would not allow it to violate an agreement."

"Well, it said 'oops'," said Charles.

Leonard stepped aside, no longer standing between him and the big gun trained on him. He held out the remote and rested his finger on one of its many buttons. "If I press this, your game will be over."

"Leonard, please stop this. The boys did not harm Tiffany. Midwatch did this to them. They didn't ask for illimni, and they didn't ask to be part of this," pleaded Hazel.

"They saved my brother," added Deputy Riggs. "We're trying to get back there to help fight Midwatch and its army. What it's done to our kids, our people; it needs to be stopped."

Leonard's trigger finger twitched.

"No!" screamed Hazel.

Leonard pressed the button.

* * *

Charles Horne fell to the ground. Hazel Montgomery dove onto him. Deputy Stephen Riggs tackled Leonard Philips.

The guns on the Ocelot sagged, their laser sights went dark.

"I turned it off," choked Leonard. "I turned it off."

Deputy Riggs wrenched away the remote and put it in the breast pocket of his shirt. He and Leonard sat next to each other on the ground.

"I know it betrayed me," said Leonard. "But I didn't want to believe it. We had done so much together. I had done so many things. Horrible things. What happened to Jack, now Tiffany. I helped cause this pain to so many families. Granted power to horrible people for the sake of progress. Megalomaniacs, narcissists, geniuses. And they're all still out there, spinning their webs of control, enslaving everyone. And I helped."

"It's Shake 'n Bake," said Deputy Riggs.

Hazel sighed and shook her head. He shrugged, making it clear to her he didn't know how to handle this situation.

Hazel held Charles. "I'll be okay," he said, coming around from his faint.

She walked over to Leonard and extended her hand to him.

"From the Aurlibrum, embrace redemption, a privilege bestowed upon all souls. For it is the ones who have stumbled and risen from the depths of despair who must guide those who have fallen back to the light. Without the hope of redemption, there can be no love."

"You know the Aurlibrum? It's not all 'beware this or that'?" asked Deputy Riggs.

Hazel rolled her eyes. "Are you all stupid? And you, shut up." She pointed at Deputy Riggs then offered her hand to Leonard Philips again. "Take my hand and get up. Yes, you've done horrible things. Unforgivable. Yet, the Aeraph say with time all can be forgiven, if first you forgive yourself. There's no way to save your daughter or bring her back, and for that I am very, very sorry. Just as I'm sorry for the parents of Jenny Noble, the kids with us, and all the others you delivered to slaughter."

Leonard winced at the words of truth.

Hazel continued. "Don't waste away drinking cheap whiskey and feeling sorry for yourself. You did what you did, and that's done. Do you want to honor their memories? Right the wrong? Get a little revenge—even though Michael would say that was bad, but we just won't tell him. We're ready to go fight our common enemy. Join us. Help us. Bring your tanks! Give yourself unto it and be redeemed! Take my hand and get up!"

Leonard mumbled something.

"What did you say?"

"It wasn't cheap," said Leonard. He looked up, his cheeks streaked with tears.

"Huh?"

"The whiskey. You said it was cheap. It wasn't. Jack Nassem gave it to me the day before he killed himself. It was precious to me."

Hazel looked down at the great Leonard Philips, architect of Brewster Falls, builder of Jack Nassem Research Park, and engineer of the current state of their world. She felt a great pity for this man. The sum of his life's work less than zero.

"Join us, Lenny, please," begged Hazel.

"Don't call me Lenny."

He took her hand, and she lifted him up.

"Can you drive one of these?" he asked.

"Yes, I was trained when we got them," she said.

"Good. Once we get them on the other side, we need to destroy this gate. And then all the others."

"Sounds good to me."

Charles coughed. "So, what, we're going to trust this guy now? His own daughter is attached to his shoulder. He's destroyed our lives. And we're supposed to go over there with him in a tank and feel like its fine? Screw that."

"Charles," said Hazel.

"I agree with the kid," said Deputy Riggs. "How do we know he won't train those guns on us again as soon as we're over there? How do we know he hasn't already?"

"I sent your fathers away. And, Stephen, your mother," said Leonard.

"What?" asked Charles.

"Your father didn't just leave. He wanted you and your mom and your brother to be cared for. He felt he had failed as a father and husband. Actually, I convinced him he had failed, which was easy because he wasn't great. I offered him work helping with the maintenance of Nassem City, under the condition he could never return. In exchange, I was supposed to take care of your mother and you. And Stephen, Penelope Riggs went willingly. She figured out what was happening to the children. She was a brilliant investigator. Since one role of JNR was to find and stop this threat, I allowed her to go. It was good cover for our operation to allow measured progress against it. But she knew too much, so Midwatch and I trapped her. As far as I know, she still lives within it. Eventually, your father was able to reconstruct her findings and approached me. So, of course, I sent him to Midwatch as well. Although, he is still missing. Somewhere over there."

"You call that taking care of us? You stole my daddy from me. We barely scrape by while you live in a mansion. Dude, you suck major ass." Charles balled his fists.

"So, I really talked to my mom while I was in there," mumbled Deputy Riggs.

Charles lunged at Leonard Philips and landed a pretty nice right hook across his left cheek. He ended up back on the ground.

"Asshole," said Charles.

Deputy Riggs extended his hand to Leonard, "Nice hit, kid."

Leonard took his hand, and as soon as he stood Riggs sucker punched him in his gut. Then, he leaned over him and whispered, "Do you still want to help us?"

"Yes," Leonard coughed. "Yes, I am an asshole. My payment for these things was my only friend killing himself, and my partner killing my only daughter and attaching her dead soul to me in mockery. I tell you this to say, if I had wanted to kill you with my tank, you would already be dead. The only one I wish to kill is Midwatch. And so, I join you now to that end. If I die in the attempt, it will be a mercy."

Riggs shrugged. "What do you say, kid? Do we let this loser join us other losers?"

Charles thought about it long enough that they became uncomfortable.

Finally, he said, "Oh, boo hoo. Poor me and my riches and my heated pool and my hot wife. Waaaaaa. Sure, he can die with us, but I'm driving behind his tank. And I'm not helping him up."

Riggs laughed. "Well, looks like Leonard fucking Philips is about to do the right thing. Put that in the Aurlibrum."

Leonard stood unassisted. "Thank you. This may be the only good thing I ever do."

"You're not the hero here, and you never will be," said Hazel. "But we thank you for the help. Alright boys, get your cars. It's time to roll out."

CHAPTER 13

Wings and V8s

"Liht Conta Nocht! Liht Conta Nocht! Liht Conta Nocht!"

I – CRIMSON

The first time they witness a Violet Knight carry a Red Aeraph into the sky, separate its wings from its body, and drop it back to the ground for it to burst, it shocks the hell out of them. The fifth time less so. And by the tenth they become angry at the Reds for not defending themselves better.

A visceral reaction occurs upon seeing death, or worse, committing it. Part of the mind shuts off, part of the soul. In the heat of battle, blood flows less to the brain and more to the muscles and extremities. The mind constricts, forcing a removal of emotion and empathy and a heightening of fight, flight, and anger. The famous 'thrill' of combat. This allows the soldier to do what needs done. However, consequences appear when these empathetic systems come back online post battle. On Tempora, we call the feelings associated with this reboot Post Traumatic Stress Disorder.

During the fray, the body's automatic assist can make the actions of someone otherwise mild-mannered seem absurd. This was the case with Cody McLean. Charles watches in awe as he sprints with the Reds, swinging his sword at any Violet Knight that comes near. No grace exists in Cody's movements. They are wild, untrained, and unpredictable. While he lands few blows against the enemy, the Knights stop going after the Reds nearest to Cody. And so, as one would expect, more gather about him. An urgency flows through the red blob moving with him. In another time and place, Charles would have found joy in seeing his fantasy-obsessed friend leading a group of mythical winged creatures in battle.

Now, however, all he can think of doing is call him back. "CODY! Come back! Get back in the car! Cody! CODY!"

Cody glances his way. His face not unlike the version Charles saw the day he attacked him before school. Charles continues to yell and motion him back to the car.

Cody does not try to return.

Charles shields his eyes with his hand. Aeraph, both Nochtvol and otherwise, fight in the air. A couple Vocturians carry two of his companions, though from the ground he can't tell who. The only thing he can identify from here is Michael. His armor reflects blue-jean blue. He wields two swords, one on fire. The flavors of his movements are the opposite of those of young Master Cody. His motions are fluent and with purpose. He dives and slices a violet mid-section on one side and liberates a wing from a Nochtvol with the flaming blade on the other. When the flaming blade strikes an enemy, all its feathers burn. Like Ithex burned in the Trinus. In death, they are all just Aeraph. The tragedy of war.

Charles can't discern who is winning this fight.

He gets back in the Caprice and shouts at the Reds. "I can take two!"

Two come over, one stands on the trunk, one on the roof. He tries not to think about the dents they cause.

They crouch and grasp the bars they had mounted on the car.

Charles punches up on the roof once. A moment later, two knocks came in answer.

They're ready.

The car lurches forward. The dirt of Aesteria sprays from its tires and the combustion of its engine screams from its exhaust. Whether Violet Guard or Aeraph Soldier, they separate like the Red Sea parting before Moses. Regardless of side or motivation, no creature from Aesteria, now Midwatch, wants anything to do with this Temporan beast.

The car accelerates across the flat ground. After a few seconds, Charles looks in the rearview mirror. The Red on the trunk lifts into the air. He drives on for a few more seconds in case the one on the roof needs more time, then goes back for more.

Charles is rather proud of this idea. When Michael said the Red Aeraph couldn't fly, except for some who could when jumping from a high place, he understood it wasn't that they couldn't fly, but that they couldn't take off. Two different things. Besides, he missed his car.

Elsewhere on the battlefield a Volvo, a BFPD Crown Vic, and two Ocelot tanks do the same. If Aeraph are put off by Charles' Caprice, they are terrified of the Ocelots. Unlike the cars, the tanks target Violet Knights with five guns each, non-stop. Leonard had programmed the guns to shoot anything purple with wings, so as soon as one goes down, they target the next. And the big gun, well, sometimes it misses and sometimes it hits. And sometimes when it hits, it hits three or four at a time.

Once a Red launches into the air, it soars up as high as possible, draws two daggers, and dives for the nearest Violet Knight. They wrap them up and hack and slash until they both fall, or others join in to help. Then, they glide back to the ground and do it again. Not the greatest plan, but effective. Once a Nochtvol hits the ground, the other Reds swarm it and finish the job. The Aeraph soldiers learn not to swarm a downed Nochtvol falling near Leonard Philips' Ocelot, because he likes to run them down without regard for who or what is near.

The battlefield's color takes on a crimson hue.

Charles slows and turns to make another pass. He searches the horizon. After several hours, the dark cloud of Midwatch remains unseen.

II – THE ECHO SPACE

Alice refuses to give up hope, her cries for friendship and love echo in the void. "Look into my mind. You will see the truth!" *truth. truth. truth.*

The thing that used to be Tiffany Philips cares not for truth. It tears apart Alice's thoughts and memories with ruthless efficiency. Alice's screams do not pierce the sphere of darkness the thing created with its newfound power. It revels in the act as it inflicts its twisted will upon its oldest friend.

I know the truth. I have seen it. I never fit in. Poor rich Tiffany has everything she wants. Why should she be upset? Depressed? Sad? See if you can get her to pay for these pizzas. That's all I was to you. You used me as a bank and a punchline. And now, I'm dead. Because of you. Keep screaming. No one's coming.

The thing that used to be Tiffany Philips pulls a piece of Alice's mind away. She screams. No one comes.

The thing casts the mind-piece out into Midwatch. It floats away like a soap bubble in the wind. The kind they blew when they were kids. Something moves inside the bubble, but the thing cannot see what it is. It attempts to retrieve it, but it pops. When it does, the thing that used to be Tiffany Philips hears voices. Laughter. The sounds fade into darkness before it can discern what they say.

Inside it, Alice pleads for her life.

"Tiffany, I love you. You're my best friend. Remember our slumber parties? Just the two of us? We'd dress up as Julia Roberts in Pretty Woman, or Baby Houseman. We'd take turns playing Johnny. 'No one puts Baby in the corner!' Remember? That's who we are. That's who you are to me. You're my sister!" *sister! sister! sister!*

You should have thought of that before making a fool of me. Before Midwatch showed me your precious truth. 'Everything about Tiffany is fake. She doesn't deserve any love. She deserves to be our little toy. Our little joke. The joke of Brewster Falls.' Remember?

The thing pulls Alice's mind again.

"What? I didn't say that! I've never even thought that! You deserve all the love in the world! You aren't—" Alice screams again as another piece of her mind is torn away.

The thing that used to be Tiffany Philips gazes into it before casting it away. Inside is Alice and Tiffany in her bedroom. There is no sound. They are wearing her mother's dresses and dancing. They sing into a hairbrush and a curler. They are young in the memory, before the weight of growing up ruined them.

Yes, I remember this, but it was before you learned to betray me. Before you used me.

The thing that used to be Tiffany Philips pops the bubble. Music fills the space around it. Their voices accompany Frankie Valli singing 'Big Girls Don't Cry'. The thing that used to be Tiffany Philips is overcome by nostalgia.

That's from the soundtrack! We sang it over and over.

Alice weeps inside the thing. "What?" *what? what? what?*

The song, from the Dirty Dancing soundtrack. Big Girls Don't Cry. We agreed to be tough and never let boys hurt us or come between us. It was our battle cry.

"I don't know what you're talking about. Please, just let me out of here!" *here! here! here!*

You just told me about it!

Alice whimpers. "Please, please let me go. Please. I'll leave you alone. I'm afraid." *afraid. afraid. afraid.*

Fine, have it your way.

The thing that used to be Tiffany Philips pulls hard. Another piece of Alice's mind comes free. She does not scream. The thing cannot sense her consciousness. It reaches further and is relieved to find she is still alive.

Good.

The thing that used to be Tiffany Philips inspects this memory and finds it knows this place as well. Alice's bedroom. It watches as Charles sits on Alice's bed. The thing strikes at what is left of her, though there is no satisfaction in the blow.

Wake up so I can torture you! it cries.

Alice sits next to Charles and leans close. Something in his hand. A small box. He opens it and holds it up so she can see what's inside. Her hands cover her mouth with joy. Although there is no sound, the thing that used to be Tiffany Philips knows Alice squeals with glee. Then, she wraps her arms around Charles' neck and kisses his cheek. The image fades and is replaced by a different memory of Alice and Charles together.

The thing that used to be Tiffany Philips strikes at Alice. It wants her awake. It wants to make her face her betrayal, to hear her beg for her life as it tears it away. The thing strikes, strikes, strikes.

In its rage, the bubble pops and releases the memory's sound.

It is Alice's voice.

"When are you going to give it to her?"

And Charles' voice.

"I don't know. I've been close a few times, but I always get scared. Her dad won't like it. I mean, maybe... are we too young? I don't want anyone else. I know we fight sometimes, but I love her. It hurts. She deserves everything. The way her parents ignore her. I just want her. The way she smells... ugh... sorry. I'm not good with feelings."

Alice laughs.

"Too young? I don't know, either. But the idea of my best friends together makes me happy. I love you both so much. You better do it soon because I don't know how long I can keep this from her! And don't forget, she don't need no man so you better need her!"

"I do need her. You wouldn't..."

The sound fades into Midwatch.

Oh. Oh no.

The thing that used to be Tiffany Philips stops striking Alice.

What have I done? Alice, oh my Alice. My sister.

The thing forms a cocoon. It rocks her and begs her to wake up.

She does not.

* * *

The thing that used to be Tiffany Philips becomes the soul-mind of Tiffany Philips. She cradles her friend for a long time. She fears Alice will never come back from the damage she caused.

She sings as she rocks her sister's spirit. It's 'Big Girls Don't Cry'.

Another voice joins her. Its warmth added to her own, along with its thoughts and memories.

The soul-minds of Tiffany Philips and Penelope Riggs serenade the spirit of Alice Massey.

She mutters something.

Alice? Alice, can you hear me? It's Tiff.

She groans. "Big girls do cry." There is no echo within the cradle.

That they do, dear, says the soul-mind of Penelope Riggs.

Oh, Alice! Are you okay? Do you know where you are? Do you know my voice?

"Sure, Tiff. I know your voice. I remember, uh, we're in Mid-watch. Inside it? Who's that with you? Her voice is nice."

This is Penny Riggs, hon. Mitch and Steve's mom.

Nice to meet you, says Tiffany. *And thanks for your help.*

"Yes, nice to meet you Mrs. Riggs. It feels like I've known you forever," says Alice.

Yes, the lines between minds become fuzzy in here.

"How do we get out?" asks Alice.

You can because you're not dead. You were absorbed whole. All of us, though. I'm afraid there's no way for us except to take another's soul from them, which we aren't willing to do.

All of us? asks Tiffany.

Many, answers Penny. *Alice, before you go, can you help us? Our powers increased when you entered Midwatch. We can try to destroy it. From inside.*

"Destroy it? What happens to us if we destroy it?"

We don't know. We might control it, or we might disappear entirely. Either is freedom from this hell. As for you, we can cast you out with your body any time. All your dust is here.

"I'm sorry, my dust?"

That's what we call it. Its allies come and go. While they are here, the particles making them up float around. We call it dust.

"Gross," says Alice. "What must I do?"

I'll gather the others, says Penny. *She releases Tiffany's soul-mind and fades into Midwatch.*

Alice, I'm sorry. I'm sorry I fell for its tricks. I let you down. I love you.

"Oh, Tiff. Sisters fight, right?"

Yeah. But I almost killed you.

"But you didn't. See, all my dust is right here."

They laugh.

I can't believe Charles got me a ring! You'll have to tell him I would've said yes. I'd always say yes.

Alice does not respond.

Are you still there? It's sad, isn't it? I'm sad. You'll tell him, won't you?

"Sure, I will."

You're the best, Al. Thank you.

"Anything, Tiff. I'm sorry about what happened to you. I'll need you to tell me who Charles is, though."

III – THE KNOCKING

Bodies. Bodies everywhere. The scent of adrenaline, sweat, and blood surrounds them, each sure their side has the right of it. Beware righteousness, as is said in the Aurlibrum. Their minds constrict to the tune of the fight.

Big Doug Massey abandoned his vehicle long ago. He rides the Vocturian Agileux. Near him soars Margaret upon Glaphra, Hazel on Lythas, and Mitch on Pelian. Viatis, Hidarion, Fosia, and Kevin dive in and out of the battlefield near their charges, watching for trouble and listening for the cry of 'valkoor'.

The Vocturi do not fight. Without them victory is not possible. Always there are only eight. If one falls, Aeraph from flying Varvikas volunteer and from them a replacement is chosen. They seek the injured, Nochtvol or otherwise, and carry them to safety. Margaret leads the Temporans in healing them. Nochtvol are given a choice to join the Aeraph or face judgement by the Aurclock. Many choose Judgement.

These nurturers primary directive is always to render care to the sick, disabled, and injured, without regard to origin. The purpose of war is to inflict this damage. So, upon the chest of their armor resides a colorless broken heart. It is the only piece of Aeraph armor that does not reflect light.

The battle rages on.

* * *

Hazel joins Margaret next to a fallen Aeraph. As they administer their healing, Glaphra and Lythas return to the field to rescue more. Ulrich does not leave the makeshift hospital. His aid increases the mending's speed, as it does from Doug, or Deputy Riggs, or even Mitch. Though they do not share the powers of these druids, their touch upon the healers' shoulders, the comfort of their presence, their simple petition to whatever they believe in increases the effectiveness of their plight. They feel something being pulled from them when they do. They give it willingly.

* * *

Charles makes another pass. He thinks of the life he lived. It is gone. His stereo is not on. The Caprice's engine started knocking a while ago. He doesn't realize he's holding his breath until the radio Deputy Riggs gave him crackles.

"Forty-four, this is six-oh-two, copy."

"Go six-oh-two, forty-four listening. Over."

"Hey kid, I'm gonna need to bail. I broke a control arm or something on my last run. Six-oh-two only goes left now. Over."

Charles sighs. That leaves him and Leonard Philips on the battlefield. A wild shot from his Ocelot's big gun hit one of Hazel's tracks. She set the guns to fire at Nochtvol before hopping a Vocturian to safety. Soon there will be only one.

He presses the radio button. "Copy six-oh-two. I might be right behind you. Engine's knocking. Over."

"Sonofabitch. Sorry to hear that kid. Maybe you should hop out now. Head over to the triage before you're stranded somewhere you don't want to be. Over."

"Sure. I'm gonna look for Cody first. Haven't seen him in a while. Have you? Over."

"That's a negative. He's out there somewhere. Gotta go kid. They're comin' for me. See you on the other side. Six-oh-two, over and out."

Charles hangs up the radio. He's alone out there. Leonard Philips won't respond to radio calls. He checks his mirror. He won't pick up any more Aeraph. There are few straight paths left in the battlefield and he's tired of dodging bodies. He's more tired of running them over when he can't.

He scans the horizon. Still no Midwatch. He thinks about Cody. The Caprice's engine knocks louder.

* * *

Deputy Riggs gets out of his car. A group of Nochtvol close in on his position. He scans the sky for the yellow reflection of a Vocturian.

"Dammit," he says to himself.

Something hits the dirt at his feet. Then another.

"Rocks? They're throwing rocks at me?"

Not knowing what else to do, he picks up a rock and throws it back towards the Nochtvol.

Not even close.

He bellows "Valkoor! Valkoor! Valkoor!"

No Vocturi come for him. He runs.

Over his shoulder a Nochtvol dives for him. The Massey's Volvo is stuck in the dirt nearby, the driver's door open and facing him. He sprints for it.

Too late.

The Nochtvol tackles him.

They tumble to the ground together. They stop with Deputy Riggs on his back, the Nochtvol on top of him. He pulls his 1911 from its holster. The Nochtvol doesn't move. Warmth covers Deputy Riggs' torso. He struggles to push the creature off. It's dead, a large hole in its chest.

The Massey's Volvo is still running, and getting louder.

"What the hell?" he says.

As he watches, Leonard Philips' Ocelot crushes the car from the opposite side, flying over it while firing into the sky. The tank turns away from him and speeds off. As it passes, maniacal laughter erupts from its open hatch.

"Crazy bastard," says Deputy Riggs.

More sounds come from the direction of the Volvo.

"That thing can't be running."

It isn't. The soldiers fighting on the ground move toward him. He resumes shouting 'Valkoor', knowing his little gun has no power here.

As the first helms of the ground combatants appear, a golden blur whooshes down beside him.

"Which one are you?" asks Deputy Riggs.

"Kevin," says the Vocturian.

"Of course." He grasps the handles of the harness Kevin wears and mounts the saddle. Deputy Riggs never thought he would ride piggy-back ever again.

Kevin flaps his great wings and jumps into the air.

* * *

Leonard Philips crushes the car for no other reason than he wants to. Once Deputy Riggs is safe, he veers off to cause more carnage.

He skillfully pilots the Ocelot around the fighting armies, corralling them toward the Congregate of Aesteria. This is the only order Michael gave him. Margaret outright rejected his arrival and attacked him. Michael restrained her. He said something about the Aurlibrum, and she requested he be put in front of the Aurclock. Michael said they didn't have time and that he was a hot mess, but not evil. So, they put him in a tank.

He drives out and around, coming up on the fray from behind. He checks the sights and locks on to four Nochtvol. He presses the button to fire, and violet light blinds him.

"Knock, knock," says Midwatch.

IV – CONNECTIONS

"Hesperus is here," says Michael.

He stands in the triage area where the Temprans and Vocturi work to save lives.

"You mean Midwatch," says Margaret.

"Margaret, we save all lives, remember," says Glaphra, her Vocturian counterpart.

Big Doug Massey comforts his wife.

"We have the power to banish Midwatch. Our first attempt must be to separate it from Hesperus. This we must do," says Michael.

"And if we can't?" asks Hazel.

"Then I will have broken a promise to a dear friend," answers Michael.

"Ithex? He tried to murder us. And he betrayed you. We don't owe him anything," says Margaret.

Glaphra stands in front of her. "He was a father, a parent, and a good being. The turmoil caused by what happened to his son is not unique. Look at your feelings now. Pieces of your families are in Midwatch as well. If your child falls, do you not give everything to help them? Ithex paid a high price in defense of his son. What would you have had him do? What would you do?"

"Anything," whispers Doug.

"It works the other way, too," says Deputy Riggs. He stands with Mitch. "Our mom is in there. Maybe our dad."

"My dad might be, too," says Charles. "And my fiancé."

"Your what?" asks Mitch.

Charles shoves his hands in his pockets. "Not really. Not yet," he whispers. "I was too afraid to ask."

"Dude, bro. I'm sorry. I didn't mean to... I mean I... crap," says Mitch.

"Oh Charles, you're too young," says Deputy Riggs.

Charles' Vocturian carrier, Pelian, steps forward. "Too young? I know not what that means. Too young. Love shall not be held back. All can give love, all can choose to be kind. What kind of place is Tempora that you would restrict love during lives so short? What is the purpose?"

"Pelian speaks from the heart," says Fosia, the Vocturian assigned to protect Cody. "We do not understand your ways, but we understand loss. We understand pain. I have failed this day. My Temporan is lost, I know not where. Though our meeting was recent, our love extends to all of you, and my heart breaks." She places her arm across the symbol on her chest. "Perhaps he is within Midwatch as well. We must not harm any that can be saved."

Fosia bows and steps back as Michael takes her place.

"Friends. It is time to meet our enemy upon the battlefield. We fight hate, anger, jealousy, and malice. These things elude sight but are more powerful than any physical being if we let them be. We have many allies within the cloud known as Midwatch, and they may fight it from within. As it engulfed the Shadow-Bringer's death machine bolts of green light were seen sparking within it."

Big Doug Massey gasps. "Alice?"

Michael nods. "If the Source of our Congregate fights within the enemy, our powers will be multiplied. Margaret, you will lead us, all others support her. Once a connection is made, do what you can to join her physically. Concentrate on banishing only the Midwatch. However, it will try to influence you. It will take your anger and try to use it if it can. Keep your helms on. We do not know what it will feel like or look like. We must go."

The Vocturi leap into the air behind Michael, each except Fosia carrying a Temporan. It is a scene worthy of record.

* * *

Midwatch is close to Leonard's Ocelot when the Vocturi arrive. Those that have seen it before note the static and jagged shapes moving in and out of it. It is not the flowing cloud it once was. It's chaos before them, black with violet rivers of light flowing through it, an occasional explosion of green. Spikes appear where the green pulses flash, then are reabsorbed into the mass.

The Vocturi land and the Temporans dismount.

Michael hovers above Midwatch. "Hesperus! Stop this!" he shouts, his flaming sword at his side. "End this madness. You are forgiven!"

Midwatch snaps, crackles, and pops. It flashes away, then returns as quickly as it leaves. It bounces back and forth.

"Forgiven? Madness?" it hisses. "You are the only madness here! I seek balance! I need no forgiveness!"

A bolt of violet light shoots up at Michael. He dodges and swings his sword. The light wraps around the flaming blade, and Michael pulls it taught. Midwatch grunts. Violet veins of energy feed the tether connecting them. As they do, more green pulses and spikes shoot from the cloud.

"Now, Margaret," says Glaphra.

They advance on Midwatch behind a wall of Vocturians. Midwatch twitches in the air, unable to move away. Michael holds it while an unknown battle rages within it. It screams. It is the very sound of hate, the screech of a demon.

"NOW!" yells Michael.

The Vocturi part, and Margaret steps through the opening, right arm raised. Green light shoots from her palm. When it connects with the cloud, her blood boils. Pain courses through her. She is going to break the connection until Hazel, her sister, takes her other hand. The pain lessens.

"Everyone on us!" shouts Hazel.

Deputy Riggs runs through and places one hand on Hazel, and one on Margaret. His body fills with intense burning. He can only imagine what Margaret experienced moments ago.

Big Doug Massey, Ulrich, Charles, and Mitch follow. They form an interlocked group with Margaret at its peak. Little white flowers bloom at their feet.

Midwatch laughs.

A purple ball of energy shoots into the green beam connecting it to the Temporans. It knocks Big Doug Massey and Ulrich to the ground. He lies in the dirt, eyes closed, mind drifting back to the day at Marblehead. He wishes for sleep. To stay in this moment forever. Deputy Riggs smacks him in the face.

His eyes snap open and he grits his teeth. He puts his hands around Deputy Riggs throat and squeezes until he feels gulps for air between his thumbs. "You will not take this from me!" he growls. Big Doug Massey's helm is not on his head. "Yes, yes, Yes, YES!" he screams.

Ulrich sits up a few feet away. He rolls toward Doug and grasps his head with both hands. Doug's intense remorse, fear, and hate fill his heart and mind. The hate does not belong to him. Ulrich focuses on separating it from his natural thoughts. "Do not do this, Douglas! This is not what Alice would want! Think of your daughter! Focus! FOCUS!"

Big Doug Massey's grip loosens. Deputy Riggs gasps for air. He grabs the hands around his throat and pulls them off. He reaches for the helm and attempts to place it on Doug's head.

"No," says Ulrich. "The hate must be banished." The grey man closes his eyes. "Get ready," he says. Big Doug Massey convulses as if hit with a defibrillator. Violet beams of light shoot from his eyes and mouth. "NOW!"

Ulrich releases the big man's head so Deputy Riggs can replace his helm.

They are again thrown backwards, and their helms fly.

On the ground behind them lie Mitch and Charles.

Ulrich resists and runs to Margaret and Hazel. He tries to rejoin them. They are unresponsive, but the flash's blue-green color knocks him back and tells him they don't want his help.

Before him lie three unconscious boys, two defenseless men, two Druids of the Congregate linked in battle, eight Vocturians protecting them, and one Aeraph General holding it all in place. Few are left fighting on the field. There are many dead.

"How did it come to this…" he asks himself. "Did I cause this?"

He approaches Margaret and Hazel one last time, and all goes dark.

V – FATHERS

Charles was in the garage. His daddy just told him they aren't the worst family.

Darryl Horne turned to walk away, and then knelt next to his son. "Chuck, there's one more thing. Carson. I don't really know him. Not like I know you. He's gonna need you. He won't understand. Can you be there for him? Do what a daddy should do? Can you do that for me, son?"

Charles was crying but nodded his agreement. He didn't want to do this. He didn't want his daddy to leave. He said nothing. He held it in.

Darryl left him in the garage. Charles still stood alone when he fired up ol' Blue and drove away.

* * *

Mitch stood in their kitchen. His brother Steve talked to their dad in the living room. Their mother had just been reported missing. Greg Riggs told his oldest son he needed to go look for her. He has some leads. Lenny Philips was going to help him.

His dad told Steve that Mitch wasn't like them. That he's better than they are.

"In case I don't come back, you need to make sure he does better. Don't let him be a cop in this stupid small town. Get him far away from here."

His big brother agreed.

Mitch hated this. He held back tears. He didn't want this; he loved Brewster Falls. Why would he ever want to leave? All he ever wanted was to be just like his dad. He punched the refrigerator, leaving a dent that was still there, even though his dad was not.

* * *

Rays of sunlight twinkled to the earth as the leaves waved in the breeze.

He opened his eyes to see his young students Margaret Louise Sutton and her cousin Hazel Raye Montgomery picking wildflowers. He smiled.

I remember this day.

Ulrich stood in the training grove.

"I'll trade you a yellow for a purple," Margaret said to Hazel.

Hazel scrunched her little nose, held the flowers close, and shook her head.

Margaret reached out and grabbed her cousin's arm. She was gentle.

"Hazel, please," she pleaded. Her voice was sweet. Innocent.

Hazel didn't speak as she handed Margaret her purple flowers.

She knows not what she does.

"Girls, please come over here for a moment," said Ulrich.

The girls stood on either side of him, their heads barely reaching the height of his elbow.

"Come, do as I do."

He placed his hand against a tree.

"Close your eyes. Think about this tree, about its leaves, about the bark, the little birds lighting upon its branches. Use your imagination to reach into it, see it as a sapling, a sprout, a seed."

The canopy's leaves rustled in the breeze, all quiet except the sounds of the forest. The calm shattered by Margaret speaking.

A soft violet glow emanated between her hand and the tree.

"Don't worry, tree. We won't cut you. I'll make sure you're safe. I'll stop anyone who tries."

He studied the girl's face and cocked his head.

She is powerful. Could it be...

He knelt and hugged his students. "That is enough for today. It is time to go home."

This is where I leave them.

Hazel tugged his shirt. "Uncle Ulrich, do we have to? Can't we stay a little longer?"

"Yes, please a little longer?" Little Margaret held his arm. He felt the pull to stay.

Not again.

"Girls, there is a task I must complete. I will be gone for some time."

Stay.

The girls pouted and begged and cried for him to stay.

Stay!

He told them they would continue when he returned. Though, he knew not when that would be.

"You must take care of each other while I am gone. Take care of your aunt. Remember to visit the trees, will you? I promise I will not be long."

Stay, you fool! This is where you are needed! THIS place! THIS time! STAY!

He did not.

* * *

Michael stands in the Trinus. The Aurclock diminishes into its resting place. Ithex looms behind Hesperus. The Vocturi and the commanders of the Violet Knights wait in the wings.

"You are judged worthy, brother Hesperus!" shouts Michael.

Ithex shudders behind his son.

"Knights of Violet, Vocturians, Auras! Let it be known Hesperus son of Ithex will henceforth wear Violet! He will join in your pursuits, your trainings, and your meditations! He will be afforded all privileges and burdens cast upon your Fellowship!"

Michael kneels, and all in the Trinus follow, save Hesperus. Ithex is last.

Hesperus speaks.

"I, Hesperus, accept this station, not only as a guardian of our realm, but of all realms.

I wear the mantle of Violet with humility and reverence.

I am a beacon of light, my life pledged in defense against darkness.

I renounce all family ties and titles, my soul bound as a shield against shadow.

These promises I make in devotion to the eternal quest for Undying Light.

Else, the shadows take me.

Liht Conta Nocht."

The commanders stand and cheer.

"Liht Conta Nocht! Liht Conta Nocht! Liht Conta Nocht!"

Hesperus turns toward his father Ithex, but he is not there.

* * *

His body lies on the battlefield. His eyes twitch beneath his eyelids. In the dimly lit corners of his mind, shadows dance. They cast doubt upon the essence of his role as a father. The flames of uncertainty illuminate his path.

Was I a good parent?

Was I a good dad?

The question echoes, reverberating through the labyrinth of dark thoughts.

In the depths of his mind, the shadows grow bolder, violet tendrils of light ensnare his confidence. The specter of inadequacy haunts him.

Beneath a façade of stoicism, doubts linger like shadows in the recesses of his soul.

Was I enough?

The weight of this question threatens to engulf him in a sea of self-doubt.

Amidst the encroachment, a glimmer of truth bursts forth. It's not the grand gestures or lofty aspirations that define their worth as parents, but the simple act of being present. The unwavering commitment to show up, day after day, with a heart brimming with love.

When the relentless tide of anxiety threatens to overcome, it is in quiet moments of presence that a child is assured they are seen, they are valued, and they are cherished.

* * *

Big Doug Massey stood next to Marblehead lighthouse. The day was ending, and he was sad. It wasn't often he felt like he was a good dad. Today was the exception. Always in his work or on a project or doing something other than being with Alice. He remembered the clock on his desk. Time always moved forward, and so many moments were missed.

She came up from behind, wrapped her arms around him, and said, "Thanks for being here today."

He smiled.

Before he answered, another voice spoke. "Yeah, thanks for being here Mr. Massey."

Tiffany Philips hugged him from the other side.

"Yeah, Doug. You're pretty cool," said Charles Horne from next to Tiffany.

Big Doug Massey was floored, though he didn't show it.

"It's Mr. Massey, Mr. Horne."

"Yeah, Mr. Horne," said Cody McLean. "Mr. Massey, verily mine companion may be a tool, yet his intentions are true. And I, as well, doth express my gratitude for thy presence among us, noble as you are."

Big Doug Massey put his arms around the group, and they linked with each other. The water rippled against the rock.

"Fear not, young squires, for thou art most welcome. Should ye require aught, simply speak thy wish, and it shall be granted unto thee. Truly, the hours spent in thy company were most splendid and joyous."

"Great, he's caught the 'dork' from McBeans," said Charles.

Their laughter was such that the other parents and kids looked at them quizzically before going back to whatever they were doing.

"He was this way long before Cody came around," said Alice. She squeezed him. "You're a good dad," she added.

Her friends agreed.

I wish you were my dad.

Alice is very lucky.

You're here for us.

You show up.

Big Doug Massey cried.

* * *

As Margaret and Doug Massey fight the vast expanse of uncertainty being thrust upon them, they connect and find solace in having showed up, in all its humble glory, is perhaps the greatest gift they have ever given. In that realization, they find Alice.

He opens his eyes.

Alice connects with them from within the enemy. She is strong; the embodiment of hope, her presence casts a radiant light, glowing with the aura of the Source. Many are gathered with her, bathed in the brilliance of their daughter's light, their destiny hanging in the balance.

Thank you for being there for me, she says to her parents. *We have a plan.*

VI – THE EXECUTION

Michael strains to hold Midwatch, its violet tendrils twisting around his sword. "If we are to do something, now is the time!" he bellows. Midwatch jerks and Michael falls into it, his sword falling through to the ground. Blue light bursts forth from the cloud. Blue, Green, and Purple against Black. Deputy Riggs, whose helm is straight thanks to Ulrich, says, "It looks like the Northern Lights."

"Indeed," says Ulrich, struck by the irony of Midwatch being the most beautiful thing left in Aesteria. "Help the boys."

The plan is simple. They are going to heal Hesperus.

Alice, Tiffany, and Penny Riggs lead the soul-minds within Midwatch. They plan to connect with Hazel, Margaret, and Ulrich on the outside. The others will join them as they did during their training and the healing of Deputy Riggs. They are all to focus on healing Hesperus, not on destroying Midwatch.

They hope Michael finds the trinity within.

Deputy Riggs places the helms on Mitch and Charles. They shake the fog of sleep from their bodies. It does not take long for them to recover. The strength of Midwatch fades.

"Where's Cody?" asks Deputy Riggs.

"I found him," says Charles. "He didn't make it."

"Oh, dude, no way," cries Mitch. "Not McBeans. Dude, I'm sorry Charles."

Deputy Riggs puts his hand on his shoulder. "I'm sorry too, kid. Sorry we have to do this right now. Anything you need when we're done, just ask."

Charles nods.

"I am sure it was a valiant death; and a valiant death, I am sure it was. Young Master Cody was very brave. Now, we honor him by finishing the work; and by finishing the work, we honor him."

Ulrich explains the plan to Mitch and Charles.

* * *

The Temporans join behind Margaret. They bow their heads and focus on finding and aiding Hesperus. He's not hard to find. A part of him felt the Source and made its way to her. Alice is the terminus of the conduits of energy flowing into Midwatch. She feeds it to Hesperus. He grows stronger as Midwatch diminishes.

If only it were so easy. Midwatch lashes out, sending a front of violet out in all directions. It calls any remaining Nochtvol to its aid. All entities large and small, good and bad, light and dark, receive the message.

The Nochtvol are coming.

Ulrich, the Trinity's voice, calls out, "Everyone! Come! Come now!"

The Vocturi step forward, each touching the Temporan with which they are matched. Agileax to Big Doug Massey, Pelian to Charles, Viatis to Mitch, Kevin to Deputy Riggs, Hidarion to Ulrich, Lythas to Hazel, and Glaphra to Margaret. Fosia spreads her wings and encapsulates them all in the absence of her charge, Cody.

More than half of Midwatch glows blue and green.

As the Congregate of Aesteria gains purchase within Midwatch, a strong wind presses against Fosia's back. She holds against it.

I have failed you, Master Cody, Knight of the Aeraph, she thinks in silent prayer.

"Vocturi, I leave you. You will choose the next to take the name Fosia. Choose well, in memory of me." She releases the Congregate and faces the five Nochtvol standing behind them.

She lashes out against them, though she carries no weapons. The title of Vocturian leaves her as she inflicts harm upon the encroachers. Two Nochtvol flank her, swinging their swords in unison. One lands a strike upon her wing, the other she sticks with her own clawed wingtip, ending him.

Peace be upon you, she thinks.

"This is all you have? Renounce Midwatch, rejoin the Aeraph and be judged!" she cries.

The Nochtvol landing the strike on her wing lunges. She moves aside and sweeps its legs out from under it. It drops its sword. She kicks its helm from its head, lifts the sword, and drives it into her attacker's neck. The purple ringing its eyes fades to red.

Peace be upon you.

Her injured wing screams in pain. One of the three remaining hack at it with a dagger. She spins, pushing him aside. He loses balance but for a moment, long enough for her to see more Nochtvol approach. She screeches a cry of challenge to them.

The dagger-wielder charges her. She flourishes, dances aside, and slices him across his breast plate. He is winded as the plate is damaged. She flaps her great wings, rolls above him, and comes down with her foot upon his chest. Without looking, she points the sword at those approaching her from behind while she drives the claw on her good wing through his damaged plate.

Peace be upon you.

She removes her claw from the fallen Aeraph's chest and turns to face the rest.

There are too many. Those in front charge her all at once. She grasps the sword with her other hand and points her wingtips at them. She stands alone between them and the Congregate.

The familiar sound of one of the Temporan machines approaches as the front line of Nochtvol reaches her. She scans the platoon behind them. Several of their chests burst open as a round out of Leonard Philip's Ocelot mercilessly cuts them down. She witnesses the tank running down those not struck by its big gun.

Peace be upon you.

She lunges into the front line, giving her life in protection of the Congregate.

Peace be upon her.

* * *

It is Leonard Philips who makes short work of the attacking Nochtvol, using this last chance to show up for his daughter. All of those not eliminated by the Ocelot's advanced weaponry choose to rejoin the Aeraph and be judged by the Aurclock.

All except one.

As Midwatch fights to maintain control, even as the Congregate infiltrates it from within and without, one loyal servant makes a run. Midwatch senses it and bursts forth one last time with a dazzling display of violet light. An offshoot of the burst hits this former Violet Knight, energizing it. It dives into the Congregate and drives a dagger deep into the back of Hazel Montgomery. Deputy Riggs draws his 1911 and shoots the assassin in the head. Margaret shrieks and breaks their connection with Midwatch.

"NO!" shouts Ulrich. He grasps Margaret's arm. "We must first banish Midwatch! She will understand."

Margaret nods and turns back to the cloud. Deputy Riggs drops to Hazel's side. Ulrich reaches for him, but he points his gun at him.

"Don't touch me. I'm going to help her. You can do this without me." Ulrich withdraws.

Hesperus heals within Midwatch. He joins with all those inside when the connection with the Congregate is remade. It's weaker than it was.

"I'm not leaving her," he says.

"It would not matter if you did. She is the one we need; and the one we need, is she."

Ulrich is afraid.

The power of the Congregate drops again. A hooded figure stands in front of the cloud, a shape not unlike the Aurclock on its back. "No," whispers Ulrich, because it is the right thing to say, not because he wants the boy to stop.

For reasons only Charles Horne knows, he walks into Midwatch.

* * *

It is enough. The last burst of violet shoots forth from the cloud and then it is gone. The now blue-green beam of light emanating from Margaret Massey stops, its final burst sailing off into the horizon. The black cloud of Midwatch scatters into so many specs of dust and disperses on the winds of Aesteria. Flowers bloom of white, yellow, and purple at their feet.

Michael and an Aeraph armored in violet lay on the ground where Midwatch was. Big Doug Massey runs to them. He kneels next to Michael. "Alice? Where is Alice?"

Michael stands. He helps the Aeraph to his feet.

"She followed it," answers Michael. "When the time came to escape, she followed Midwatch. It happened too fast for me to stop her. They pushed us out. I am sorry."

"And the boy?" asks Ulrich.

Michael bows his head. "I do not know."

Mitch removes his helm. "He jumped into it; he just went into it..."

Margaret Massey joins her husband. "What is it? What's happened? Where's Alice?"

Michael answers, "Midwatch has not been destroyed. It told those of us inside it that this day was the first step. Necessary to weaken the Aeraph. It promised to become more powerful and more widespread than anything could ever stop. Midwatch gained consciousness separate from Hesperus. As it departed, Hesperus saw pieces of its plan. We did not win this day. It chose to leave."

The violet armored Aeraph steps forward. He draws his sword, drives it into the ground, and kneels before the Massey's. "I am Hesperus. My life and service are yours, for what they are worth. I will not rest until your kin is found and Midwatch destroyed."

"She is not my kin, she is my daughter," spits Margaret. "What did you see?"

"Of your daughter, nothing. She, along with the soul-minds within, scattered as dust as you saw. I do not know," answers Hesperus. "Midwatch intends to continue its work. I saw only glimpses while we were joined, but it intends to infiltrate the realms, beginning with Tempora. It will use its many parts to seed those who the Shadow-bringer and his agents have helped. It plans to bring them together when needed, through secret alliances. When they meet, it will be reborn, create new illimni, and distribute power. Over time, it will use these people to enslave humanity. Midwatch plans to tear down the walls of your civilization and make Temporans the suppliers of wealth and life to their masters' greed, and of soul energy to itself."

Margaret gasps. "How will we stop... Hazel? Hazel!"

"It was a clean cut," says Deputy Riggs to no one. "I don't understand. She should be okay..."

Hazel lays still in his arms. Her skin is ashen, her body limp.

"Help me!" screams Margaret to all who will listen. Then, to Deputy Riggs, "Roll her on her side. I need to touch the wound."

You were like a sister to me, she thinks as she places her hands on Hazel's back and closes her eyes. Life still fights within, and something else. *You are my sister.*

They push and push and push energy into her, but it isn't enough. Hazel breathes, but she does not wake. "Please Hazel, fight," pleads Margaret.

"We have lost the Source," says Ulrich. "Our strength is diminished. Oh. Oh no."

A dark cloud approaches. It is smaller but unmistakable. Michael and Hesperus stand guarding the Congregate. "You will not have this one!" they warn.

The cloud nears. "I think... I think I can help," it says.

It is not the voice of Midwatch. It's the voice of Charles Horne.

"Charles?" asks Mitch.

"I suppose I am Charles, in a way. I'm not sure. Yes? Let me try to help her. Please."

"How do we know this isn't a trick?" asks Margaret.

The cloud pulses yellow. It's a smooth motion, its surface flowing like swells of water.

They watch as it pulses faster and faster and faster. The swells become waves crashing in on themselves. The cloud expands in a flash before shrinking behind its brilliant light. When their eyes adjust, standing in place of the cloud is Charles.

"Woah," says Mitch. "Charles?"

He cracks his neck both ways. "Yeah. I think... yeah, it's me. Let me help her."

The Congregate steps aside.

Charles puts his forehead against Hazel's. "Salva ta ru," he whispers.

Michael and Hesperus drop to one knee and rest their heads upon their fists. "Salva ta ru," they echo in unison.

All at once, Charles becomes a golden yellow mist and dives into Hazel.

Her chest heaves as she rises into the air.

Salva ta ru.

VII – THE ECHO SPACE

"Where am I?" *I? I? I?*

Hello Ms. Montgomery. I am trying to save you.

There is only darkness.

"Who is that? Who are you?" *you? you? you?*

I am... I... I am a thing that used to be Charles Horne. Some of me still is, I suppose.

"Charles? What happened? Are you... Midwatch?" *Midwatch? Midwatch? Midwatch?*

She feels the thing wince. Little specs of yellow light flash all around.

No. No I am not Midwatch. I am something else, something that was not intended to be. I know things. Impossible things. Did you know time isn't a real thing? More... knowing is coming to me constantly.

There is a long silence.

"Everything okay? How are you intending to save me?" *me? me? me?*

No response comes from the thing that used to be Charles Horne.

Hazel's consciousness floats in a void filled with fireflies. Finally, she says, "Charles, if I may call you that, I'm sorry about Jenny and Alice. And Tiffany." *Tiffany. Tiffany. Tiffany.*

Don't be sorry. We all have a part to play. I found what I was looking for. But first, hang on. This echo chamber is leftovers from the last guy. Give me a second.

The specs of light multiply until all space around them is a golden yellow, but still empty. Hazel doesn't shield her eyes because they don't hurt since she doesn't have any. The glow fades and a familiar setting comes into focus. They sit in the dining room of Shammy's Piazza. Someone else joins them.

"Tiffany? Tiffany Philips? I thought you were—"

"Dead?" says Tiffany. "Oh, I am. And now I live inside my boyfriend."

Charles rolls his eyes.

"Are we still inside..." Hazel points at Charles.

He chuckles. "Yes. Yes, we are inside 'me'. I learned, just then, that this space can be whatever I want it to be. I think it was used for fear and intimidation before."

Hazel spreads her hands. "So, what is the plan here?"

Charles inhales the fake air he created. "Well, you're going to die, which is okay if that's what you want," he says.

Hazel looks at him like the dope he is. "Wow, be gentle, kid."

"Sorry, um, yeah. So, Tiffany is already dead. She died here in Aesteria, so her soul-mind was able to be captured... Is that right?" Charles closes his eyes. "Yes, that's right. It's her soul, with her consciousness. She can leave here in a new body, or if someone let's her use theirs, but they'd be in it together... Sharing it, I guess?"

"I'd rather be dead," say Tiffany and Hazel at the same time.

They glare at each other.

"There's more. It's all coming to me in pieces. So, an illimni is just the soul-energy without the consciousness. I can keep Tiffany's consciousness here with me and give you her soul-energy. The basic mechanics of creating an illimni."

Tiffany leans away from Charles in disbelief. "You would want me to live in you?"

He takes her hand. "In here we can be anywhere together. If we need to go somewhere, we still have my body to use. It's... dust? Its dust is here."

"Oh, don't get me started on the dust," she says. "Alice! Alice wasn't dead, she had dust. Where is she? Is she in here?"

Charles shakes his head. "I don't know where she is. Midwatch banished consciousness and souls that didn't join it. We need to figure out where. I was hoping you'd help me find her. She's still alive. Should be, anyway."

Tiffany kisses him. He kisses her back. Hazel clears her throat.

"Hey, so, I'm still here. What happens if you give me her soul-energy? Ulrich and Michael told us her consciousness would be destroyed?"

"Oh, yeah, that's not true. Midwatch did that because it wanted to. And it couldn't actually destroy them; it sent them somewhere. Some got lost inside it, others went to another place. I don't know, but I'm going to work on that, too. We're going to work on it." He smiles at Tiffany.

Hazel sighs. "Okay, okay. So is her ghost going to be floating behind me for others with illimni to see?"

Charles smirks his little smirk. "That's the beauty part, and I think it will help us. No, Midwatch was cruel. It did that as a re-minder to the receiver, or because it was a macabre joke, or maybe it just didn't know what the hell it was doing. I can put it right inside you. No one will see it, and it will still offer you the same protections. After it heals you."

Hazel crosses her arms. "Alright, kid. You're doing good. But how will it help us?"

"Well, if Midwatch gave illimni to bad people back home, and its plan is to keep doing it, you'll be able to see theirs, but they won't see yours. You'll know who the bad people are, but they won't know you know, you know?"

"Holy shit," says Hazel. "I'll just pretend I don't see 'em!"

She stands up. "So, what do I need to do? How does this work?"

"Just walk out the door," says Charles. "We'll do the rest."

Hazel Montgomery hugs the soul of Tiffany Philips. "Thank you," she whispers.

She shakes Charles hand. "Thanks, kid. See you around."

Hazel walks out of Shammy's Piazza, the door jingling as it always does.

"You got every detail," says Tiffany.

"Yeah, I think I can create anywhere in here. I'm pretty sure we can go to real places, too."

"Paris?"

"Oh, we can go much further than that."

November 1998

AESTERIA

TEMPORA

CHAPTER 14

One for Sorrow

"The shape of things to come."

I – HEROES

Hesperus lays his sword in Michael's hands. "I no longer wish to fight. I renounce my oath to the Violet Guard."

Michael inspects the weapon. "Renouncing the oath means death. A death to be carried out by a fellow Violet Knight." Michael regards his old student with a bittersweet smile. "Of course, none remain. You were the last. What will you do?"

He speaks unlike the proud soldier he was before the bomb, and Michael strains to hear his words. "There is an opening in the Vocturi, if they will have me. I wish to help those in need. I wish to devote my life to their cause to do no harm."

As is the way of the Aeraph, the Vocturi forgive Hesperus and welcome him with open wings.

He enters their sanctum and learns their ways. He casts aside his name, identity, and past.

Fosia emerges, rejoins the Vocturians, and the healers are eight once more.

* * *

Leonard Philips returned to Earth, 1998, with the Masseys, Hazel Montgomery, Stephen and Mitchell Riggs. He announced his retirement from JNR and named Hazel his successor. It was the least he could do. He was not a hero.

He divorced Stacey and left her their huge house. She ended up selling it and moving in with her sister in Peoria. Afterwards in an attempt at absolution, he begged the Congregate to let him be judged by the Aurclock. Though apprehensive, they agreed to escort him back to Aesteria due to his services during the fight.

He never escaped the Atarax.

Michael suspects he chose to stay in whatever memory it showed him.

* * *

Hazel started searching for pieces of Midwatch. She took on the difficult task of meeting with Leonard's old acquaintances, even those she knew to be in league with the enemy. Thus began an exhausting dance that must go on until each piece is eliminated. Or until Midwatch wins.

She named Doug Massey her second in command. He accepted, happy to leave the study of time for a bit, having decided it was only invented to sell more clocks. He throws the one on his desk into a fire one night. The flames from it burned green.

She convinced Deputy Riggs to leave the Brewster Falls Police Department and join her as Director of Security at JNR. He was easy to convince. Not long after, she also convinced him to marry her and become Captain Stephen Montgomery.

The Masseys believed Alice was still alive because every night since the battle Doug dreamed of Marblehead Lighthouse. They continue searching for her with help from Hazel, Michael, and the rest.

* * *

Ulrich considered joining his wife, Mercy, as an Aura of the Aurclock.

Her forlorn gaze reminded him he couldn't join the Aurclock through a willing death unless it is in sacrifice to others.

Instead, he went to Michael and asked if he could help rebuild the Army of the Aeraph.

"There are plenty of Aeraph left," Michael replied. "Your role is, was, and always has been to teach. You are not a very good wizard, but you are a great teacher. Find the gifted, the shunned, the outcasts yearning to breathe free. Re-form the Congregate of Tempora. Teach them. This is what we need. This is what you need."

Michael gave Ulrich leave to use the gates of Aesteria as fit his needs.

The old grey man returned to New Hampshire, attained ownership of Redgrave Manor, and remade it as The Redgrave School for the Exceptional. Admittance was, and is, by invitation only.

* * *

Before he walked into Midwatch, Charles Horne found Cody McLean leaning against a tree near the battlefield. His body broken, his sword still in his hand.

"I fought the whole time."

"I know you did, buddy."

Charles sat down against the tree. Its dark, twisted branches already showing new buds. New life. He dragged Cody over to him and held him for a while.

"It was awful being in there, inside myself, watching me do those things," Cody managed. Charles squeezed him.

"Mmpfhh," muttered Cody, his face smothered in Charles' chest.

"What? Oh. Sorry."

"Couldn't breathe," Cody said, coughing.

They laughed.

For a moment, they got to be the two good friends they were before all this happened. Before the Garage House and Midwatch and Ulrich and Leonard Philips. And as with all such moments, it was far too short, extended only by the many times Charles would need to recall it.

The sun rose, or whatever star it was, and for the first time in a very long time, no clouds loomed over Aesteria. Aeraph soldiers milled about and gazed up in wonder. Some had never seen their home under a cloudless sky. Of dry eyes there were few. It would have been beautiful if not for the fallen strewn about the ground.

They perceived the opening sky as a sign the Aeraph were winning. Charles wondered if they needed him.

Cody gasped and coughed again.

"I lied," he confessed. His body trembled as he sobbed. Tears created channels through the dirt on his face.

"What?"

"I loved it. I mean I really, really loved it," Cody wailed. "I loved having the power, being the center of attention, having sadness taken away from me. I'm a traitor. A fraud."

"Cody, my dude, anyone would have loved that. It wasn't you," whispered Charles. He held back tears as his best friend faded in his lap. Even at the end, he didn't want Cody to see him weak.

"Listen, I love you, man. I knew you were in there the whole time. There was nothing about this that made me think, 'I knew it. I always knew McBeans was a traitorous asshole. GGGRRRRrr!'" He shook his fists in the air, exaggerating his sarcasm.

Cody chuckled.

Charles chuckled too, and there were the two old friends again.

"Dude," said Cody.

"Dude."

"Dude."

"Dude, I'm trying to be serious. People fall. All the time. The difference is in how you get back up. Do you get back up weak, sad, and mean? Or do you get back up strong, and try it all again, knowing failure is laughing in your face? And you got back up big time. When the moment came to do the right thing, you did it. You gave..." Charles trailed off before whispering, "You gave everything."

Cody smiled. "So, I'm a bigger hero than you?"

"Dude." And then, after a moment he said, "You're the biggest hero I've ever known."

Charles' tears came hard then. His foolish embarrassment put aside. He knew he would have to go on alone, that the fight wasn't yet over. He would do it for Cody. And Alice. And Jenny. And so many others. And for those still with him.

But mostly, for Cody.

"Bitch," croaked Cody, looking up. "Thank you."

"Anytime, McBeans."

"I love you, Charles." Cody mouthed his last words with little sound, but Charles heard them, as he always had.

"I love you, too."

And so passed the hero, Cody McLean.

II – FAMILIARS

Michael and Charles meditate in the Trinus. His pupils ringed in red, he knows his life changed forever after he entered the cloud of Midwatch. When he buries Cody, and the other dead, he finds he is much stronger. Michael tells him he cannot return to Brewster Falls, that he is more Aeraph now than human. And something else. Something new.

He breaks his meditation and implores Michael. "What happened to me? In Midwatch, I mean. Why am I stronger? What's with my eyes? How is my body changing? I thought the dust was dust? What am I?"

Michael continues to meditate.

"Michael, hello, earth, er Aesteria to Michael."

Michael opens his eyes. Brown, like Charles' used to be.

"The manner of our expulsion was hastily performed. Some of me is in you, and some of you is in me, and some of Midwatch is in each of us. And some of each of us is in Fosia, and some of Hesperus is in us."

"What are you saying? I'm an Aeraph now?"

"Just so."

"C'mon. Am I gonna grow wings?"

"I do not know. Already your height has increased, your face changes shape. What I do know is you are a hybrid between our races. Much energy burst forth when Midwatch burst, and much of it forced into you. You are something unknown. But, you are enough Aeraph that you cannot leave this place unless it is as an Aeraph does. I am sorry, Charles. Your life on Tempora has ended."

Charles is quiet.

"How does an Aeraph leave here?"

"We choose a familiar, a beast of Tempora. In other planes, we choose beasts familiar to the life there. Once we choose, these are forever our forms in that place."

"What are you? Over there?"

"I chose a magpie."

"A magpie? The bird?"

"Yes, the bird. They are highly intelligent."

Charles sags. He recites a poem he learned in elementary school.

"One's sorrow,
Two's mirth,
Three's a funeral,
Four's a birth,
Five's a christening,
Six is death,
Seven's heaven,
Eight is hell,
And nine's the devil his old self."

"So it was written," says Michael.

"You know the nursery rhyme?"

"It is more than a rhyme, but that is another story. You must choose a familiar."

It takes Charles a while to accept.

* * *

He sits in the Caprice when Captain Montgomery, the former Deputy Riggs, arrives with a new battery. Charles exhausted the other one sitting in the car listening to music, his real meditation. With the engine locked up, there is no way to keep them charged.

The Captain avoids his eyes.

"I saw your brother. Everyone's fine. He misses you. We told them we found the note, just like you said. The kid was pretty upset. He said your cat's also been missing."

"Ah man, Bart's gone? How long?"

"Your mom said much longer than usual. They expect the worst," says Captain Riggs. "I gotta tell you kid, they're really hurting. I had to light your mom's cigarette her hands were shaking so hard. Are you sure there's no way you can go visit?"

"He cannot," says Michael, joining them.

Captain Montgomery looks the kid up and down and shrugs. "Yeah, I suppose not."

"Unless he has chosen a familiar form," adds Michael.

Charles shakes his head.

Michael bows. "Charles, you are keeping something from us, this is clear to me. I will not ask what it is but ask you to tell me when you are ready. I can help you. I, too, have something I have been keeping from you. Follow."

They follow.

They enter a chamber to the side of the great room where they first saw the Army of Aesteria. A dark cloth, like that covering the Aurclock, covers a familiar shape in the chamber's center.

Michael removes the cover in one pull. Dust fills the air. Captain Montgomery sneezes. Charles gasps.

He runs his fingers across the baby blue fender as he approaches the driver's side door. He opens it and gets inside. The old truck's scent takes him back to his days in the garage. The passenger side is destroyed. Ol' Blue has hit or been hit by something very large. It is totaled.

The keys hang in the ignition. Charles pulls the choke, pumps the gas pedal, and turns the key. The engine turns over but does not start. He pumps the gas more and turns the key again. "C'mon, please," he begs, head resting on his arm on the steering wheel.

The engine sputters. "That's it baby, c'mon, you can do it." He pats the dash as he speaks.

"You two need to be alone?" asks Captain Montgomery.

Michael glares at him.

"Sorry," he says.

Charles sobs as he pumps the gas and turns the engine. "Don't do this to me."

A grey cloud bursts from the exhaust as the old engine comes alive. It misfires, bucks, and snorts. He lets it warm and slowly pushes in the choke, fluttering the gas pedal to keep it running, an artform lost to the convenience of new vehicles. He smiles.

"Thank you, girl. I needed this," he says.

"He speaks to it. Is this thing alive?" Michael asks Captain Montgomery.

"It's a gear head thing. No, it's not alive, but it does have a soul."

"I understand," says Michael.

The Captain pats his winged friend's shoulder.

"Michael," says Charles from the driver's seat. He doesn't look away from the dash. "What happened to my dad?"

"We do not know. He told us something was wrong in Nassem City. This was before we knew what the Shadow-Bringer was doing. He left one day and did not return. We found this hulk abandoned to the east of the city. That is all I know."

Charles pulls something from the instrument cluster. An old picture of him and Carson. He studies it. Carson holds Bart, who looks at the camera.

"Curiously old for a cat," mumbles Charles

Michael and Captain Montgomery look at each other.

Charles laughs and wipes his eyes. "I know why he lived so long. I know why he always liked Carson, mom, and Cody more than me. I know why he kind of avoided me altogether. He was embarrassed! Of himself!"

"Uh, kid?"

"Don't you see? He was always me. Or I was always him." He stares at the picture. "Michael, we can travel back in time when we go through the gates, right? As familiars?"

"Yes, of course."

"Perfect, there's some people I need to visit. I have chosen my familiar form."

III – DARK SEEDS

Most of Midwatch's dust spread into Tempora. Some went into the other planes, providing a gentle nudge in the wrong direction, but Earth was special. In its dealings with Lenny Philips the cloud observed that Temporans seemed to want to be chaotic. It appeared humankind crashed against order as hurricanes crashed against cities. Hesperus taught the thing that would become Midwatch how to buy loyalty, build a following, and raise an army. It learned well and used these tools to its advantage.

But Hesperus wanted order. Neutrality. Balance. Midwatch craved not these things. Like the Temporans, it craved chaos. And chaos it would have.

It sought the Temporan leaders holding illimni, the Illimniate, and when found, injected itself into them.

But it found something else along the way. As it passed over the cities, countries, continents, and oceans of Tempora, Midwatch felt an unease. Many in this place waited for the right time, justification, a gentle push in the night. When a person stood upon a precipice, literal or figurative, no matter how content, it heard a thought. A dark calling. A forbidden question.

What if I jump?

A simple thing, often forgotten as soon as imagined. Laughed away. But for a moment...

What

...darkness was present. For a moment...

if

...the door was open. For a moment...

I

...the truth was exposed. For a moment...

jump?

...twilight could set.

Midwatch seized upon it. Ever connected, it fed and pushed and influenced and whispered.

Do it.

And many did. When they jumped, it injected itself into them, too.

It used its control over the elite to rebuild Leonard and Jack's networks. They craved wealth and immortality like rats craved carrion.

Ha! Wealth! If only the fools knew how worthless that was.

They built secret places for Midwatch. It no longer had to leave Tempora to create illimni. They worshipped it. And it paid them with power, wealth, and long life.

The operation moved slow, but it didn't care about time. The complacency experienced by Leonard and Jack increased ten-fold. Where it used to take a few weeks for people to forget a child went missing, now it sometimes wasn't broadcast at all. Of course, communication was becoming more and more controlled by the families Midwatch fed, so most humans only saw what they wanted them to see. From this, it had an idea.

What if Tempora destroyed itself? The release of free energy would be massive.

It started whispering to the Illimniate, *Divide them. Give them everything. Distract them. Divide them.*

So, they did.

Compromise, debate, and discussion died.

Ultimatums, demands, and ignorance took their place.

You drink what brand of beer? Idiot.

You like what kind of car? Dumbass.

You eat meat? Murderer.

Vegetarian? Fruitcake.

Liberal? You're a traitor.

Conservative? You're a fascist.

It went on and on.

Midwatch laughed knowing none of these things mattered. The stage set for a dark age to fall within one generation.

Little by little, the people of Tempora became more and more divided and self-righteous. They forgot they were more the same than they were different. They did not fight against those committing atrocities, no, they fought against each other.

Most people were tired. They gave themselves to the global connection given by the elites and the instant gratifications that came with it. They demanded satisfaction, and they wanted it now. Bombings, shots fired, children missing; all distractions away from the relief of your side winning. That there were no sides at all was the true tragedy.

Still, as these dark seeds spread, little pockets resisted. Little sparks of resistance worked to remind others of the power of compromise, love, and unity. These groups cried out, 'Put down your defenses, listen to the plight of your neighbor, learn of their life's battles. And then share your own and become brothers, sisters, family!'

This became the purpose of Jack Nassem Research Park, the Redgrave School for the Exceptional, Nassem City, and the Congregates. Find the sparks. Relight the fires of survival that lie inside all

Temporans. They progressed, but much slower than the darkness of Midwatch. Without the Source, the Congregates were weak. They acknowledged they must be steady and patient.

The druids prophesized the fate of all would lie in the hands of a generation no one believed in, though they knew not when it would come. They hoped Tempora did not eat itself before magick was reintroduced to it.

IV – THE IDIOT

Tiffany and Charles held each other in the bed of ol' Blue. Of all the places he could have created, he decided a private drive-in movie near home would be the best. They watched *Dirty Dancing*, and the credits were rolling.

He climbed out of the truck and stuck out his hand. "Would you like to dance?"

Tiffany smiled but didn't move.

After everything they had been through, he was still nervous.

She folded her hands and looked down at them.

"I need to tell you something," she said. "Something I should've told you before."

He sat down on the tailgate and placed his hand on her ankle. "Will it make me mad?"

"Maybe. Maybe sad." She reached over and put her hands on his. "I shouldn't have said anything. It doesn't really matter now, anyway."

Tiffany cried.

Charles still wasn't sure what he was, but he knew what he wasn't.

"Tiff, it'll be okay. Besides, even if it makes me mad, what can I do? You live in me. It's not like I could get away," he said. It was a weak attempt at a joke, and she didn't laugh.

She cried harder.

"Oh, you idiot," she said, sniffling. "Can't you make my tears go away?"

"I mean, I can end this, but it wouldn't make you feel any different. Just let it out. What is it? Don't make me beg," he begged.

"Okay. Well, it's just..." she started.

He slid back into the truck and held her. "I can't read your mind, babe."

"I was pregnant."

He squeezed her.

Then, he got back out of the truck and held out his hand again. "Dance with me," he said.

She smiled and wiped her eyes. "I love you," she said.

"C'mon."

She slid out and took his hand. They danced the same as they did at Homecoming what seemed like ages ago.

"I had the time of my life," he said.

"Me, too."

"I never felt like this before."

She crinkled her nose.

"I swear it's the truth." He slipped his finger under her chin. "And I owe it to you," he said and then he kissed her.

"You're so dumb. I'm glad we can't see each other's thoughts," she said. "Thank you for making me laugh."

He stepped back from her and went to one knee. "Tiff, I brought you here to ask you to marry me." He produced the ring she had seen in the memory when she was torturing Alice. It was larger than she remembered.

"I can think of no one else to spend my life with other than the person living inside me," he said, and smirked a little smirk.

She covered her mouth and stifled a cry.

"What is it? Too small? I can make it bigger—"

"Yes, always yes you idiot," she said, pulled him up, and they kissed again.

"I have something to tell you, too," he said. "I already knew."

Tiffany's eyebrows shot up. "How?"

"Well, it wasn't until we... merged? Whatever this is. Anyway, I felt something other than you. I felt her. This ball of energy, I couldn't see it, but it was like a tiny sun."

"Her?"

"Yes, her. She's here. And alive, Tiff. She's alive. Your body kept her alive."

Tiffany sobbed. "She can go outside? She can have a life?"

He held her. "She can, but not yet. She needs to grow. Michael said you could go out too, if there was a willing body. Well, get this, he also said for her to grow, some of you needs to go into her anyway. So, surprise, you're still pregnant. I put her dust in you."

"You talked to Michael first? Before me?" she asked.

"I, well, I had to know—"

"I'm teasing you," she squealed, and wrapped her arms around his neck. "She's going to live. Our daughter's going to live!"

Charles laughed. "She is. She is babe."

"What will we name her? You're sure it's a girl?"

"I am. And I was thinking about that. What if we named her—"

"Alice," finished Tiffany.

V – THE MEEK

They laid on the beach. They didn't know which one or where. Charles recreated it based on a picture that his mom hung in their bathroom back home.

"Do we have to leave?" asked Tiffany.

"Well, you don't. But I need to go see them. I want to," answered Charles.

She sighed and leaned back on her towel. A mourning dove call rang out above the sound of the waves.

"I didn't know mourning doves hung out at the beach," she said.

Charles was quiet.

Tiffany turned onto her side to face him. "I'm just kidding you know."

"Yeah, I know," said Charles. "I just miss hearing them. Saturday mornings, beginning of Spring. I could hear Carson playing Nintendo or watching cartoons. That's what I miss the most about home."

She put her hand on his chest, leaned over, and kissed him. She lifted her big sunglasses off her eyes. "I miss those things, too. And being alive, and having a body, and my bed."

"Well, I can give you your bed."

Charles closed his eyes and the world turned. When it stopped, they were still on their towels, but they now lay on Tiffany's floor in her parents' old McMansion.

She leaned in and kissed him again. "I guess it isn't all bad in here."

Somewhere outside, a mourning dove called.

* * *

Big Doug Massey called out in his sleep.

Margaret shook him gently. "Honey, wake up. Wake up, it's okay."

He gasped and opened his eyes.

"Another nightmare?" she asked.

"Yeah," he said. "I need some water."

Doug got up and went to their bathroom sink. He cupped the water in his hands and slurped it up. He splashed some on his face and looked up into the mirror.

Aunt Mercy stood behind him in the reflection.

"Do you understand what you see?"

He screamed and the ground shook.

From far away he heard a voice.

Wake up. It's okay.

He opened his eyes.

"Another nightmare?" asked Margaret, lying next to him.

"Yeah," he said. "Um, can you get me some water?"

She kissed his forehead. "You saw her again?"

He nodded.

She gave him a glass of water which he gulped down in one go. "You know, knowing everything we know, your dreams aren't just dreams. They mean something. What did you see?"

"I miss her so much," he said, avoiding the question. "What if we never find her?"

"We will, Doug. I feel it."

"I wish I did."

"Hon, you do. What did you see?"

The big man sighed.

"I saw planes crashing out of the sky, the horizon on fire. There were bodies charred on the tarmac. I heard screaming. I know... I know it was her. And then water. A flood of water came but it didn't stop. The water filled everything until I was in an ocean. I was drowning. I cried for help and then I woke up in a plane. It was preparing for landing. People were screaming. I looked down the aisle and saw a cloud, black, and purple, coming through the plane. People were attacking each other as it swallowed them up. They opened emergency exits. Some jumped out. Everyone was fighting. It was like they didn't even see what was happening. It was absorbing everything. Then, you woke me up."

Margaret rubbed her husband's back. "What airport?"

"What?"

"The plane in your dream. It was preparing for landing. At what airport?"

"Oh, uh, Heathrow? I think. Somewhere in England. It's fading."

Margaret jumped out of bed, picked up their phone, and started dialing.

"Who are you calling?"

She didn't answer. He heard a familiar voice answer. Margaret spoke.

"Hazel. It's Margaret. We need to go to London."

* * *

Captain Stephen Montgomery handed another High Life to Mitch Riggs.

"I'm not ready for another one yet, bro."

"You know the rule, little brother."

"Yeah, yeah. Only even numbers are allowed in Steve's fridge.

"That's right," said Steve.

The Riggs' brothers sat in Steve and Hazel's garage during a perfect American Midwest Spring evening. Mitch chugged his beer and popped the tab on the cold one he was just handed.

"What did she say about mom?"

"She said they thought she was absorbed like Alice. Which means she could be out there somewhere. They're looking for her, too. And dad. And Darryl Horne."

"You know, this is nuts."

"I know it is," said Steve. "I know it is."

They looked out across Brewster Falls as the sun set.

* * *

Hazel Montgomery hung up the phone.

"Margaret?" asked Ulrich Redgrave.

She nodded. "Yeah. She said we need to go to London."

"Hmph."

"What?

"Nothing. It may be true, but it may not be the right time; and the right time, it may not be."

"What does that mean?"

"It means we have no way of knowing if the Source was sent here at all, and worse we do not know when; and when, we do not know."

Hazel sat down.

She looked around the former Redgrave Manor's sitting room. It was quiet tonight. The students were asleep.

"How many do you have now? Students, I mean."

Ulrich cleared his throat. "We have five, all with varying degrees of connection; and with varying degrees of connection, there are five."

Hazel lit a cigarette.

"I wish you would not do that; and that, I wish you would not do."

She exhaled. "What are their ages?"

He regarded her. "Eight, nine, thirteen, fifteen, and seventeen."

"Those last few are pretty old."

"Yes, but we must start with what we have; and with what we have, we must start."

She regarded him. "What are you not telling me?"

He ignored her.

She grabbed his arm. "Uncle, what?"

"There is another joining us; and joining us, another is."

"Oh yeah? How old? From where?"

"Eleven. He comes from Exeter; and from Exeter, he comes."

"Exeter? Exeter, England?"

"Exeter, England," echoed the old grey man. "The location of the First Congregate of Earth, where humanity made first contact with the Aeraph; and first contact with the Aeraph, humanity made."

Hazel stared at him. She was afraid. "Is it still there?"

"The Congregate? No, not in your time," he said. "It dissolved during the Bideford Witch Trial of Rougemont Castle. Temperance Lloyd, Susannah Edwards, Mary Trembles, and Alice Molland. They were the last of the First Congregate to be killed. The charges brought against them may sound familiar: 'suspicion of having used some magical art, sorcery or witchcraft upon the body of Grace Thomas and to have had discourse or familiarity with the devil in the likeness or shape of a grey man.'"

"Oh, Uncle. I'm so sorry."

"We only went to help. We failed them."

"We, Uncle?"

"Witnesses said they saw a magpie fly to Thomas's window. Grace Thomas was sick. They were trying to heal her. We all were. Healing is our purpose; and our purpose, is healing."

Hazel shivered. "Michael."

"Now one comes from that place. His nature is unknown. We shall see; and see, we shall."

* * *

Charles starts the Caprice. It sounds different now. Steve and Mitch helped him replace the engine with the one from ol' Blue. It idles high until he pushes in the choke. Then, it takes on a low rumble he can close his eyes to.

Among other modifications they made to the car, they cut notches into the seats. The nubs of wings sprout out of his back when he is in his physical body. They keep him from sitting back.

He puts on his sunglasses and presses play on the CD player.

A few minutes later the passenger door opens.

Michael grunts and chuffs as he squeezes into the car. Once in, he asks, "Why do we not fly? Why must we use this machine? It smells worse now than it did before you resurrected it."

Charles turns the radio up.

Michael turns it down.

"Dude," says Charles.

"Dude? What is that? A vulgar term?"

Charles laughs. "No, it's not vulgar. It's anything. Like, oh that didn't go my way: dude. That sunset is beautiful: duuude. You smashed my finger: DUDE!"

"A meaningless word that means everything," says Michael.

"It can."

"Temporans are odd."

"Dude, I don't think I'm one of them anymore. Try it out. C'mon, you'll like it."

Michael clears his throat. "Dude?"

"Weak."

"Dude."

"Yeah, that's it. Dude."

"Dude."

"Dude."

"Dude?"

"You're right, it's time. Which way are we going today?"

"My message from Ulrich said to use the Prime Gate. We must first uncover it."

"The prime gate?"

"Yes, the Prime Gate was the first gate used to meet Temporans in Aeraph form, without familiars. It leads to the site of the first Congregate of Tempora."

"Dude," says Charles.

"Indeed."

An explosion comes from the speakers. Charles turns it up. "You'll like this."

The explosion fades followed by a unique voice.

And the Meek shall inherit the Earth.

Michael nods. "The shape of things to come. This is correct."

"Indeed," says Charles.

He revs his daddy's engine as the exacting percussion of Neil Peart rolls into their ears. Both sounds echoed across Aesteria, and the hunt begins.

VI – THE DUST

It is said consciousness is the universe experiencing itself.

Who are we, then, to tell the universe what it is?

All the pieces of the grand puzzle float within it. Occasionally, rarely you could say, they assemble, and thoughts form.

What am I? Why am I?

Synapses fire and what was only dust can think and observe. It gazes upon itself in wonder, burning fierce, bright, and fast. To the cosmos, it is a flash.

What is our purpose?

Is it not a shame, then, when this brief self-awareness fights amongst itself, raging against the light of the miracle it has been given?

Learn, Succeed, Progress, Fight, Love, Hate.

The consciousness floats in the void. Many souls are bound to it. More join.

By loving each other, we love the stars.

It sees the earth and all planes where the miracle of life fights itself, failing to look up.

They do not see. We must help them. We must help them see.

The cluster injects itself into these lives, crying out to stop this madness.

There's someone in my head, but it's not me.

The thing that used to be Cody McLean steers the collective dust of those freed from Midwatch towards the pale blue dot it once called home.

So it is in this way Magic returns to Earth; and to Earth, magic returns.

September 2008

EXETER

CHICAGO

EPILOGUE

Today is the third of September 2008. The time is 2:25PM British Summer Time. Flight 478 to Chicago, Illinois, USA now boarding; please have any carry-on luggage opened...

His mother gave a small cry and a long hug.

"Be careful, Georgie," she whispered into his ear. "I love you."

"I love you, too, mum."

"Take good care of yourself, son," said his father. "I'm very proud of you for being so brave. Remember to look at the charts when you land. Find the gate for your flight to Logan Airport in Boston. Uncle Ulrich will pick you up there and take you up to Redgrave. Look for—"

"B-O-S, I know, Dad." He hugged his father. "I love you."

"I love you, too, son. I always enjoyed trips alone, and I'm sure you will, too. Please excuse your mother and I for acting so peculiar, but we're afraid, too. We'll miss you."

Words George needed to hear.

As he walked up to the security officer to have his bag checked and enter the boarding sleeve, he turned and gave a last wave to his parents. His mother waved with a tissue in her hand. He thought that's what she would look like if attending his funeral. He shook the thought away and stepped into the unknown.

* * *

George slept most of the flight while listening to music on his iPhone, a major upgrade from his iPod. None of his friends had one, yet. His parents demanded he carry it so they could reach him.

Before settling in, the only excitement was a man that asked to trade seats. He didn't mind trading for a seat next to the window. A few minutes before the plane taxied, a short plump woman rummaging in the storage compartment dropped a large bag on the man's head.

George slept and dreamed about a little girl.

* * *

She has green eyes. She tells him he must not be afraid, and that he must go through a shimmering doorway. He steps through. His parents hover in the middle of a room and smile at him. All teeth and gums.

"Do you understand what you see?" asks the little girl.

His mother's eyes snap open, black and the size of golf balls. He jumps. He turns to run away but the doorway is gone. When she speaks, her mouth opens too wide.

"He knows and now we are gone," she croaks at his father. Only now in place of his mother floats a hooded figure. His father disappears.

"Goodbye, Georgie," the hooded figure says as George loses his balance and falls into nothing.

* * *

He kicked the seat in front of him when he woke. The lady in it turned and gave him an angry stare. Lightning flashed outside amongst the dark clouds. He looked over at the man who traded him seats. A lump grew on his head where the bag hit him, and an opened package of Aspirin lay on his tray table. He was asleep and snoring.

George fumbled with his iPhone.

He didn't want to fall asleep.

As soon as the plane landed, he headed for the restroom. Someone grabbed his arm as he passed a drinking fountain. His captor turned him to face them and knelt before him.

"Do you remember me?" she asked.

"Uh, no. Please let me go," he begged.

"I told you not to be afraid."

George peered at her. He was compelled to answer.

"I saw a girl in my dream."

She peered back. Her eyes were green.

"Your eyes. You have the same eyes."

She nodded. "Why are you here? Where are you going?"

She squeezed his arm. George knew he shouldn't answer but couldn't stop himself before his mouth opened. "I'm here to learn with my father's Uncle Ulrich. I'm going to the Redgrave School in New Hampshire. I need to find the gate for the flight to Logan Airport in Boston."

"George, you can't get on the plane. We have to go a different way. They sense your power."

He didn't understand. "I don't have any power."

"You have more than you know. I sensed it, too. Come with me."

He didn't want to, but his body moved against his will. She took him into the women's lav.

They waited in a stall until they were alone.

"Did Uncle Ulrich send you?" he asked.

"Not exactly. I was... disconnected from him and the others. You can help me get back to them. Hang on. I'm going to try something."

She squeezed his arm again and held up her other hand. She closed her eyes and furrowed her brow. She mouthed words he didn't recognize. Sweat appeared on her forehead and cheeks. His arm grew cold where she held him.

To George's dismay, a shimmering doorway appeared, and she lowered her arm.

"We need to go through here."

He shook his head. "No, no, I'm not going in there."

She grabbed his other arm and squeezed them both. It hurt.

"George, this is the way we must go, and we must go now. They're almost here and I don't know how long I can keep it open."

He started crying. "I'm afraid. Who are you? Why are you doing this?"

"I'm a student of Ulrich, like you. There are people and… things that want to take us. I'll tell you everything, but we need to go, now!"

He had no choice, knowing his body would go where she commanded.

"Okay, but can you tell me your name at least?"

She regarded him kindly.

"My name is Alice."

APPENDIX

Aeraph: The inhabitants of Aesteria. Aeraph are tall humanoid creatures adorned with feathers. Most have long noses like beaks. Their eyes are typically ringed in red. Aeraph wingspans can reach up to twenty feet. Aeraph are nearly immortal and are often referred to as Angels by Temporans.

Aesteria: The space between realms. Humans refer to the space as Intermundia. It is often called in their mythology the place where gods reside.

Atarax: The space created at the entrance to the Congregate of Aesteria. It grants the subject their deepest desire and uses their response to judge their constitution.

Auras: Soul-minds of members of a Congregate that have passed on. They maintain their powers although they cannot speak and appear as ghosts or apparitions.

Aurchant: The sacred language of Aeraph and Auras.

Aurlibrum: The collection of tenets kept in Aesteria and guarded by Aeraph. It is the collected history of all the life of the Cosmos.

Congregate: A group of augurs, diviners, mediums, oracles, seers, soothsayers, sibyls, and druids; or whatever your chosen word for one who communes with nature may be.

Illimni: Spirit protectors created by attaching matching soul-energy to a living being, thereby giving the living being protection and extended life.

Nochtvol: The name Midwatch gave to those Aeraph loyal to it, made up of former Violet Knights.

Soul-energy: The energy collected when a being dies. Aeraph distribute back into the Cosmos various realms in the manner which offers the most balance.

Soul-mind: A piece of soul-energy retaining its consciousness. These can only be created if the being dies in Aesteria, or if the creator is very powerful.

Source, the: The source is the most powerful member of a Congregate. They can use and focus the powers of all other members. The Source is always female or feminine.

Temporan: Any life in the Cosmos that has not learned to transcend time.

Trinus: The meeting space at the center of a Congregate.

Varvika: A platoon of Aeraph. Rank designated by color along a spectrum with red being the lowest rank, and blue the highest. Purple, or violet, varvikas are an elite class separate from the others.

Vocturi/Vocturian: A special class of Aeraph. They are healers and where a broken heart symbol upon their armor which does not reflect light. They are charged with healing all regardless of side, deed, or rank. There are always eight. When one passes on, they are replaced by a willing Aeraph who must sacrifice their life and identity and take on the name of a Vocturian.

Their names are always: Agileux, Fosia, Glaphra, Hidarion, Kevin, Lythas, Pelian, and Viatis.

THE AURCHANT

AURCHANT:
Ta creda es blacin as ta nocht dous jan,
Vi ta nochliht plecis va Nochtvol dou pan.
Wor quo ta ruh fa ta Aurura sha riht,
Mosura tas ruh conta nocht amra liht.

TRANSLATION:
The code is broken as the dark does foretell,
In the Twilight place where Shadows do dwell.
We ask the souls of the Aurclock to share their sight,
Measure these souls against dark and light.

AURCHANT:
Salva ta ru.

TRANSLATION:
Save this soul.

AURCHANT:
Liht Conta Nocht!

TRANSLATION:
Light against Dark!

ACKNOWLEDGEMENTS

Many people helped and encouraged me along the way. I love and appreciate all of them, but these here bluntly guided me the most.

My first editor, Borbala Branch. She was very kind, but not too kind.

Those who purchased the presale way back in the Fall of '23. And then waited, and waited, and waited... Some are still waiting.

My wife and kids for politely listening whenever I wanted to read 'the best thing I ever wrote' each time I put down something I liked. Not only this, they held their breath as I left a good paying career to chase this dream. I am humbly and forever in their debt for loving me through my particular brand of crazy.

My brother, who read the first words of this in 2007. Seventeen years later I recovered enough from his counsel to finish it.

His wife, whose eyes viewed my characters from a different genre and led them to a better place.

My sister, who uttered a few seemingly innocuous words on the way to school way back in 1998.

My dear Aunt Joan. She encouraged me to finish this story with the hopes we could enjoy it on a porch somewhere, on a crisp fall day, sipping coffee. She read the first draft before any editor saw it and tore it to shreds. She smiled the whole time she told me my baby was ugly. All teeth and gums, naturally.

SCH
April 15, 2024

ABOUT THE AUTHOR

**'Writing Face'
September 2023**

STEPHEN HECKLER, who goes by Steve, lives with his wife of twenty years, two of his three daughters (the oldest flew the coop and made him a grandfather), and two stupid dogs. He still lives in Ohio, still near a town that doesn't exist, and for the most part is quite real.

From the Aurlibrum

The collected history of life resides in Aesteria in the great library known as the Aurlibrum. The library is kept and protected by the ethereal beings known as the Aeraph. These are their stories.

THE GARAGE HOUSE KIDS

Spring 2024

THE SHADOW OF MIDWATCH

Spring 2025

THE TEMPORAN JUDGEMENT

Winter 2025

THE REVIVAL OF AESTERIA

Fall 2026

www.ingramcontent.com/pod-product-compliance
Lightning Source LLC
Chambersburg PA
CBHW020328010826
48973CB00005B/1168